C000174529

JESSE JAMES

& THE SECRET LEGEND OF
CAPTAIN COYTUS

ALEX MUECK

iUniverse®

JESSE JAMES & THE SECRET LEGEND OF CAPTAIN COYTUS

Copyright © 2016 Alex Mueck.

All rights reserved. No part of this book may be used or reproduced by any means, graphic, electronic, or mechanical, including photocopying, recording, taping or by any information storage retrieval system without the written permission of the author except in the case of brief quotations embodied in critical articles and reviews.

iUniverse Star
an iUniverse LLC imprint

iUniverse books may be ordered through booksellers or by contacting:

iUniverse
1663 Liberty Drive
Bloomington, IN 47403
www.iuniverse.com
1-800-Authors (1-800-288-4677)

Because of the dynamic nature of the Internet, any web addresses or links contained in this book may have changed since publication and may no longer be valid. The views expressed in this work are solely those of the author and do not necessarily reflect the views of the publisher, and the publisher hereby disclaims any responsibility for them.

Any people depicted in stock imagery provided by Thinkstock are models, and such images are being used for illustrative purposes only.
Certain stock imagery © Thinkstock.

ISBN: 978-1-4917-8791-5 (sc)
ISBN: 978-1-4917-8792-2 (e)

Library of Congress Control Number: 2013917957

Print information available on the last page.

iUniverse rev. date: 3/18/2016

For you, my sweet Melissa

In memory of our loving dog, Paola.
You'll be in our hearts forever.

PART I

CHAPTER 1

PRESENT DAY

It had to be a practical joke.

Professor Gladstone peered at his prized book collection through horn-rimmed glasses and scratched his sparsely covered scalp. He'd already methodically searched every other square inch of his Harvard office in Robinson Hall. Thus far, the only unaccounted thing he'd uncovered was a used marijuana joint in a carinated pottery bowl dating back to Stonehenge; it had been in the room for over a hundred years. The used narcotic was certainly not his. He supposed it might have been left behind by someone who'd cleaned the office at some point over the past century. If he had to guess the culprit, it was probably a professor during the 1960s. Horrible decade. Back then, the faculty was full of hippie stoners.

They could have gone all-out and planted a camera, and a listening device was possible. With today's technology, stealth devices could be miniature, as fine as a fiber optic wire. Yet he doubted they would have gone through all the trouble to get something overly sophisticated. Besides, nothing looked out of order. No sudden appearance of a clock on the wall with a secret camera lens inside or a newly mounted, two-way mirror.

The faculty knew better than to mess with his rare collection of books and plant a monitoring device between book bindings. The cracked leather binding of Ptolemy's *Cosmography* winked out from the glass-encased shelf. Only two copies in private collections existed, and the book was valued at close to $750,000. In total, his personal rare book collection was insured at over $3 million and was protected with a security alarm, something well known across campus.

No secret monitoring devices had been found.

What now? In fifteen minutes, a student of his, Ulysses Hercules Baxter, would be here. How was he to play this?

Gladstone believed Baxter's ruse had to be a clandestine Harvard custom of which he was unaware. Some secret fraternal ritual orchestrated by the faculty elite. He wondered if every new Harvard chairman was subjected to such an elaborate prank, or whether this was the product of the twisted academic minds in the history department.

A month before, Gilda Busby, the department chair, had been killed. She'd been in Bahrain, researching a book on the social impact of Western technology on Islam, when she was crushed under the weight of a camel as it tried to mate with her.

Gladstone was saddened by the news and later horrified when a student spammed an e-mail prank referencing the camel and part of the foot anatomy. Sick, perverted bastards. Yet her death left a vacancy for the chairman of the department, and Gladstone was the anointed heir-to-be.

Gladstone peered down at his desk and focused on the centerpiece of the charade: Ulysses Baxter's thesis paper. It was a hoax, but unlike *The Hitler Diaries*, the thesis was so preposterous that it offered no pretense of legitimacy. Baxter was the perfect setup man. He was not some fourth-generation Harvard blue blood whose credibility would have been blown were he to attach his name to such nonsense. No, Baxter was a jokester, hardly Ivy League material. A few unqualified students always slipped through the door, especially if Daddy volunteered—with no preconditions, of course—to help finance the largest modernization update in American university history.

Baxter was almost the perfect buffoon; everyone would acknowledge him as the author of such rubbish. With his family wealth, the lad did not take school seriously. His work—up until then—had been unexceptional.

Indeed, Gladstone's fellow professors had found the perfect conman for their joke.

Although Gladstone considered Baxter the best setup man the

faculty could find, he also noted that up until now—despite Baxter's underwhelming grades—the student's work had never been fraught with fiction. Baxter performed poorly because he was apathetic toward his studies and spent his free time in bars chasing girls.

Gladstone pondered. *What fun is a joke if the perpetrators cannot witness the reaction?*

With nothing found in his office, only one option was left: Baxter would be carrying some sort of surveillance equipment. Gladstone would observe the lad closely and take measures to thwart that ploy. Once Baxter made to adjust his equipment, the reality that *it truly was a prank* would be apparent.

Actually, Baxter's paper might be more than a prank, and their meeting might be in fact a test of Gladstone's fitness to assume the role of chairman of the department. Thus, he would be sure to angle the conversation so that it turned the tables on his colleagues, making them the butt of the joke.

Gladstone grinned. *This meeting with Baxter is the perfect time for me to strut my stuff.*

Like most history professors, Gladstone was well versed on a range of topics, but his area of specialty—one where he had authored eleven books and had been used as a consultant for a major Hollywood movie—was the Civil War. He also happened to know quite a bit about the famous American outlaw, Jesse James. Still, anyone with an educational pedigree above a fourth-grade reading level and an IQ over sixty would spot Baxter's revisionist history of Jesse James as a work of juvenile fiction. It was one thing to take a position on disputed historical matter, such as claiming that Lee Harvey Oswald had not acted alone in the assassination of President Kennedy, or theorizing something new, such as Gavin Menzies's proposal that the Chinese were the first visitors to the New World, but it was something quite different to reinvent indisputable history.

Baxter's work was pure poppycock. The title of the thesis alone portended the delusions within: *Jesse James and the Secret Legend of Captain Coytus.*

A knock came from Professor Gladstone's office door.

CHAPTER 2

Gladstone eyed Baxter as he sauntered into the office. The boy carried a carefree confidence and a large duffel bag. If the paper was Ulysses Baxter's alone, then he should have been a trifle more apprehensive; the thesis and its evaluation would determine whether or not he graduated. Gladstone's suspicions grew, since in all the times he'd ever seen Baxter, he barely recalled him carrying his books, let alone an oversized bag.

Gladstone grinned. *What's in the bag, Baxter? Maybe some digital recording equipment?*

"Professor Gladstone, so good to see you."

So good to see you? This was quite unlike Baxter. The only time he looked pleased in a classroom (when present, of course) was when the class ended. His attention was always focused on the ladies, not the lessons. No, the boy was not smart enough to hold up the faculty's charade, and now they all would pay. Gladstone would start with a little deception and see how quickly the straw man crumbled.

Baxter nodded to the open chair across the desk from the professor. "May I?"

"Baxter, my boy …" Gladstone spun around the desk like a race car around a turn in the track. "Let me take that duffel bag from you and put it over here."

Naturally, his sudden offense flustered the student, who stood with his mouth hanging open and eyes slanted. Baxter looked more than shocked; he was aghast.

Gladstone smiled. *Gotcha.* He judged the bag to weigh a few pounds and sensed some motion within, which suggested that more than one object lurked inside.

Gladstone took the bag to a small coat closet, set it down, and shut the door. Victorious, he returned to shake Baxter's hand. "Take a seat," Gladstone commanded, with a stern sense of authority. He wanted to keep Baxter rattled and off-script.

Seated once again, he took stock of Baxter. He understood the reasons his student captivated women. His hair was just long enough to be risky, yet short enough not to look degenerate. A perfect mess, one that took no time grooming, yet it worked. He wore faded blue jeans and an olive T-shirt that depicted a dog with one hind leg raised. Like his casual attire, Baxter himself was ill-suited for the occasion. Gladstone would undress the faculty's con-artist.

A puzzled expression crossed Baxter's face. Flustered by the professor's masterstroke, the hustler had been hustled. Gladstone swelled inside. Surely Baxter was aware of the professor's intellectual superiority and was further intimidated. Unable to maintain his composure under Gladstone's steely gaze, Baxter seemed afraid to speak.

With the mysterious bag sequestered in the closet, Gladstone believed he'd nullified the faculty's attempt to listen in. At first he had planned to play it up and put on a show, to impress them with his oratory prowess, yet he did not want to come across as pompous. Better to ditch the possibility of any recorded account of his dealings with his student.

Gladstone's eyes bore into Baxter's as he toyed with the button on his sports jacket. He imagined himself as Porfiry Petrovich in Dostoevsky's *Crime and Punishment*, with Baxter playing the part of the criminal, Raskolnikov. It would only be a matter of time before the rascal confessed, and if the boy looked away from the steady glare, he'd be providing a telltale sign of deception. Yet the boy maintained a steady gaze, while his mouth curled at the corners as if amused. *Well, the joke's on him*, Gladstone thought, but with less certainty.

Gladstone decided to open the dialogue. He spread his hands and said, "Mr. Ulysses Baxter, where to begin?"

Baxter's eyes brightened. "Amazing, wasn't it?" The enthusiastic tone evidenced his reply was not a question. "Dare I say brilliant?"

Unbelievable, thought Gladstone. *The gall. The balls. How does the lad put his trousers on in the morning?* Maybe the faculty had found the right man for the job after all. Baxter was a bullshit artist of the modern variety. He could spray flowery shit around, but it was abstract illusionism. Now was the time to peel the paint from this forgery.

Referring to the faculty's game afoot, he said, "I know."

Baxter almost levitated from his chair in excitement. "I hoped you would agree. I knew the thesis was unorthodox, and yet I believe it will go down in history as a landmark paper." He nodded and pressed his lips like he was proud.

Gladstone gawked. Either the boy did not comprehend or he chose to continue the faculty's scam. He wondered what the boy was getting in exchange for playing the conman. At least he hoped the interview was a scam. It had to be. While Baxter was not overly bright, the boy was not insane, and that's what his paper was—utter insanity.

Doubt resonated. Rather than parry what he believed to be a ploy by the faculty, he was more concerned about getting to the bottom of things.

Gladstone's eyes no longer pried, and his voice hitched up an octave. "I know this is a joke," he said, though more as a question.

"It's not a joke, Professor Gladstone. And if I may comment, you're acting a little peculiar." He paused to glance back at the closet door. "Are you okay?"

Professor Gladstone ground his teeth in frustration. Perhaps this was not a faculty prank at all. If that were the case, then the matter was easily dealt with. "I want to know one thing right now. Did someone put you up to this?"

A sly smile crept across Baxter's face. "What are you saying?"

"You know what I'm saying," Gladstone said, though he no longer was certain of his read on the matter.

The younger man puffed air and scowled. "The only one who put me up to this was a source that wanted to let the world know about the Captain. Anything else is a figment of your imagination."

Gladstone shook inside. The nerve of the boy to brazenly suggest something was a figment of his imagination, even though that well may be the truth of it. Even more absurd was his mention of this *captain*. A fictional character if there ever was one. Baxter was either a shyster or mentally unbalanced. Whichever, his old man had wasted a lot of money, because his son was about to fail his history thesis and not graduate.

The professor considered himself kind when it came to evaluating his students. Sure, few were gifted enough to earn an A, but it had been a long time since he had flunked a student. Under normal circumstances, the ones who did poorly at least presented factually accurate work. This was different. Gladstone had neither qualms nor pity in leveling with Baxter.

So he cleared his throat. "Well, then." He picked a pen off his desk and scrawled a big F on the cover of the paper. "Here you go. Hope you thought the joke was worth it. You failed."

Baxter took the paper, gawked at the grade, and then glowered. He leafed through the paper, at first slowly and then in rapid succession, looked up, a trace of anger forming in the lad's countenance. "There are no comments. You usually mark my papers up. Did you even read this?"

The lad submitted a pile of rubbish, and now he has the audacity to question an esteemed professor? Today's generation had no respect. "I read enough to know that it was unworthy of a passing grade." Gladstone stopped, realizing Baxter obviously wrote the paper, seeking some perverse pleasure. There was no need to encourage him.

"This is unacceptable!"

"Excuse me?" Gladstone replied. He blinked in rapid succession as he pressed the frame of his glasses back. "Who are you to question me? Your name will be synonymous with lies and deceit."

Baxter grinned. "Your name, *Glad*-stone, *is* synonymous with happy-rock."

Gladstone bristled at the mockery. Unless this was a faculty prank, the boy's behavior was grounds for expulsion.

Baxter sat back, relaxed his posture, and said, "All I'm asking for is feedback on my work. This is my graduate thesis, and I deserve as much."

Gladstone sighed and tried to rub the migraine from between his eyes. "Perhaps you could have passed had you majored in creative writing, but this is history, where facts are facts. You submitted something you found amusing, yet it is beyond even being historical fiction. It's historical fantasy. Your unconventional footnotes detailed personal peccadilloes, not historical references. The paper is riddled with ridiculous clichés. In over thirty years of teaching, I have never read such a pile of shit! Excuse my French."

A sick smile formed on Baxter's thin lips. "*Que?* My apologies, Professor Gladstone."

Gladstone was pleased the charade was near an end and that his student finally expressed contrition. He rolled his hand for the lad to continue.

"Footnotes are annoying. No one wants to keep reading fine print at the bottom of every page. You historians, however, insist on trying to blind us with information that a skilled hand could incorporate into the body of the story. My infrequent footnotes illuminate."

"Your footnotes are further evidence this thesis is a spoof."

"As for the clichés, they originated from the primary-source document, so I was forced to incorporate them." Baxter rolled his eyes. "Although I found your classes dull and uninspiring, I'm aware that you are some superelite tenured professor. Thus, I half-hoped you would comprehend the magnitude of this masterpiece."

Gladstone glowered. The insult. The audacity. Before he could speak, Baxter forged on.

"I know I took some literary liberties, especially in the paper's prologue, because my source was a secondhand account. The rest of the paper, I assure you, is derived from primary-source documents. Every historian should be allowed some educated conjecture, especially when the story benefits from different points of view." He jutted his jaw. "I also presented my work in novel form, rather than some boring, stuffy history book that no one wants to read. You know all about those, right, Professor Gladstone?"

"Literary liberties?" he coughed out in dismay. He wanted to address the insulting insinuation of his own acclaimed work, but Baxter was quick to reply.

"Here and there, but it's all true, starting with the death of Major Johnson."

"I know all about Major Johnson."

Baxter actually laughed at him. "Do you, Professor Gladstone?"

The moron, thought Gladstone. The boy's innuendo was a reference to some ridiculous connection premised in his thesis. At best, he should have ignored the conjectured connection. "Yes, and while that part where Jesse James kills Major Johnson is certainly factual, much of the rest is balderdash. There was no Captain Coytus."

Baxter appeared crestfallen and bit his lip with a blank stare. Gladstone felt like he had just explained to a child that there was no Santa Claus.

Then the lad's eyes sparkled. "I'm sorry to say, Professor Gladstone, but you're dead wrong. The *no-longer-*secret legend of Captain Coytus is very true."

"Horsefeathers. You're mad."

Baxter glanced at the closet, leaned closer, and tapped the desk. "What if I can prove it?"

PART II

CHAPTER 3

THESIS PAPER
PROLOGUE

SEPTEMBER 1864

The soon-to-be most famous outlaw in American history gazed his blue eyes at the Missouri night sky. Venus shined bright; its synodic cycle had the planet positioned within the constellation Sagittarius, yet the lad knew nothing about astronomy. He's a fair-haired scrappy ruffian, not a seafaring navigator.

Campfires partially illuminated the gathering of over three hundred strong. He thought of the war gripping the nation. A nation that must split in two, one with slavery, and the other with *whatever the hell they wanted.*

He thought about his mother, Zerelda. If she had been a male, she'd have been the fiercest Bushwhacker of them all. She had cannonballs, that one.

He thought about his stepfather. Humiliated and hanged from a Union noose, Dr. Samuel had relieved his bladder before allowing relief from strangulation. He lacked a pair.

His true father, a hemp farmer and Baptist minister (talk about high on God), died in California searching for gold, and his son conjured an image constructed solely from a photo.

Next, he considered his family's slaves, all of whom had been treated well, even better than cattle. Especially Charlotte. He even liked Charlotte.

The sixteen-year-old reflected on his prior deeds. While serving under the most famous Bushwhacker of them all, William Quantrill, he learned about killing and about being shot, which had become the only way of life he understood. He'd already deduced that killing was considerably more fun than being shot.

The Union's Provisional Militia had brought the war to his farm and had separated him from his family. Several men dragged him across a hemp field like a tilling garden hoe. The memory angered him. He was no hoe. He was a Bushwhacker.

He had been away from the farm for weeks and missed home, his mother, and the privacy of the family outhouse. Well, except for the time someone put a beehive down the privy hole just ahead of his using it.

He spit into the campfire and glanced around, spotting the man responsible for the assembled militias, a former Quantrill lieutenant, Bloody Bill Anderson. Bloody Bill was decked out in black garb, the shirt embroidered with decorative patterns. He had long, full hair, and a beard framed his jaw.

Also present was the lad's older brother, Frank, who took his looks from his mother, with the dark, wavy hair, sunken eyes, and the fact that neither was generally attractive. The two siblings would later, allegedly, form the most famous outlaw gang in America history. For some reason, no one cared about Frank. Think loser brother.

Nearby, Little Archie Clement fingered his pistol. Clement stood five feet short and weighed a buck-thirty wet. Think Little Archie.

The plan was set. They would break camp at dawn, and something told him tomorrow would change his destiny.

CHAPTER 4

Centralia, Missouri, was a small, quiet town with a dozen buildings. Centralians were not an alien race, but rather hardworking folks who enjoyed the benefits of westward expansion. The town had a hotel, two general stores, and a railway line that helped keep the stores stocked, and the hotel's beds occupied.

A few residents had bank accounts in Callaway County, a new concept from the Unionist Northeasterners. Nonetheless, Centralia was a one-horse town if there ever was one.[1]

The early-morning calm broke with the sound of hundreds of galloping horses and the yelps of a marauding force of guerrillas. Bullets crackled skyward as the Bushwhackers swarmed like locusts to every building. They reappeared with loot and hostages.[2] The sound of an approaching locomotive interrupted the revelry. Bloody Bill shouted orders, and his men stacked wood ties on the railway tracks.

The train squealed to a complete stop.

The guerrillas boarded the train. Inside the cargo hold, they found

---

1   For instance, to this day, Centralia still does not have a Starbucks.

2   One general store owner was robbed of his money. A few goods (not soap) were also taken, including a British gentleman's magazine on colonial American fur trapping with a special feature on beaver pelts. Also missing was a salve moisturizer.

thousands of dollars of newly issued greenbacks and other valuable loot, including twenty-three soldiers wearing blue uniforms—Union Army men.

Bill Anderson ordered the soldiers off the train.

Two men protested. "We're veterans of Sherman's army and are traveling home on our furlough. I demand we be treated as proper prisoners of war," one of them said.

Bloody Bill spit on the ground and shot them dead.

At gunpoint, the soldiers were instructed to strip to their underwear.[3]

Bloody Bill conferred with Little Archie, who was known as the brains of his clique.

"Kill them all, but one hostage."

Bloody Bill nodded and approached the Union soldiers. "Is a sergeant in your rank?"

No one moved.

He asked again. This time, Thomas Morton Goodman stepped forward, and a few guerrillas pulled him from his fellow soldiers.

Bloody Bill addressed the remaining men. As he spoke, his men gathered around him, firearms aimed at the unarmed soldiers. "From this day forward, I ask no quarter and give none. Every federal soldier on whom I get the jump shall die like a dog. If I get into your clutches, then I expect death. You are all to be killed and sent to hell."

The guerrillas opened fire. It was like shooting a herd of buffalo.

Somehow a few soldiers survived, writhing in pain. The guerrillas surged forward and put them out of their misery with a gun barrel to the skull or a knife across the throat. Scalps were snatched as souvenirs.

They stripped the dead soldiers of their Union uniforms while other men torched the train and town buildings. Bloody Bill then ordered the men to retreat to the predesignated rendezvous point.

---

3   The men's undergarments were like today's long johns, except the older model was equipped with an emergency trap door.

CHAPTER 5

Major Andrew Vern Emen Johnson, nicknamed Major "Ave" Johnson, surveyed the wreckage: the frightened Centralians; the burned locomotive; the looted store; and the swag-less, dead Union soldiers, killed in their underwear. Such destruction angered the large man, not because his undergarments lacked the emergency trap door, but because he was a soldier. War was hell, but there was morality to combat too. What he saw was senseless carnage—uncivil war.

The townies gave him an estimate of the size of the guerrilla force, and he realized they outnumbered him by more than two to one. His battalion of the Thirty-Ninth Missouri Infantry was made up of volunteers, primarily men without much combat experience.

Major Johnson gazed at his troops. Young faces, some around the same age of his oldest son. He was responsible for their lives and accountable to their loved ones (except, perhaps, to the pet sheep with whom one of his soldiers was anxious to reunite).

As a veteran soldier, he was compelled to take action not only for the deaths of his fellow Union blue coats but also for a *United* States. A nation's blood should never be shed on its own soil unless in defense from a foreign force. He believed in the promise of America and the importance of victory in this war. Though the odds were against his men, he was governed by a sense of duty for these ideals.

Thirty men stayed in town while the rest saddled up to search for the Bushwhackers.

CHAPTER 6

The soon-to-be most famous outlaw in America sat horseback and digested Bloody Bill's plan to deal with the approaching battalion. They were stationed at an expanse known as Young's Creek, a few miles as a crow flies from Centralia, but in the morning dusk, no birds were visible.

A Bushwhacker named Dave Poole was drenched with the responsibility of acting as bait. Poole was known to get heated, even pissy, with children around. Still, he was well suited for the job at hand.

Poole's team would wade out to meet Major Johnson's men, make some waves, splash a few shots, and retreat up a ravine to Bloody Bill's company. On either side of the gulley, more guerrillas were stationed to pounce on the unsuspecting Union troops.

The soon-to-be most famous outlaw surveyed the saddled men around him, many with human Federalist scalps strapped to their horses. The men were ready. Bloody Bill's eyes shined with night fever, and they strayed across Little Archie, who looked like Lilliputian Archie, seated on his stallion.

Frankly speaking, he loved his brother, but was glad that it was he who was blessed with the good looks, brains, and charisma instead of Frank.

The soon-to-be most famous outlaw pondered one last thing before he ventured into battle. This was Missouri and would be a slave state no matter what President Lincoln and the newly formed, Negro-loving Republican Party had to say. He felt intellectually superior, having gained his ideals from the Know-Nothing movement, even though he was a

Democrat. He, like all men, had to fight for what was right and proper. If war was an end to a means, so be it. He slapped his horse, ducked, and charged into the fray.

As Bloody Bill predicted, the Federalists tried to pick off the Bushwhackers with rifle shots. The inexperienced infantry made a rookie mistake when shooting uphill. He heard the bullets fly over the approaching stampede.

The soon-to-be most famous outlaw in America spotted his target, namely, the decorated uniform. He aimed his pistol and fired.

The decorated man's eyes grew with surprise and then narrowed in resolve. Their gazes locked, and Jesse Woodson James approached the wounded man. He did not look away as he fired the round that killed Major Ave Johnson.

PART III

CHAPTER 7

SEPTEMBER 1864

Out of habit, the stranger checked his gold watch as he entered Booneville, Missouri. The journey had been long; days had gone by without signs of civilization, yet he had also labored for food and board as he traveled. Nine months later, some of his female employers would be in labor themselves.

Although alone, he was not out of place or mesmerized by Booneville's revelry. The city had celebrated a Confederate victory with a parade and was bursting with townies and out-of-townies.

The stranger's contact briefed him before he entered town.

Representing the Confederate Army was Sterling Price. He had served in the Mexico-American War, was former governor of the state, and now a major general for the Confederates.

When Bloody Bill's Bushwhackers rode into Booneville for the celebration, chaos almost erupted. The Confederates were horrified to see scalps hanging from horses, the stolen Union uniforms, and the rebel ragtag attire. The Bushwhackers were like a band of land pirates minus the parrot and cool accents.

Sterling Price had ordered Bloody Bill to clean up his gang's image before they addressed the Confederate leadership, and of course, Bloody Bill obliged. When he returned, he presented Price with a box containing two silver-laced pistols. Every man has his *price*, especially when it's named *sterling*, the Captain had mused to his informant.

Sterling Price realized the Bushwhackers were a necessary evil. So he secretly met with Bloody Bill later that day. After the celebration ended, most of the Bushwhackers and Confederate soldiers pulled out of Booneville.

The stranger steered his horse to a shanty-looking saloon. Dismounted, he waved in vain at a swarm of flies and grabbed a large cloth bag he'd strapped to his oversized horse. Despite his horse's well-deserved moniker and stubborn personality, Fly Bait was the perfect ride. The stranger was a big seventeen-year-old boy.

He glanced about and did a double take. Down the snow-less street stood a man on skis dressed in fur and heavy wool. He put his hands to his mouth and yodeled. The stranger turned back to the saloon. The skier must have sampled some fine moonshine to be in that state. Even so, the stranger was surprised by the skis, which were the first pair he'd seen in the New World.

He parted the swinging doors and entered the saloon. Conversations ceased. No glasses rose. Nary a gastronomical event was evident.

They saw his size and uniform. No one from the Union Army could be that brave (although statistically speaking, being suicidal was a possibility). Instead, he was pegged as a Bushwhacker—a rebel.

"We're not looking for any trouble here," the burly bartender commented.

The stranger smiled and removed his Stetson boss-of-the-plains hat, revealing a full head of dark, clean, shiny hair. "Just here for the party. Trust me; I'm not here to tangle with any men." He flashed a grin full of boyish charm.

The bartender gestured toward the stranger. "What's in that there sack?"

The stranger put his cap back on and brought the cloth satchel from behind him. Several patrons reached for their guns.

The stranger brushed his hand along the bag, and a muffled twang resonated. He smiled broadly. All his teeth were evident—white and straight as the nation's politicians, except perhaps former President James Buchanan Jr., who was rumored to play the other way.

"My only weapon is a guitar. I need a few drinks, but if you like, maybe I'll play for you all."

His words, plus the fact that over thirty armed Confederate soldiers were in-house, snapped the silence. Chatter stirred, and people went back to enjoying their drinks. All eyes remained on the stranger as he sauntered to the bar. As though they were still unsure of the well-groomed, strapping, young lad, the patrons cleared a path for him. Along the way, he paused to make eye contact with a few female saloon employees. Each got a wink and a smile.

He reached into his overcoat, and again a few pistols were aimed in his direction. Out of his jacket, he pulled a gold bar. He slid the bullion on the bar top to the bartender. "That buys everyone in here a drink and then some."

The saloon once again fell quiet, and the bartender seized the gold. He inspected it and grinned. "Courtesy of the gentleman in blue. A glass of whiskey for every man in the house."

A loud cheer erupted.

"And every woman, if they do so indulge," corrected the stranger.

A less raucous feminine applause reverberated.

The stranger took a whiskey glass and raised it to the crowd. "Let's party."

CHAPTER 8

All eyes were still wary of the stranger, but none more focused on him than three men who sat at a table in the back shadows of the establishment. Bloody Bill Anderson had left Little Archie and Frank James behind in Booneville to meet the third man at the table, Major John Newman Edwards.

Edwards, dressed in a sack coat, sported a ridiculous walrus-like mustache and held considerably more power than his rank and pinnipedian visage suggested. He was General Shelby's right-hand man and chronicled his triumphs in the press. Edwards's plan was to fight the Civil War with his pen and make heroes of those fighting the Confederate cause. To that end, he wished to form a newspaper.

"You sure you don't know him?" Edwards gestured to the bar, where the stranger danced on the bar with three women.

His Stetson now sat atop a curvy blonde who sported a nasty black eye. The drunken crowd cheered and then rejoiced louder when he ordered yet another round for everyone.

"Never laid eyes on him," assured Little Archie.

Edwards shrugged. "He's wearing a Union uniform. Like you Bushwhackers after your glorious victory over the Unionists at Young's Creek," egged the Walrus.

Little Archie addressed Frank. "Have you ever seen him before?"

He shook his head. "Never."

Then Little Archie eyed Edwards. "He never rode with us."

Edwards peered over to the bar again. "Is that brunette up on the bar the sheriff's wife?"

"Indeed, it is," confirmed Little Archie.

Edwards frowned. He valued the Bushwhackers' brutal means in the war and wanted to keep unity between the Confederate Army and the bands of rebels under men like Bloody Bill Anderson. While Little Archie might not know the stranger, he was a rebel of sorts.

Edwards scanned the crowd. "Where's the sheriff?"

Little Archie stifled a laugh and pointed. "The drunk's passed out in a pile of puke."

The men watched the sheriff's wife perform a do-si-do around the stranger.

"She'll catch quite the beating when he hears of his woman's conduct," Edwards prophesized.

"No business of mine," Little Archie commented. "The last sheriff of Booneville was killed when he signed up for the Confederate Army. This lazy lard ass owns the largest pig farm in town and used his influence to become the new sheriff. The man needs slaves to make his money, yet he does nothing to support our cause. Fuck him. I hope that big ole Bushwhacker gives it to his wife good."

"The boy has size. Maybe we should talk to him and find out what faction he fights with," said Frank.

Little Archie grinned. "That's exactly what I'm thinking."

Edwards gave a knowing smile. "That's why they say you're the brains of your outfit."

Frank James nodded. "It's true." He patted Little Archie on the shoulder. "Arch is a genius. His brain is bigger than even a whale's."

Archie shook his head like a bug had flown across his visage. "Thanks, Frank. Think you can rustle us up a few of those free drinks?"

When Frank was out of earshot, Little Archie said, "Frank means well, and he's the guy you want by your side in a fight, but he's as dumb as a buffalo's ass. His brother, Jesse, in contrast, has brains to go with the balls."

"I'd like to meet this Jesse." Edwards pointed at a newspaper on the table and frowned. "The Republicans are a traitor to the white man. Hope someone kills Lincoln."

Little Archie pressed his lips in consternation. "Me too, but it'll never happen. We have to win this war. Trust me; no way in a million years is anyone getting to him."

He nodded. "You're probably right. After all, you're the brain."

Little Archie winked in modest agreement, used to high praise. "Another example of how stupid Frank is: We were talking about the war, politics, and what happened if we lost. You know what the moron said? He said things would change over time. He actually claimed one day there could be a Negro president of a *United* States."

Edwards slapped the table and laughed with his hand over his ample belly, his mustache tusks bobbing in amusement. "You're right. He's dumb as dirt."

"It gets better! He went further and suggested the Negro president could even be a Democrat."

The two men fell into combustible laughter. Edwards resuscitated first. "That's the dumbest thing I have ever damned heard. Good thing you make the decisions. If you listen to a guy like Frank, you'll quickly be killed in this war."

Edwards's eyes slid to the bar after. "What's Frank doing?"

Little Archie stared at a spectacle. "Shit on your mama's linen if I know."

Frank James was upside down, trying to do a headstand against the bar. Two ladies helped brace his legs. The stranger kneeled down, placed the whiskey bottle to Frank's lips, and pumped a fist in the air.

"Go, go, go, go!" the stranger cheered, and the chant became a chorus.

After about ten seconds, the alcohol bubbled from Frank's mouth. The stranger flipped Frank back to his feet, and the girls helped spin him in quick circles.

"This looks like fun." Edwards eyed the female company the stranger had attracted.

Little Archie grunted. "It does, but I have a bad feeling about this."

Frank was spun like a pulled thread spool. Laughter sounded

throughout the bar, none louder than his. It was like the children's game, Yelp-Piggy-Yelp.[4]

"Stop," yelled the stranger, and they released Frank. "Return to your table, now!"

On the first misstep, Frank's legs turned rubbery. He thrust his arms out in the open air for support, and his lips twitched in shock when he found nothing but gravity to brace him. He tried to recalibrate his body, but the adjustment sent him spiraling into an occupied table.

---

4   Children's games are a blast. Who didn't play Hide and Go Seek or Duck, Duck, Goose or Blind Man's Bluff? Yelp-Piggy-Yelp was a new one for even me, so I thought I'd explain. One person is blindfolded and plays the farmer. Everyone else is a pig, and they scuttle about. The farmer then points in a direction and says, "Yelp, piggy." If he guesses the person's voice, that person becomes the farmer. I always thought college would be more interesting if we could slip some games in like we did in kindergarten. It sure beats reading narcoleptic novels written by the professor.

CHAPTER 9

Three townies wiped ale from their dirt-stained, bacteria-incubating attire in disgust. They glared down at Frank, who lay on the floor, holding his head in pain, while laughing. The largest of the three townies sneered, "Rebel mudsill."

Edwards motioned to Little Archie. "You may need to step in here."

He shook his head. "Wait a minute. Let's see where this leads first."

Frank got to his feet and slurred an apology of sorts before trying to shuffle away.

The largest townie interceded and put a hand on his chest. "I ought to slap you around with my pecker."

"Actually, you ought not to do that at all," said the stranger. "Looks like he lost a tooth in the fall. Your willy might get stuck in the vacant wedge."

The large townie stared at the stranger and snarled, "Who said that?"

"Unless someone's a proficient ventriloquist—or your hearing's impaired due to a candle's worth of wax buildup—I'd wager the speaker was I," the stranger said. He stood at complete ease.

The townie glanced back at his two pals and puffed his chest like an overfed turkey. "And who the hell do you think you are?"

The stranger removed his Stetson and spread his hands peacefully. "I know who I am. Who are you?"

The townie screwed his face up and spit on the floor. "Friends call me Badger Bob, but you're no friend of mine."

The stranger appeared to accept that. "True, so what's your God-given name then?"

"Bob Shortwood," the townie said and spat again.

A sly smile crept across the stranger's lips. "Is there any way we can become fast friends? I'd rather run Badger than have to gag over Shortwood."

The townie scowled, but the stranger quipped, "Please accept my apologies for this man's actions," pointing to Frank. "We were having some fun, and it got out of hand. Let me get you gentlemen a drink, and let's forget about the whole thing."

Frank liked the idea. "Yuuuuh."

The townie nodded. "I reckon I can pull in my horns. I don't want to have to hurt you none. But there's one condition."

The stranger waved the townie to continue as he went to fetch the men new beverages.

"Stay away from that woman." The townie pointed to the blonde with the black eye, and a malicious grin spread across his wrinkled face. "She's my new girlfriend. Had her in my clutches last night."

The stranger looked at the blonde.

The blonde shook her head in dismay. Even with her bruises, she was the most beautiful women Edwards had ever laid eyes on, and no doubt the stranger thought the same. Her skin glowed like a full moon, her features dainty, yet she carried strength about her. To see her present state upset him, judging by the twitch of his lip and the darkening of his glare.

The stranger brought back three drinks for the townie trio. "Thanks for the warning."

The tension broke when he handed the glasses over, and the patrons returned to their conversations.

Frank arrived back at his table without the drinks. "Lil' Arch, you have to try that sometime. It's like riding a bull, except it's your own legs that throws you to the ground."

"Maybe next never, Frank. I need to stay in control of my faculties."

Edwards leaned in. "Did you ask the stranger who he rides with?"

Frank shook his head. "I whispered to be careful with the sheriff's wife and volunteered for his game."

"Looks like he did not heed your warning," Edwards said.

The sheriff's wife was in deep conversation with the stranger.

CHAPTER 10

The stranger listened to the sheriff's wife.

"Susanna's a friend of mine, and she didn't sleep with Badger. Like a caveman, he struck her a few times and carried her upstairs. Everyone knows he's got sexual diseases. Dr. Gant's wife warned us gals. Said her husband claimed the Badger has more warts than a bloated toad. Susanna's a virgin and not married. So she climbed out the window and jumped."

The stranger frowned. "Why don't you tell your husband to have a chat with Bob Shortwood?"

She glanced over to her husband, who was snoring at a table, drool hanging from his lip to the gold-star badge on his chest. "He was here when it happened. Badger's a friend of his."

First confusion wrinkled his brow, and then anger.

She grabbed his wrist. "I know you will think I'm an evil woman, but every time my husband goes hunting, I pray he does not return." Her eyes flickered to the floor with shame. "I can take his fists, but my son's skin is too young to be burdened with scars of his drunken discipline."

Silence hung between them as the stranger pondered the tidings. "I think someone mentioned he runs the largest pig farm in the area?"

"Yes ..." She hesitated out of confusion.

"Maybe there's something I can do."

Her visage relaxed, and hope glimmered in her gaze as she released her hold. "Thanks," she whispered and floated away.

The stranger went to an open corner and took out his prized Martin guitar. All eyes turned upon him, and he addressed the onlookers. "It would be my honor to entertain you all. Just need to warm up a tad."

Framed by his large physique, the guitar looked like a ukulele. He brought his left hand to the guitar's neck and his right to the front of the bridge and then strummed, and a rich sound thrummed from the rosewood-and-mahogany body. His fingers moved around the frets flawlessly, and he ended with one note of clear sustain.

CHAPTER 11

The patrons looked on, especially Little Archie and company. They had discussed Edwards's vision of his newspaper, and Little Archie was impressed, but he was more awed by the stranger's skill on the guitar. "That boy's got the devil in his fingers."

The stranger cleared his throat. "The first song I'd like to play you is relatively new. Not sure if you've heard this yet, but it's called, 'With a Banjo on My Knee.'"

A few cheers were heard, mostly from the remaining Confederate soldiers.

He strummed a chord and held everyone's attention. Then a deep baritone voice sounded through the bar with the beckoning call of a church bell.

> *I come from Alabama with my banjo on my knee*
> *I'm going to Louisiana, my true love for to see*
> *It rained all night the day I left*
> *The weather, it was dry*
> *The sun so hot, I froze to death*
> *Susanna, don't you cry.*
>
> *Oh, Susanna,*
> *Oh, don't you cry for me*
> *For I come from Alabama*
> *With my banjo on my knee.*

Several voices joined in on the chorus. Hands clapped, heads bobbed, one couple started to dance. The joint was a-rockin'. Back at the Bushwhacker table, a drunken Frank James was on percussion, stomping both his feet and slapping his thighs. Edwards played rhythm, strumming his walrus mustache.

Little Archie did not join the jam. He wondered if the opening song was a coincidence. The Badger glared at the stranger, seemingly ready to strike. Susanna, on the other hand, tried to act uninterested but was consistently guilty of stealing a glance at the stranger, who was less discreet. His ogling eyes rarely wavered from her.

When the song ended, the stranger played a few Confederate favorites, including, "Goober Peas,"[5] "Stonewall Jackson's Way," and "Dixie's Land." Little Archie reconsidered the stranger's intentions. Even the Badger appeared mollified, although Susanna rejected his offer to dance.

The stranger announced, "This will be the last song before I take a small break."

Shouts resounded across the room. No matter the words, the initial tones rang of disappointment but changed to cheers and applause as he bowed.

He took several sheets of paper and a pen from his guitar case. "Feel free to write some requests, and I'll see what I can do."

The stranger then looked at Little Archie's table. "I would like to dedicate this song to the rebels of this war. You're heroes." And he saluted them. "This one's called, 'Riding a Raid.'"

Little Archie gushed. "I love this guy. I think we have just found ourselves a new member of the gang."

A skeptical crease formed on Frank's brow. "You sure, Little Arch?"

He snorted away the doubt. "If he says no, then I'm a Negro."

---

5   In case you were curious, the song "Goober's Peas" has no connection to Goober's candy. Goober's is a movie staple along with popcorn, but in research, I determined the candy name is derived from the Gullah word, *guber*, meaning "peanut."

CHAPTER 12

"I appreciate the offer," the stranger said, "but I ride alone."

Frank James chuckled. "Little Arch, I think your skin turned a shade darker."

"Shut up, Frank," he seethed.

The stranger huddled closer. "Don't mistake my words. I'd like to work with you." He paused to put his arm around Frank. "You're my brothers, but here's the scoop. I don't take orders well, and I sure as hell don't like spending my nights sleeping with a bunch of guys in the open plains. I prefer a covering over my head and a woman in my arms."

The three men nodded, as if they dreamed of the same thing.

"We can have an alliance of sorts. When I fight with you, I will take orders from whoever your leader may be." He stopped to point at his Union uniform and said, "Sometimes one man can do things an army cannot. Be in a place where the enemy congregates, you know, espionage and sabotage."

Impressed, Edwards preened his mustache. "Brilliant. If only we had more men who thought like you did. If I may ask, you appear to carry an education. Can you read and write?"

"*Ipsa scientia potestas est.*"

Edwards's eyes dilated.

The stranger illuminated, "'Knowledge itself is power.'"

Edwards's jaw hung down in awe before he explained his plans to start a newspaper. "Maybe we can work together too. Our work won't require outdoor sleepovers."

The stranger seemed to mull over the possibilities and grinned. "A splendid idea." He gave a conspiratorial glance. "There might be some trouble. I'm not asking for your help. I just want a neutral corner I can have my back to."

All three men agreed, but Frank did so with the most enthusiasm. "Tell me who to kill, if you need help."

The stranger left the awestruck trio and spotted the sheriff. Badger must have woken him up, and they were in deep conversation. He headed in their direction.

Badger stopped talking when he saw the stranger approach, but he showed no sign of malice. "You can play, son," he said and walked back to his friends.

The sheriff sized up the stranger. "You've made quite a scene here tonight, boy."

"I'm glad I brought some excitement to your mundane village."

The sheriff's face tightened, and he appeared prepared to comment but paused, his eyes narrowed. "I'd like to ask where a boy your age got this gold you've been flashing about."

"So ask."

"I'm asking."

"My father, God rest his soul," he said and crossed himself.

This seemed to soften the sheriff's mettle, who mumbled something that sounded like a condolence.

The stranger brightened, though there remained a hint of sadness in his tone. "There's a lot more gold where that came from. I inherited a fortune that my father made raising pigs."

The sheriff looked eager and incredulous at the same time. "A fortune with pigs? I raised pigs my whole life and made good money but am hardly rich."

The stranger drew the sheriff in closer. "Neither did my father, until he heard about the great Massachusetts famine and their boundless need for pork. Sure, he kept the enemy alive, and I was against it, but he rationalized it by charging ridiculously exorbitant prices. It's weird, but they love ham;

it's like sex to them. Those dumb Mass-holes were unloading bank vaults for father's pigs." He sniffled. "But when he got back, someone tried to rob him, found no gold, and killed my pa."

The sheriff mumbled another condolence but got to the matter of his interest. "I never heard about this famine."

"Some disease wiped out all their livestock, yet somehow pigs imported from the west are resistant. Father could not meet their demands." Pause. "I suppose at some point the opportunity will pass. On the return trip, we saw other pig farmers heading east."

"Where would I go?" the sheriff demanded.

He smiled. "Almost everywhere. You have a map of Massachusetts in town?"

"I believe we do."

"I only ask so you can verify what I am saying—and am about to show you—is true." He pulled a journal that he had retrieved from a satchel hung on his horse, Fly Bait. "In here, I have a map of Massachusetts, since I was recently there with my father."

The stranger opened the journal on a table, and a map appeared. Several cities had been circled. "Some towns even changed their names to advertise their plight." He pointed at a circle. "This is the town of Needham. How much more blatant can they be? They desperately *need ham*."

The drunken sheriff squinted over his round, red cheeks at the drawing and smiled. "Would you look at that?" he gushed.

Again, the stranger pointed. "Here you have Dedham. These folks will be dead if they don't get their ham." His finger moved. "This is Wareham. Where's the ham? That's what these folks want to know. This is Stoneham, which never changed their name."

He met the sheriff's eyes. "The people of Stoneham are R-I-C-H, rich. And the town specialty was stone-cooked ham. One destitute restaurant owner offered his four daughters as concubines for a few pigs. Father declined. Although he was morally right, I have to admit I had my eye on one with red hair. Then, over here, we have Wantham."

The sheriff's watery eyes focused. "Looks like Waltham."

"I believe the map's been smudged. Or maybe that ridiculous Massachusetts accent caused a mispronunciation. You know: *I traveled fah in a carriage cah, to get a drink in a Bahst'n bah*," he scoffed. "As I said, Yankee Mass-holes."

The sheriff squirmed like a fish caught on a hook, and his mouth gaped, and his lips twitched about.

"Did I mention Hingham?" inquired the stranger.

The sheriff shook his head, swallowing the bait further.

"You probably have heard of the Ching, Qing, and Ming Dynasties of China."

The sheriff shook his head. "The only china I know is in my cupboards."

"Well, the Hing Dynasty lasted only one year. The rulers plundered the wealth and were forced to flee the country. They ended up in Massachusetts." His right eyebrow angled upward. "You can't make pork fried rice without pigs. In fact, you might want to start in Hingham. Oh, and the town of Raynham? *Let it rain ham*," sang the stranger.

The sheriff bit his lip and shifted from foot to foot. "I reckon I'll need some hands. My boy is too young. I'll cut you 20 percent of the profits if you lead me there."

"I'd love to, but I'm here to fight this war." The stranger gestured toward the table of townies. "Why not take Badger Bob and his two cubs with you?"

"That's almost a great idea. The Badger may be a friend, but I can't trust him with this. But the other two, Cooter and Billy Bob, are the type to take orders. In fact, I could talk to them without the Badger sniffing about."

The stranger silently cursed. He'd tried to kill two dodo birds with one stone, and now his mind galloped. "I have an idea. I'll cause a scene. When Badger reacts, grab his men and get out of here."

The sheriff nodded.

"I have one favor to ask, though."

"Anything."

"Give me your badge. Make me sheriff in your absence."

CHAPTER 13

The stranger held his guitar and the bar's undivided attention. He sifted through some scraps of paper. "I see we got a few requests. Since three are for the same song, I'll start with that. This song of the savannah is for Roscoe, Earl, and Clint. It's called, 'Old Rosin the Beau.'"

By the time the second verse began, almost everyone sang along. Drinks were raised high, and people swayed to the rhythm of the music.

> *When I'm dead and laid out on the counter,*
> *The people all making a show,*
> *Just sprinkle plain whiskey and water*
> *On the corpse of old Rosin, the Beau.*
> *I'll have to be buried, I reckon,*
> *And the ladies will all want to know,*
> *And they lift up the lid of my coffin,*
> *Saying, "Here lies old Rosin, the Beau."*

When he finished the song, he scowled at the next request. He always hated the song's lyrics, but for some reason he could not quite put his finger on, he liked the song's title: "Jenny, Get Your Hoecakes Done." Scrawled next to the request was "Zeke."

Again, he found himself looking at Susanna. Like a rose among weeds, she was a goddess, the nectar of life. He had to turn away in order to concentrate on some of the stupidest song lyrics he'd had the misfortune of memorizing.

De hen and chickens went to roost,
De hawk flew down and hit de goose
He hit de ole hen in de back
I really believe dam am a fac,
Oh, Jenny get de hoe cake done my dear,
Oh, Jenny get de hoe cake done.

As I was gwain' lond de road,
Past a stump dar wad a toad.
De tadpole winked at Pollewog's daughter,
And kick'd de bull frog plump in de water.
Oh, Jenny get de hoe cake done my dear,
Oh, Jenny get de hoe cake done, love!

People danced about in drunken celebration. Several sang along with a mocking Negro accent, and fervent applause greeted the final note.

The next request was made by Lyle. It was a ditty called, "John Brown," but he chose to skip it. The stranger knew the twisted words well.

Oh, there is great news come from Charlestown:
Tis all about the hanging of old John Brown;
He tried all his best to set the niggers free,
And for it he had to hang upon the gallows' tree.

It happened at Harper's Ferry, as you already know,
He tried all his best, but he found it was no go;
He gave to the niggers spears, pistols, and guns,
And in the struggle he lost his two sons.

So, all you old men who wish to set the niggers free,
Just think of John Brown and the gallows' tree;
And oh ye, abolitionists, before it is too late,
Think of John Brown and of his sad fate.

The next request was one that he'd personally slipped in. He'd been working on a melody, and suddenly the lyrics had come to him.

The stranger waved down the saloon's appreciative volume. "In the spirit of humorous songs, next comes a request I'm only vaguely familiar with. I'll do my best." He looked down at the paper. "It's an anonymous dedication. It's called, 'Oh Susanna,' except in this version there's no 'banjo on my knee.'"

> *Oh, Susanna, forgive me please,*
> *Did I mention I have sexual diseases?*
> *You're so pretty, and I was drunk.*
> *I'm just a redneck scalawag punk.*
> *Oh, which diseases you may ask?*
> *There are many; the list is vast:*
> *Syphilis, gonorrhea, and the clap.*
> *If only I had my willy wrapped.*

The stranger was quick to notice a hush come over the bar. Some people still clapped along, but most squinted in puzzlement. Apparently, talk like "hanging Negroes" was perfectly acceptable discourse, but public sexual commentary was not.

He took stock of those he'd met. The sheriff retreated to the corner, and there, he poorly faked his prior comatose state. His wife was amused, and her hand did little to stifle giggles. Little Archie sat stoically. Flabbergasted, Edwards twiddled his mustache. Frank number-one-fan James was whooping it up good—all limbs in motion.

Susanna radiantly stood out among all. Like a cat, her green eyes appeared to casually take everything in. Her lithe body was at ease but in a blink of an eye, ready to pounce. Her blank expression tried to portray disinterest. Still, the stranger could read the emotions behind her mask. She was both scared and amused, but the small bat of an eye and nod of the head suggested she was also flattered.

Badger Bob was also an easy read. He was trying to act as if the words had no meaning to him, but the pursed lips, determined jaw, and steely gaze suggested otherwise. It was like he was afflicted with a fierce gastro anomaly but trying to be a gentleman about it.

The stranger strummed his way to the second verse.

> *Oh, Susanna, forgive me please.*
> *Did I mention I have sexual diseases?*
> *You're so pretty, your body so firm.*
> *I'm the man with viral sperm.*
> *Oh, which symptoms you may ask?*
> *There are many; the list is vast:*
> *Crabs, cankers, and scaly warts.*
> *An ax should make me eunuch short.*

"Probably already is." (Laughter.)

> *Oh, Susanna, forgive me please.*
> *Did I mention I have sexual diseases?*
> *You have nice curves, I love your shape.*
> *I'm a loser who's forced to rape.*
> *Oh, how could he, thou wonder why?*
> *I beat on girls; check your black eye.*
> *I'm no gentleman, just a scofflaw slob,*
> *Or better known as Badger Bob.*

At the song's conclusion, there was a smattering of applause, unheard whispers, and a few raucous cheers from Frank James. When it died down, Badger Bob rose to his feet, took two steps toward the stranger, pointed, and barked, "Let's take this outside."

CHAPTER 14

The stranger gawked at the stocky but flabby townie with bewilderment. "If you don't mind, I'd prefer to play indoors. It's a bit nippy, and I can't see why everyone should move outside."

Badger Bob took another step, his voice now a deep growl. "Me and you are gonna draw."

He scratched at his chin. "Charitably, I may be called a musician, but I am certainly no artist," he said with almost credible sincerity. He reached down, gripped his pen and paper, and gestured toward the lug. "But here—draw until your heart's content."

Badger Bob stomped his foot.

The stranger grinned back. "If I may point out, the lighting is better in here, so if I were you, I wouldn't go outside either. May I commission you to draw me playing guitar?"

Frank James called out, "If you have time to draw two pictures of him, I'd sure as hell pay something for it."

The sheriff's wife made no attempt to stifle her laughter.

Knuckles cracked as the insulted man curled his fists. "I'm talking a gunfight. A contest. See who the better man is."

The stranger's head rolled on its axis. "How about we arm wrestle instead? Bet I can take you."

"I'm talking a contest for men, not little boys."

"Is thumb wrestling out of the question then? Hmm, what about chess? That's a man's game. I'll whoop you good in that too."

Badger Bob was steaming to a rapid boil. Sweat beaded on his forehead. "*No games!* A gun duel."

The stranger smiled and nodded his Stetson-covered head. "Like a cock fight?"

"That's right."

"Except there's no birds."

"Outside. *Now.*"

The stranger held his hands up. "I'm unarmed."

The other man squinted. "You got no weapon in that coat?"

"Nope."

"Nothing in your pants?"

The stranger sighed. "Well, yeah, but—"

"So pull your weapon out, and let's step outside."

"Er-r-r, I'd rather not do that, Bob. There are women here."

A whip of his hand to his holster revealed the six-shooter, which he aimed at the stranger. "No more buffalo chips. Get your piece out or I'll shoot you now."

The stranger looked around the saloon. "My apologies, ladies and gentlemen." He unbuckled his pants and let them drop. He'd once sported the trapdoor underwear but left them in a barn when a wife's husband rushed in with a pitchfork.

Spontaneous reactions echoed from the timber roofing all the way to the cellar.

"Oh my god, Wilbur! Do you see the size of that thing?"

"Look away, Sally!"

"Holy horse meat."

"That boy's hung like old John Brown."

"Hmm, he looks white to me."

"You better not touch a hair on that boy," a female voice called from out of eyesight. "He's the one who left Jefferson City weeks ago. My sister, Claire, said such wonderful things about you."

The stranger finally located the source of the voice. "Well, then, please send Claire my regards. And tell her that the meal was delicious but the dessert even tastier." He winked.

Then he turned toward the Badger. "Hey, Shortwood, if it's all right with you, I'd like to pull up my pants."

"Make him wait ten more seconds," his female advocate snickered.

The Badger motioned his gun upward. "Someone give this man a gun."

The stranger pulled his pants up. "Here's the thing, Badger. You don't want to duel me, and here's why. I have perfect aim. I could shave a herpes wart off your scrotum and save you a doctor's bill. Or, I could put a bullet through your heart. But to me, a real man's game is a fight without weapons. So if you're such a tough guy, how about drop that gun and bunch them fists."

The Badger thought it over but shook his head. "No."

"He's scared. I think he's afraid you'll beat him with that club of yours," Frank James whooped.

"That I'd like to see," cooed the female advocate.

The bartender slammed the counter. "No trouble inside, men."

As the bartender uttered his last word, the Badger sprung into attack with the barrel of the pistol raised in his hand, as if he intended to bludgeon the stranger with the wooden grip stock.

The stranger stepped to his right and grabbed at the extended arm with his left hand. The right, clenched in a brick-like fist, smashed into the side of Badger's rib cage. The torque of the blow elicited cracking, a sharp intake of air, and a few feet of altitude as Badger glided through the air before he crashed to the ground in a heavy heap. He moaned through labored breaths.

The stranger felt no remorse; this was just the beginning. Before his heart could thaw, others would burn in hell.

CHAPTER 15

The sheriff was serious about his pig pilgrimage. By the time Badger Bob was on the receiving end of the punch, the sheriff had altered from stupor-man to superman. With arms around both Cooter and Billy Bob, the sheriff escorted them to the saloon exit.

Then he reappeared just as fast as he'd gone. "A personal matter has forced me to undertake a long journey. In my absence, I appoint him," the sheriff pointed at the stranger, "acting-sheriff of Booneville."

Through gasps, the sheriff made his way to his wife. They chatted briefly, and then he departed without another word.

The stranger flashed his newly acquired sheriff's badge and some teeth. "If someone thinks they can do a better job than me, let him step forward now. We'll arm wrestle for the badge."

No one took the gambit, but Frank James commented, "At least the odds appear better arm wrestling than a cock fight."

With her husband gone, the sheriff's wife howled in laughter.

The stranger found Susanna's eyes, shrugged, and looked back at Badger Bob, who was still on the ground, sucking air. "Can I get a few volunteers to take that stinking heap of dung to the doctor?"

More than a dozen men jumped into action before they realized, despite the Badger's girth, it was no more than a four-man operation.

The stranger made his way to the Bushwhacker table, where Frank greeted him with a hearty handshake.

Little Archie stared at the acting-sheriff in wonder. "I'm impressed. Envious, even."

Frank James chuckled. "I've seen you naked before, Arch, so I do empathize."

"Shut up, Frank. I'm talking about how he handled things. He walked in a stranger, took over the bar, entertained us, clobbered a large man, and became acting-sheriff in less than a few hours." He whistled. "Badger didn't look too good. He'll be all right?"

"No," informed the stranger.

"That's what I thought."

Edwards wet his fingers in his mouth and fingered the ends of his mustache. "You're the kind of hero I'm looking to chronicle—a man of peace and justice." He stopped twiddling his whiskers and his brow knit. "We don't even know your name."

The stranger feigned consideration. "As I mentioned, I work undercover, and not just in a bedroom," he said with a sly smile. "You can call me Coytus. Captain Coytus. C-O-Y-T-U-S."

"That works. I like it," approved Edwards.

"Me too," marveled Little Archie. "*Coytus* has a certain refined purity to it. Is *Coytus* a Scottish name?"

The captain raised his eyebrows. "I think it was copulated in Karma Sutra."

Little Archie's eye's drew together. "Karma Sutra? I think I heard of that island. It's real far away, near Australia. *Coytus* is likely a British name." He paused and then asked, "You like tea?"

"Love it."

"That seals it." He tapped at his temple. "British. I knew it."

Frank leaned in. "Funny, but *Coytus* sounds like a dirty word."

Little Archie shook his fist at Frank. "Fool, please do shut up. You know nothing."

"When I move on from being sheriff, how can I find you boys?"

Edwards rubbed his nose and then played with his mustache. "How long are you acting-sheriff?"

"I sent the old sheriff on a wild-goose chase. He won't be back for a while, but I am not long for this job. I'll find the right replacement and move on within a week."

"You're sticking around to get with Susanna," declared Frank. "I can tell you like her."

The Captain was going to acknowledge that truth, but Little Archie interjected.

"Frank, for the final time, shut that flap trap of yours." He turned to the Captain. "My apologies. He should be a southpaw, 'cause he never does anything right." He cast an admonishing eye at Frank before returning to the Captain. "We're headed back to Clay County."

Edwards scrawled something in a journal and then tore out a sheet of paper and handed it to the Captain. "Leave word for me here, and I will find you."

"Thanks. Hey, were you men part of that raid on Centralia?"

Little Archie grinned. "Yes, we were. Were you there too? Is that where you got that uniform?"

"No. I got this by other means."

The Bushwhacker gleamed. "You missed one hell of a fight; it was a massacre." He pointed to Frank. "His brother, Jesse, was the one who killed the Union major." In a gesture of camaraderie, he patted the Captain's shoulder. "You should have been there."

"Oh, I wish I had been," he said with firm sincerity as he rubbed his chin and gazed into the other man's eyes. He rose from the table. "Gentlemen, we shall see each other soon."

CHAPTER 16

The sheriff's wife smiled coquettishly. "Where did you send my husband?"

"Massachusetts," the Captain answered. "The swine's probably on his way now."

"Do you need a place to stay, or am I going to have to misbehave and have you arrest me?" She bit her plump lip and batted her eyes. "I've always had a fantasy of being a prisoner but never envisioned my husband to be the one to render justice upon me. But you …" She let the implication speak for itself.

"I'm likely to accept your most generous offer. I'd also like to talk to Susanna, but not for the same reasons."

"I understand completely. That's the girl to go for. I just can't help myself for trying."

The Captain thought of his mission and shook his head. "I could never be with her now. How about we meet at the jailhouse? Probably better if you get a head start."

She beamed and chuckled. "Bring that nightstick with you."

The Captain found Susanna cleaning a table but almost hesitated to interrupt her. He enjoyed watching her work, her fine features accented in fierce determination as she scrubbed.

"Need a hand?"

She turned to him. No anxiety or favoritism showed on her face. "Isn't the sheriff's job to cleanse the dirt from this town, rather than this saloon?"

He took the rag from her hand and pressed it over the persistent stain she was having some difficulty with. "I thought I had cleansed this town of at least *some* filth."

She nodded, her curls bouncing with the motion. "You sure did. And thank you, but just so you know, I can take care of myself. Badger was going to have to kill me before he ever had his way with me."

He believed her and told her so. Satisfied with the job he'd done cleaning the table, he handed her the rag. "I wanted to ask you something."

Without pause, she replied, "You want to bed me. You think I'm impressed with your song serenades and winning a fight." She snapped the ratty rag down.

He was surprised but impressed by her resilience. This was not a weak woman. "While I admit I fancy you, I do not want to bed you. That is not my agenda."

Susanna turned away. Even though the Captain could no longer see her face, he was sure he'd seen an expression of hurt flicker across her brow. Yet when she turned back, her face was a firm mask of indifference. "I see. Already made plans with Katherine, the sheriff's wife."

"I did," he confessed.

"I see," she said and went to another table, where she began to scrub.

The Captain followed. Again, he took the rag from her and wiped the table. "What I wanted to ask was if we could spend some time together tomorrow."

A comical expression arched Susanna's eyebrows. "So you want to get some tonight and sow new ground tomorrow?"

The exchange amused him. "As a gentleman, I swear I have no intention of improper conduct. To the contrary." He stopped scrubbing, drew closer, and then looked down to her upturned face. "I confess I am something of a scoundrel."

Susanna looked right back at him. Her eyes attached to his, but it seemed not out of desire or defiance, but curiosity. "I know. Betty told me. She's that gal over there that voiced support for you. She says her sister refers to you as the Casanova Cowboy."

With a blush, the Captain broke their orbital connection. "This sheriff is guilty as charged. I'm not going to lie to you, but hear me out. I think you are the most beautiful woman I have ever laid eyes on."

She turned her head away for a second and then returned her eyes to him.

"You're different. Someone I'd like to get to know," he said. "Although I would love nothing more than to *bed* you, I will not under any circumstances. At this time, I cannot offer you the things you so richly deserve in a mate."

Intrigued, Susanna went to speak but stopped. Her front tooth pinched her lower lip in consternation.

The Captain filled in the void. "I'm on a mission filled with peril and folly. It is not right for me to try to win your heart under these circumstances. I want you to think of me as a rogue. Maybe, if I succeed with my mission, and we do develop a mutual fondness, then you will consider making an honest man of me."

Susanna appeared almost speechless but looked as though the many thoughts racing through her mind needed to tumble out. "I know I should be flattered, and the truth is I am. You're the one that's different. Your way with words, your looks, physical size, hygiene, plus you can sing and play guitar. That you seek the company of women, I cannot hold against you. Most men do. The difference is women desire you, and so it all comes too easily to you."

The Captain waved away the character profile, although he figured she nailed it just right. "Who's the flatterer?"

"Well, I'm not done just yet. Here's the bad part," she said, her voice several octaves lower. "I don't support your mission or your cause. This war took my father. My mother and I barely get by. I'm not looking for a fighter, a barroom brawler, a rebel, a scalper, a Confederate, or a Union soldier. And I don't want to marry a murderer." A small smile curled her lips. "So I thank you for your honesty. For that, I will agree to spend time with you tomorrow."

Like water removing the grime off his body, the Captain felt cleansed. Her words were a revelation, a song that captured his inner voice. They shared the same sad melody, and so he steered her farther from the crowd.

"I'm sorry for your loss and plight. Tomorrow, we can talk more about that. But if the lady is not offended, may I ask how your father was killed?" With a tight jaw, he passed a grave frown her way.

She swallowed and bit back anguish. "Our family had slaves too. We needed them to keep the farm going, but Papa made sure they were treated fairly. They became part of our family. When the war broke out, Papa did not believe in breaking the Union over the issue. Besides being morally wrong, he saw a future where modernization would replace the need for mass labor. He also remembered stories from his father. How when England had changed kings, his religion then fell out of favor, and the persecution began. That's why his father fled to America. What applied to freedom of religion should govern skin color and both genders as well."

She swallowed again, as though her mouth was dry with cotton. "Everything would have been okay if Papa just kept his feelings to himself, but that wasn't his way. Word got around, and he was branded a nigger lover."

This time, Susanna let the emotions escape. Her breaths came rapidly, and tears welled in her eyes. The Captain placed his hand over hers.

She found strength in the touch and continued. "We found his scalp on a fence post, his bullet-riddled body out in the field."

The Captain tensed his hand over hers. "My father died in this war too. He was a Union soldier who also believed in freedom for all." He pointed at his blue uniform. "This, I did not get off the body of a dead soldier. It's my father's old uniform. I know it will sound evil to you, and I fully understand your hatred toward violence, but I plan to avenge my father's death." He paused and pursed his lips. "Maybe I can avenge another."

Incredulous, Susanna shook her head. "First, I will not have your death on my hands. I am done with this eye-for-an-eye business." She took her hand out from under his and rested hers on top. "Do you mean to tell me you rode into Booneville for the biggest Confederate celebration statewide, and you're fighting for the Union? Are you crazy?"

"I am not truly fighting for the Union, but I do have contacts to help me succeed. And yes, I may be a little bit crazy." His voice softened. "I loved my father."

Both clasped their hands together.

Her jaw firmed. "As did I." The words came out a whisper but strong with mettle as she inched her hand away. "I must get back to work. Meet me in front of the church tomorrow at noon."

As they walked back into the crowd, Betty, the vocal advocate, approached. "Sorry to interrupt you," she said to Susanna, "but I have to ask him something." She slurred her words, likely feeling the booze.

Then she turned to the Captain. "Most men name their thingy," she said and pointed to his crotch. "My last lover called his *Thor*." She giggled. "I was wondering with your size and reported abilities, if you had a name for it?"

Susanna turned away and tucked her chin, embarrassed.

The Captain shifted in discomfort. He'd never thought about such a silly thing, but a moniker suddenly occurred to him. He gave Susanna a knowing glance and smirk before he answered.

"In honor of my late father, I named him *Major Johnson*."

CHAPTER 17

PRESENT DAY

Baxter boasted, "If you Google the slang word for *Johnson*, you will find it's synonymous with *penis*. The source of the reference is murky, and there are lots of theories, but the first recorded reference was in the 1860s. I believe I have now uncovered the origin of this urban legend."

Professor Gladstone sighed, shrugged, and brought his right hand to his forehead as if he had a migraine. The summarization of the bar scene alone had Gladstone thinking of some good scotch he had back home. He half-wished he were drunk now.

Even if he'd been inebriated, he was not some sorority hussy. He could never fall for Baxter's bullshit. Silly songs, college bar games, saucy dialogue, and nudity—the paper reminded him of some cheesy porn script covered over by a few historical clichés.

He recalled camping in rural Maine. At the one general store, one could get live bait, along with an assortment of goods, including playing cards, booze, condoms, and the four-pages-only local newspaper. It also had a small selection of rentable movies, half of which were porn.

Then he had been revolted by some of the titles: The perverted Dickens, *A Tale of Two Titties*; the Huxley bondage epic, *Slave New World*; the heroine Indian gangbang adventures of, *Poch-a-Hotness*; the make-love-not-war lesbian drama, *Daughterhouse Five*; Surecock Holmes in the "whore done it?"—*The Mounds of Baskerville*.

It was all so vile, but no more so than Baxter's thesis.

Baxter had more to say. "All those songs were real, Professor Gladstone, except of course the one *he* made up on the spot. All those people, John Edwards, Little Archie, Frank James, Badger Bob—they existed."

Professor Gladstone took his hand from his head and pointed at the student. "The first three names I'm well familiar with, but this Badger guy is likely your own creation—along with the rest of the bit characters."

"What about the main character, Captain Coytus?"

The pounding against his skull intensified. He closed his eyes for several seconds and willed this nightmare to end. Continual harping about this Captain Coytus reminded him of a matter with his only son, Theodore. For almost a year, his son had insisted a monster lived in his closet. No matter how many times the room was inspected and the closet cleared, when the lights dimmed, the monster returned.

How much more must Baxter's frightful tale continue? The comparison brought something else to mind—the closet. Behind his office closet door lurked another monster, a deposit of Baxter's mischief.

He spread his hands. "Mr. Baxter, I really have had enough for one day. We don't need to rehash this sordid story. I'm at the point where I'll give the paper a D- grade just for your conviction. Will a passing grade and graduation from Harvard be enough to send you on your way?" His furrowed brow etched with hope.

"It certainly will not," an insulted Baxter replied.

Professor Gladstone massaged his temples. "How about a C?"

Baxter straightened. "For this *magnum opus*, I will take nothing less than an A+."

With vigor that bordered on panic, Gladstone shook his head, holding both hands in a stop motion. "An A+ paper will be seen by fellow professors. If *this* was ever to see the light of day, I would be ruined with ridicule."

The student grimaced. "I plan on publishing this. Consider yourself lucky that you got a sneak peak."

"Publish?"

"I owe it to the academic world. I came here expecting at minimum, praise, but I never considered that you'd be envious of my work."

Heat swelled into his cheeks, and he gripped the armrest of his chair until his nails turned white. "Envious?"

Baxter nodded. "Jealousy is the only explanation I can fathom for pretending to ignore the obvious." He paused, raised an eyebrow, and asked, "You're not trying to play dumb, only to steal this scoop for yourself, are you?"

To think he, a *professor*, would ever author something so maniacal! "I would never—"

Baxter cut him off. "It's unethical." And tapping his chest, he continued. "Unlike me, you do not possess the evidence to make the case."

Like an electrical eel that keeps shocking its already-dead prey, Baxter kept zapping away. Professor Gladstone's brain buzzed but felt short-circuited, as though he couldn't quite bridge the gap between what was happening and what should have been happening.

"Anyway, at least I don't have to offer you the privilege of penning the foreword. I felt obliged, being your student. There are plenty of other more acclaimed historians who surely will jump at the chance of having their name associated with this surefire seller."

Baxter paused for just a second and continued. "I could have placed a review from you on the back cover. Naturally, I would have been happy to return the favor for one of your future endeavors, but it's your loss on mutual prestige."

This was beyond cocky; the lad suffered from delusions of grandeur.

Yet he wasn't finished. "I can see the book tours. I suspect you could meet a lot of women on the road. They dig that intellectual, author thing." He stopped to observe Professor Gladstone and then quipped, "Well, usually."

After leaning back and with a cocky smirk, he shrugged. "If you ditch that comb-over and your Mr. Rogers's sweater-thing, you might reel in a few ladies yourself. Try suspenders; they seemed to work for Larry King. Speaking of which, he might come out of retirement just to interview me."

Professor Gladstone instinctively moved his wedding-ring-less hands below his desk. His marriage lasted six years, gave him a son, and then his wife left him, claiming he was a bore. He took Baxter's insults like the anesthetized take pain. The absurdity was heaped in such rapid fashion it was mind-boggling. Nothing registered. The boy had to be done with this bravado … he hoped.

Baxter preened. "I'll do what J. D. Salinger should have done—quit after the first book. Sometimes you only have one classic in you."

"Indeed," Professor Gladstone offered at last. "What is this proof you speak of? I want evidence that this captain of yours existed."

"Speaking of Captain Coytus, it's time I got to the meat of the story, a saga that will fascinate not just historians but also the public."

The migraine stiffened. "I'll give you a B. Please take it and leave."

PART IV

CHAPTER 18

September 1864

Deputy Richard Less arrived at the jailhouse like he did every day—late and without expectations. War ravaged the nation; rebel factions fomented local injustice. In short, Booneville was virtually lawless, which meant Deputy Less had little to do, with which he was quite content.

He noticed several things when he entered. The smell of sex clung to the air, the Badger was behind bars, sprawled on the ground moaning in pain, and a large, young man, dressed in a Union uniform, was seated in the sheriff's favorite chair, swinging a timepiece.

Something odd was going on. Deputy Less opened and closed his eyes as if the visual might be a mirage. "Do you know you're sitting in the sheriff's chair? He won't even let me sit there."

The stranger was no dummy. He nodded and, as expected, rose to vacate the chair. Then he said something unexpected. "It's a chair, not a throne." The Captain's eyes rolled to the rickety old stool. "Take a seat. I have to say, it is damn comfy."

Deputy Less whipped his head from side to side. "The sheriff will thrash me if he finds out."

"I don't think he will. In fact, I promise."

Badger Bob stomped his feet on the ground. "Dat becuz dat fukin ahole," inhale, wheeze, inhale, "is da nuuu sheeerif!"

Deputy Less strained his neck toward the cell. "Sorry, Badger, I couldn't quite make that out. Can you repeat that?"

He groaned and leaned forward, resting his arms on his knees and his head in his hands.

The Captain smirked. "It's okay. He needs to rest, but I'll roughly translate that for you. He said, referring to me, 'That asshole is the new sheriff.'" He pulled out the dirt-smudged badge from a pocket. "Take a seat."

Deputy Less's brow lined like conflicted factions on a battle map. He had no love for his boss, but he needed the job, and as long as he did nothing, it was his to keep. Yet this new sheriff offered up the chair. Maybe change was no change, and there was no reason to be worried. He wandered over, smiled with confidence at the new boss, and took a seat. He closed his eyes and dreamed of the status quo. He opened his eyes, hopeful.

"I'm Captain Coytus. Everything you know is about to change."

The deputy's stomach lurched, and he jumped up as though he'd been sitting in a Judas chair. "How so? And where is Sheriff Graft?"

"He went to Massachusetts on a business trip."

"Dat hor—" cough, "sheet."

Deputy Less tilted his head as he tried to process the words.

The Captain grimaced. "I think he said something about the 'whore shits.' Not sure if you know, but Badger's got some venereal diseases. Messes with your innards," he said and waved his arm in a circle around his lower midsection.

Badger Bob groaned.

The Captain picked up several wax-sealed envelopes. "The first order of business is ensuring these envelopes arrive in Massachusetts before our friends get there. I want Cooter, Billy Bob, and the sheriff to be greeted with the hospitality they so richly deserve."

"Dat becuz uw ah fukn' iz weefe," stammered Badger Bob before his face grew red from the lack of oxygen.

Deputy Less cast a puzzled glance and raised eyebrow to the Captain.

The Captain tilted his head from side to side. "If I didn't know better, I think he said, 'That's because he's fucking his wife.'"

Deputy Less sniffed the sex-fragranced air again. Although that was how he'd translated the Badger's words, he winked and replied, "No. I think I understood him this time. He said he's looking for a fucking wife. Think ole Badger's been looking to settle down."

"You may be right. He was quite garbled that time."

Badger Bob beat his fists on the ground.

Deputy Less could tell the big townie was in some pain. "What happened to him?"

"Doctor says he broke a few ribs."

"How did that happen?"

The Captain pointed to a journal next to the envelopes. "I wrote an incident report."

Deputy Less was flummoxed. "A report?"

"Yes, but I'll save you the details. Citizen Bob Shortwood threw a punch at me," the Captain said. "In self-defense, and after several prior attempts to avoid violence, I threw one punch in reply."

Deputy Less rubbed his chin and leaned back on his heels, impressed. "He's a tough bastard. You did that to him with one punch?"

The Captain shrugged. "So here's the deal, Deputy Less. Wait, if we're going to work together, I need a first name."

"Richard."

The Captain blinked. "Richard Less?"

"Yeah, why?"

"Just hope you got some balls. Are you willing to bring change to this town?"

Apprehensive of doing anything without the previous sheriff's knowledge and of doing anything at all, really, Deputy Less frowned. If he actually had to work, then this job could be dangerous, but he considered what his wife needled him about morning, noon, and night—that he lacked confidence and self-worth. Maybe this was exactly what he needed.

Deputy Less offered his hand. "I'd be proud to serve under you."

The Captain shook hands before motioning at the envelopes. "If you can do me a favor, get those letters mailed. Later, I'll need you to tell me where I can get a canvas-covered wagon. Oh, I also could use some large mirrors, but we'll talk about that later."

Deputy Less was curious about the mirrors. His new boss obviously had a strong sexual drive. "Sure thing, Sheriff Coytus," he said as he saluted.

The Captain leveled his gaze with Deputy Less. "You're on a five-day trial."

Deputy Less's stomach jumped, but he dismissed the wobbling of his guts. "I need this job, so I am going to do whatever you say. You want me to shovel horseshit, you got it."

The Captain shook his head. "You misunderstand. I'm leaving town. If you do right by me, I'll appoint you sheriff of Booneville. A lot depends on what you do in the next five days."

Deputy Less's jaw dropped, and his eyes bulged. He could not wait to tell his wife. There was no way he could blow this opportunity.

"You need me to break more of his ribs?" Deputy Less gestured to the injured man on the floor.

"Uk uw," mumbled the Badger.

The Captain scowled. "Was that 'uck ew'? Really is difficult to comprehend."

"He was never articulate to begin with, but now …" agreed the soaring deputy.

The Captain smiled, but his visage drew grim. "I have five days to solve a murder. Getting to the bottom of that goes a long way to making you the next sheriff."

Deputy Less offered a lopsided grin. Permanent sheriff had a nice ring to it, but solving a murder in five days was another matter. Crime, especially murder, was low in Booneville. In fact, the last victim Deputy Less recalled was when Skip Walker was found dead, naked, and scalped. Days later, half his personal items were seen on several men around town. The matter was never investigated. Walker owed everyone, except his mother, money. She knew better.

Frontier justice meant the guilty were not always charged. So Deputy Less was curious what matter the new sheriff referred to. "What murder case are you on about?"

"You know this local gal, Susanna?"

Deputy Less sped his gaze from Badger back to the Captain. The words came slow and in a mumble. "Yes, I do." His eyes flashed back to the Badger.

"Well, it sounds to me like you know what I'm talking about then," leveled the Captain.

Less's emotions teeter-tottered from happy to melancholy. Forget telling his wife a thing. The job was not worth it. He leaned close and whispered, "I need to be alive in five days to get the job. I might as well commit suicide." He rolled his eyes again toward the Badger. "For one thing, he'll talk. He was one of several guys in on it. So were Cooter and Billy Bob. Everyone knows about it."

The Captain snarled, "Well, you have a choice to make. Don't worry about the dirty work; I'll take care of that. I only need to know that you won't betray me."

The new sheriff was morally right, but there would be consequences. The dynamic would change when Coytus left town, and Less wasn't about to risk his life for something like this. Still, he grabbed the envelopes. "Let me get these letters out and think about it."

The Captain seemed satisfied. He motioned toward the Badger. "Don't worry about that loser. He won't be alive to tell anyone a thing."

"Doc say he's a dead man?"

"Not really, but there will be a long recovery."

"Huh?"

The Captain walked over and unlocked the cell door. Loud groans came from the Badger as he was rolled onto his back. The Captain took aim and connected a thunderous punch. The Badger's body coiled from the force of the shot, and a small gasp snapped through the air. The Captain knelt and felt for a pulse, frowned, and delivered another blow.

With the cell door once again locked, he walked back. "Benjamin Franklin once said, 'Three men can keep a secret, if two are dead.' Deputy, I want you to prove our founding father wrong."

CHAPTER 19

After a day's ride, Little Archie and Frank James reunited with Bloody Bill at the Bushwhackers' camp just off the bank of the Missouri River. Bloody Bill's men traveled apart, but parallel to General Shelby's Confederate force. Despite the alliance, each viewed the other unfavorably.

Little Archie explained their meeting with Edwards and his plans to bolster their cause through the media.

Bloody Bill thanked Little Archie. "I needed someone real smart to handle Edwards. Good job." He walked away to confer with another gathering.

Little Archie turned to Jesse James. "We met this guy. He's about your age and as big as an outhouse. Nothing scares him." He detailed the encounter in the bar.

"When he heard you were the man who took out that Union major, he seemed impressed, and he does not look the type to impress easy," he continued and solicited a nod from Frank. "I think that was the final selling point in his agreeing to join us, like he was dying to meet you."

Jesse James smiled and said, "You always have great intuition, Arch."

Brother Frank James jumped in. "I love this dude, Coytus. Know what's weird, though? I happened to be thinking of him when we passed two rattlers, and they were both curled in a way that reminded me of two, Cs—Captain Coytus. I took it as a bad omen."

Little Archie gave a backhand smack to Frank's chest. "Bad omen? Who do you think you are? Nostra-dumbass?"

Frank James acquiesced. "You know best, Arch."

They turned west to link with Major General Price's men, but the Bushwhackers got lost and descended on a farm, where they rustled out the owner, a recently emigrated German. They grew abusive, since most of the German immigrants were strongly pro-Union and strong abolitionists.

Little Archie declared, "I hate these German do-gooders. Always sticking up for the minority types."

"Hey, you never know," began Frank. "Their sympathies may be temporary. A time could come when the German people would target a race of people. I mean, you never know."

Little Archie aired an exasperated sigh. "The Germans? Ha, they're not the type to wage any aggression. Take my last name, however, Clement, which is French. Surely history will show them to be the fiercest of warriors. The French do not know the definition of surrender. Not even God could conquer Paris."

Little Archie addressed the quivering German. "Here's the deal, Hans. Lead us west to the Crooked River or *eins, zwie, drei,* you die."

For four days, the Bushwhackers rode. The German led them through forests, up and down gullies, and across valleys. They forded rapid streams and sniffed out faint wooded trails. Little Archie started calling the man Hans Boone for his navigational prowess. On the fifth day, however, they broke camp, and the German led them to a rocky dead end, where they were forced to retreat. The guide scoped the area, muttering in German.

"I think your buddy, Boone, is lost," Frank chided.

"Thanks, Captain Clairvoyant," Little Archie huffed, and he slipped behind the German with a raised sword. "*Eins, zwei, drei*, off your head flies."

He swung the blade at the man's neck, once, twice, three times. After severing the last few straggling tendons, Archie placed the head on the man's chest. The arms propped the head in place.

Little Archie snickered. "Let's *head* out of here."

Chapter 20

Deputy Less delivered the mail, and there was one upside in that endeavor. Logic told him to report the new sheriff's crusade to the men responsible for the crime. Since their identities were not all known, they could dispose of the new sheriff by surprise. This way, by tipping the men off, Deputy Less would enhance his status and could easily become the new sheriff. That would be the smart thing to do. His gut told him so, but he was also a man who lacked guts.

He continued his inner debate as he arrived at the general store. The vendor did not have the mirror dimensions the Captain wanted, but he thought he could put it together in a few days.

Afterward, he slowly made his way back to the jailhouse. He liked the new sheriff but was not convinced that this man would emerge victorious. Although the Captain showed compassion by offering the chair, he proved how ruthless he could be with his fist work on the Badger. The deputy's feet felt shackled as he trudged the last few steps, and he did not make his choice until he stepped inside.

The idea flashed into his brain from out of nowhere, and he smiled. Badger's cell was vacant, and the Captain was seated with a guitar. He strummed a chord, held the note, and smiled.

Deputy Less declared, "I've chosen to betray you."

The Captain raised an eyebrow. "I'm listening."

"I have a plan," he proudly offered. "I go to the men who did this, and

I tell them you're after them. Then we can pick a time and place, and you could be ready for them."

The Captain grinned. "Why wouldn't I prefer being the only one with the element of surprise?"

Deputy Less suddenly didn't feel so great about his plan. "I figured word would get out and make the job more difficult, and with your limited time, you could ambush them."

The Captain bobbed his head back and forth. "Or, this way you thought you'd curry favor with each side. You did stack the odds against me a bit. I did not foresee you as underhanded, Deputy."

Deputy Less's shoulders sagged. His plan had already failed miserably, and his misery worsened as he gazed at the young man before him. There was no anger. Sour disappointment was found in the lines around his tight mouth. It was time Deputy Less went with his heart, time to have some balls, as the new sheriff had demanded.

"You're right, of course," began the deputy. "You have every right to hurt me, and I'd offer no resistance, not that it would likely matter much."

The stranger rose from the prized chair. "Take a seat, Deputy."

Grateful because his legs felt wobbly, Deputy Less did as instructed.

The Captain leveled. "If you were truly diabolical, then you would have gone to the men responsible. With their numbers and the element of surprise, I'd likely be dead, and you a secure sheriff. I'm sure you thought about it."

"I did. I'm a coward."

"And why didn't you act on it?"

Deputy Less's face grew taut. "I know your cause is just. While I don't know any founding father quotes, I'm no Benedict Arnold. I was afraid, but I do want you to win."

He watched the Captain closely as he spoke. Without any bitterness, the deputy was envious of the aura the new sheriff carried. He was huge, good looking, and just maybe too smart for his own good. Deputy Less shrunk into his seat as he awaited the reply.

Seemingly satisfied with what he heard, Coytus nodded. "Franklin also said, 'Tricks and treachery are the practice of fools that don't have brains enough to be honest.' You acted wisely, Deputy."

Despite the gratification of knowing he wasn't going to catch a beating, Deputy Less's innards quivered in shame, and his eyes drooped downward. The Captain's words edged his focus upward.

"You acted out of fear, and that is nothing to be ashamed of. Graves are filled with brave but stupid men. I'll need those mirrors and a few more supplies. I'll also need to know the names of the men involved and where they live."

The Captain explained his idea, which turned out to be basically the same plan as what Deputy Less offered, just delayed a few days so the Captain could prepare. The best part was that the deputy was told he could leave town after the plan was properly set.

When Deputy Less had entered the jailhouse, his legs were wooden, but his stride buoyed him. He left for the wainwright and wondered why the Captain requested mirrors that were the same dimensions as the wagon. The young man clearly had an imaginative libido.

CHAPTER 21

"Did Katherine ride Fly Bait?" Susanna asked as she lathered the horse's coat in front of the jailhouse.

"Err, no. Why do you ask?"

"He's a big fella," she said, patting the horse. "I saw Katherine this morning, and she was walking bowlegged." She cast a sly smile Coytus's way. "Suppose it must be on account of your personal horseplay."

Susanna saw discomfort in the retreat of his eyes. She eased up. "I'm joking with you. Never saw her at all."

He smiled in relief, and they both laughed.

"That should do it. This cider-vinegar tonic I put on his coat and the garlic mixed into his feed should keep the flies away." She patted the horse on his neck. "Maybe the garlic feed would keep the women away from you, but I doubt it."

"Hmm," he replied. "Last I heard, you were jumping out windows to escape stalkers."

The slight reference to the Badger knit disgust in her brow. "How's he doing?"

"Not well. He's dead. We'll get to that later."

For the moment, Susanna let it pass. Instead, she asked, "Are we ready?"

They mounted Fly Bait and headed west, toward a rocky hill formation. Within a few minutes, they crossed a stream that fed a larger river on the right. Ahead loomed a sheer rock wall and a hill that rounded to the east. He brought Fly Bait to a stop.

After helping her dismount, he declared, "This is perfect."

Susanna could tell by the way he surveyed the terrain that he was not only talking about their picnic spot. She chose not to validate her intuition. It was more important to see what he'd reveal on his own. Questions could always come later.

He kicked away a few rocks and took a large blanket from a saddle bag and then spread it on the ground. He placed a canteen, a jug of wine, a block of cheese, bread, and guitars on top of the blanket.

"I can't wait to see you play your dad's guitar," said the Captain.

Usually mention of her father brought anguish, but this time the memory of him conjured a smile. "I can't wait for you to hear the song I wrote for you."

He appeared to shake away some comment. From the wry smile, Susanna guessed it was some juvenile suggestion. She credited him for holding back his usual bravado around her. It meant respect; however, she supposed she would have reveled hearing his retort.

When he answered, he simply said, "Right after I get a fire going." He pulled out his timepiece, checked it, and put it back in his jacket. Satisfied, he went to gather wood.

Susanna spread her dress out and sat on the blanket, where she watched him work. He was so masculine she could envision him pulling trees from the ground. Instead, he came back with several sticks and a few sturdy logs. He set the wood down on a large, flat rock, bundled them together, and then pulled cloth rags and a pack of matches from his jacket.

When the fire reached an ample blaze, he rejoined her. The Captain pulled out a knife and cut wedges of cheese into a wooden bowl. He selected a piece and offered it to her mouth. She accepted and felt like a mouse knowingly taking the bait. She was happy to be trapped with him and wished she was his prey.

He chewed more than the cheese as he looked at her. She noticed his eyes drifted to her bodice and then upward, but it was more reflexive than leering. He nodded up and down and then back and forth as if debating with himself. Finally, he faced her and said, "I can't lie to you. I killed Badger."

Susanna waved away his obvious guilt. "It's not your fault. You hit him one time. Not like it was murder."

The Captain pressed his lips and then said, "Hear me out. Badger was one of the men responsible for your father's death. That information was given to me in his presence and compromised the situation." He drew a deep breath. "I hit him a few more times—ruptured his lung."

Susanna thought she would have been angry with his tidings. Clearly, she'd expressed her views on violence and revenge, but his rationale seemed reasonable under the circumstances. She had no love for the Badger prior to his implication in her father's death, and a sense of vindication warmed her.

Reading her, he added in a tentative tone, "I have the names of the other men responsible."

Her ears tingled, and she brushed her hair back. "I don't want you playing a hero. I don't even want to know their names." The words were flat as a chessboard.

"I have a plan. In a few days, Deputy Less is going to incite these men. If they come for me here," he gestured to the land around him, "I will protect myself." A boyish smirk erased the lines around his forehead.

She swatted his leg. "This is not a game, and what do you mean *here?*"

He motioned to the horizon and beyond. "This place is perfect."

She took in the rocky rise ahead and the river on her left—two places that proved impassable. On her right, the terrain was unhindered but difficult for horseback travel. There was only one easy approach, and he'd picked a good spot to defend an ambush. Smart, but then she lamented that this picnic location had not been selected solely for its romantic appeal.

She met his gaze. "All right, tell me who killed my pa."

The Captain reached into his jacket pocket, pulled out a folded sheet of paper, looked down, and read, "Brock, Butch, Clay, Cody, Forrest, Hunter, and Wyatt." He waved the paper and smiled. "Are they members of the town's outhouse-tipping team?"

Susanna chuckled and then grew serious. "I expected a few of those names, if not all, but this is not funny. They're a dangerous bunch. Brock is almost as big as you, and you're outnumbered."

"Don't worry about me, Susanna. I ask you to trust me on this."

She trusted him and his confidence, but that did not mean she believed the outcome would prove favorable. "You told the Badger you had good aim. How well can you really shoot? Cody won the town marksmanship contest five years running."

Blood drained from her cheeks as he answered, "Not good. But I don't fight with guns." His sheer size and confident tone backed his conviction.

Yet she was not convinced. "What are you going to tell them? 'Please put down your guns'? These men don't fight fair."

"Neither do I," he assured her.

The strength of his aura was an irresistible pheromone. Suddenly, she felt different about the notion of revenge. She wanted to help him in some way.

"Do you even have a gun?"

He giggled. "Not yet, ma'am."

Her eyes bulged. "You're on a dangerous mission, and you're unarmed?"

"It has a way of working to my advantage."

Susanna scoffed. "Please close your eyes and turn your head. I'll let you know when you can look again."

The Captain did as instructed.

She reached under her dress and pulled out a Colt pocket revolver. "I'm decent."

He turned to face a pointed gun. "Hmm," he said, lips curled up like the smoke rising off the fire.

"No matter how strong you are, even a girl like me could kill you with this gun," Susanna said, rotating her aim across his body. "My father taught his girl to defend herself. Before Badger ever had his way with me, he would've gotten a taste of this." She jerked the pistol a few times, simulating fired shots.

"Good for you."

She opened her purse and plucked out several bullets, rose to her feet, handed him the gun, and set off. Along her journey, she picked up a fist-sized rock. Fifteen feet out, she sat her rock on a much larger stone. She lifted her dress and daintily sprinted back.

Susanna gestured to the target. "Let's see what you got, tough guy."

The Captain grinned at her and then focused on his target and fired. The bullet went low and wide to the left. He shrugged. "No guy is as small as a rock."

Susanna took the gun from him. "In a fight to the death, aim is everything. There's a difference between taking a bullet in the leg or the skull," she declared and pressed the trigger. The rock went flying from the boulder.

"And I thought the only danger was your beauty."

Her eyes fluttered, her heart sputtered, but she remembered his declaration and packed the compliment in deep storage.

The Captain continued his target practice. The first shot hit the boulder well below the rock, his second went too high, yet on the third shot he grazed the rock. The two then set out for the stream, where the Captain caught two fish. As he cooked, she took out her guitar.

"I started to write a song last night. It's not complete yet, but I'd like to play it for you."

Thrilled, he said, "Nothing would please me more."

Susanna chugged a chord progression that sounded like galloping horses. Her voice broke the quiet like a songbird.

> *This is the legend of Captain Coytus.*
> *The Casanova cowboy that turned women's hearts to dust.*
>
> *The legend began in a small western town.*
> *A man rode in on horseback as the sun set down.*
> *First he entered a shanty saloon,*
> *And suddenly everything stopped like it was high noon.*
> *All eyes followed the debonair stranger.*
> *Here was one strapping stud lone ranger.*
> *Went to the bar, ordered everyone drinks,*
> *Gazed at every woman and gave them a wink.*
> *A townie got jealous and challenged a draw;*
> *The Captain laughed, and he said sure.*
> *When he unzipped and showed the size of his gun,*
> *The girls said, "Woo, you are the one."*
>
> *Oh, Captain Coytus, a legend in lust.*
> *Oh, Captain Coytus, his work was always just.*

Susanna watched his face shade red and was pleased with the trait it exposed. Humility.

CHAPTER 22

In the early dawn, the ex-sheriff's wife, Katherine, and her friend Marge departed from the jailhouse. A short while later, the Captain appeared with a shovel and two buckets filled with Susanna's garlic mix feed. He emptied both in Fly Bait's trough. With the empty buckets in hand, he went behind Fly Bait and cleaned up after him. After the horse had been well fed, the Captain grabbed both filled buckets and set out to the farmhouses outside town.

He cocked his head to a scratching sound, like something was being dragged in the road. Ahead, a shape came out of the dawn. At first he thought it was an upright bear, but then he realized the full head was a fur cap. From one side of the street to the other crossed the man in skis. He yodeled and trudged into the front door of one of the better-sized homes.

The Captain shook his head and continued down the road, where he found the run-down farmhouse he was looking for. Weeds filled the farmland, and no animals grazed. He spotted the stone well and rode over, dismounted, and dropped a third of the bucket down the well.

He repeated that same maneuver at five other farmhouses. At his sixth and last stop—because both buckets were now empty—he backed Fly Bait's rear over the well's stone precipice. After a few minutes, Fly Bait's tail went up, and a splash was heard from the water below. The Captain waited until the horse fully flushed his system. He rode back to the road, gazed at the fading stars, and waited.

A girl appeared from the farmhouse and came toward him. The Captain called out to her.

"Jasmine?"

The girl's visage twitched from being startled to having a small smile. "Yes. Are you the new sheriff?"

"I am. Need a ride to town?"

She looked back at the house. "I probably shouldn't. I'll walk but would be delighted if you'd escort me."

They began their short journey, and the sheriff reflected that Deputy Less was right. Hunter's girl was pretty. Her dark, straight hair fell to her shoulders, lining a sharp, small nose and a fierce chin pinched by deep dimples.

She turned up to him. "I've heard quite a bit about you."

"I hope the chatter's been compliments aplenty."

The dimples appeared alongside white teeth. "Depends who you ask. The women seem to fancy you, but not so much the men."

"Must be the cologne," he replied with a grin.

He changed subjects. "I hear congratulations are in order. My deputy tells me that you're to be wed to Cody."

A small frown etched her brow. "I want to leave this boring town. Now Pa wants me to marry his friend," she said and retched. "How could he want me to marry that wretched man? I got work at the church and plan to save enough to take a train east and escape."

"I'll give you the money," he offered.

Her jaw dropped. "You wouldn't?"

"I would."

"I know what you'll want for the money."

The Captain removed his Stetson and put it over his heart. "A thank-you will do, ma'am."

Jasmine pulled on his dangling leg. "No, it won't. Let me leave this town an experienced woman. Help me up on that horse so we have more time."

He pulled her up and playfully slapped Fly Bait. "Go!"

The horse broke into a strong gallop. From the corner of his eye, the

Captain saw the man on skis slide down a slanted roof and land perfectly. A yodel followed.

An hour later, the sun peeked over the horizon. The two lovebirds flew the jailhouse coop. With Jasmine successfully mounted, he rode her over to the church. She planned to leave town the next morning.

Jasmine purred, "See you tomorrow before I leave?"

"Same time, baby. Remember what to tell your father if he asks you about the Badger."

"You got it." She smoothed her Sunday dress and licked her lips, eyes glittering in the dark.

The Captain returned to the jailhouse where he thanked the horse for his duty in the day's deeds. Once inside, he fell into the chair and took a nap.

Too short a time later, he woke to the sound of Deputy Less's arrival. He rubbed his eyes and yawned. "You ready?"

"It's that time," Deputy Less said, sniffing the sex that still hung in the air, which reminded him of a brothel his father had taken him to when he turned fourteen.

The Captain held up a hand. "Before we go, what's the scoop on this chap I've seen around town in skis?"

Deputy Less offered a tepid grin. "That's Ingemar Skidmark."

"Swedish?"

"Yes, sir."

"What's he doing here? And why is he wearing skis when there's no snow?"

Deputy Less sucked air and whistled. "Ingemar was a prodigy of this sport, skiing, which I know nothing about. His family moved to Switzerland so Ingemar could ski the Alps."

The Captain nodded. "I'm familiar with it. Go on."

"Well, he was caught in an avalanche. A rock struck his head, and he passed out. Weeks passed, and he was presumed dead. One morning, a gaunt boy stumbled into town with a malnourished mountain ram at his side. It was Ingemar, but he was different."

"Different?"

Deputy Less made a fist and knocked his head. "His mind is mush.

He claimed the mountain ram got trapped next to him and kept him alive with his warmth. Though he was nearly starved, he never killed the ram, even when a passage opened to escape the mountain."

The Captain rubbed at the rough stubble on his chin. "So how did he end up in Booneville?"

"Someone killed his ram, and then Ingemar murdered him. His parents fled Switzerland and settled here."

"Has he caused any problems?"

Deputy Less's head teetered. "Depends who you ask. If you ask me, he's as friendly as they come, but he had a thing for the sheriff."

The Captain leaned off the back of the chair. "This I have to hear."

"On All Hallow's Eve, some kids picked on Ingemar.[6] They threw chicken eggs at him. Before anything could happen, the sheriff arrested him."

"Did Ingemar get violent?"

"Nope, but the sheriff said he could not take a chance," Deputy Less said and then stopped for a lopsided grin. "The sheriff's costume on All Hallow's Eve happened to be a Viking. On his head was a helmet with two horns."

The Captain gave a throaty chuckle.

"Ingemar believed the sheriff was the mountain ram reincarnated. Inside the cell, he begged the sheriff to snuggle with him. Thereafter, he blew kisses at the sheriff every time he saw him." Deputy Less mimicked the gesture, and through a sly grin, he said, "In the middle of the night, he'd serenade the sheriff's house with yodels. It drove the sheriff crazy, but Ingemar's parents paid him to look the other way."

The Captain left the chair to slap Deputy Less on the back. "Good story, friend. Is Ingemar going to the funeral?"

"No."

"Too bad."

The two men rode to the cemetery. A small gathering stood around

---

6   All Hallow's Eve is Halloween. Each year, my friends come up with a costume theme. We did uniforms, women, and pirates. Last year, the theme was a costume to make you lessen your chances of bringing home a girl. The costumes ranged from priests and skinheads to rednecks. I went as one of my history professors.

a grave. The minister, the doctor, as well as Brock, Cody, Clay, Forrest, and Hunter were in attendance. No women. As the Captain and deputy approached, a few odd looks were cast in their direction.

The Captain removed his Stetson and bowed his head at the gathering. "I admit, I feel awkward being here, but I'd like to say a few words. I've never killed a man before. Although I tried to avoid the confrontation, it does not change the fact that your friend, affectionately known as the Badger, is no longer with us. In his memory and at the location that brought this moment upon us, I thought it would be a tribute to the man to have a postmemorial celebration. Any friend of the Badger's will drink free until dusk at the town saloon."

Badger's friends perked up. Although they hardly appeared grieved, they had been unsettled by the Captain's arrival. Now they smiled and licked their lips, already tasting the booze.

He eyed the Badger's friends. "So let me finish by saying, although I did not know the man, some say you learn a lot about a man by the company he keeps. You look like fine gentlemen." He paused and bobbed his head a few times. "I did get to bond with Badger back at the hoosegow where he confessed to a few things."

Badger's boys shifted and began mumbling to one another.

The Captain smiled. "He told me how much he loved women, which is something we can all appreciate." For a few seconds, he stopped and surveyed the gathering. "Is someone here named Brock or Hunter?"

A large guy whose face held so much weight his eyes squinted back from deep caverns stepped forward. "Brock's my name."

A tall, thin man, with a large head, making the Captain think of a sunflower plant, nodded. "Hunter."

He beamed at the men. "Gentlemen, Badger said he literally loved Brock's wife and especially raved about Hunter's daughter."

The two men's lips peeled back in disgust.

The Captain focused on Hunter. "Your daughter named Jasmine?"

"Err, uh, yeah."

"That Badger, such an eye for detail. He marveled over a large birthmark on her firm left buttock. Said he felt like an artist as he traced the tanned mark with his tongue."

Hunter and Cody scowled at each other, and Brock spit at the grave.

"Badger also let me in on a secret. Said he has a buddy, Clay, whose father told him that his mother died in childbirth. But he said it was a lie; Clay's mother was a Negro prostitute his father met in St. Louis. The father named his boy Clay due to the mixed pigments." The Captain shook his head back and forth in consideration. "However, as friends of Badger, maybe we should keep that secret with us. This feller, Clay, might be offended if he heard these tidings."

"That's horseshit. I ain't no Negro," a voice cried out.

The Captain opened his mouth wide and put his right hand over it. "Oops. I'm terribly sorry. Being new in town, I should have realized you may have been present." He clasped his hands in prayer-like fashion. "He also claimed that you personally made him think that Negroes are just regular people like white folks. Being Clay was good through and through."

Clay kicked dirt at the grave. "That son of a bitch. I don't take horseshit from no one, let alone a dead man." Then he too spat on Badger's grave. "I wish that fucker was alive today so I could kill him."

The Captain shrugged. "Hmm, I guess I shouldn't mention the time he won a lot of money off some sucker playing cards with a marked deck?"

A man with pasty white skin and yellow teeth started wheezing like he'd completed a pony-express route on foot. "I always knew that bastard cheated. I ought to . . ." Cody said and tugged his pants down. He urinated on the grave, pissing away whatever miniscule elegiac sentiment existed.

The horrified minster seemed poised to react, but icy stares kept him frozen in place.

The Captain put his Stetson back on his head. "As a reminder, there will be free drinks at the saloon in honor of your dear friend, Badger Bob."

CHAPTER 23

The Captain smacked Brock's wife, Gaby, on the behind. "Thanks for the hospitality, ma'am."

Gaby's face gleamed with perspiration and bliss. "You can lasso me anytime," she panted. "And I'll remember to tell my husband Badger had his way with me and vowed to kill me if I uttered a word of it."

Back aboard Fly Bait, the Captain was keenly aware that flies no longer swarmed the horse. Perhaps the stallion deserved a name change.

The Captain had one more stop to make on his tour. He spotted the largest home in Booneville, a Victorian. The homeowner, Butch Dyke, had come to Booneville three years prior from Georgia. Butch inherited a fortune but moved west to be closer to his beautiful wife's family. He met his spouse while she attended the first chartered college for women, Wesleyan Female College.

The Captain knocked on the door. When opened, it confirmed everything Deputy Less had said, but for some reason, the Captain had been dubious. Butch Dyke's wife, Gretchen, was stunning. Her red hair was not fiery but burned a low, deep ember, and her face shined a soft, translucent white. Green eyes sparkled with beguile. "Are you here to rob me, my dear sheriff?"

Delighted and confused, the Captain stammered, "E-excuse me?"

She grabbed him by his jacket, pulled him inside, and then shut the door behind them. "Steal my heart, Adonis. We don't have much time. Butch can't drink, and he will be the first back from your saloon party."

The Captain snapped his fingers. Butch had to be the lightweight.

She smiled. "Would you like a glass of water?"

"No, thanks. Did you drink water from the well today?"

She grimaced. "Funny you ask. It didn't taste right."

The Captain snapped his fingers once more, but in annoyance. He was too late. What a shame, too, as her mouth longed to be kissed. "I would avoid well-water for a week. Think the aquifer is contaminated. I have one last supply of fresh water to keep you satisfied. There's probably not enough for your husband, however."

She shrugged dismissively. "Butch is a bad egg. He's rotten and smells. Last time we had sex was our wedding day." She stopped to cavort around in a circle. "So let's get to it."

She grabbed his hand, led him through the house, and out the back door. They passed a field where two slaves worked. The Captain noticed Gretchen make eye contact with a large male as they approached a barn.

Inside, she steered him to a bed of stacked hay and pointed. "That's Butch's prized pistol and favorite riding saddle. I had a few fantasies in mind," she said and pushed him back. She disrobed and placed the saddle on his midsection. With the pistol in her right hand, she mounted. "After I play with his gun," she said and caressed it down her midriff, "I want to play with yours."

An hour later, they dressed. Gretchen grinned at the Captain as she laced her bodice. "You're even bigger than Rodney, our house slave." She shook her head in wonder. "When can you visit again?"

The Captain buckled his trousers. "Not sure I'll be able to."

"Actually, you'll be back tonight."

"I will?"

Gretchen's dimples grew. "We'll need the sheriff to investigate my husband's stolen gold." She pointed to a sack on the barn floor, leaning against the pile of hay. "Don't worry. He hasn't looked at this stash in weeks. I'm going to say Badger stole the gold and threatened to rape and kill me if I told Butch."

She handed the sack of gold over. "This should more than pay for Jasmine's exile from Booneville." She leaned in to kiss him, which he dodged, and her tongue ended in his ear. She came back into focus, her eyes full of wanting lust. "The tea I'll serve my husband will knock him fast to sleep. Then perhaps we can start your investigation back in this barn." She flashed a coquettish smile. "With a firm lead, we'll work every angle to exhaustion."

CHAPTER 24

eputy Less arrived to find his new boss asleep in the chair. From the sheen on his face, the deputy first thought the man ill, but the familiar fragrance in the air told him he was likely tuckered out. A dozen sharpened sticks were stacked against the wall.

Deputy Less coughed, and the Captain woke, blinking several times as he stretched.

"Good news," the deputy announced. "Your canvas-covered wagon is complete, and the mirrors have been cut to specification."

The Captain yawned into his first words. "Napoleon once said, 'Never awake me when you have good news to announce, because with good news, nothing presses; but when you have bad news, arouse me immediately, for there is no instant to be lost.'"

The deputy's face drooped, and the Captain sprung from the chair and gave his companion a strong hug. "That's fantastic news, friend. I always thought Napoleon was a wanker, anyway."

Deputy Less breathed a sigh of relief. "I'll bring your horse over and get the wagon hitched and then stop to get the mirrors." He eyeballed the Captain. "You could use some rest."

He playfully punched his deputy. "You might be surprised to learn I've had a case to solve."

Deputy Less arched his brows in question.

"Butch Dyke got robbed. A stash of gold's gone missing."

Deputy Less noticed the Captain's eyes wander to the table as he spoke, upon which sat a bulging sack.

The Captain refocused on the deputy. "Turns out Badger Bob seduced Butch's wife, and she hated her husband so much she gave Badger the gold."

The other man scratched his head in thought. "Really? Butch is no prize, but I can't picture Gretchen going for Badger."

The Captain pointed. "There's hope for you yet. She gave the gold to me but told her husband Badger stole it and threatened to rape and kill her if she confessed."

"I think you've given me more than enough ammo for tonight."

The two men discussed the deputy's talking points. "When you're done meeting them, you can clear out of town. Tomorrow, no matter the outcome, you'll be the sheriff of Booneville."

Deputy Less left the jailhouse to get the wagon and mirrors and took with him a new outlook on life. In a matter of days, his mundane life had changed. Soon he would be sheriff. All he had to do was tell Badger's gang things the Captain had done.

He'd be sending wolves to the lair of the man who wrought this opportunity and newfound confidence. These thoughts weighed upon him as he brought Fly Bait to his new burden.

CHAPTER 25

Susanna arrived at the jailhouse, thinking of how much her life had changed. The Captain had flung open a window that illuminated her dark, suffocated world and brought with him fresh air, a new horizon.

Her reverie broke when the Captain emerged from the jailhouse. "Susanna. You look radiant, my sunshine."

She wore her finest dress, one her mother had made for her seventeenth birthday. Her blue bonnet was decorated with blue and yellow pansies she'd picked that morning.

He led her around back of the jailhouse to an already blazing fire with a blanket positioned upwind. Susanna's mouth watered as she watched him turn ribs over the fire. Red meat had been scarce since Father passed.

"You're smart. Have you ever thought about attending a university?"

Like tugging a loose thread, a grimace unraveled his stoic visage. His words dropped like soft cotton. "Education was important to a kind neighbor," he recalled. "I was tutored by a member of the British Royal Society. If not for Father's death, I reckon I'd be sipping tea in England this very minute."

Susanna wished her father was alive. Protective of his daughter, he stared down any man who peered her way, yet she was certain he would have approved of this one. "You must have seen a lot. What fascinated you the most?"

"You."

His reply surprised her. She wanted to dismiss the reply as flattery, something he said to all the girls, but his words came natural and without a trace ambiguity. Still, she forced herself to store this memory in her mental locker.

"Be serious. I meant something you gleaned in your education."

"I was serious, but I will answer your question in the manner requested." His eyebrows arched to their natural zenith. "Imagine having the power to induce another person to do whatever you desire."

Susanna scoffed. "Are you claiming an academic rational for your conquest of women? Nice try."

He feigned a look of surprise as his mouth stretched in a circle. "My tutor once attended a lecture by a man named James Braid. He reached notoriety, although not many subscribed to his theories, which are built off the work of Abbé Faria, and before him Franz Anton Mesmer." He paused after the name drops; Susanna's eyes did not dim but twinkled.

"Mesmer is where the word *mesmerize* comes from. Braid took underpinnings in those theories in conjunction with studies of near and Far East religions, such as yoga. Based on science rather than the occult, Braid claimed he perfected the ability to place a subject under a hypnotic state."

She grinned. "Are you claiming you're using alcohol to bring women to this hypnotic state and thus mesmerize them?"

A deep laugh rolled from his chest. "Works on men too. Drunk, I'm as easy as a summer morning snooze in a hammock."

"You're easy sober."

"True."

"Except with me?"

"Err …," he stammered. "Nice try, honey cakes."

One of her father's expressions came to mind: *off the hook*. She'd release the Captain from his discomfort on this topic. "What is so interesting about Braid's theories?"

With boyish enthusiasm, the Captain replied, "Braid and other researchers believe the mind is capable of incredible things under a hypnotic state. They're found a way to induce a person to answer any question, even the most closely guarded secrets. Later, when released from the dream-fugue, the subjects were unaware of the inquiry."

"Incredible."

The Captain nodded. "Furthermore, it's been suggested that a thought or any fabricated notion could be embedded in one's memory, only to be pulled from the subconscious by the use of a trigger word or image."

He stopped to invite her input.

A male who cares what I actually think? Hogwash.

Susanna shuddered and chose her words carefully. "Frightening. While education does lessen ignorance, it does not whitewash evil. Can you imagine a sinister genius using these techniques for ill-begotten means?"

He grinned at her.

"Why are you smiling?"

"Your feminine perspective. It's refreshing."

Although pleased, she replied, "Either you are a foolish flatterer or you must have low regard for women."

Her reply appeared to put him on the defensive. She wondered why she gave him such a hard time. A few theories came to mind, but she pushed them away as he replied.

"I am not sure about all that, sugar sweets, but you fascinate me."

"Then you are amazed far too easily." She realized the weird arrangement between them had her unsettled. If he was simply hers and hers alone, she doubted she'd be so petulant.

"You fend away compliments like the garlic lotion repels flies," the Captain said and laughed. His smiled straightened. "Women often exhibit the best of humanity. Too often their voice is neither spoken nor heard." He shrugged. "Tis a shame."

For once, Susanna did not have a curt reply. It wasn't his physique or hygiene alone that captured women's hearts, but rather his ability to understand the fairer sex. Maybe it was time she played fair with him.

"Thanks for actually caring what us gals think."

He laughed. "This time I shall parry your compliment. My tutor assured me testing done on males and females showed no edge in intellect. Some boys are smarter than some girls, as some girls are smarter than some boys. Education is vital, even at the earliest stages of childhood. Just as some people are tall, some folks are just naturally smarter than others, or are predisposed to certain fields, such as mathematics or the arts. Men are generally physically stronger than women, and as is the wont of human cultural nature, we exploit the advantage." He paused, still grinning. "Speaking of which, shouldn't you be serving me a meal, woman?"

Flabbergasted, Susanna was again left speechless. She realized for the second time, he'd cooked for her. Besides her father, she had never seen a man cook before, and she wondered if he cleaned, sewed, gossiped, and enjoyed shopping all day at the same three Booneville stores. Perhaps the perfect man existed after all.

He flashed an impish grin at her. "My sugar of the earth, lunch is ready."

There was no such thing as *the perfect man*, yet the Captain was damn close. A perfect rogue would do for now. She studied his carefree manner as he set the meal of corn and ribs down. On the side, he placed a plate of vegetables. Despite his size, he had certain limberness to his motion, as if he moved to an inner beat.

She was conscious of how messy the meal was. Fortunately, he had several cloth napkins handy.

The Captain removed his Stetson, placed it on the blanket, and sat beside her. He asked, "You want any of these vegetables?"

Susanna loved vegetables, but they had been her entire sustenance of late. "There's enough on my plate as is, but kindly, thanks." She hoped the sincerity in her words rang as true as the gratitude she felt in the core of her being.

"I'm not having any of them, either. Rabbit food," he said in mock disgust. He brushed the blanket and lifted his Stetson. A brown bunny rabbit bounced out of the hat.

Susanna gawked.

His face firmed. "I also studied illusionism. When I meet your father's killers tonight, I'll have a few tricks up my sleeve."

CHAPTER 26

"I'm bored," Frank James declared.

For five straight days, the men had holed up in a drafty barn. The region had been besieged by fierce rainstorms and heavy winds so intense that the rain fell almost parallel to the ground. The sight of a rampaging twister had been enough to convince the men to wait out the weather.

For once, Little Archie agreed with Frank James. They were men of action who did not enjoy idle chatter or banal frivolities of the average American. They were Bushwhackers, serious people.

Frank James sported an eager grin. "Let's play a game, everyone. Duck, Duck, Goose, perhaps?"

A small murmur of agreement died when Little Archie groaned his disapproval. "Schmuck, Schmuck, Vamoose." He sighed. He felt like a chaperone of morons. The scary thing was Frank was actually one of the sharper tools in his gang.

Frank asked, "How about we play Hide-and-go-Seek instead?"

Many faces turned to Little Archie. Some squinted with doubt, while others remained hopeful and faced him with puppy eyes.

Frank jumped up and down. "It will be fun, Arch."

Little Archie frowned as he sized up the James brothers. Frank's head was squatter, perhaps on account of baby Frank being dropped one too many times. He addressed Frank and then the hopefuls. "Anyone who wants to play, leave the barn and hide somewhere outside. In a few minutes, I'll come a looking for you."

Frank pointed. "Little Archie's 'it.' Let's go!"

He watched as the majority of the men started to venture out in the storm, presumably to crouch behind some shrub or climb up a tree. These were his dumb disciples. The few still seated were men of better judgment—an important distinction a leader needed to make.

One man sat on the floor with his arms tied behind his back. A smirk split his lips. "Can I play too?"

Little Archie laughed. He knew their captive said it in jest. James Cowley was a militia man they'd forced to lead them through the region. Thus far he'd proved a better scout than the German, and therefore Mr. Crowley's head still rested upon his shoulders.

Little Archie shook his head. "No one's going anywhere." He stopped to scold the men who snapped up his bait, especially Frank. "I should let you morons rot in that storm out there. Hide-and-Go-Seek my butt cheek," he muttered, incredulous. "I'd eat horseshit before you could get me out in this weather."

The standing men withdrew from the entrance, except Frank who said, "I think Mr. Clement is like the weather—inclement." He gave Little Archie a goofy smile.

Archie bristled inside but laughed when he saw Bloody Bill appear in a state of haste.

Agitated, their leader clapped his hands rapidly. "A large pro-Union militia force is headed this way. We need to pull out now."

"In this weather?" Frank asked.

Little Archie groaned.

"We have no choice," Bloody Bill reasoned. "There's too many of them. We live to fight another day."

Frank nodded. "I only asked because Little Archie vowed he'd eat horseshit before he'd face the storm." He made a scooping motion. "Thus, I wanted to shovel up some dinner for him."

Bloody Bill's laughter pushed outward to the barn's stooped walls and drowned out the storm's roar. His lips smacked a sound of sarcastic pity. "Frank always seems to get the best of you, Little Archie."

Aghast, he froze his expression. That Bloody Bill had made the observation was disconcerting.

The captive, James Crowley, led the Bushwhackers several miles from the farm, though the going was slow and tedious. The storm made travel nearly impossible, so Bloody Bill opted to set camp.

Frank helped pass the time by singing nursery rhymes. By the time Frank got around to "Pat-a-Cake, Pat-a-Cake, Baker's Man," Little Archie had enough of being a captive audience, yet glancing at Bloody Bill, he chose to keep his cool. *Always stay in control.*

A loud whistle shot through the pounding storm. The men listened as a large force thundered their way. Bloody Bill seized Crowley by his shirt. "If you want to live, get us out of here."

Crowley claimed, "If a few men stay behind and fire shots from the copse of the trees, it would give the rest of the party enough time to escape."

Bloody Bill mulled the plan over. "We need two brave, clever men to stay and cover our flank."

Little Archie contemplated whom he should pick.

Impatient at the pending delay, Bloody Bill resolved the matter. "Might as well have the James boys stay behind. Everyone else, pull out now."

CHAPTER 27

"My wife ain't spreading 'em," Brock complained.

"Mine neither," seconded Butch.

Hunter huffed, "Where's my daughter?"

"Son of a bitch," the men cursed in unison as they sat in the back of the saloon.

While they waited for Deputy Less to return from the bar, the assembled crowd of Brock, Butch, Clay, Cody, Forrest, and Hunter reflected on recent peculiarities.

Brock declared, "Someone done slept in my bed."

Butch held up his saddle and pistol. "Holy haystacks. Who stained my saddle?" He pointed to a white discolored stain and waved his gun. "Something fishy is going on around here."

Cody's eyes drew together. "My well water stinks."

Several men agreed. "Tastes like shit," Butch bitched.

Brock shook his head in disagreement. "Our fresh water got mixed with mineral water. It just adds a little flavor." He rubbed his belly. "Personally, I've been guzzling the water like an exhausted draft horse."

"You've been drinking horseshit," Deputy Less declared.

The men looked stupefied with their slacked jaws, bulging eyes, and hands that scratched either heads or tails. Several said, "*Horseshit*," although the word *shit* grew each time, with the letter *i* stretched to a long finish. By the time the word circled to Brock, he had "*Horseshiiiiiiiiiiiiiiiiiiiiiiiiiiiiiiiiiiiiiiit*" down to phonic precision.

"That's right, men. Horseshit, which means you're afflicted with diarrhea of the mouth," Deputy Less said through a snicker. The Captain gave him the line, and it always made him giggle when he envisioned the delivery. He watched the men before him, glad that he had their attention, possibly even their respect.

"What you sayin', moron?" Brock barked.

Okay, respect appeared a stretch. Attention would do for now. Deputy Less realized he was not scared in the presence of these ruffians. In fact, he felt emboldened. "I said your well water has been tainted with horse manure. So if you thought the water tasted better, Brock," he said and intentionally coughed twice, "ahem, then it is you who wins moron of the millennium."

Brock started to make a threat as the other men raised their questions, but he was cut off.

Deputy Less put up his hand and shouted over them all, "I called you here to tell you this, not to argue. I'm not your enemy."

Brock's friends murmured agreement and emptied their canteens out a nearby window while Brock himself studied the discolored stream.

Hunter asked what they all wanted to know. "How did horse manure get down our wells? Was it one of those flying horses? You know, *Unicorns*, or something like that?"

"*Dem* things ain't real," chastised Clay.

Wyatt nodded. "Yeah. Those things are ex-*stinked*. Think the Greeks killed them off."

Everyone seemed to agree with the reasonability of Wyatt's theory.

Deputy Less shook his head. "It was not a flying horse. A man instructed his earth-plodding horse do this."

"Why?"

"For a laugh. He's also the same man who had his way with your wife, Brock."

Before Brock could interject, Deputy Less continued, "As good as Gaby was, he claimed Gretchen was better. Called her a filly. Said she saddled up and rode like a wild horse of the apocalypse."

"Son of a whore."

Deputy Less focused on Butch. "If you're wondering about the saddle stain and the missing glitter of gold, the same man is responsible."

Butch seemed more upset about the money than his wife. "My gold!" he snarled in shock. "Who's this man? He's a dead 'un."

"He's the same man who broke the virginity of Hunter's daughter," Deputy Less said as he focused his attention on Cody. "Sorry, buddy, but your bride-to-be is long gone."

Hunter and Cody looked equally thunderstruck with their mouths gaping. Hunter managed, "What do you mean, *gone?*"

"He paid Jasmine's way to New York. Well, actually Butch paid, but that's just semantics, being his gold was stolen. Jasmine had dreams of big city life. She also had nightmares of seeing Cody naked. Hence—"

"Who is this man?" Hunter seethed. "I'll fix his flint."

Fix his flint? Deputy Less smiled. This was going well. He could almost feel the Captain speaking through him. He wished his boss was an *eye* on the wall. Or was that *fly? No,* eye *makes more sense,* he reasoned.

"The man responsible for these actions is the new sheriff," he informed them, though almost in a whisper.

"Son of a bitch," rang the quorum chorus.

It was going too well to quit, so he drawled, "He murdered Badger Bob and then told all those lies at the funeral when he was the guilty party. But it gets worse. Much worse. Due to his affection for Susanna, he plans to charge you with the murder of her father."

The men grew angry and talked animal excrement all around. "Horseshit," "pig shit," "bull shit," "lamb shit," "dog shit," "chicken shit," "rooster shit," "geese shit," "buffalo shit," and "mouse shit." "Shit on ice," "shit on a skillet," "shit up a creek," "shit in our wells." Each man had given two shits.

Brock took stock of his friends' feelings and faced the deputy. "Say, you shitting us?"

"I shit you not."

"Then why are you telling us this?"

Despite the contrived act, Deputy Less felt bad slighting the Captain. He was not the best liar and hoped his performance would be convincing.

He drew an even stare and focused on the back wall. "Well, it's this simple. If you kill him, then I'm the new sheriff."

The seven rednecks mulled over the deputy's words, and before long, Brock snorted, "He's a dead man. I'll see that he's hung."

Deputy Less grinned at a non-prerehearsed reply. "Actually, Brock, your wife can already attest to that."

CHAPTER 28

"Are you sure you don't need a glass of water, Sheriff? You look a tad parched."

The Captain shook his head. "No, ma'am."

He had no qualms that Forrest's wife, Anne, was also a victim to his well-water degradation stunt. Deputy Less referred to her as "Anne the man." Susanna called her "Forrest's fire." Katherine, the ex-sheriff's wife, eloquently described her as "She-devil cunt."

Anne was known to run a tight farmhouse. Her slaves were routinely whipped, and if she got wind that one had romantic interests in another slave on their farm or elsewhere in town, then she sold him. She believed the Negro race should have their breeding controlled to keep a viable workforce, but not one more. Even in a town sympathetic with the South and its proslavery platform, her stance was extreme.

While she was by no means an unhealthy specimen, her cruel countenance voided much of her femininity. Like a hungry attack dog, her face was in a perpetual snarl.

The Captain had to give Anne some credit, though. Thus far, her behavior was cordial. She even tried to be accommodating when she dropped a suggestive hint: "Please bed me before Forrest gets home."

The Captain knew she'd get around to her desires. Five women from the quilting bee club had previously stopped by the jailhouse. After testing the new quilt to ensure it was bed worthy, one of the women had mentioned Anne was having fantasies of her own. All of them involved a blindfold.

The Captain smiled. "What do you have in mind?"

When she spoke, she growled like a bear. "I want you to make love to me while I am blindfolded."

The Captain's visage feigned seriousness. "First I have to ask you a question. Your husband, Forrest? Is it true that you can see a forest through the trees?"

"Huh?"

"Never mind." The Captain checked his watch. Satisfied, he unbuttoned his pants. "I just want to show you what you won't see," he said with one wide eye.

Anne grinned while she pulled out a scarf she had tucked in her pocket. He made sure the blindfold was wide and tight, and then, all of a sudden, he began to cough. "Sorry, ma'am, bit of a cold," he said, and fell into another coughing fit.

The back door opened. The house slave, Big Tempy Larod, crept into the room with considerable stealth for a large man. He stood beside the Captain; the men shook hands and mouthed greetings.

The Captain's eyebrow arched, and he motioned for Tempy to pull down his pants. As Tempy obliged, the Captain said, "Anne, open your pretty mouth. Give Major Johnson a kiss for me."

Anne kissed Tempy's measurement. The Captain coached her further, and the attack dog gorged the bone, turned on by his directness.

The sound of hooves approached. The Captain started another coughing spell. He guessed he had about thirty more seconds of coughing left, and he hacked his way for the duration. "Sorry, my lady. Bad cold." Then he sauntered out the back door.

The front door opened, and in walked Forrest. His eyes opened like clams as he watched his blindfolded wife perform fellatio on their slave. "*Son of a bitch*," he roared.

Anne's lips quivered as she became unencumbered. Then her jaw tightened with resolve. As she pulled the blindfold off, she said, "Sheriff, you can kill my husband." Startled, she stared up at Tempy. Her head twisted about like a weather vane.

Tempy smiled at his two owners, gave a curt wave, and ran through the back door. Screaming, Forrest followed. On the other side, he was met with a large fist, and he dropped like chopped lumber. Anne followed out next, and the Captain clamped his hands over her mouth.

"Listen closely. Your husband is either going to die or spend a long time behind bars, it matters not to me. But here's what does matter. I'm setting your slaves free with transport out of the state."

She cursed.

"Woman, you have nothing to be bitter about, so wipe that sneer off your puss," he warned. "You've used the sweat of slaves to do your dirty work while you sit your ass in a tub of butter, sneering through life. Yet it's the slaves who can be heard sharing a laugh, singing a song, or beaming a smile. You could learn something."

She kicked the ground. "You deceived me, scofflaw!"

"And that's another thing. You loved every inch and minute with Tempy, right?"

Tempy said, "The lady gobble like a turkey, Master Coytus."

The Captain shook his head. "No, Tempy. *Mister* Coytus, not master. You're a free man. Take Forrest's horses and travel to where I told you to go. Take everyone."

"Thanks, Mister Coytus," Tempy said as he turned his attention to Anne. "Thanks, lady. I ain't had me no sex since you sent my girl, Thelma, to Texas." He grinned and gave his farewell.

Anne cursed again and grimaced at her unconscious husband as a trickle of drool ran from his mouth. Then she glared upward. "We'll just buy more slaves. Forrest is a rich man." She paused to flash a triumphant smile. "You stupid nigger lover."

She then pushed away from the Captain and rolled toward Forrest and his fallen gun. After grabbing it, she rushed a shot at Tempy. The Captain dove and knocked her arm as the gun fired. She missed.

The Captain knocked the gun to the ground and rolled his eyes. "Some people never learn. Too bad, because I believe in second chances."

CHAPTER 29

"The deputy tells the truth," professed Clay. "Forrest was afraid and decided to flee Booneville, but there was no sign of his wife, slaves, or horses."

"I told you," Deputy Less attested. "Everything I've been telling you is the truth." The deputy had confided to the Captain his trepidation in lying. The Bible said it was a sin, but the Captain had rationalized that they were doing God's work, and the good Lord was inclined to look the other way in such matters.

The rednecks pondered the news and muttered to one another before Brock sighed and said, "I always had my questions about Forrest."

"Me too," agreed Deputy Less.

Brock quizzically stared at the deputy. "What questions do you have about Forrest?"

"If a tree fell in a forest, would it make a noise?" Deputy Less grinned as crooked as the men before him.

Brock grunted like a displeased pig, and the men huddled. After a minute, Brock said, "Sheriff Coytus is still outnumbered." Almost as a foreshadowed destiny, he paused to puff his chest like a frog ready to croak. "We don't need Forrest; we're tough guys."

The deputy's brow slanted. "How come you're not heading there until after midnight?"

"I don't want him to see us coming and escape. And I don't like you claiming we're scared."

"You did *like* your water mixed with horseshit."

"What?" Brock raged and stepped toward him.

Days ago, Deputy Less would have flinched like a mouse caught in a cat's shadow. Now he refused to do as much as blink. With a small grin, he replied, "I'm just pointing out that not everything you like may be right. I'm not accusing you of being a coward."

He knew when to cut bait. Well, not literally. He was hardly an outdoorsman, unskilled in fishing, hunting, or trapping. "I need to be going. Good luck, fellers."

CHAPTER 30

Hours after the deputy departed, the men saddled up and galloped off. A few miles later, they saw the wagon lit from at least three campfires' glow. For a quiet approach, they decided to dismount and travel the rest of the way on foot.

As they got close to the wagon, the men began to spread out like a paper fan. They stopped about twenty feet from the wagon.

Brock called out, "Sheriff? Sheriff Coytus?"

From the wagon came a groan.

The men smiled at each other. This was going to be as easy as a three-piece jigsaw puzzle. They cocked their guns.

"I got some bad news for you, Sheriff," Brock said.

Another groan came from the wagon, this time louder and pronounced. "Don't tell me your wife has syphilis, Brock head?"

The men peered at Brock.

"She does?" Wyatt inquired.

"Of course not, you moron," Brock snapped. "The sheriff thinks he's a jester. This time he's going to get a taste of his own medicine."

A voice came from the wagon. "You want me to drink muddied, horseshit well water? No thanks, Brock. You seemed to enjoy the taste so much, I'd feel like a leech to deprive you one precious drop." A throaty chuckle sounded.

Brock spit at the ground, but most of the saliva found his right foot. "Sheriff, you're a dead man."

"Wooo, wooooo … boo!" moaned the voice. "Does that mean you're talking to a ghost?"

Brock gritted his teeth. "It means you *will* be dead."

"Oh my, that does sound dire. Do I get one last request?"

"That depends."

"Can I get one last roll in the hay with each of your wives?"

Clay stepped forward and yelled, "Enough. Kill him!" He pointed his gun and fired into the wagon. His lightning-quick strike was followed by thunder from the other men's guns. The men stopped to listen. Silence.

"Sheriff?" Brock called out. Still silent, he smiled. "Look at the bottom corner. That's blood."

The men nodded with grins.

He waved his gun at Wyatt. "Open that wagon. We got you covered."

Reluctantly, the other man trudged to the wagon. He poked at the fabric like it was some mortally wounded predator. Nothing happened, so he went to the front and peered in. "Someone's under a bloody blanket."

Brock snorted with exasperation. "Pull the blanket off," he said as if speaking to a child or imbecile.

Wyatt complied and removed the cover before he jumped back. "Oh my god."

Bound under rope was a kneeling Forrest. His wife Anne was tied with her backside to him. They looked like a bloody—and very dead—pantomime horse.

A loud splash broke the silence followed by a crackling hiss. The air filled with smoke, and the breeze carried it right at the men. They flailed about until Brock ordered everyone not to move.

"Don't panic. He's playing games, trying to separate us. The smoke will clear. He's got no balls." Then he felt a shotgun barrel press into his crotch.

"The irony," the Captain said before he pulled the trigger.

Brock fell back with screams of agony, but his cries died quickly with him.

Chapter 31

For the past few days, the Captain had dug tunnels deep enough to crawl through. Then he'd filled the top back up with wood boards and rocks, leaving a few prairie dog holes covered with brush.

He crawled back through the tunnel toward the wagon and came up underneath, where he tugged the second string. A bucket tipped, dousing a part of the fire with water and sulfur. He yanked another string, and a group of stacked rocks tumbled onto a metal pan. The men turned toward the clatter.

He heard Clay mumble, "What the Dickens, and Twain, is going on?"

The Captain slid mirrors along the frame of the wagon, where within he was hidden in plain sight. He pumped the shotgun and fired three shots as the barrel shifted from his left to right. Three men dropped. The two left standing fled out of the trajectory of the wind-funneled smoke. They didn't travel far before they disappeared, as if consumed by a parched tract of earth.

The Captain waited for the smoke to clear.

CHAPTER 32

Deputy Less heard the sound of shotgun fire and hastened his pace.

At one time, he had celebrated his cowardice. Tonight, he just had to stay out of the way, and he would become sheriff. It was the best plan ever.

This time, his spinelessness did not sit well with him and showed in his hunched posture. The only time he drew erect—besides when his wife dusted their home in undergarments—was when he conjured thoughts of being a hero.[7] Like a soldier who had never seen battle, his metal needed to be forged.

The Captain had the element of surprise in his favor. How much that parried being outnumbered was as debatable as whether the chicken or the omelet came first.

The wagon was visible as he came around a rock clearing, yet from the distance, the fires offered little clarity in the smoke. The terrain was sloped and uneven. Gunfire thundered ahead. Deputy Less stumbled as he hastened his pace. As he rounded another turn, he felt the steel of a gun barrel press against the back of his head.

---

7   For the record, a stale breeze could have aroused the deputy. A Victoria's Secret lingerie show using only undergarments in the 1860s would have been safe on *Nickelodeon*.

CHAPTER 33

The Captain assessed the situation. Four men were down. Brock was as dead as a doornail, despite a nail never being a mortal entity.

Grounded, Butch, Clay, and Wyatt were all in varying degrees of pain. Wyatt was near death, his body riddled with buckshot. Clay slowly crawled, dragging his lower half across the dirt and rock. Butch was bloody, but on his haunches, his gun aimed toward the wagon, trying to find a target. That left Cody and Hunter still in the covered ditch they'd fallen in—one screaming in pain, the other silent. The Captain was pleased. Everyone suffered some measure of agony.

He yanked the last string, and the air again filled with smoke. He aimed the shotgun at Butch, the healthiest of the trio, and pulled the trigger. Then he fired off two more shots in the direction of Clay and Wyatt. Two shots were returned in his direction. *Had to be Clay.* The Captain again waited for the smoke to pass. When it did, he saw that Clay was on all fours scuttling sideways like a fleeing crab.

After jumping from the wagon, the Captain broke into a sprint. Before Clay could properly grip and aim his pistol, the Captain brought the shotgun stock down on his skull. A concussive sound followed with a *pop*. The angle of the wood stock cracked Clay's skull, and the wound gaped like a mouth in the back of his head.

The Captain headed toward the trap he'd previously dug. A pair of hands appeared on the ground ahead. Cody's head followed as the townie climbed from the hole.

Wounded and dog-tired, Cody gasped, and his face buckled as he saw the Captain approach. His hands went up in surrender. "Please! I did not harm Susanna's father. I said at the time there was no need for violence. You might not know it yet, but I'm a swell chap," he said with a hand pledged in the air like he was under oath. "I'm a man of peace."

In pain, Hunter coughed from the ditch.

The Captain snorted. "Then why are you even here, unless it was to kill me?"

Cody's head wobbled back and forth like the last few revolutions of a spin-top. His wide eyes and oval mouth suggested the mere thought was scandalous.

The Captain snickered. "What about all the bullets fired into the wagon, which killed Forrest and his wife? No malice there?"

Cody's lips bunched. "I told them it was a mistake, and we should sit down and discuss the matter with you as just and honorable men." His hands clasped in prayer.

Hunter again coughed from the ditch.

"You did?" the sheriff voiced, rising an octave higher like a bullshit thermometer. "That's mighty kind of you."

Cody's face beamed with hope. "Thanks. Can we be friends?"

Hunter snorted like a pig.

"Friends?" the Captain said with a haughty chuckle.

"How about we head back to town, and let me buy you a beer?" Cody bargained, hands outstretched like he wanted a hug. "You know, shoot the shit."

The Captain appreciated a little woolgathering. He was known to spin a few loose yarns himself. "You're trying to sell me a big bag of wank," he said as Cody's head began to titter again. "But for the laugh you provided, I might let you live." He aimed the pistol. "Give me any weapon you're carrying. I'm going to check, so if I find something on you, I will kill you."

Cody handed over a gun and a knife, and then the Captain patted him down. Satisfied, he said, "Stay out of the way." He gestured for Cody to stand a few yards back.

The sheriff looked down the ditch. Hunter's leg was impaled on one of the several stakes lining the bottom, and his face must have slammed against a stake or rock. Hunter's mouth was filled with blood, the majority of his teeth gone except a few jagged pieces that hung like the last few autumn leaves. He tried to cough blood up at the Captain, but it fell short, and much of the trajectory landed back upon him.

"It's not polite to spit, Hunter. At least your daughter knows better."

"Where's ma *dawta*?" the wounded man garbled. This time he spat blood downward.

Before the Captain could give an informative, nonsarcastic reply, a bullet ricocheted at his feet.

Cody's voice menaced from behind him. "Drop the shotgun, Sheriff."

The Captain wondered how he didn't find the gun on Cody when he noticed Butch's body nearby. In what might have been his last act alive, he must have crawled over and thrown the gun to Cody.

"We still on for beers, my dear fellow?"

"That's not going to happen. Drop the gun, now."

"What if *I* treated?"

"Maybe I'll let you live if you do what I say. You spared my life; I'll spare yours. You had your victory, but it's over. So either drop the gun and split toward town or I'll shoot you."

The Captain mulled it over and dropped the gun. The steel clanged against the rocky terrain.

Hunter screamed from the ditch, "Kill him, Cody. He's got no gun!"

The Captain turned and focused on Hunter's mouth. "And you have no central and lateral incisors. Cody is clearly a wiser and better man than you."

Cody chuckled. "What if I'm not?"

He shrugged. "Then I reckon you're a dead man."

Cody blanched, his eyes straying from the gun he was holding to the one the Captain had dropped. The Captain's hands remained empty. Hunter beckoned him. Cody's color returned, and he aimed the pistol. "Sorry. Guess I'm not half the man you are."

"Don't take it personal. I'm freakishly endowed."

"That's not what I'm talking about."

"Oh."

Hunter called out from his grave, "Cody, you cock knocker—kill him!"

The Captain arched his left brow. "Last chance. You let me live, I'll let you live."

Cody shook his head. "You're bluffing."

"You don't know squat, and—come to think of it—I don't know anyone named Squat either." The Captain motioned to his opponent's feet and then held his hand upright. "I'm not bluffing, feller. The choice is yours."

He hesitated, but Hunter's demands broke his indecisiveness.

"Cody. Pull ... the ... damn ... trigger!"

When Cody aimed the gun, the Captain brought his raised hand down. Bullets peppered the ground at Cody's feet.

The Captain tilted his head. "Still think I'm bluffing, buddy?"

He offered a sheepish grin. "We still on for them beers? I could definitely go for a drink myself."

The Captain drew a finger across his throat. "Sorry. Think I found better company." He gestured beyond Cody. "Turn around."

Crouched behind a large rock huddled Deputy Less and Susanna. They fired, and Cody fell. With surprising speed, Susanna ran up to the fallen townie, her face cold and flat like a winterized cliff wall. "For my father," she declared and put a bullet in his head.

A voice called from the ditch, "Wench."

Susanna's pretty face crimped.

"Hunter's down in a hole," explained the Captain. "He doesn't look too good. Want me to put him out of his misery?"

She shook her head, and her voice came resolute. "It has to be me."

With purpose in her stride, Susanna went to the ditch and looked down. Without delay, she fired. Satisfied, she walked back to the two men and fell into the sheriff's arms. Her eyes grew misty, and she rubbed them into his chest. After she composed herself, she said, "Lucky we both decided to come to your rescue."

"I had it all covered."

"Poppycock," she mocked as she eyed the deputy.

Deputy Less cleared his throat. "Sorry, boss, but the lady's right. She actually snuck up on me, and I would have been dead had I not convinced her I was here to help you."

With blushful appreciation, the Captain tethered his eyes to hers. "Beautiful, can I offer you a glass of wine before I escort you home?"

CHAPTER 34

She knew this might be the last time she would ever see him. This boy, who rode into Booneville less than a week ago, was now a man leaving town with a permanent residence in her soul but a vacancy in her heart.

She continued the relationship as it was but longed to be in the sanctuary of his arms, her head nestled back against his chest. She desired him to take her but resisted these emotions. She had to, since his leaving would only be worse. That had been his rationale for shunning romance. He was right, she knew, but her true feelings were a stubborn weed that kept blooming no matter how hard she tried to pluck the roots from her soil. She plowed away the seeds of discontent and maintained a sunny disposition.

"I worked a little more on my song last night," Susanna said as she sipped a glass of wine. They sat on a blanket near a campfire. The Captain had dumped all the posses' bodies in the ditch—out of sight and hopefully out of mind.

The Captain's hand jerked. Wine curled to the brim of his glass. "Which song is that, honey pie?"

She batted her lashes. "The satirical tribute I'm writing in honor of you."

His face greened, and in chameleon-like fashion, his visage morphed into a rosy blush. "Err ... I'd like to drink more wine before being privileged with your sweet serenade." The Captain downed the rest of his glass and refilled.

"Good call. Drink up," she said with a light chuckle. "My song reeks of ribald revelry. I am not sure what it says about me as a person, let alone as a lady, to conjure such impure poetry, but I'm having fun with it."

The Captain laughed, stopped, and then laughed again, this time harder. "You're having fun at my expense."

Susanna realized how much she loved his laugh. Deeply infectious, she was compelled to chortle along with him. He pointed an acknowledging finger at her for joining him, and this made them both cackle louder. The Captain was in such hysterics he began to gasp for air like a fish at a lake's summer surface. Susanna fell onto the blanket, her hand to her stomach as if trying to dam the chuckle dyke.

In the midst of the joy, Susanna realized that she had not laughed this hard in many years, if ever. She killed two men tonight. The only other mammal she'd ever killed before was a rat that had charged at her and caught a boot to the stable wall, which was lined with protruding nails used to hang tools. She knew that after the Captain left town, she would need to face her own demons. For now, he kept her heart filled with light.

When they both composed themselves, Susanna asked, "Where did you get this French wine? The saloon doesn't stock this."

He looked at the wine in his glass and then took an appreciative slug. "Remember I told you about mesmerism and hypnosis?"

Coyly, she replied, "Is this where you tell me you have me under some spell?"

"I wish," he muttered and blushed.

For some reason, she liked how the big galoot was easily embarrassed. She again took him off the hook and purred, "Tell me what you were going to say, please."

The Captain's swagger returned. "I used Forrest and Anne as test subjects, and I learned a few things."

"What?"

"If he wears orange hunting clothes, then you would definitely see Forrest through the trees," joked the Captain.

"Ha. What a knee-slapper."

The Captain brought his right hand up and down on his thigh. Susanna shook her head at his antics like she was a naturalist observing *genus Buffoon*.

"Mesmerized, I also learned Forrest likes to dress in Anne's clothes and masturbate with animal lard."

Susanna retched. "Yuck. Tell me you're joking."

He sucked in air. "It's the truth, sugar loaf, but as for your question about the wine, turns out Brock and the boys robbed a stage coach caravan destined for St. Louis. Inside were two cases of Chateau Lafite Rothschild."

"Sounds and tastes expensive."

The Captain shrugged. "The wine possesses silky undertones despite a firm tannic structure. Concentrated layers of black currents are mixed with vanilla, leather, *framboise*, and cedar. Long finish," he said and inhaled. "It's a hedonistic monster, the nectar of gods."

He reached for her hand and kissed it. "*Raison d'être, Mademoiselle.*"

Susanna swooned. "How do you know all of this?"

"Education and a gastric Frenchman, Pierre. If you think I could really taste all that in this glass of wine, I'm sorry to disappoint you."

Susanna was not disappointed, rather, enthralled with his zestful energy. She sensed a nervous energy about him, though. She thought it must be the song she wrote about him but hoped the unease was something deeper.

They talked about things she had never discussed before. It started with the pyramids of Egypt, shifted to Charles Goodyear and the future use of vulcanized rubber, spun over to Eli Whitney's cotton gin and the unforeseen effect it had on profitability, and the subsequent explosion of slavery.

They also engaged in small talk. Susanna was fascinated by the stages that led to the flight of a butterfly. They both liked to snuggle under a blanket on a cold, winter day and discussed the preferred way to eat corn—going in a circle or straight across (they both munched the kernels vertically).

When he tried to refill her empty glass, she stopped him. "If I drink any more, I won't be able to play you my song."

He responded with a mock-sinister laugh, "That's my plan."

She clucked her tongue at him. "Your plan's not coming to fruition." Then she pulled his guitar from the canvas case and strummed a few chords. "You want me to start again from the beginning or just the new stuff?"

"The new stuff will be fine," he said. Despite being several feet from the fire, a sheen of perspiration had formed on the Captain's forehead. He drew his finger across his brow and flicked the moisture to the ground.

Susanna stood with the guitar, her body outlined by the fire behind her. "This is for you, hero of Booneville."

> *Soon all across the great prairies*
> *The legend grew like a gigolo tooth fairy;*
> *The scandals became sown in country lore.*
> *He was like Robin Hood behind bedroom doors!*
> *He stole from the rich and gave to his whores;*
> *He was the burglar of sexy women's drawers.*

Susanna puffed her chest and, through the next verse, sang in different mock-men's voices.

> *My wife ain't spreading 'em.*
> *Mine, neither.*
> *Where's my daughter?*
> *Son of a bitch!*
> *Someone done slept in my bed.*
> *Holy haystacks!*
> *Who stained my saddle?*
> *My well stinks.*

Susanna returned to her normal voice.

> *What made this cowboy so unique?*
> *This hygienic hombre did not reek.*
> *His horse now pulled a canvas-covered wagon;*
> *He was out back, doing some shagging.*
> *Women from a-far came for rodeo lessons,*
> *He gave free rides and never lost his Stetson.*

Oh, Captain Coytus—a legend in lust!
Oh, Captain Coytus—his work was always just!

The posters read, "Wanted, dead or alive!"
Once he had his way with a city sheriff's wife.
"Oh, Captain Coytus," the woman sung.
The men were angry because he was hung.
A cry went out. 'Kill Coytus!' the men stormed.
They grabbed their guns, a posse was formed.

Once again, Susanna drew herself into a masculine posture.

He violated my wife!
Mine too!
He desecrated my daughter.
Son of a bitch!
He soiled my sheets.
Pierce my pistol.
He branded my wife!
His horse shat in my well!

Susanna switched to her feminine voice.

Oh, Captain Coytus—a legend in lust!
Oh, Captain Coytus—honored with marble bust!

So in this small village
The Captain's work was finally done.
Belles sighed in bliss
As he rode off into the rising sun.
He headed off to his next town
But would always be fondly reminisced.
Nothing touched this sexual legend,
Not even syphilis!

If you listen to the wind,
It still whistles his name.
All hail Captain Coytus!
Damn Jesse James.

In the early stages of the song, the Captain's face crimped with light discomfort, and during her renditions of the male mob, he laughed heartily. Yet on the last line, "Damn Jesse James," his face froze. As if he didn't want her to notice, he let the emotion pass and clapped his hands. "Bravo."

Susanna, like a lighthouse in the fog, clouded her internal glow. She wrote the song to impress him in a way other women perhaps could not. He, the musician with the razor wit, applauded her. Speechless, her mouth turned dry.

"Sugar blossom, I'm starting to wonder if our meeting is no mere coincidence and instead was orchestrated by my teacher. You assuredly are his guru, and this is a test I'm failing miserably. I've fallen victim, mesmerized by the master."

His playful smirk showed the satire in his comment, but his words and delivery brought her to a near-cadaver state. Her breathing slowed, and she corked her emotions for fear she'd erupt in a bubbly tearful spray.

He seemed to sense her true feelings, and he brushed his fingers across the top of her hand. Their fingers intertwined.

"I have no right to, but I have a favor to ask."

"Anything."

"I like orgies. You ready to do what it takes to please your man?"

Repulsed, Susanna frowned. "Really?"

He let rip a mock-laugh. "Of course not, silly. I had to say something stupid to break the mutual awkwardness. I have no right to make such a request, but I'd like to bank your heart for one year. By then, my mission will have been a success or I'll be dead. If you find a better man, by all means, but if not, and you can look past my indiscretions—"

"You mean *whoring!*" she retorted.

The Captain gulped and cleared his throat. "Uh, part two of my mission is to return to Booneville and make you an honest woman."

Susanna faked a glare. "Are you claiming I'm dishonest? A hussy?"

"No," he assured. He shook his head. "Why do I feel so mortal around you?"

Without thinking, she replied, "Because we belong together." Her own words shocked her. The cork twisted loose, and she unleashed her true feelings.

Her words seemed to please him, and his eyes sparkled. White teeth flashed. "So you'll give me twelve months?"

He sounded a tad desperate, which Susanna viewed favorably. "I will, but I have one conditional request."

"Huh? What's that?"

The cork popped. "I'll need a twelve-second kiss. One for each month I must endure purgatory waiting for you."

CHAPTER 35

"Fuck Lincoln," Little Archie snapped at the mention of the president's name. "That top hat must be hiding brain damage."

Frank shrugged. "Maybe he always wears the hat because the Foo-Foo bird defecated on his head."

Little Archie's eyes bulged. "The Who-Foo-what bird?"

"You don't know about the Foo-Foo bird, Mister I-Know-Everything?"

Little Archie ground his teeth.

"Actually, it may be a myth."

"Tell me."

"It might take awhile," Frank confessed.

He surveyed the night sky. "We have time before we get some shut-eye."

Frank James took a long slug from his canteen and grinned as twelve of the men gathered in around him. Jesse angled his face away from his brother and bore a tight-lipped smile.

"About two hundred years ago, the Osage Indians sent several tribesmen on an expedition on the Platte River.[8] They never returned. Speculation was a rival tribe took the small party out. A force of over two hundred men was dispatched to find out what happened to the missing tribesmen.

"Adept at tracking, the missing party was found dead. The strange

---

8   Interestingly, it appears the Osage word for woman, is *WAKO* or Wak'o. I believe the correct pronunciation is "whacko." But I may also be wrong.

part was this: they found no sign as to the cause of death. No wounds were visible. No tracks, animal or human, were present.

"While they puzzled over the fate of their men, a distinct bird call broke the men's confusion—*'Fuuuuu, fuuuuu.'* Twelve men cursed in disgust; they'd been shat upon. While these men wiped themselves clean, once again, *'Fuuuuu fuuuuu,'* sounded from the sky. The men looked up, and an extremely large condor-sized bird circled above them. Another sixteen men were rained upon. As they cleaned themselves, the first twelve men fell to an instant death. A minute later, the next sixteen perished."

Frank paused and took a slug from his canteen. "One hundred and fifty men died before the remaining Osage tribesmen fled the open skies as if their lives depended on it. And, well …

"In the end, only thirty men returned to their village, six of whom died later. The shamans assumed the bird's excrement passed on a plague. As a precaution, the river camp moved inland, under tree cover too formidable for the flight of a large bird.

"About a year later, a survivor of that massacre, Strong Wind, ran in pursuit of a boar his party had wounded. Exposed on the open plain, he saw a shadow move across the tundra. *'Fuuuuuu, fuuuuuu.'* Three of the five tribesmen were shat upon. They wiped themselves clean, and within two minutes, they died. Strong Wind pointed to the other survivor and then to the closest cover. 'Run!' he yelled.

"The men were mere strides away when they heard, *'Fuuuuuu, fuuuuuu.'* Then they felt the splash. The other man wiped the shit from his neck, hoping to get the plague off in time. Strong Wind didn't even bother. In a minute, his friend moved to the spirit world. Minutes passed, but Strong Wind didn't. More time elapsed, yet he remained alive. A thought occurred to him.

"Strong Wind became the chief of the Osage tribe, and his tidings on surviving the Foo-Foo bird were passed to the others.

"Forty years later, two French explorers, Louis Jolliet and Jacques Marquette, entered the region. They had been perhaps the first Caucasians to cross the Mississippi River. They were shocked to find that the native Indians wore bird shit like it was war paint. A perpetual insect storm followed the Indians like harbingers of the reek that followed. Even the five

Indian guides they'd brought with them from the shores of Lake Huron were perplexed. They questioned the locals but received no satisfactory answers.

"The French tandem eventually came upon Strong Wind's village. The elder tribesman was still alive but frail as a snail. Speaking of snails, Jolliet and Marquette inquired if they could procure a few dozen for escargot, as well as some healthy-legged frogs. Strong Wind obliged but apologized for having no wine and cheese to offer.

"At the banquet of honor, the men discussed everything about the region: the geography, precious metals or lack thereof, weather, and wildlife. When asked for locations to trap fur, the Indians gave locations where they knew the Foo-Foo bird dwelled.

"Days later, Jolliet and Marquette were setting traps when they heard a strange, shrill call. *'Fuuuuuuu, fuuuuuuuu.'* Their Indian guides were spooked when they saw the bird's tremendous wingspan overhead.

"Before the bird flew out of eyesight, the two Frenchmen and five Indians were shat upon. Immediately, the Indians went to clean themselves. When Marquette pulled out his handkerchief, Jolliet thought of the bird-shit-covered Indians and grabbed Marquette's wrist. He whispered, 'Wait.' Realizing they needed guides, he managed to deter two Indians before they fully cleansed themselves.

"Jolliet's premonition proved accurate when the three clean Indians fell over. Jolliet explained his theory, and Marquette and the two Indians agreed with his logic.

"Wearing little clothes, the Indian's had Foo-poo stains on several body parts. Jolliet, however, had only a spot on his head while Marquette had a splatter on his nose and atop the crown of his scalp. While in Illinois, a huge storm hit the party before they could find shelter. The rain washed the Foo-Foo-poo stains off the Indians, who succumbed as they guided the canoe. Jolliet and Marquette took over and managed to get to shore and shelter. For better or worse, Marquette's nose no longer sniffed a stench with every inhale.

"When they reached Michigan, the men were traveling horseback when a huge gust blew the cap off Marquette's head. It fell off a cliff and into a fast-moving river. At the drop of a hat, the two men set off to a trading outpost to get Marquette head cover. Before they could get there, a storm moved in. Marquette draped his coat over his head. Jolliet wanted to take his off to his friend's bravery, but he didn't want to die, so he kept his lid on tight.

"Marquette's coat soaked through, and at age thirty-eight, he died near a place known as Starved Rock.[9] Jolliet, however, lived on for many years. In fact, he was never seen without his trademark fur cap. He later forged another expedition down the St. Lawrence River and into Canada, and despite the Foo-Foo-poo, he completed the journey without incident. Years later, he married."

Little Archie coughed to interrupt Frank. "Hmm. Maybe we don't have so much time. Want to wrap this ridiculous story up?" He poorly stifled a yawn.

A few men who enjoyed the flight of fancy hushed him.

"Almost at the end, buddy," replied Frank. "Louis Jolliet was embarrassed by the fact that he lived with bird shit on his head and had neglected to tell his wife the truth. In all the years of marriage, he had never removed his fur cap. His wife questioned it, but he claimed he had some rare scalp disease and preferred to keep it covered.

"One evening, and twenty-five years after Marquette died in the violent rainstorm, Jolliet passed out from a hard night of drinking. His curious wife slowly removed her husband's cap, and there she found a crusty stain. She decided this disease could be cured with soap and water. Louis Jolliet woke before she completed the job and told his wife about the Foo-Foo bird."

Frank took a long slug from the near-empty canteen. "The official story is that Jolliet went on a trip to Anticosti Island and was never seen again. But many years later, there were whisperings that he actually went missing in search of the Foo-Foo bird. He was apparently after a fresh coating to replace the small smudge he had left."

Frank spread his hands and brought them together as if he was drawing the matter to a close. "Whether true or just a legend, myths usually impart

---

9   Jacques Marquette reportedly died of dysentery that he contacted in his Missouri travels. Could it be ...?

a lesson learned. Here, the Foo-Foo bird brings to mind another fairy tale, *Cendrillon*, with a poetic twist of words."[10]

A grin chiseled his countenance as Frank's eyes darted about his audience. "The moral of the story is, 'If the Foo shits, wear it.'"

Little Archie groaned. "Do you want me to kill you now or have mercy and slay you in your sleep?"

---

10   *Cinderella.* I love fairy tales. I'd love to write one someday.

CHAPTER 36

John Edwards twiddled his mustache as he joined the Bushwhackers for breakfast. After their meeting with Sterling Price, Edwards and Bloody Bill Anderson rode to the Bushwhacker camp. Edwards's mission was to redefine how the Bushwhackers were perceived, to turn them from murderous thugs into honorable victims. If the Confederate forces were made up of men like these rebels, then they'd never lose the war.

Quite a challenge for Edwards, actually, since the assembled Bushwhackers were not exactly poster boys for a gentlemen's society. These were rough customers, and without the sexy bad-guy allure. Bloody Bill with his wild mane-like hair and bedazzled, embroidered garb looked every bit the ruthless villain he was. Still, Edwards needed to find a way to sell his story and pull the hearts and minds toward the Confederate cause.

His eyes settled on the reason for his visit: Jesse James. The boy had a regal air about him, far different from Frank, his stumpy-dumpy brother. Jesse had piercing blue eyes, high cheekbones, groomed hair, and a good complexion. The James family also had a story to sell. They had been abused on their own farm by the Union Provisional Militia and were truly victims—righteous victims he could sell.

As Edwards procured the newspaper he'd brought with him, he thought of Captain Coytus. There was another possible prop in the propaganda war. The Captain had that good-looking, country-boy thing working for him and had proven to be especially articulate for a Bushwhacker. Plus, he'd expressed an an interest in assisting the journalistic apparatus of Edwards's vision.

Edwards handed the *Daily Missouri Republican* to Little Archie.

He frowned at the paper and handed it back to Edwards, who read out loud. "Abraham Lincoln said, 'My dream is of a place and a time where America will once again be seen as the last best hope of earth.'"

In a calm delivery, Jesse James said, "Fuck Lincoln's America. I believe in a nation that is truly free … without government interference and oversight—a place where every *white man* can prosper. A country that follows the founding fathers' wisdoms indoctrinated in the Constitution and the subsequent changes made, such as the Second Amendment, whereby men have the right to bear arms."

Frank shot his pistol into the morning sky. "In other words, brother, you stand for the Democratic Party platform. To hell with them sissy Republicans!"

Edwards clapped a loud percussion beat and then went back to fingering his greasy mustache. "Lincoln is a saboteur to the government our forefathers blueprinted."

Jesse ground his teeth as if he had a small quibble to nibble. "Although, I must say, I see zero merit to the Third Amendment."

"Really?" Little Archie questioned. "I never heard *you* take the Lord's name in vain."

"That's the Ten Commandments, not amendments," interjected Edwards.

Archie scowled at the correction.

In deft fashion, Edwards smacked a backhand across the newspaper and changed the focus. "Shit on a kebob. Lincoln actually asserted, 'Better to remain silent and be thought a fool than to speak out and remove all doubt.'"

"You'd think the gangly scarecrow would follow his advice," Little Archie sneered.

"He must be smoking buffalo chips," Bloody Bill chipped in.

"As I theorized, he's gone insane from carrying the burden of the Foo-Foo bird," Frank chirped with a smirk.

"The only explanation is the man is a mute, and these perverted parables were birthed from an inkwell," Jesse interjected with a coy smirk.

Impressed, Edwards studied the younger James boy and wondered how Little Archie was known as the brains of the clique.

"I'll bet you any amount of money that President Lincoln is one of them homo …" Little Archie stuttered.

"Sapiens?" Frank answered.

Little Archie agreed. "Yeah. Them sinners."

A small smile crept across Jesse's lips. "You're always right, Little Archie. I wouldn't bet against you there."

Edwards and only Edwards snickered.

He fell into the newspaper again, and this time he pulled out, "Listen to what else that Homo Sapiens said. 'The shepherd drives the wolf from the sheep's fold, for which the sheep thanks the shepherd as his liberator, while the wolf denounces him for the same act as the destroyer of liberty. Plainly, the sheep and the wolf are not agreed upon a definition of liberty.'"

"Holy hornswoggle," Edwards huffed.

Bloody Bill cupped his crotch with his right hand and piped in, "Lincoln, put this in your pipe and smoke it."

"*Fuuuuuuu, fuuuuuuuu,*" chirped Frank.

Everyone laughed except the shortest guy in the crowd.

Jesse chuckled, the deep sound resonating across the group and helping to stifle the laughter. "It's a clever Aesop's fable-type passage but a metaphorical lie. Speaking of sheep, Lincoln is trying to pull the wool over the nation's eyes. He's the wolf, and the South's the slaughter. The sheep must become the ram. Our heads are hard, our hearts warmed by a righteous dignity in our traditions and way of life. Let's not further tilt the economic scales to the Yankee imperial bank barons. Let not our children wonder why the dreams and freedoms of a new nation were squandered and strangled by voices who no longer live off the land, but rather off the sweat of the farmer and frontiersman. Let no one but God almighty judge us."

Bloody Bill let a scream rip, and then he clapped. He walked to each man and looked him in the eye. Each man so gazed upon him and then clapped along until every Bushwhacker was whipped into frenzy dance state, almost like an American Indian celebration. Frank decided to do his rendition of a war dance and crashed into his fellow Bushwhackers, knocking several to the floor. At one point, the only man standing was Edwards, who kept his hands at the ready and away from his mustache for a record-setting time.

The scrum ended when Little Archie screamed in pain from the bottom of the pile. "I'm being crushed to death!"

While Little Archie attended his ailments, Frank brought the talk back to Lincoln. "Remember, if we don't win this war, Lincoln might go down in history as a great president. Parks, schools, new towns, and even cities will be named after him. The fucker will probably have a memorial in the nation's capital built for him when he dies."

Little Archie scoffed. "Where do you come up with this shit? He will never be accepted by half the country." He kicked at a piece of unused firewood with his Brogan boots. "He'd be lucky to have a log named after him."

"My brother may or may not be right," Jesse said with a defiant shake of his head. "We must never find out. We need to win this war."

CHAPTER 37

Terror gripped her, and Susanna could not escape its pursuit. The dead called her name, but it sounded like a hiss, as if spoken from a reptile or perhaps some dude with a whiny voice afflicted with sinus problems. "Sissss-u-anna-sisss," over and again.

Cody and Hunter were dead. She didn't feel guilty or remorseful for killing them, yet the deceased townies tormented her sleep for the second straight night. The first night, the Captain had been there. In his arms, her inner demons stayed in the distance, afraid to venture closer, as though they took a peek at the Captain and decided to pass.

"Susanna!"

This time the voice was normal and feminine. "Susanna. Wake up, sunshine. A storm's coming our way. We need to get the laundry in," her mother said.

Susanna needed sleep, but when dreams are nightmares, early-morning chores can seem a perfect respite. She helped retrieve the laundry and then pulled water from the well. She plucked weeds from the small garden and managed to feed the chickens before the first drops began to fall.

Thunder crackled overhead when they settled inside for a cup of tea. The house was scented from a cooling loaf of bread. Both women were dressed in full blue skirts, hemmed with dark trim that they had made together several months prior. The only difference was Susanna's was longer to match her several-inch height advantage.

"You miss him, don't you?" her mother asked.

Susanna didn't answer. Instead she said, "He avenged Father's death." She explained how the Captain killed the men who had murdered Father.

Mother didn't rejoice or grieve; her attitude was simple. "Nothing can bring him back. Anything else is immaterial to me."

Her mother had heard the gossip about town regarding the Captain's exploits and his fancy for Susanna. She assumed her daughter was another sexual conquest, but Susanna assured her otherwise. "Too bad," her mother let slip, and they laughed like young girls.

"He reminds me of Father," confessed Susanna.

Mother and daughter both knew in each other's gazes that they missed what Badger and the boys stole from them. The intuitive link ended with synchronized sobbing. Mother offered her hand, and Susanna accepted, allowing the embrace to pause the painful memories.

"You'll wait the year for him?" her mother asked, though it was more a statement.

Susanna didn't need to think it over. "I will. Taking aside my expectations from a relationship with a man I met only a week ago, who else in this town could I possibly be interested in?"

"What about the Ryder boy? He's so nice," Mother endorsed with the conviction rate of a liberal judge.

"Rod is nice, Mom, but he doesn't like women."

Mother blinked, and then the revelation seemed to register. "Okay. What about the Poole boy? He's a strong lad, much like your captain."

"Mom, have you ever talked to Gene?"

Mother's head seesawed in consideration. "Well ..."

"Mom," Susanna replied, half-exasperated, half-amused. "Who's Gene's father?"

"No one is sure, actually."

"Exactly. Once you get past Gene's, 'Good morning, ma'am,' you'll soon realize he's an in-bred freak."

Mother frowned. "I take it the Small's youngest boy doesn't measure up?"

"Willy?"

Mother smiled. "Okay. You're right. No one here is worthy of your affections."

Susanna decided to ask what plagued her mind over the past year. Until this reawakening, her mother resisted voicing her emotions. "Do you wish Father was less vocal about his stance against slavery? I know this is selfish, but sometimes I do. He'd probably still be alive." Guilt leaked from her subconscious like ink-stained water as she sobbed.

Mother shook the *what if* away. "There was no changing him. It's who he was. The only reason we had slaves was they'd end up somewhere else, somewhere worse. He ensured some were at least treated with dignity."

She huddled closer and put her arm around her daughter. "Let me tell you a story. When your father was a young boy, your grandfather took him on a hunting trip with several men from their outpost. There was an incident with some Indians, and the men fled back to the safety of their fortified village. Your father was accidently knocked down a hill as the men retreated. By the time they figured out he was missing, the town was surrounded. The standoff lasted days, but eventually the Indians were placated with gifts only the white man could offer: guns, liquor, and syphilis.

"The village men went out to search for your father, but they did not find him. A week passed when two black men came into town. On one of the men's shoulders sat your father. When he'd fallen down the hill, he banged his head and blacked out for some time. When he regained consciousness, he was unable to walk on the twisted ankle the fall caused." Mother paused. "That's why he always walked with a limp."

She took a deep breath and forged on. "Injured and unable to move, two runaway slaves come upon him. He begged for their help. He promised if they'd rescued him, his father would help them reach safety.

"The two slaves were lavished over. Your grandfather, the thankful man he was, hid the runaways in his home and had his wife prepare a large meal. Your father could not thank his two rescuers enough. They were heroes.

"Just as the meal was served, several men stormed the residence. They were from a posse in search of the runaways. With considerable force, they reacquired the two slaves. Your father screamed for their freedom and then mercy but was stopped by his dad. When the men left, his father smiled and explained. As it turned out, he'd received reward money for returning the runaways to their *rightful* owners."

Mother brushed her hair back, trying to wipe away the bad memory. "Your father never forgot the look of betrayal on his two saviors' faces."

Susanna said the first thing that came to her mind. "I love Daddy. He was the way all men should be."

"Agreed. So if you see your father in the Captain, I think you should allow him the time to make good on his promised return."

Susanna emptied the teapot in both cups. "Let's just hope his real name is not Ulysses, because I'll end up Penelope, forever awaiting his return."

CHAPTER 38

PRESENT DAY

"Wink, wink, Professor Gladstone," Baxter said. He blinked twice in exaggeration. "You sense a pattern here?"

Gladstone leaned back, his head lolled to one side. His mouth hung open, and his eyes clouded like heated water. He felt either medicated or lobotomized. At this point, he would have signed up for either.

He thought of dental surgery. Novocain-numb, he endured the needling, the drilling, the probing, helpless surrender. He inspected his seat to ensure it was not his dentist's. Nope, more likely it was an electric chair. If only it were an ejector seat.

"Are you okay?" Baxter needled.

"Huh?"

The student brought his hand to his forehead in shock. "Do I have to connect the dots for you?"

Gladstone was beyond taking umbrage at the baited insults. "What are you on about now?"

The boy huffed a condescending gasp. "What's my first name?"

The sound of a dentist drill buzzed in his mind. "Ulysses," he answered with the enthusiasm of a doctor delivering news: *We caught the testicular cancer in time to save you, but ..."*

"Very good. What's my father's name?"

"Ulysses?"

128

"Yes, Ulysses *Zeus* Baxter. You're on a roll, Professor Gladstone. Can you venture a guess what his father's name was?"

Gladstone played along and answered the obvious. "Ulysses?"

Baxter grinned. "Actually, it was Joe."

"Really?" the crestfallen professor replied.

Baxter shrugged and laughed. "You're right. I fibbed, rare as that may be. His name was Ulysses *Apollo* Baxter."

"Humph."

"Now, here's the bonus question. What Fortune 500 company did my family start?"

"Ulysses Voyage, USA."

"And how could you miss? The logo of the *V* bookmarked by the two *U*s is suspiciously reminiscent of a cornucopia or a gynecological diagram. The company is in almost every home. They make commodes, sinks, bathtubs, as well as a variety of paper products, such as tissues, toilet paper, and tampons. Through acquisition, they also manufacture soaps, shampoos, deodorants, and other general hygiene items, such as early-pregnancy-test kits, jock-itch salves, contraceptives—some made for her pleasure—and lip medication for cold sores, meaning," *cough, cough,* "herpes. Yes, Ulysses Voyage, USA, is an American institution."

Baxter paused for a moment to let the enormity of the institution sink in and then asked, "Do you now grasp my personal connection to this story?"

Gladstone lurched. Surely he wasn't suggesting …

Baxter apparently read his thoughts. "Shall we say my family has a vested—or, *in*vested—interest in the revelations revealed in my thesis paper? It explains how Ulysses Voyages, USA, started and where the seed money came from. Then you have the whole matter of the famous outlaw, Jesse James. My family is willing to let skeletons surface."

"Is that so?" Gladstone replied, weary and exhausted by this point.

Baxter smirked. "We can call my father, and you can pass along some of your insults about the veracity of my thesis. I'd love to be a spectator to the flogging you'd receive. You're lucky I'm such a swell chap. My father can be a real ball-buster."

Gladstone declined the offer. "I'll take your word on the part about your father. Tell me about the evidence you have to prove these claims."

He turned and nodded at the closet door behind him. "In my bag is ample evidence to convince even the Apostle Thomas that my assertions are true."

Despite Gladstone's reservations that this "evidence" equated to nothing but more chicanery, his interest was piqued. He imagined he was a scientist who received deep core samples from the moon and discovered our lunar cousin was made of cheese. Could Baxter's hunk of cheese have some historical merit?

So he went to the closet and returned the duffel bag to his student-turned-teacher. The boy put the bag on the ground and pulled out a large, plastic zipper bag.

"Please don't take it out yet."

Gladstone held the parcel—a battered leather case with an inch of thick parchment within the cover. "What's this?"

"Susanna kept a journal. This is one of several in my family's possession." Baxter reached into the duffel bag and pulled out two latex gloves. He snapped them on and smiled at Gladstone with his hands up, fingers wiggling. "You seem a little anal, I must say. When's the last time you had your prostrate checked?"

Gladstone's eyes bulged.

Baxter chuckled. "Just kidding, Professor." He left his seat and stood along Gladstone's desk. With the gloves on, he opened the seal and gradually pulled the journal out. With care, he opened the binding. "I assure you, the paper and ink will pass any scientific scrutiny."

Gladstone squinted at the journal's pages. The handwriting flowed crisply feminine, and he recalled seeing a TV special about an apparent alien autopsy from around the period of the reported Roswell incident. The camera, film, and props used suggested authenticity, but it was an elaborate hoax.

"Baxter, my boy, I trust you're aware historians are routinely presented with fakes and forgeries. The infamous *Hitler Diaries* comes to mind."

"Are you *serious*?"

"I'm merely stating that paper-and-ink tests are not enough to convince a peer review on the validity of documents."

He shrugged and motioned to the yellowed journal. "I understand, but why would I go through the time and expense to do all of this?"

"Playing devil's advocate: to pass my class and graduate?"

Baxter laughed. "I could pass this class with my brain tied behind my back. And if I thought I couldn't, I'd pay someone to write my thesis paper. It would be far cheaper, and the topic matter far more conventional."

"True," Gladstone conceded. The kid had a point. The cheaper, easier thing would have been paying a ghost writer, and the boy was spot-on with his commentary on the unconventional subject matter and bizarre methodological treatment.

Gladstone decided today was the worst day he'd had since the *New York Times Book Review* declared his latest book, "disappointing" and "dull," claiming he was "losing his touch," and the worst of all, "superficial."

Baxter gingerly turned several pages of the journal and pointed. "See!"

Centered on the parchment was the vile song Susanna had supposedly written for the Captain. He had no idea what to think it all meant, let alone say anything.

Baxter shined. "So how about awarding my work an A+, and we can call it a day?"

Gladstone refused to go that far, and the thought of the repercussions made him shudder. "I am willing to go as high as an A–."

Baxter's shine turned to gloom. He pursed his lips, sniffled, shook his head, and then slid the journal back in the plastic and pressed the seal close. The boy's eyes drooped. "I suppose I understand your reservations, but then again, I don't. Something is holding you back."

Gladstone had to deliver here. He needed to convince the boy to take the A–. "For starters, you're not good enough of a writer to warrant a better grade."

Baxter face grew placid, calm, and conciliatory. "A fair point, but I would think the magnitude of this magnum opus would overshadow any limitations on the author's behalf. Not all historical treasures were created by literary geniuses. Take Hitler's *Mein Kampf*. Even fellow fascist, Mussolini, panned the book, saying it was 'a boring tome I have never been able to read.' Yet it's a famous historical work because the hate foreshadowed the coming evil."

Gladstone had to seize the momentum back. "That may be, but those works were not a graded test. I also doubt any examples you may cite are filled with juvenile sensationalism, abundant clichés, and ridiculous footnotes."

The criticism seemed to amuse the now-smiling Baxter. "I read other history books. I wanted to avoid writing anything that could ever be labeled as dull or superficial. I added a splash of modern jazz and 'cooled' the story up."

Gladstone winced. Surely, Baxter referred to the review of his latest book, but this was not the time to defend his honor. "What about the vulgarity and violence?"

"Dear Professor Gladstone, history is filled with violence and vulgarity. Would you have someone write an expose on September 11, 2001, and tone things down by comparing the Twin Towers' demise to the collapse of Jenga blocks? You have to tell the truth and let the morality chips fall by the wayside."

Gladstone gagged like he was caught in an ocean undertow that pulled him toward deeper, darker waters. "That may be so, but the obvious fake names like Gene Pool and Deputy Richard 'Dick' Less detract any sense of seriousness. It's beyond a James Bondish farce."

Baxter scoffed, "That's your opinion. Later on in the story, we meet Dick Liddil, whom I'm sure you're familiar with."

Gladstone knew of Liddil but said nothing through the boy's long pause. He didn't want to set the table for one of Baxter's barbs. He nodded instead but kept his lips tight and his eyes narrowed.

Baxter pointed at Susanna's journal. "Every name is taken from primary-source documents. You can make the claim that Susanna invented these names though. It would appear she had a devilish sense of humor from the song she wrote about the Captain." He tapped the journal. "Her account will prove accurate."

PART V

Chapter 39

October 1864

There's nothing like a family barbecue, and the James family loved to throw a proper Confederate shindig. An effigy of Lincoln and an arsenal of sticks entertained the younglings. The women stayed busy ordering the slaves around, while the men were free to enjoy the feast and discuss some of the hot issues, while ordering both the women and slaves about.

Little Archie questioned Edwards. "What's the chance of voting Lincoln out of office?"

"Or impeachment?" Bloody Bill said as he used his short sleeve to wipe swine grease from his maw.

Edwards dismissed the wishful thinking with a wave of his callous-free hand. "The only way is to win the war. We need to be cunning, more ruthless than the enemy."

Frank James belched. "Can you imagine if we lose? Negroes might vote one day. Heck, someday we'll be at a similar crossroads, and women will be able to vote too."

In his haste to reply, Little Archie hacked several kernels of corn into the face of Edwards. He didn't apologize. "Neither is going to ever happen, but if there were a first, our white sisters will earn the privilege before any Negro."

"You never know," Frank replied.

Little Archie tapped his temple. "I know. In our good state, Negroes are not allowed the right of assembly, even in a church, unless a white man is present."[11]

The head house slave, Charlotte, brought the men pie. She smiled at Jesse as she gave him the largest slice and then moved to leave, but Little Archie grabbed her wrist.

"What do you think, Negro woman? Who deserves the right to vote first, your Negro brethren or white women?"

Charlotte grinned at the men and then Little Archie. She shrugged. "What do I know? I'm just a Negro. And a woman."

The men laughed.

Charlotte smoothed her apron and pointed at the younger James boy. "My answer is whatever Master Jesse thinks. The good Lord blessed that boy with wisdom."

Little Archie turned to Jesse. "What do you think, *Mastah Jesse*?" he said, imitating Charlotte's accent.

He cradled his firm chin with his hand and pondered. "I think Negro men will get the right to vote first but have less social freedoms and face more heated oppression than the women. If that makes any sense."

"It doesn't," Little Archie commented.

"Actually it does," Edwards contradicted.

With a satisfied smirk, Charlotte slid from Little Archie's embrace and went back to the house.

A Bushwhacker on lookout yelled, "A man approaches with a canvas-covered wagon. He's wearing a Union uniform."

"He's one of us," Bloody Bill said. "Or he's one unlucky son of a bitch. Gather a few men and greet him."

The lookout summoned five men, and they marched out across the open plain. The lookout beckoned, "Are you a Jayhawk or a Bushwhacker?"

The Captain tipped the brim of his Stetson at the men. "Neither. I am certainly not a bird, but boy wouldn't it be exhilarating to fly? And, to be

---

11 In 1847, Missouri passed a law that blacks did not have the right of assembly, even in a church, unless a white official was present. Christ almighty!

honest, I'm not a Bushwhacker. I always detested yard work. Landscaping is not my thing. In fact, city life seems so much easier, doesn't it, guys?"

The reply unsettled the men, and they looked at each other with pinched, confused brows. The lookout drew his posture up as if reminded they outnumbered this one man. *Unless …* "Say, is there anyone else in your wagon?"

The Captain nodded. "Just a girl."

"Your wife?"

He whistled through a head shake. "Nope. I met her several miles from here. Told her where I was headed, and she begged for a ride." His lips curled up with mischievous intent.

The lookout pointed at the wagon. "We need to check inside."

He held a finger in the air, turned his head, and said, "Dawn, you decent back there?"

"Sure am, my stallion," purred a giddy voice.

"That sounded like …," the lookout said as he went to the back and peered inside. "By golly! It's Krackov's daughter, Dawn. Your father's at the Jameses' farm."

Her voice chirped from the wagon. "I came here to tell him that Mama ran away with Dick Powers."

This news caused a stir, and the lookout's face jolted as if he'd been slapped. "Dick's poor and has a face only an inebriated mother could love. The boy must have hips like the devil's fire."

The Captain smirked. "How about letting Dawn and me pass? I'm here by invitation of John Edwards, Little Archie Clement, and Frank James."

"Who are you?"

Dawn answered from within the wagon. "Don't you dummies know? This is Captain Coytus! Every woman's dream and every man's nightmare."

The Captain snickered. "We good to go here?"

Still, the lookout frowned. "Why are you wearing a Union uniform?"

"It's comfortable as far as military uniforms go." He rotated his shoulders and tugged his sleeve. "Guys my size have a hard time finding clothes that fit. And if I dare say, the women tell me this Union blue draws out my eye color."

"Really?"

He dipped his Stetson and said, "You bet," and he brushed his hand down the uniform. "I wear this to go behind enemy lines. I do my best work undercover."

"He certainly does," Dawn called out.

The lookout squinted. "Your accent. It sounds Yankee. You're no puke."[12]

"No, and I'm not gutless either."

"Huh?"

"Listen up, chum." The Captain pointed over the man's head to the Jameses' farm. He smacked one of the saddle bags strapped to Fly Bait. Inside was a forged document Susanna helped him create. "I carry information regarding the Union Army's plans. I'm pretty sure Bill Anderson won't be happy to learn you've delayed him receiving this news."

A grin split the lookout's face. "Maybe I'll take the information from you and give it to him myself. Get in his good graces and all."

The Captain snorted. "The only thing you could take from me is an order. You're lucky I don't smack you around with my pecker."

The voice from the wagon said, "You better let the man pass. That's some weapon he's packing."

The rift was distracted by the sound of galloping horses, and three men approached on horseback. The Captain could see one of them was Frank James, and he took the Stetson from his head and waved it at Frank.

Frank's mouth opened, and he pumped a fist in jubilation. He leapt from his horse with the grace of a clubfooted acrobat and hit the ground tumbling, but with youthful exuberance, his energy carried him toward Fly Bait. "You're here! Captain Coytus, my hero."

"Mine too," cooed the voice from the wagon.

Frank blinked a few times but refocused on the Captain. "What's the hold up here?"

The Captain gazed at the lookout and shrugged.

The lookout shrunk under the sudden glare Frank sneered his way.

---

12   A "puke" was a Missourian, "The Puke State" was the state moniker. Missouri officials later upgraded the state with a new nickname, "The Show-Me State."

"Holy tumbleweed tits, you're even dumber than me." Frank smacked the guy across the chops and then remounted his horse and gestured to the Captain. "Follow me. I can't wait for you to meet my brother, Jesse."

CHAPTER 40

More than a month earlier, the Captain had begun his mission to avenge the death of his father. Here he finally was surrounded by the men responsible: Bloody Bill Anderson, who orchestrated the Centralia massacre, and his lieutenant, Little Archie Clement. His focus, however, was on the lad who shot and killed his father—namely, Jesse James.

Frank had drawn them together like they were destined to be friends. Jesse's blue eyes flashed an icy current but exhibited a warm glow like the bottom spectrum of a flame. He appeared thoughtful and well mannered. Among the riffraff, he came across as almost debonair. Almost, because he was still a little backwoods and outdated by the Captain's more urbane standards.

When they separated so he could explain his gambit to Edwards, Archie, and Bloody Bill, the Captain was slightly pained. As far as initial impressions went, Jesse seemed a decent chap, yet it did not matter. Even a good man could be a dead man.

For privacy, the men walked over to a large, gnarled oak tree and sat in its shade. The Captain pulled out a journal and handed it Bloody Bill, who opened it as Edwards and Little Archie peered on.

The Captain began his spiel while eying Bloody Bill. "As I told these two men back in Booneville, I have my own way of fighting this war. I might not be some backwoods warrior, but I can still be useful to your cause."

Edwards beamed as though this was music to his ears, being a man who used his pen over a rifle. "Don't kid yourself, Bill. He can take care of himself."

Bloody Bill's lean, bony frame looked malnourished next to the Captain. He grunted his acknowledgment.

The Captain opened the journal to a map of Missouri. "War is not only won through combat. It also comes down to economics—everything costs money. The North has an advantage, being backed by Yankee banking barons. That needs to change."

Little Archie scoffed. "You want us to build a bank?"

The Captain rolled his eyes. "No, I don't want you to build a bank, genius. I'm talking about disrupting their money supply. Taking their wealth and using it to finance our cause."

Bloody Bill cast a stone face at Little Archie, affirming the chain of command. He scratched his scraggly beard. "Keep talking."

"Gold is delivered from St. Louis to Union generals, such as Francis Preston Blair Jr., to keep his soldiers armed and fed. The gold is discreetly brought by four men. I know their route and a spot where we can ambush them."

"Brilliant," assessed Edwards.

Bloody Bill had a devilish glint in his eye. "Aye."

Little Archie gushed, "You want us to kill them and take the gold? Great idea."

He shook his head. "No killing."

Bloody Bill waved a hand of silence at Little Archie and then looked back to the Captain. "Why? Every dead Union soldier helps our cause too."

"It's simple. You'll kill my source. This could be a repeat operation. Why derail the gravy train? I would make the ambush a standard robbery, not a Confederate-Bushwhacker action."

Edwards was quick to reply, his words directed to Bloody Bill and Little Archie. He jutted a finger at the Captain. "We cannot compromise his spy work."

The men went back to the map, and the Captain gave them the time and place to stage the ambush.

Edwards requested a moment alone with him. After the two

Bushwhackers left, he asked, "Have you ever thought about joining the Knights of the Golden Circle?"[13]

"Can't say I have," the Captain admitted. "Don't think I'd be interested, though. I'm kinky as the next guy, but a circle jerk golden shower party is just not my thing."

"Huh?"

"But if you know of any club like Nights of the Nubile Circle, I'm interested. A charter member, even."

Edwards's eyes registered alarm. "You misunderstand me. The Knights of the Golden Circle is a secret society of Southern gentlemen who want to ensure that, if we lose this war, the South continues to prosper. In other words, men who don't trust Yankee bank barons."

The Captain feigned surprise. "Oh. That is a little different. Sign me up."

Edwards's face smoothed in relief, and he toyed with his mustache. "You still have an interest in helping my journalistic endeavors?"

"You have no idea how much I do. No offense to them Bushwhackers," he said and pointed over to a group of men shooting in-season pumpkins, "but you're obviously more refined, cultured."

Flattered, Edwards tinted crimson. He ignored the praise and continued his vision. "The American revolutionaries used the colonial press to turn the public against the British. We need to do the same with this war. We do that two ways. First, we demonize the opposition, weaken their standing. Second, at the same time, we will glorify our cause. Make heroes of our men. The public loves a hero."

Edwards went on and on … and on with his Machiavellian journalistic hegemony. The Captain was impressed with the plan, as well as Edwards's ability to ramble on incessantly. A walrus must be able to stay under water a long time, because Edwards had an overabundance of oxygen. In fact, the Captain wondered if the man was paid by the word.

13　In 1864, US Judge Advocate Joseph Holt penned a report that warned Secretary of War Edwin Stanton of the dangers posed by the Knights of the Golden Circle. Due to actions against the order and internal bungling, history has written off the ideals of the secret Southern society. Today, tractor pulls carry more influence in the South than the KGC.

He finally interrupted Edwards's marathon mouth. "That sounds great, feller, but I'm parched and could go for some whiskey. Want to head back over before it gets dark?"

Edwards took the comment in stride and strolled back at a slow pace with the Captain at his side. They passed a row of target pumpkins. One bullet-ridden gourd was painted with sideburns and a beard.

Charlotte walked by carrying dishes back to the house. The Captain took in her fine figure and ample chest.

He motioned toward Charlotte and said to Edwards, "Check out the pumpkins on her."

Edwards twisted his face in disgust. "I will not. She's a Negro."

"Really? You wouldn't sink your tusks—I mean fangs—into that?" He hoped Edwards did not get the import of his gaffe.

Edwards flapped his hands about as if he was batting away a sudden swarm of insects. "I would do no such thing."

"Hmmm. Sorry, I did not envision you as the picky type."

He shook his head. "I'm not being picky. It's immoral."

"I bet you'd screw Little Archie if he was dolled up in a dress."

Edwards's jaw dropped like the Captain's sanity went cliff diving. "I—I …"

"I should perhaps clarify. Provided the little guy shaves his ass," the Captain added as he maintained a straight face.

Edwards's fleshy countenance contorted and creased.

He spared Edwards further insult. The Captain had some journalistic ideas and did not want to jeopardize his plans, so to calm his new companion, he put an arm around Edwards. "I'm playing with you, big guy."

Relieved, he chortled, "You had me going. I almost thought you would sleep with the slave woman."

The Captain shrugged. "Damn straight I would," he said as Edwards's skin whitened. "You see that body? Something so perfectly sculpted is surely blessed by the creator, no?"

Edwards shook the horror from his face and adapted to his professor walrus persona. "God created everything. That does not mean I approve of dalliances between the races."

The Captain thought of the interlude he'd orchestrated between Tempy and Anne. Both parties, at least for a while, seemed happy. "Suppose you were blind, and you believed you were talking to a white gal, but in fact she was black. Do you think if you took a roll in the hay with her, you'd enjoy it any less?"

Edwards snorted the supposition away. "Even if I was blind, I would know. And if forced at gunpoint to submit to such a vile act, I would detest every second of it."

The Captain nodded. "Fortunately with you, the hate will likely be short-lived."

CHAPTER 41

The rain fell lightly onto the canvas above them. The patter sounded like the fall of heaven's tears tapping a melancholy tale to earth's departed soul mates. Well, that's what Charlotte said. The Captain's imagination conjured no such descriptors.

The sex had been like two combatants waged in battle; no quarter given, nor asked—a victory for both parties. Her physique and fierceness was akin to an Amazon warrior on the throes of an eternal quest for orgasmic utopia. Or, perhaps those thoughts exhibited the limitations of the Captain's hormone-imbalanced imagination.

Either way, it was the best sex in a while—for him anyway. Charlotte was a little older and likely more experienced, at least regarding girth. He wondered if she was equally satisfied.

His mind returned to his agenda.

"Tell me about the family. Zerelda the zealot, what's she like?"

She arched her back into his fingertips. "She works us hard, but she's a fair woman."

"Her skin color seems the only thing fair about her," Captain commented.

Her eyes rolled up to him. "If you do what you're told, she treats you well."

He snorted. "That's mighty white of her. I figured you'd despise her."

"Why, because I'm a slave?"

The Captain felt as if he just graduated from the University of St. Augustus the Obvious. "Well, yeah. She hates your whole race."

"What do you know about hate, white boy?" Her elbow struck his ribs. "Zerelda thinks we're inferior, but she doesn't hate us. There is a difference. Trust me, I know."

The Captain got the import of her message. What did he honestly know about hate? The path of life he traversed was unencumbered—a free and straight journey. No roadblocks.

He tightened his arms on her. "I understand. I just figured that if someone looked down on me, I would hate them for that."

Charlotte turned within his arms, face-to-face. "I have a roof over my head and three meals a day. I can freely attend church. They allowed me to marry, and when my husband was dying of consumption, they sent for the best doctor available.[14] Without their support, I could never have raised my daughter alone. The boy, Jesse, even reads to my little Elizabeth."

The Captain understood, but only to a point. The Jameses were fierce Confederates.

She seemed to read his thoughts. "What good is hate, son? Years ago, I did things to get revenge." She paused and flashed a pearly grin. "One time, my daughter played a prank that backfired. She jammed a beehive down the outhouse privy hole. Mr. Samuel always rose first, but on that day, young Jesse woke with a bad stomach," she said and shuddered. "He's a sweet kid."

More Jesse accolades, which angered him, although it reconciled with his own impressions.

"Are you aware he's killed people?"

Charlotte's questioning eyes penetrated, and she seemed to find her answer. "So have you. How can you thus judge Jesse?"

Like the sex, the Captain sensed she was getting the better of him. "Anyone I killed was a bad person. They deserved it." His voice betrayed the justice he wanted to project.

---

14 Consumption was the common term for tuberculosis. If you're like me, you thought he died from the bottle.

She patted his arm. "It's all a matter of personal or cultural perspective, now isn't it?"

Talk like this went against the grain of his timber. Again, she was right. Many societies throughout history performed rituals or committed certain atrocities, yet on an individual basis, the citizens were kind and decent. He figured a conversation with Charlotte would have stoked the engine of his fury, but instead his inertia cooled, his cause derailed.

The Captain rallied his thoughts. "What if I offer you freedom? A place of your own?"

She looked at him as if he were crazy, but when his face did not falter, she smiled coyly. "Just because I gave you some good loving doesn't mean you need to take care of me. It'd been a while for me, so maybe I used you."

A voice called out. Zerelda James. "Charlotte? Charlotte, are you in there?" The back of the wagon ruffled as a hand went to open the flap.

She tensed in his arms. Her eyelashes fluttered against his chest before she withdrew from him. The whites of her eyes radiated fear. "I'm dead. You're dead. We're both dead."

The Captain remained calm. "I'll take care of this." He opened the custom trap door and gestured. "Go."

Charlotte kissed him on the lips and descended beneath the wagon.

The flap opened, and Zerelda's face appeared. "Now I've got you!"

The near-naked captain dangled a gold chain from his hand. "Can you look up? Yes, eyes up at this timepiece, not the codpiece. Very good."

Zerelda's eyes fluctuated north and south before she focused on the gold.

"Now I am going to count down from a hundred to zero."

A half hour later, the Captain looked into Zerelda's vacant eyes. "When I countdown from ten, you will forget everything I told you. Only when you hear the secret password will you act as instructed. Ten … nine … eight … seven … six … five … four … three … two … one! Now, send Little Archie to me."

The Captain holstered his pocket watch inside his trousers and snapped his fingers.

Awakened, her eyes settled on his nakedness, and she screamed.

CHAPTER 42

After lunch, the wholesome farm fun continued. Many of the male adults and children decided to cool off in one of the pigs' mud pits. They came out looking just a smidgen dirtier than beforehand. The women sat on the shaded porch and quietly discussed what a stud the Captain was.[15]

Frank and Jesse's mother, Zerelda, patrolled the compound like a rabid watchdog. Unattractive, her physique was akin to a fruit bowl. Her body was shaped like a pear; her head, like a shriveled, dried-up apple. Frank, unfortunately, resembled his mother.

Zerelda was strongly pro-Confederate. The prior year, she was taken into custody for a full month of questioning. The authorities only released her after she signed a loyalty oath to the Union. Zerelda would have made a determined soldier, but her duty was confined to housing and feeding the Bushwhackers.

The men gathered around Fly Bait, and Bloody Bill patted the horse appreciatively. "This is some warhorse. Biggest damn stallion I've ever seen."

The Captain scratched Fly Bait's head. "He sure is."

---

15   It should be noted that this commentary was not written by the author of the journals chronicled in this story. Rather, the subject of the female chatter was written in the margins by another hand. The writing appeared masculine and was initialed *C. C.*

"He sure *isn't*," Little Archie sneered. He pointed at Fly Bait. "Where are the scalps a real warhorse would carry?"

The gathered men peered at the Captain.

"Sorry, gang, scalps aren't my thing. I just cured this feller of his fly-magnet problem." He pointed at a horse adorned with multiple scalps and said, "For instance, look at that swarm." A cumulus insect cloud hovered around the animal like a shield.

"Hey," Little Archie defended, "that's my ride. Scalps are badges of honor—shows I'm a man to be feared."

"Maybe I'll start my own trend. Instead of scalps, I'll hang ladies' undergarments for all my victims." He saluted and winked.

Bloody Bill laughed. "You are different."

Frank James walked over, covered in mud and pig excrement.

Next to him was someone who looked like his brother, Jesse, except he was paler and dressed in all black. Jesse, sporting a white cotton shirt, was in the foreground talking to Edwards. *Must be another brother*, the Captain figured.

Frank noticed the Captain's pinched brow and cleared the mystery. "This is my cousin, Jesse *Mason* James. He looks more like my brother than I do."

The cousin turned his nose up at the Captain as if the mere introduction were a chore. His eyes scattered about, suggesting there were more interesting things to visualize than this guest. The two men wandered toward the well to wash off.

Edwards called Bloody Bill, Little Archie, Jesse, and the Captain over. When the Captain arrived, much to his chagrin, Jesse offered a firm hand and a kind smile.

"Hey, brother Coytus,"

The kindness flustered the Captain. Again, he sensed the man who murdered his father was not the devil reincarnate. Still, he promised he'd get Jesse talking about the Centralia massacre. Assuredly, his recount would bring the hatred forth.

Edwards clasped his hands. "I have friends at the newspaper, the

Lexington Caucasian.[16] Until my paper is up and running, they're going to help me get our side of the story out."

Frank returned by himself with a lit cigar protruding from his lips.

Bloody Bill asked, "Have you thought about a name for your future newspaper? The *Caucasian* is a tough one to beat."

"Indeed, I have," said Edwards. "Rather than tie my paper to a city, I want an international audience. I was thinking along the lines of: *W.W.W.— World White Web*."

Little Archie snorted. "You're a little old fashioned, gramps. Three Ws might sound cool in the days of dinosaurs, but it seems primitive and immature using all the same letter."

Frank cocked his head. "I would not be so overtly partisan using words like *Caucasian* or *white*. I would be sly and name it after an animal, such as *Fox News*."

Little Archie scoffed. "People hate foxes. Also, 'sly as a fox' is not exactly a cipher puzzle in partisanship. The fox name-brand could never be successful."

Frank shrugged. "How about, *MSNBC* for *Missouri State News by Caucasians?*"

"That's even worse," Little Archie derided. "All news is by Caucasians. Too many letters is confusing."

Frank's eyes sparkled with a new idea. "*CNN* for *Caucasian News Network?*"

"Give up, Frank." Little Archie hocked phlegm to the ground.

Edwards tilted his head as though he were listening to some inner thought. "I liked *Fox News* and *CNN*. You have any better ideas, Little Archie?"

Little Archie puffed his chest. "Yeah, how about a name that exudes professional trust? A paper that focuses on facts, not sensationalism. The *National Enquirer.*"

Edwards didn't reply and instead focused on Jesse James. "Any ideas?"

---

16   The *Lexington Caucasian* was a real newspaper. You might not have guessed, but the newspaper was stridently pro-Confederate.

"I would use the word *Confederate*, followed by either *Times, Journal,* or *Post*. A dignified way of representing the paper's allegiance."

Impressed, Edwards's lips were pursed and eyes sharpened. He turned to the Captain. "You got any thoughts?"

"I'd keep it simple and represent Southern gentlemen. For some reason, *Playboy* appeals to me.[17] I could see it filled with titillating stories."

Edwards swallowed, digesting the information. "Generals Shelby and Price want me to report your deeds and help make more rebels from the populace. I'll do that. But there is something else I need to talk about. What will you do if the North prevails?"

"We'll fight to the death," Bloody Bill vowed.

"I understand, but I want to give you an alternative back-up plan. This comes straight from Generals Shelby and Price. Do any of you know anything about Texas?"

Several men went to speak, but the Captain's voice drowned out the others. "Texas won its independence from Mexico in 1836 and stayed an independent republic until 1845, where she became the twenty-eighth and largest state in the union."

Edwards interjected, "Very good. What foreign nation does Texas border?"

"Mexico," the Captain answered.

He prodded for more. "And do you know the current situation in Mexico?"

The Captain nodded and said, "The whores are cheap, and the guacamole's fresh."

Edwards stuttered. "Well, yeah, but—"

"Oh! They have this amazing blue agave plant," the Captain replied. "If you squeeze the juices and ferment it with yeast, you can make one amazing alcoholic beverage called *tequila*. One time, I drank so much I thought I was dancing with a bunch of hot babes, when I'd actually

---

17 *Fox News, CNN, MSNBC,* and *Playboy* …: The author admits he took literary liberties with this passage. The source document referenced a *Skunk News*, the *Confederate Caller,* the *Whipping Post,* and *White Is Write.*

wandered into a nunnery. They had fun with me, but when I stripped to the buff, I scared a few away." He paused to wink. "But not all."

After the laughter ended, Edwards continued. "Price and Shelby are veterans of the Mexican-American War and have contacts in the country, especially with Archduke Maximilian, namely, the man Napoleon III put on the throne. We can head there and help him maintain his domain. We'll live like fellow royalty."

Bloody Bill grunted his displeasure. "I can only speak for myself, and I *will* fight to the death."

Skeptical with the answer, the Captain gave a sideways smirk at Bloody Bill. "Did I mention the tequila and cheap whores?"

CHAPTER 43

The next morning, the Captain woke to the greasy aroma of sizzling bacon. He fed Fly Bait some apples and joined Edwards and the Bushwhackers for breakfast. Assembled was Bloody Bill's trusted crew: his lieutenant, Little Archie; the James brothers; their cousin, Jesse Mason James; and the three Younger boys—Jim, Cole, and Bob.

The Captain grabbed a plate of bacon and eggs and managed to squeeze a seat next to Little Archie. The men were discussing women.

He suddenly gagged and chugged water to unclog himself. "Wait," he sputtered. His eyes circled the table. "You're all virgins?"

"Fuck, no," Bloody Bill snarled. "I'm married, and I've raped a few gals along the way."

The Captain gulped, unsure how to respond, but it was another justifiable reason for Bloody Bill's soon-to-be death. "I suppose that counts."

He examined the rest of the men. "Any other rapists here? No? Virgins. Hmm." He sighed. "No wonder you're so tense. You need the company of a woman. Nothing's better."

"Hogwash," Little Archie scoffed. "Better than Mom's French cooking? Never."

"I'll take sexy legs over frog's legs any day," the Captain croaked.

"Yeah," Jim Younger said as he stroked his chin. "What about a winter snowball fight? That's the best."

"No, actually it's not, Jimbo."

"Yeah, dummy," said Frank. "It doesn't even snow in most Confederate states."

Jim picked at his nose and nodded.

"No," Cole Younger challenged. "Cow tipping. Truly, is there anything more fun?"

The Captain rolled his eyes. "You lads rather go cow tipping than bed hopping? No wonder women throw themselves at me."

Bob Younger, who was younger than the other Younger brothers, put both hands up. "You're trying to tell us bedding a girl is more fun than whipping a Negro? How dumb do you think I am?"

"Did you ever meet the Swedish skier living in Booneville, Ingemar Skidmark?"

Bob's eyes seemed to reverse, as if he was looking within himself. "No," he finally said.

"Hey." Little Archie scowled. "He's the village idiot."

The Captain shrugged.

Jesse James clapped his hands. "I'll tell you what's better than sex. Gold. When you're rich, you can have all the women you want." He cast a friendly and charming smile at the Captain, who was torn between hatred and smiling back.

Edwards refilled his plate and said proudly, "Remember, the gold is for *our* future, the Knights of the Golden Circle."

The Captain squinted at him. "Can we vote on a name change? This Golden Circle doesn't sit well with me. I had a few thoughts. How about A.S.S.E.S? Alliance of Southern Sons Equals Success." His face gleamed with pride.

"I don't think so," Edwards muttered.

"S.S.S. The Southern Stud Service?"

Edwards shook his head.

The Captain nodded. "True. Not with this crowd."

He chewed as he spoke. "The Knights of the Golden Circle is a fine name."

"I disagree. You're not knights, for starters."

Edwards's face flushed like he'd never considered such. He composed himself and said, "At the top of the command, there are rituals that foster knighthood."

"Until I see a sword and shield, I'm calling that bogus." The Captain dismissed him with a wave of his hand. "And why a golden circle instead of silver square?"

Edwards dropped his fork and bit his lip in thought.

The Captain filled the void. "The Pseudo-Knights of the Red Rhombus would make a welcome change."

"I don't think so."

"Tangerine Triangle?"

Frank James snapped his fingers. "I like that!"

Edwards tapped a nonrhythmic, frustrated beat on his plate. "Let's get back to the plan to rob the gold."

Bloody Bill took control. "I've decided Jesse will lead this mission."

This surprised everybody, including young Jesse. During the commotion, the Captain leaned into Little Archie and whispered, "Benedict Arnold."

Bloody Bill silenced the men. "The James and Younger boys will all go. Little Archie and I will wait for you here."

Little Archie glared at the Captain, rose from the table, and then went to the other side, next to Bloody Bill. He pointed a finger at the Captain. "How do we even know we can trust him? This could be a trap."

The Captain tried to appear shocked and insulted. Hand over his heart, his voice rose. "I'll tell you what." He gestured to Little Archie and Bloody Bill. "I'll be your hostage until these men return with the gold. If these men don't come back, then kill me."

Bloody Bill nodded. "Sounds fair, Little Archie."

Little Archie inhaled through his nose and then hacked to the ground. "It would be a loss of five of us versus just him."

The Captain addressed Bloody Bill. "With all due respect, sir, if desired, I could have systematically killed half your gang last night. Heck, I'd easily maim this guy," he said, pointing to Little Archie, "with a shake of the hand. Small little bug that he is."

Then, without even thinking about what he was going to say, the Captain fingered Jesse James. "I wouldn't send this good man to his death."

"I believe him," Jesse said.

Little Archie grumbled, "That's because you're young and naïve."

Bloody Bill smacked the table and stared at Little Archie. "What's gotten into you?"

"I'm supposed to be the brains of this group, and it's up to me to think about these things."

"True, but you're acting like a baby. I'm ready to summon your mom for breast-feeding."

Little Archie slapped the table. "Jesus hates Christ."

The Captain took his timepiece from his pocket. The sun glinted off it, casting a beam and interrupting Little Archie. "I feel like a reverse Benedict Arnold."

Little Archie's eyes glazed over.

The Captain drew Bloody Bill's vision to the silent man. "Speaking of the Revolutionary War personalities, Benjamin Franklin once proclaimed, 'The worst wheel always makes the most noise.'" The Captain snapped his fingers.

"Huh," Little Archie mumbled. "What did you say?"

"You need to go back to bed and wake on the right side," Bloody Bill scolded.

Chapter 44

Zerelda James sat in her rocker, angry and defiant.

She'd recently returned to the farm after being detained for a month for aiding the rebels and was released only after she signed a declaration of loyalty to the Union, with a promise not to aid the Bushwhackers. Missouri was now governed by Union General Thomas Ewing's General Order Number Eleven, which was famously memorialized in George Caleb Bingham's painting.[18]

Back home, Zerelda ignored the oath, and her farm became a rebel refuge.

She passionately discussed current events with Bloody Bill and Little Archie, and she was so ruthlessly anti-Union the two men appeared like ascetic Buddhist monks by comparison. Her husband, Dr. Samuel, sat like a mummy, offering no opinions.

But as the hours passed, Zerelda fussed like a mother hen as she sat and brooded over the vacancies in her roost. Every sound heard from outside drew her beady eyes to the living room window.

The Captain pulled out his pocket watch and jumped into the conversation. "I agree. Lincoln is a modern-day Benedict Arnold."

---

18 General Order Number Eleven was a directive of Union General Thomas Ewing that forced residents from western Missouri to evacuate their homes. If they signed an oath, they were allowed to live near their homes in a community governed by Union rule. If no oath was signed, the resident was expelled from the state. Many years later, Ewing's order was modified and rebranded as the Patriot Act.

Little Archie twitched like a mouse alerted to danger. He spied the Captain as if he was bait set in the trap. Slumber-faced, he pointed his finger like the grim reaper marking his next victim. "If they don't return, I will kill you myself."

Zerelda tensed like a cat poised to pounce when the Captain captured her attention. "They'll be back."

Charlotte broke the friction when she walked in with a plate of pork lard cookies. She dazzled in her blue dress with yellow trim on the sleeves.

The Captain figured it was time to get rid of Mother Z. for a while. Truthfully, Zerelda scared him in ways none of the Bushwhackers did. Bloody Bill was a skinny stalk of wheat, and Little Archie was a Lilliputian loser. Zerelda was a pistol-packing piranha.

Bloody Bill and Little Archie conversed in hushed tones.

He flashed Zerelda with his timepiece and said, "Vacation day."

Zerelda rose from her rocking chair, approached Charlotte, and took the serving tray from her. "Dear woman. Please take a seat in my chair. It's been a long, hard day."

Charlotte's mouth opened in bewilderment. "Madame?"

Bloody Bill and Little Archie rubbed their eyes.

Zerelda steered the smaller woman into her rocker and then wagged a finger at Charlotte. "All the work you slaves do has made me lazy. Look how fat my behind is." She patted her rump, pirouetted for all to see, and then gesticulated to Charlotte. "Look how thin and shapely you are. I want to look like that again. A young gal's figure."

Dr. Samuel snapped out of his fugue aghast. "Darling, what has gotten into you?"

"You know very well. I see you eyeing every other woman." She said this without malice, but rather with understandable sadness as she sat next to her husband. "I want to give Charlotte and the slaves some days off, for *our* own good. We're growing old and soft, and they are lean and strong. There is something to a hard day's work."

Zerelda grabbed her husband from the couch. "To take our minds off waiting for Frank and Jesse, we'll clean the kitchen."

Resolute, Dr. Samuel said, "I will not."

She yanked him along. "Who do you think calls the shots here?"

His head drooped. "Yes, honey."

On their way out, Zerelda stopped before an awestruck Charlotte. "Enjoy the cookies and the boys' company." To the men, she said, "I expect you to treat dear Charlotte with the respect and dignity she deserves."

When they departed, everyone looked at one another as if confirming what they'd witnessed was real and not mass hysteria. No one moved or spoke until the Captain took the serving tray and passed it to Charlotte. "Try one."

Charlotte judged him with a crooked gaze.

He let a small smile form on his lips.

She tilted her head as she reluctantly took a cookie.

Charlotte's presence made the two Bushwhackers uncomfortable. The Captain wanted to take their attention from her and motioned at Bloody Bill.

"Where do you stand? Seems Little Archie don't trust me."

Bloody Bill had likely thought this through. "By morning the latest, I'll have the answer."

Little Archie sneered, "Before we acquire your scalp, I'm personally going to torture you. Your body will be an experiment for the pain a human being can endure."

The Captain sighed. "I hope them boys return soon, because your silly tough-guy talk is torture enough, Tiny Archie."

"That's Little Archie."

"Small Archie's a no-go?"

"No!"

"They're just synonyms, Short Archie."

"*Little!*"

Recognition etched across his visage. "Gotcha. Didn't think you'd be so particular over an adjective most men would avoid association with. That's the long and short of it."

The Captain got up and went to a knotty pine table. There, he opened a glass decanter and poured himself whiskey. He jiggled the tumbler at Charlotte. "Want one?"

She shook her head and put a hand to her heart. "No thank you, sir."

The Captain checked his timepiece. "Ma'am, if I may ask. Of all the chores you do, which one do you prefer the least?"

Charlotte's head wavered as she considered the outrageous amount of duties to attend to. The Captain planned to give her a well-deserved break. Plus, he didn't want her too tired in the evening.

"I like feeding the farm animals but sure don't enjoy cleaning up after them." She cast him a quizzical expression, as though she knew he was leading to something.

The Captain returned with his drink. From his jacket, he pulled out a cloth sack. A black silk cord tied the top, and he unfastened the knot and withdrew a few gold coins. He passed one to Bloody Bill for inspection. "I'll tell you what, Ant-sized Archie," the Captain said and shook the sack. "If those boys don't return, this gold is yours. If they do, you're on poop patrol. You clean the stables and pigpen."

Little Archie tapped his temple. "Why would I be dumb enough to agree with that?"

"You're the smart one—the brain of the Bushwhackers. You've figured me out as the stranger who lied. Your friends were set up."

Little Archie nodded along with the Captain's summation.

He appealed to Little Archie's vanity, taking things a little farther. "Since you're never wrong, what do you have to lose?"

"Nothing! I just want to point out your proposal did not trick me to bargain what I already know."

"Of course not, buddy. So we have a deal?"

"Yes. The James and Younger boys should have been back three hours ago. I'll be rich, and you'll be dead."

The Captain stared at Bloody Bill. "He's accused me of scandal and betrayal. I expect him to honor our agreement."

Bloody Bill scratched at his beard like his pet tribe of lice was on the march. "A man is only as good as his word."

"While we wait, would you mind if I asked dear Charlotte for a dance?"

Bloody Bill grinned. "You most certainly can."

She, however, was not as amused and kept her fanny rooted to the chair in protest.

The Captain was hoping to slip in a few dances before the men returned at the prenegotiated time he'd set with Jesse.

Everyone's head cocked as they listened to the beat of galloping horses. Jubilant cries rang out.

Bloody Bill smiled at the Captain and frowned upon Little Archie. "Sounds like they got the gold."

"Sounds like they got laid to me," the Captain replied with a wry smile.

Zerelda and Dr. Samuel rushed into the room and opened the front door.

A dripping, sarcastic cough came from the Captain. "Well, well. I guess when you talk shit, you deserve to shovel it."

Little Archie glared. "You may think you're as smart as a steel trap, but you'll get yours."

Charlotte fidgeted in her chair.

The Captain whispered, "Wagon. Two hours."

She gasped.

Their attention turned when Zerelda called out, "My boys!"

Charlotte excused herself and bustled out the back door, but not before the Captain shot a suggestive wink her way.

The hooting and hollering continued as the boys filed through the door.

Zerelda was still mesmerized. Rather than call Charlotte, she pulled her husband into the kitchen.

Bloody Bill approached the men, his face beaming with pride. They grinned back in the delight of pleasing their chieftain.

Zerelda emerged moments later with trays of cured meats, slabs of cheese, and mounds of sliced bread. Dr. Samuel carried two pitchers ripe with condensation.

After the cursory greetings, Zerelda and Dr. Samuel left, and the men got down to business.

Jesse gushed. He pointed at the Captain. "It was just as he said. We ambushed them. Caught by surprise, they dropped their weapons and surrendered. We stole the gold, told them we supported the Union but support ourselves first, and left."

Little Archie grunted with displeasure. "Then what took you so long? A squadron of snails would have made a more expeditious round trip."

The men giggled, but Little Archie's glare silenced them.

Jesse stood tall. "We made a small detour."

"What?" His eyes bulged.

"The war has left several towns bereft of men," Jesse explained with a devilish smirk. He saluted the Captain. "He told us about this Union gold route, and he was right. He told us about Missouri towns that are filled with lonely, anxious women. Right again."

"What towns?" Little Archie's cheeks bulged like a bullfrog.

"There are several. The Captain gave me a list of towns worth stopping by." Jesse pulled out parchment and unfolded it. "These towns: Butts, Buttsville, Cherry Box, Crumpecker, Good Night, Hooker, and Split Log." He folded the paper and put it back in his pocket. "Fidelity he listed as a town to avoid—says a preacher corrupted it."

"Where did you go?" Little Archie's pants bulged like his eyes.

Jesse ran his fingers through his short-cropped hair. "One town was close to where we intercepted the gold. So on the way back, we stopped in Knob Lick, Missouri, for an oral history of the town."[19]

The men snickered.

The Captain's laughter rumbled like thunder. "Look how happy they are. There'd be no wars if the leaders of two opposing sides met in a brothel where the women were affordable and the whiskey free."

---

19 All the towns referenced above exist. From what I gather, they are no longer hot spots for the enterprising bachelor.

CHAPTER 45

The Captain unhitched the wagon from Fly Bait and rode against the rising sun. Destination: Kansas City.

The Bushwhackers were happy. They had more gold in their possession than the rest of Clay County combined. With the exploits in Knob Lick, only one virgin remained. Little Archie bristled when the Captain voiced the observation.

Charlotte was also happy. She spent the night with the Captain, and the next day Little Archie was on duty.

So everyone but Little Archie was elated.

The Captain left under the pretenses that he needed to spy and find the time and place for the next gold run. Instead, he met Union Lieutenant Colonel Samuel P. Cox on the outskirts of the city along a bank of the Missouri River.

"I've earned their trust," he informed him.

Twice the Captain's age, Cox scratched at the grayish red stubble on his chin. "I have no idea how you did it, son. We had snipers waiting to kill them Bushwhackers should they harm any one of my men, but they listened to you."

He ignored the praise. "Don't think I've gone soft carousing with the enemy, but heavy-handed tactics by our side only embolden our opponents and turn public sentiment against us. General Ewing's General Order Number Eleven is a farce."

"I agree. That's why this fight is so personal to a man like Bloody Bill."

He did not understand what Cox meant. "How so?"

Cox's face revealed sympathy, and he looked back toward the growing city. "His sisters were prisoners in the building that collapsed due to negligence. One died, the other's a cripple now. It was stupid to round up women."[20]

"Strange. Bloody Bill never mentioned this," the Captain said almost to himself.

He liked Cox. Both men were comfortable in supporting the general Union ideals; however, they understood that the human element to royally fuck things up pervaded both sides. It wasn't as much good-versus-evil as right-versus-wrong.

Cox's tidings gave him a different perspective of Bloody Bill. Like the Captain himself, Bloody Bill was motivated by revenge for a family member. The thought made him pause until he realized his mission did not include raping and scalping.

Cox mirrored the Captain's thoughts like a Janus facing both ways but seeing continuity in transition. "There's no going back for men like Bloody Bill Anderson. He will kill until he's killed."

The Captain nodded in agreement, but his thoughts turned to his father's killer. Was there no going back for young Jesse? Or, was he a different breed than Bloody Bill? The question was: did he even want to know the answer?

Cox pulled an envelope from his jacket. "This is for you."

His heart skipped a beat as he took possession of the letter.

Cox mounted his horse. "Anything else you need?"

The Captain had almost forgotten but pulled out a list of his own and said, "Yes. Do me a favor and try to find some of this sheet music."

"Sheet music?" Cox took the parchment. "Anything else?"

---

20   Union General Thomas Ewing, whose order incarcerated the women, blamed the collapse on the prisoners, who tried to carve a tunnel under the building. The claim was made despite common knowledge that the women were stripped of all possessions once inside their sleeping cell, and this was before the invention of *Lee Press On* nail enhancements.

He grinned. "In about a month's time, I'll need the services of a Negro prostitute. She needs to meet certain criteria."

Cox cupped his hands under his breasts. "Big udders?"

"Let's call that optional equipment. She needs to have sexually transmitted diseases. As many as possible."

CHAPTER 46

The Captain stopped Fly Bait only a hundred yards from where he left Cox. From his saddlebag, he pulled the envelope. His finger traced the wax seal willfully, like it was a strap from the author's undergarment.

As eager as he was to read her thoughts, he was nervous in equal measure. Normally, he was content playing the Jolly Roger. What his lovers thought was not that much of a concern to him, as long as both parties were satisfied.

Susanna was different.

He broke the wax and lifted the parchment, which unfolded like wings freed from a cocoon. Despite the cool October morning air, his hands grew damp as he read.

> To my captain,
>
> Make believe for a moment that you were not raised by your parents, but by another mother and father. Maybe they don't love each other. Maybe they don't love you. How much different would you be? What if you were born in Georgia, and your father had been killed by someone from the Union? What then?
>
> What circumstances shape a man? At what stage does one reach a tipping point when life's fulcrum is permanently off kilter? Did I have to kill those men the

other night? Is revenge a dish better not cooked, served, or sampled at all?

I will not bore you with thoughts of my feelings for you. I will, however, encumber upon you other burdens of the heart. I killed other humans and wake each night with these thoughts.

Would my father approve of my actions? Would God? *Doubt* is the last thing I should add to your mission, but you're different than most men. You may be macho, but I know you're a big softy inside. You need to think about your mission's endgame, because the ghosts will come.

Business is slow at the saloon. You killed off our best customers.

Oh, it seems Booneville is struck with a syndrome that has afflicted several of the town's women. The symptoms are akin to a feline in heat. Doc Grant has termed the ailment *Coytus Fever.*

Write back to me. I need some color to work on the next verse of your tribute song. And don't lie. I know your shaggin' wagon has already been battle tested. Poor Fly Bait. Give him an apple for me.

Oh, and Deputy Less misses you. You made a man out of him! His wife gives her thanks.

There's so much I'd love to say, but I lack the paper to detail all my mad ramblings, nor would it be right.

I miss you!
Susanna

CHAPTER 47

No longer looking through a short-sighted lens, the Captain scrutinized the Bushwhackers. The majority was still a motley group of ragamuffins, murderers, rapists, and racists, but the tidings from Lieutenant Colonel Cox and Susanna's letter framed them in less filtered light.

He had arrived back at the Jameses' farm the prior evening. Charlotte visited and sensed his unease in their lovemaking; his exploits distracted him and made him timid.

She said, "Whatever is bothering you will resolve itself in good time but not here or now."

The Captain rallied somewhat, but after she left, he brooded over the mission. He had taken Susanna's letter to heart—Bloody Bill and Little Archie were way past their tipping point. One thing he had resolved: both these men would die. He originally thought Little Archie might be salvageable, but the shrimp was such a sheep-shagging schmuck, his days were a finite number. His father's killer, Jesse, was another matter.

The eager men waited for the Captain's report while the slaves served them breakfast.

Frank called for a prayer and asked the newcomer to do the honors.

The Captain confessed to not being an overly religious man, but Frank insisted, so he bowed his head, and the men followed in kind. The Captain raised his head for a brief glance, as did everyone else. All eyes were on him. He bowed again.

Father, I thank you for the tasty dessert late last night.
Father, I thank you for the morning feast at first sunlight.
I thank you for the company of these brave men,
Whose exploits brother Edwards will put to pen.
Glory be to the virgin Mary and the virgin Archie.
Ahh-men, ahh-woman, *ahh-choo!*

The Captain sneezed, and while doing so, he coughed out Little Archie's trigger phrase—Benedict Arnold.

"*Gesundheit*," Frank said. "God bless."

Little Archie wagged a finger at Frank. "Don't bless this wicked devil."

The Captain zeroed on Little Archie. "I trust you thoroughly enjoyed cleaning the stables this morning."

Little Archie bucked from his chair like a jockey dismounting. Bloody Bill's arm stopped the momentum and reversed the inertia, and Little Archie's rear found wood.

"You deserve it, my little buddy. Plus, he's twice your size."

Little Archie tightened his lips as if to stem a flood of hate.

The Captain's face slackened and drooped like that of a morose beagle. "Let's acknowledge the corn and then butter up our differences.[21] I offer my apologies."

As programmed, he would refuse any truce. "You can acknowledge my corn hole and stuff your apology there."

Bloody Bill pointed a finger at him. "It takes a man to apologize and a bigger man to accept the apology. Maybe there's a reason your short in stature after all." His voice dripped with disappointment.

Little Archie bristled and went to speak but was cut off.

"Say another word, and you'll never ride with me again." Bloody Bill's proclamation hung in the air like a black cloud in an otherwise blue sky. He shrugged and looked at the Captain. "Tell us about the next gold heist."

The Captain explained. "The Union is taking extra precautions once the gold leaves St. Louis. An expedition scouting group will precede the

---

21 "Acknowledge the corn" means to acknowledge a mistake and cop a plea. It's a silly expression that understandably fell out of use.

men with the gold. If ambushed, they'll fire a warning shot." He paused. "These gold runners won't turn craven like Benedict Arnold reversed." Little Archie's posture went from erect to squishy like someone pulled a wood stake from his bum.

"Let me explain the merits of disrupting this gold supply—something y'all might not have figured out. Stealing their gold is like killing hundreds of men," Bloody Bill declared. Most of the men looked stupefied, except the Captain and Jesse James.

Bloody Bill continued. "In these parts, they can't find men passionate enough to fight on behalf of the Union. They rely on paying wages, literally bribing the poor to take up arms. These men don't believe in the cause they fight for. That's why we beat their sorry asses every time we meet in battle." He paused to gain every man's attention. "If we steal the Union gold, they'll never recruit the manpower to take Missouri."

He stopped to wipe some swine grease into his beard and gesticulated to the Captain. "This man has given us a way to hit them where it hurts. Missouri will be a slave state. We'll be so rich we'll own the bloody show," he said with a sly snicker.

The Captain bit his lip to hide his disgust. "I do not have the rendezvous date yet. The Union leadership was trying to keep that a secret, but my contact will have the information in a day's time. My contact claimed that due to prior robbery and a strong push by Union generals to crush the rebels, this delivery was to have over three times the weight in gold."

Bloody Bill clapped his hands over his empty plate. "Fantastic." His head cocked like he heard an inner voice. "The James family has been courageously gracious in hosting us. Thus, I promised Momma Zerelda one of us would clean the outhouse, which is only fair after the filthy lot of us defiled it. Being one of us is already experienced—and has a penchant for kicking up a stench—I volunteered Little Archie's services."

Confused, Little Archie blinked like being woken from a dream.

"That's mighty kind of you, Little Archie," Frank said as he spooned the last of his baked beans in his mouth. "Mind if I use the privy one last time before you start?"

CHAPTER 48

Little Archie stood like a eunuch in a room full of eager concubines—impotent, deflated, and ultimately undesired. He'd lost the respect of his men. Worse yet, he'd become the butt of jokes, something that erstwhile had been inconceivable. Glowering at the Captain only distracted him as the new addition to their gang gave a young Negro female a piano lesson on the front porch.

Yes, Little Archie's downward spiral, he recognized, had begun the day the Captain arrived. The worst part, however, was that he could not remember the details of his own downfall. Everything seemed murky, and he almost did not believe Bloody Bill's account, until his apparent reprehensible actions were corroborated by others.

One thing was certain: Jesse James would not lie unless it was to the Union.

Little Archie sidled up to the Captain, well aware that many eyes, including Bloody Bill's, followed him. He thought of his mentor's prior words about accepting an apology. When had Bloody Bill uttered them?

"I want to say I'm sorry. I hardly remember—"

The Captain held up a hand and halted the apology. Then he winked as he lowered his voice. "We'll talk later," he said as he scanned all directions as if he wanted their conversation private.

Little Archie's maw puckered like a pike. "When?"

"Why don't you accompany me when I meet my Union contact? I'll leave you about a mile back, but trust me—that's for your safety."

Surprised, Little Archie nodded and muttered, "Thanks." Then he rejoined the men.

CHAPTER 49

The Captain returned his attention to the ten-year-old piano prodigy, Charlotte's daughter, Elizabeth. After a quick lesson, she played "Oh, Susanna" with ease. He relished the thought of teaching her Chopin, Liszt, and other pianist geniuses.

Most of the Bushwhackers tapped their feet and nodded their heads along to the melody unleashed by Elizabeth's fingers. They were getting keyed up for a game where they rode pigs around the mud pit. The last one still mounted would win an extra ration of beef jerky every night of their next campaign.

Bloody Bill walked onto the porch, pointed to Elizabeth, and said, "I'd wager that if you gave enough monkeys a piano, inevitably one would create a concerto worthy of Bach." His slanted eyebrows and sinister laugh suggested he was pleased with his sarcastic wit.

The Captain grinned back, knowing the terror before him would be dead by dawn.

Bloody Bill leaned closer. "Did you ask Little Archie to accompany you?"

"I did."

When he did not expand on the answer, Bloody Bill gave a dark, grave look. "You plan to kill him, don't you?"

The accusation caught him by surprise, but after further consideration on Bloody Bill's way of thinking, it was all quite logical. "Honestly, the thought never crossed my mind. I wanted to make amends. I'd be more worried about Little Archie shooting me in the back than anything else. To be safe, why not send Jesse and Frank along?"

Bloody Bill shook his head. "For his mother and Edwards, I'll leave Jesse *Woodson* behind. You can have his cousin Jesse *Mason* instead."

Disappointed, the Captain merely shrugged.

Bloody Bill's eyes narrowed. "You sure about the gold quantity? That's silly money."

"No, it's not. They'll be carrying United States bank gold deposits, not Chinese currency."

Bloody Bill shook his head. "*Silly money* is just an expression."

"I know."

A puzzled expression crossed Bloody Bill's visage like he was asked to recite the alphabet backward.

The Captain produced a sheepish grin and chuckled. "Just being stupid. I'm used to relating to less astute company, but you're clearly more rank and defiled."

Bloody Bill thumped him on his back. "Thanks. You're going to be a legend among the Knights of the Golden Circle."

Elizabeth switched back to a familiar song, "Mother, Oh, Sing Me to Rest."

The Captain shook his head in appreciation. "Her fingers move with the power, speed, and grace of a svelte jaguar. Amazing."

Bloody Bill cast a steely glower. "The way you speak, I'd almost think you were a Yankee. Don't tell me you're against slavery."

A flash of sadness crossed the Captain's visage, only to be replaced by a determined resolve. "I am," he said and held Bloody Bill's gaze. "My motivation for joining this war is for personal reasons."

"What reasons?"

"The same reasons I assume motivated you. Am I wrong that it's not your passion for slavery, but rather another cause that brought the rage?"

Just like the Captain, Bloody Bill frowned as his eyes lost focus, and then a snarl split his face.

The Captain nodded; his voice came forth like he was quoting from a well-rehearsed dream. "I lost my father, and the men responsible will die, one by one." He paused. "It's personal for you too, isn't it?"

Now Bloody Bill nodded. "I knew I felt a brotherly bond."

He shivered.

"How did you find out?" Bloody Bill asked.

"I've been trying to infiltrate the Union to get closer to the men responsible for my pa's death. My contact is a Union cousin. He's one of the gold runners. That's why I insisted on no killing. He told me about the building collapse and your sisters." He cast his eyes down, partially to hide the lie. "I'm sorry for your loss."

Bloody Bill hugged him. The Captain made a mental note to take a bath as soon as permissible.

Bloody Bill turned to leave but stopped. "Too bad you didn't want to stick around on a permanent basis. I might be looking for a new second-in-command."

He shook the offer away. "I am honored, but Little Archie passes the sniff test to make a perfect number two."

CHAPTER 50

Charlotte mixed the mosquito repellent and helped the Captain lather up Fly Bait.

"Thank you," she said. "For my daughter."

He sponged the horse's powerful hindquarters. "Are you kidding? She has a gift. Not just musically, either. She's a special person, beautiful inside as she is outside."

Charlotte swooned and almost dropped the bucket. "She adores you too."

A blissful silence passed between them. Somehow his hand slipped from the horse to her bottom. "Oops, sorry," almost worked on the first grope.

When they finished, the Captain returned a promise. "I'll ensure your daughter grows up a free woman."

He walked Fly Bait over and joined the Bushwhackers. Little Archie, Frank, and Jesse Mason were ready and stood by their mounts. Jesse Woodson helped Frank pack some food their mother prepared for the journey. With a glint in his eyes, Bloody Bill rubbed his hands together.

"God speed," he said.

The four men were merely a few miles from the Jameses' farm when the sound of an approaching dog bark caught their attention. Through the brush came a bloodhound, his tail happily gyrating behind him. The hound's ribs stretched over the skinny frame. The Captain reached for the saddlebag for some pork jerky when his ears were assaulted by gunfire.

On the horse next to him, Jesse Mason held a still-smoking pistol. Like a lightning bolt in a pitch-black sky, a twisted grin lit his pale face.

The Captain glared at Mason. "What the hell did you do that for? He wasn't rabid."

"It's just a dog. Max was his name." His voice swelled with pride.

Frank coughed and edged his way into the conversation. "Max is one of the Jones's hunting dogs. He'd been missing. Looks like he found his way home." Unlike Mason, Frank's drooping eyes and somber voice evidenced compassion.

Even Little Archie, a practitioner in the art of human scalping and other feats of barbaric cruelty, scolded Mason. "Dog was defenseless. No valor in taking its life."

The corner of Mason's lips curved further north. "I killed him to spite Jenny Jones. She laughed at me when I asked her to the county dance. Jenny loved Max like the *thing* was human."

The Captain calculated the merits and demerits of the Bushwhackers. When Little Archie questioned the morality of someone's actions, then you knew the devil had an eye on you. Jesse Mason James was speeding up the kill chart.

If only Mason had been his father's killer.

Further down the road, the men came upon a white farmhouse. Three children played in the yard, and a squat man in a large Stetson walked out to the road.

Frank lowered his voice and directed his words for the Captain's benefit. "Woof, woof. That's Mr. Jones."

Almost as if he'd read Frank's lips, Mr. Jones asked, "You see a dog? Mine's been missing for over a week, and I just heard his bark, then a gunshot."

"No, sir," Mason replied without remorse.

Had the Captain not witnessed the killing himself, he'd swear Mason was telling the truth.

"Damn," muttered a disappointed Mr. Jones. "My family loves that dog. Heck, I love the beast myself."

The Captain dismounted and worked his hand into his saddlebag and came out with a cloth sack. He walked to Mr. Jones and bent his head. "Err, your dog, Max. He's dead."

"What?" His face bunched with bewilderment.

"I'm going to tell you something that will make you angry, but for your children's sake, I'm going to ask you not to react. Hear me out. Okay, friend?"

He offered his hand. Puzzled, Mr. Jones accepted.

With his free hand, the Captain pointed at Mason. "That man killed your dog."

Mr. Jones took a step forward, but the Captain's prior words—and grip—stopped him.

"I empathize, sir. Apparently, my acquaintance was miffed your daughter had the good taste to reject his advances."

"Don't listen to him. He's lying," said Mason.

The Captain cocked his head. "Tell the truth or I'll call off our mission."

Without pause, Little Archie pointed at Mason. "He killed the dog."

"That bastard," Mr. Jones said. "You sure I can't kill him?"

"Maybe some other day. The important thing is not letting him get the satisfaction of upsetting your daughter. Tell your children we saw Max with a wealthy family aboard a caravan headed west." The Captain reached into his purse and handed over a gold coin. "Get a new pet. They'll miss Max, but the new puppy will make things better."

Mr. Jones glanced back to his children who stared with nervous, wide-eyed curiosity. He examined the gold coin. "Why are you doing this?"

"Because it's the right thing to do. But I do have a favor. With highest respect to you, good sir, and with the best intent of a gentleman, would you allow me to ask Jenny to the dance?"

"Scoundrel," Mason snarled.

"You may. I trust Jenny. She's sensible." He called his daughter to join them.

Jenny scuttled over, her steps as unsure as her pinched-brow expression. She wore a red-and-white-checkered dress with a cream silk ribbon at her neck. A yellow bonnet, with a red marigold pinned above her left ear, graced her head like a star on a gingham Christmas tree.

The Captain went down on one knee.

"I killed Max," Mason barked. "So fuck you all."

Jenny's hand went to her mouth.

Mr. Jones's hand bunched to a fist.

Mason tapped his pistol.

The Captain rose off his bended knee and walked toward Mason.

Jesse Mason turned his horse so that the steed's head faced the oncoming Captain. His hand rested on the pistol grip, but the gun remained holstered. "Don't think I won't shoot. I will, but I promise it won't be a kill shot. We still need you or it would be."

Frank and Little Archie appealed for calm, and Frank patted the air down. Little Archie cussed.

"You can have my gold, but you must apologize to Miss Jenny Jones." The Captain lightly tossed the cloth sack up to Mason.

As soon as instinct took Mason's hand from his pistol in an effort to catch the incoming object, the Captain ducked left and then came up with a furious lunge that knocked him from his horse.

The Captain smacked the stallion on the behind. "Get," he said, and the horse trotted several paces away. He retrieved a stunned Mason by the cuff of his collar, and like a dog on a leash, he walked Mason over to Jenny.

With a smack to the back of the head, the Captain demanded, "Apologize to the lady."

Mason did not oblige and received a second whack.

"I'm sorry," he growled, with the hollow conviction of a convict.

With ninja-like speed, Jenny's right foot greeted his privates. He groaned, dropped, and writhed on the floor.

Mr. Jones's face glinted with pride.

Mason was down and splayed like a fallen scarecrow.

The Captain smiled. "Appears you taught Mason-head a lesson."

Jenny grinned upward. "Thank you. Who are you?"

He removed the Stetson. "Call me Coytus. Captain Coytus, if you please, my lady."

"Coytus. Hmm, that is an unusual surname."

Little Archie grunted in agreement. "It's actually British. He's from the Island of Karma Sutra."

Both father and daughter fixed uncertain expressions. "Never heard of it," Mr. Jones asserted.

"Anyway," the Captain said in an effort to change the conversation. He went back to a bended knee. "Miss Jenny Jones, if your head and heart allow, I'd love to take you to this county dance."

Jenny turned to her approving father and then performed a curtsy. "I'd be delighted to accompany you."

Jenny skipped back to the yard while Mr. Jones shook the Captain's hand farewell.

If Frank or Little Archie found the Captain's action disagreeable, they chose to withhold comment.

He stripped Mason of his weapons, and satisfied, he lifted the injured man to his horse like he was stocking a store shelf with shoddy merchandize.

CHAPTER 51

"Do you love pork?" Frank asked the Captain.

He found the question odd, but Frank's face and voice appeared sincere. "I suppose so."

"Ah, that explains it."

"Explains what?"

"I heard, on more than one occasion, Charlotte refer to you as Mr. Sausage."

The Captain flashed a sheepish grin. "'Slam Some Ham' is practically my motto."

The horseback-mounted men continued down the road, and Frank smiled as wide as his saddle.

Little Archie sat on his mount like an annoying kid on a rocking horse, kicking his legs back and forth, back and forth while clinging to the reins.

Mason stared straight ahead, quiet as a slaughterhouse mouse.

As the men forged on, the Captain explained his plan. "In case you have to move from the rendezvous point, can any of you replicate bird calls?"

"I'm not good with birds, but Charlotte taught me the roar of a lion," Frank informed. He let rip a hearty growl that sounded feline and feral.

"That's aces, Frank, but I'm fairly certain lions don't roam these parts," he pointed out.

Little Archie brightened like an idea took flight. "I'm good at imitations."

"Hmm. What's your specialty, a dodo bird?"

"A what?"

The Captain pondered. "I wonder if my buddy Mason could do a humming bird and follow with a swallow."

Mason did not flinch. His sight was firmly glued to the horizon.

"We can whistle 'Dixie,'" Frank gushed. "I can do that as good as my lion."

"We're trying to be a little more evasive, Frank."

Little Archie tilted his head back and howled like a wolf. Impressed, the Captain settled on the wolf call.

Proud, Little Archie puffed his chest.

"This is where I say farewell," he said as they ventured into a copse with a clean-water stream for both man and beast.

"I hate good-byes," pouted Frank. "How about a group hug?"

"I'll be back in three hours, Frank. Be strong."

"I'll sure try."

The Captain, gratefully, left the Bushwhackers. A cigar added to the tranquil enjoyment of riding on alone.

He had lied about the three hours' round-trip travel time. On the previous jaunt to Kansas City, he'd been at a farmer's market and seen the backside of a woman who appeared so alluring that the Captain had maneuvered to get sight of her face. What he visualized repulsed him. By all accounts, she should have been beautiful. Instead, her eyes were blackened and puffy, shifting about, while her maw quivered like a mole sensing sunlight.

The Captain forced conversation on her. He learned her mother died young, and six months ago, her father fell to consumption. Her older brother had gone east to fight the war and had not been accounted for in over a year.

Desperate times took desperate measures, and she agreed to a marriage with a man in town not based on love, let alone affection. He had money and could provide. While it was not uncommon for husbands to smack their wives, it was another matter to beat a woman to a bloody pulp. On one occasion, she damn near perished from internal injuries beyond her doctor's medical means.

The minister prayed to God for her well-being, and God blessed her recovery. She was thankful, but the minister's prayers and talks with her husband produced no further miracles. The sure hand of God did not intervene and protect her from the coarse hand of her husband. The Captain liked to think God picked him to handle the earthly chore.

The Captain walked up a cobblestone path to a large white-folk Victorian. He climbed three steps to a rectangular porch, where a wood bench rested against the house and a swinging chair hung from an overhead hook. Between them lay a square oak table. Indian corn was fastened next to the front door where he knocked.

A beefy man with no discernible neck and an isosceles-triangle snout answered. He reminded the Captain of an animal he'd read about: a penguin. Maybe he knew Edwards the Walrus.

The man squinted, and his eyes almost disappeared in the folds of flesh. "May I help you?"

"Are you Chet Owen?"

Owen's jaw protruded. "You are?"

The Captain flashed his best smile. "Terrence O'Dourke. I understand you married my sister."

Dumbfounded, Owen's mouth hung open. The Captain could picture him swallowing fish whole like his animal twin.

"You're Janet's brother?" He stepped out to the porch and shut the front door behind him.

"I am."

"Did you receive word of your parents' fate?" Owen's voice lacked empathy.

"God rest their souls, I did."

Owen took a few steps from the door to the top of the porch stairs. "What happened to you?"

"We won some, we lost some. I went as far as Georgia and then got myself shot. I recovered. Now I'm back." The Captain spoke a little louder than normal and noticed alarm set into Owen's eyes.

Owen thumped down a few steps.

The Captain did not follow. "Can I see my sister?"

He groveled like a dog caught stealing human food. "Uh, err, hmm. She's not here."

"Where is she?"

"Yeah, well, you know, right, yeah."

The Captain snapped like a shark hungry for penguin poppers. "What the 'yeah-well-you know-right-yeah' does that bloody mean?"

Owen fixed the Captain with his beady penguin eyes. "She's not available at the moment."

"Is she sick?"

"Not exactly. She fell off a horse and is bedridden."

The Captain snorted. "My sister? Ride a horse? By God, she's frightened of the beasts."

The fat man swiveled his head. "Not anymore."

The Captain's face grew with desperation. "Surely, I can check in and let her know I'm here."

"Doctor's orders. She's not to be disturbed."

The Captain drew frantic breaths and cried out with an anguished heart, "I love my sister." He fell into an exaggerated sobbing fit.

A cracking noise came from behind. The front door opened, and out came a woman who was hunched over, a hand pressed against her abdomen. "Terrence? Oh, Terrence, is that you?"

The Captain ran to Ginger and steered her to the wood bench, where he put his arm around her. "You fell off a horse?"

Ginger shook her head, confused. Her husband discreetly nodded for her affirmation.

She had prepared for this moment earlier. "No," she said as she pointed at her husband. "He did this to me."

The Captain frowned. "Ginger, a *real* man does not savage a woman, unless they've misbehaved in some unseemly fashion. Did you commit adultery?" he accused with a cross expression.

"Surely not!"

"Return to your bed," Owen ordered his wife.

The Captain canceled the order. "Stay. What wrongs have you committed, sister?"

Rehearsed, Ginger replied, "The first time was when I made lemon macaroons. Chet became displeased that mine were not quite up to his mother's standards. I tried to explain that she had an advantage, being they grew up in Florida with fresh sugar and lemons."

The Captain shook his head. "I love lemon macaroons. Damn sin if they don't taste right. We might be building a case here. What else did you do wrong?"

"I did not solve the nine-word square puzzle in time."[22]

The Captain scratched his head. "I need some more color, folks."

Owen took the request literally, and his ashen face reddened.

Ginger spoke before her husband could. "He had a bet with Joe Cole. You remember Joe."

"Of course. Wealthy man."

"He is. They'd been wagering on the weekly puzzle. Apparently, my dear husband was winning on puzzles I'd solved for him. They upped the ante, and I was unable to solve it before Joe."

The Captain's eyes crossed in confusion. "You're telling me Joe Cole bested you in a nine-word puzzle? I almost feel like clubbing you. He's thicker than horseshit, and his money is inherited."

"Joe paid a cryptographer to help him."

"Oh. That explains it. Word that he used a cryptographer assuredly came out after your thrashing?"

Ginger batted a puffy eye. "It didn't."

"Guess that doesn't explain it," the Captain said with a shrug. "No matter, you still lost. What else did you fail at?" He smiled at Owen.

Owen offered a reserved laugh. The lopsided expression confirmed he had no idea this was a charade.

Ginger kept the hits coming. "Occasionally, I've talked in my sleep."

He rolled his hand. "Did you call out another man's name?"

"Nope."

---

22   The square puzzle was the precursor to crossword puzzles. I once tried to do the Sunday *New York Times* crossword puzzle. If I was locked in a room without references and told I could not leave until I finished the puzzle, I would have served a life sentence.

The Captain clucked his tongue. "Well, whatever you said, I'm sure your discourse was disrespectful."

"Whatever I said, it was incomprehensible gibberish."

The Captain patted Owen's back. "I understand. A working man needs his sleep. Last thing he needs is a wife who talks his ear off, even in her sleep."

"My husband does not work. His money is inherited too, and the incident in question was an afternoon nap. I was nursing a fever."

"Really?"

"He beat me because my babble must have been devil talk. I apparently communicated with Satan in my dreams."

"Humph, there you go—perfectly illogical. What else have you done wrong, my dear sister?"

"Men have looked at me."

"They have?" He squealed in shock. "Say no more. Don't you know a good wife must stay invisible? You'll have to do better, Ginger."

"One time, I did not know what he was thinking." She grimaced.

"And what was he thinking? Or, do I not want to know?" the Captain said as he grimaced back.

"He wanted a glass of whiskey. I thought he wanted, well, you know," she said and stared at the ground.

The Captain inhaled like he considered a weighty matter. "Sorry, Ginger. A dutiful wife must be clairvoyant. A beating might have been a tad harsh, but you must strive to perform the impossible."

Ginger sighed in near-defeat but gave it one last go. "One time, I spilled milk. He cried like a baby and then beat me so bad I near died."

The Captain rounded on Owen. A punch brought the portly penguin down. "You cried over spilled milk?"

CHAPTER 52

The Captain left the Owens' residence an hour later. He continued to Kansas City, confident that relations between the couple were forever improved. He implanted a charm on Owen the same way he had with the others and planned to drop in occasionally to ensure that his marriage-counseling skills had not been for naught.

He found Colonel Cox in the saloon, sipping whiskey and drumming an imaginary beat on the bar. He stood next to a large Negro woman with smiling eyes.

Cox introduced her. "Here is Miss Veronica Mosley, lady of the night and day—if you're inclined to pay. She's just as you wanted. Doctor certified."

The Captain took in Miss Mosley. She had big curves everywhere and a kind countenance despite the hardships she assuredly endured. He empathized. Born into a life where a human believed their best viable option was selling their body, degeneration and disease were just two of the lousy perks that came with prostitution.

And here the Captain was, ready to use her again. He rationalized away some of the guilt, hoping it would be the last time she'd have to turn a trick. He explained his need for her services and apologized for doing so. He promised her an incredible sum of money and upfront gave her several *Stellas*—four-dollar gold coins—which were more than she could make in a lifetime of tricks.

Miss Mosley was provided a time and a place and left the bar with a slow sway.

The Captain concluded his planning with Cox and handed the colonel an envelope addressed to Susanna. Cox scribbled a hasty letter of his own and gave that to the Captain.

"One last thing. Make sure no one shoots me," the Captain said. "I'll be wearing this Union uniform and this large Stetson."

Cox laughed. "It's easy. Don't shoot the big guy."

The Captain slammed an empty glass of whiskey down and left the bar. A few buildings along the road, he knocked on a door. Upon entry, he greeted Edwards, who wore a three-piece suit with a flat-topped derby. He appeared rather dashing for a middle-aged walrus.

"Coytus," Edwards huffed as though he'd just swum five leagues, full flipper speed.

"Wal—I mean, Edwards."

Edwards motioned to a chair and took one himself. The room's Spartan décor was limited to three desks and a small Confederate flag discreetly hung from the open back door.

"You're looking at the future site of my newspaper," he boasted while playing with his shirt collar as though it were a badge of the privileged.

The Captain gazed around. His first thought was arson. "I see a bright, blazing future."

Edwards slapped his flippers. "Oh, goody, I have great news for you. I've secured a job for you with the *Lexington Caucasian*! How sweet is that?"

"Sweet as a lemon," the Captain quipped. Truthfully, he was genuinely excited about the opportunity. He unleashed his best smile, all white, straight teeth on display. "Thank you."

"Hone your skills with the *Caucasian*. When I'm ready to start my paper, you'll work with me."

The Captain brought out his timepiece and held it by the chain, and the gold circle arced slowly back and forth. He yawned, long and pronounced. "I'm excited. Mistrust me."

The Captain's last words did not register with Edwards. His eyes fluttered. Under the Captain's spell, Edwards's mind was opened to suggestion. The Captain rerouted some thoughts, memories, and inhibitions—and planted the trigger words.

Mesmerized, Edwards admitted that his disgust with interracial sex was a façade. In fact, he fancied Negro women. "If only there was one around right now, my loins burn with desire."

A knock came from the door.

"I'll get that for you," the Captain said and grinned when he opened the door. "Hello, my lady."

In strutted Miss Mosley. She turned and addressed Edwards. "At your service."

The Captain laughed. "I'll leave you two love birds together. I'll be back when you're finished." He checked his timepiece. "Say, one to two minutes?"

Miss Mosley looked at the Confederate flag and then sized up Edwards. A smile crept across her lips, and she took him by the hand. "I'm all yours, mister."

The Captain bid farewell. Eighty-seven seconds later, he opened the door. He held a large wooden box with a tube sticking out of the center and pressed a button of an early camera he'd made himself using a pewter plate and bitumen.

He snapped several shots from various positions and angles, all the while thinking about drawing whiskers on the walrus, but realized it would blow the ruse.

The Captain returned the camera to the saddlebag and said the magic words. "Reverse: naughty for Negroes."

Edwards snapped out of his charmed fugue, naked and straddled over Miss Mosley, who was pressed atop a desk.

Edwards stumbled back from her. "What the backwoods blazes?"

"You stallion," the Captain said with a hearty chuckle.

Miss Mosley grinned at the Captain and began to dress.

Edwards yanked his trousers up from his ankles. "I can explain," he asserted, but the panic in his face said otherwise.

Fully clothed, Miss Mosley sauntered over to him. She blew a kiss. "Thanks, sugar."

"You get away from me!"

Miss Mosley laughed and left the building.

Edwards folded his hands in prayer. "Please, please, please, don't tell anyone. The Knights of the Golden Circle can never know."

The Captain made a promise he intended to keep. "I swear my lips will never betray you."

CHAPTER 53

The Captain was plotting future journalistic endeavors for the *Lexington Caucasian* when he heard the Bushwhackers ahead. Little Archie was so enamored with his wolf call, the Captain made sure he would not get to use it. He rode along a babbling brook to mask Fly Bait's hooves, and then he yelled, "Go," and the mighty stallion broke into a thunderous gallop.

The Bushwhackers were caught by surprise.

"Coytus!" Frank rejoiced from his position midway up a tree.

"Great job on lookout, Frank," Little Archie yelled upward. "If he was with the Union, we'd all be dead now."

Frank shook his head. "I spotted him, but when he slowed and took an indirect route, I kept quiet, thinking he might have a tail behind him."

Frank wiggled down a big white oak. Mason the mute offered no greeting. He bit at his fingernail and used the shaving to pick at his teeth.

Frank bound over. "You get the gold info?"

The Captain nodded. "Not a bad idea to keep a lookout. Mason, watch the trail over there." He pointed the way he'd come.

Mason grunted and sauntered off, seemingly happy to be away from present company.

The Captain unfolded a map and pointed. "Here, the men will come this way in three days. They'll have two men ahead. You need to stay hidden and let them pass. If a gun is fired, then the gold convoy will retreat. Once the two pass, four other men will come with the gold. That's when you set the ambush."

Little Archie grinned. "We can't go wrong."

"You can," the Captain warned. He pointed back at the map, his finger in Gentry County. "Do not pass the city of Albany to get to the ambush spot. The Union has a large force stationed there. They're running patrols, looking for men just like you."

"Maybe we kill some Union *reckies* while we're at it," Little Archie proposed.[23]

"Not this time. Steal the gold and get away. I'll meet you back at the Jameses' farm in a few days."

He agreed. "Yeah, that's right. Take the gold, destroy the Union Army. Good strategy—get rich and win a war."

"You bet," Frank said.

The Captain leveled his gaze at both men and pointed again at the map. "Remember, come this way, not past Albany."

Little Archie grinned. "We can't get that wrong. It's out of the way to pass Albany."

He shook hands and hugged both men. When he embraced Little Archie, he whispered, "Benedict Arnold."

Little Archie's eyes glazed over. The Captain bid his farewell and rode back the way he'd come. He once again came upon the white Victorian home and knocked.

Mr. Owen answered, dressed in an apron and a black eye. He had a feather duster in his hands. Scrumptious smells wafted by draft of the open door. "I just baked lemon macaroons. You must try one," Chet Owen said dutifully.

"I will, thanks," the Captain said and walked into the kitchen with Owen. "Where's my sister?"

"She's out back catching some late-afternoon sun. I made a bed of hay and feathers and served her lunch in bed as she took in the fall foliage, in particular a Cooper hawk's nest in the tree over the barn." He handed the Captain a still-warm macaroon.

---

23 "The term *rookie* comes from the Civil War term *reckie*, which was short for *recruit*." Snapple Fact Cap #863.

"These are good," he said after he swallowed his whole.

"Not as good as my wife. She's my princess."

A self-satisfied smile broke his face. The demon had been exorcised, and this house, cleansed.

CHAPTER 54

Back on the road, the Captain left the Owens' residence, assured that Chet was a reformed man. Submissively doting, he was obsessed in ensuring that his wife was satisfied in all matters, especially sexually. Owen practically begged the Captain to pleasure his princess. Exit Corporal Cuckold; enter Captain Coytus.

Within eyeshot of the Jameses' farm, the Captain spotted another testicular-challenged husband, Dr. Samuel. His wife, Zerelda, bustled behind him as he walked to the stable, carrying a large satchel. Jesse James stood on the porch, watchful and poised. He waved a hand at the Captain.

Jesse's usual calm demeanor appeared weathered like the gray of a fleeting storm. The Captain dismounted and strode up the porch, where he greeted his father's killer. He had to keep reminding himself that. Thus far, he'd found Jesse and Frank to be the most likeable of the Bushwhacker lot. They were like two gold coins stuck down the privy hole.

Dr. Samuel led a horse from the barn. Slung across his shoulder was a large wood stake. Zerelda met him with a cross necklace.

The Captain gestured to the barn with a puzzled crease in his brow. "Huh?"

Jesse's voice came low. "Mason's family dog transformed into a vampire."

Something odd was in the air, but this was battier than expected. "Please, do tell."

"Mason always had a thing for vampires."

"That's bizarre."

"I think so too, but Frank sees the allure. He likes scary stories and believes vampires could spawn sagas of storytelling."

"Hmm, maybe."

"Little Archie thinks hobgoblins are much more practical and pointed out Shakespeare's *A Midsummer Night's Dream* and the character Puck. Hard to argue with him there."

The Captain was impressed the Bushwhackers knew of Shakespeare. Despite being ruthless, and in some cases evil, these were much brighter men than the Booneville buffoons.

"To be honest, I think I'm going with Frank," said the Captain. "What about Mason's dog?"

Jesse's voice sounded soft despite his steely visage. "I heard about what happened between you and Mason. He came back angry and vowed revenge."

The Captain nodded for Jesse to continue.

"He said you were strong, but a vampire was stronger, and set out to a nearby cave. He said if bit by a special bat, he'd finally become the vampire he always dreamed of. Except the only one bitten was his dog, King. Mason's mother came to our farm, hysterical, saying King had gone mad, but Mason told everyone to relax, it was just a phase until the canine became a vampire. He claimed he did not think a by-product of the wolf family could become a vampire, being they are more akin to their shape-shifting lycanthrope werewolf cousins. Yet the hound's transformation was undeniable proof."

The Captain shook a thought away. He should let King turn wild and bite moronic Mason, but innocent bystanders might incur harm. "King is no vampire. Your cousin has bats in his belfry."

The Captain waited for Dr. Samuel the Vampire Slayer to make his approach. Horseback and unbalanced, he teetered from side to side. With his sparse hair, mustache, and wood stake, he looked like Don Quixote set for a foolhardy quest.

"You're tilting at windmills, Dr. Samuel," the Captain said.

The bad doctor grew confused, but Zerelda spoke. "This vampire business is your fault."

He wanted to reply but decided not to pick a fight at this time. "You may be right. Right now, though, we have a problem to deal with. First, you can put the stake and cross away; King is not a vampire."

Zerelda protested the claim, but the Captain focused on Dr. Samuel and appealed to his medical side. "King's got rabies, a disease passed from the saliva of an infected animal. Rabies comes from a Latin term, *to rage*. King is exhibiting symptoms consistent with this disease. He needs to be killed. If he bites anyone, they'll be infected. There is no cure."

"That sounds like bull," Zerelda spouted.

"Put a nonsilver bullet in King. If he rises, then you can lasso my pecker with a thorny vine."

Only the men gasped.

Dr. Samuel cleared his throat. "I've heard of this 'rabies' before. Some Italian doctor discovered the disease."

"Correct," the Captain said, keen that Dr. Samuel made the connection. "Girolama Fracastoro also discovered syphilis, so his diagnosis of rabies should not be discounted."

Jesse stepped off the porch, approached his mother, and pointed at the Captain. "He's right. I can feel it. You know in your heart it's not his fault. Mason is a bad seed. The Captain, in contrast, has been honorable and a boon to our Confederate cause."

Her rigid face softened as she mulled over her son's reasoning. The woman might have been ornery, but she wasn't stupid. "You're right."

Jesse took the reins from his stepfather. "Let me deal with King. They know I love the dog, and I'll tell them this rabies theory came from you, Dad. It's best we leave the Captain out of this mess."

Zerelda walked over to her son and hung the cross around his neck. "Take this anyway. Make your momma happy."

The Captain clapped Jesse on the shoulder. "I appreciate the cover, but I'm coming with you, partner."

CHAPTER 55

The two young men rode in great haste to Mason's farmhouse, which was a few miles south. Like cool, crisp cotton, the weather soothed the men's skin as they pushed their horses faster. They were racing each other as much as time.

The Captain was a far heavier handicap for Fly Bait to carry, but the horse was a much bigger stallion, so it balanced out. Jesse was a natural in the saddle, with the instincts of a savvy Indian. He also knew where the hell they were going and gradually took an increasing lead.

The Captain followed Jesse's wake as the leader plotted the best course. When they neared a run-down ranch, angry barking was audible. The barking came from inside the weathered barn, and smoke seeped through spaces in the wood panels.

"Leave the horses here. It's not their fight," yelled Jesse. He leapt from his mount and landed with feline grace.

The Captain, less gracefully, tumbled from Fly Bait like a bear that lost its underpinnings atop a broken tree branch. He followed Jesse to the barn doors but plowed into the lad, who had frozen in his tracks.

King had his back to the two boys. The mastiff's hair was raised, and he snarled at the quarry pinned to the far barn wall. Mason stood with a pitchfork thrust in front of him. From the metal prongs dangled a large silver cross. His younger, petrified sister kneeled behind him. It wasn't the weapon or cross that held King back. Rather, his path was blocked by a line of hay fire. The blackened bale husk and dwindling flames suggested the deterrent was close to an end.

Mason cheered the arrivals. Well, at least one of them. "Jesse!"

King appeared cheered by the arrivals as well. He turned to the young men, bared his teeth, drooled, and growled with an underworld force worthy of all three heads of Cerberus.

"So much for a sneak attack," Jesse muttered in the direction of Mason.

"Attack?" said a perplexed Mason. "He's turning into a vampire. We just need to stay out of his way for a little longer."

Jesse looked at the Captain. "If it wasn't for his sister, Dottie, I think I'd let this fool die."

The Captain mulled killing Jesse along with Mason but resisted the notion, telling himself he could not do so in front of young Dottie. As his mind swirled over completing his mission, King charged.

He moved right, Jesse went left. King decided to challenge the large alpha male and veered for the Captain, who reached for his gun but fumbled as he pulled the weapon free. The fact that he wasn't a great shot raced through his mind as King bore down. Before he could pull the trigger, a shot rang out.

Still going from the forward momentum, King landed dead at the Captain's feet.

Mason screamed, "Don't kill him!" He jumped through the flames and sprinted over.

"Too late," Jesse said.

"I told you he was turning into a vampire."

The James lad shook his head. "No, my father's a doctor. He said your dog had a disease called 'rabies.' There is no cure. He had to die. Anyone he bit would die too."

"No! Anyone bit by King would also become a vampire."

"Then why were you hiding from your darling dog?"

"Because he wasn't a vampire yet," cried Mason. He went down on a knee, petting the dead dog.

Jesse snorted, "Then I couldn't let him savage someone waiting for *this* change."

"Thanks," the Captain said. "I think King was past the stage where 'Sit, King. Good boy,' was the solution."

Mason glared at him.

Angry with his cousin, Jesse did not even acknowledge the Captain's gratitude. "You're wrong. King had a disease. My pa told me to kill the dog before he kills others."

"I despise you." Mason's words were not directed at the Captain.

"Of course, you do," Jesse amended. "I have bested you in every competition since we were young'uns. You're jealous."

Mason's hands were coated with blood, and he smeared them across his face, leaving streaks of crimson. "One day, I'll get the better of you. You'll see. I'll become the famous Jesse James. You'll end up like your *real* father, dead and forgotten."

Jesse lunged at Mason, but Dottie's scream and the Captain's arm held him back.

"He's so not worth it," the Captain attested. "You're better than that." He meant what he said, though he was again reminded the praise was bestowed to his father's killer.

Jesse relaxed. "You're right. Even if he doesn't know better, we probably saved his and Dottie's life. Let's go."

Dottie walked past her brother. "Thanks. Do you know where my momma is?"

Jesse crouched down eye-level with her. "She's at my place and very worried. Would you like me to take you to her?"

Dottie fell into his arms, crying, "Please," between sobs.

Jesse picked her up and glared at Mason. "I reckon vampire or not, King sure ain't coming back to life. He was a good dog. Give him a proper burial."

With Dottie's arms secure around Jesse's neck, they turned back to where they left the horses. A question of doubt passed through the Captain's mind. If Dottie was not with them, would he have killed Jesse Woodson James? If so, would it be sudden, without warning? Or would he confess the reason for wanting Jesse dead? If he allowed an explanation and found one that suited him, would he grant Jesse clemency? His reverie was broken by a pitched voice.

"Who's he?" Dottie asked.

"Him?" Jesse said with a laugh. "Why, that's Captain Coytus. He came with me to rescue you."

"Thanks," she said with a twinkle in her moist eyes.

Jesse winked and pointed at the Captain. "He's my new best friend."

CHAPTER 56

Jesse brooded.

The two boys sat on the porch of the Jameses' farm. Dottie's euphoria in reuniting with her mother provided enough magic for the boys to bask in the afterglow. The warmth lapsed into an icy silence.

"Why are you so glum, chum?" asked the Captain.

Jesse sighed, his hands perched into a tight steeple. "Nothing," he muttered.

He sensed Jesse's unease but didn't probe. "You don't fool me, but it's okay. If you want to talk about it, my ear is as long as my penis." He beamed a toothy grin.

Jesse snapped out of his funk and laughed. "So I hear. My brother told me in some detail about the night at the Booneville saloon."

"Rather embarrassing, but I did get to meet Frank, and now I met you," he professed.

Jesse's complexion tempered. "It's what Mason said about my father."

The Captain had figured as much. "You know better than to listen to Mason-head. You're twice the man he is."

"That's not saying much," Jesse said with a smile that turned to a frown. "I never knew my pa. I was three when he left us to find gold in California and died there of an illness. We never received his body or had a proper funeral. It was like he abandoned us. I hated him all these years, and Mason knew that."

"Forget Mason. Your father did not leave for another woman. Like a lot of men, he went west for the glory of gold. Now he's up in heaven, proud of his son."

Relief formed on Jesse's face. "Your father is the toast of heaven; his angelic son is living proof of the goodness of God."

The words stunned the Captain. Not for kindness, but the irony.

Jesse took a sip of water and continued. "Bloody Bill told me about your father. I hope you find the men responsible and exact revenge. If you need help, let me know."

His confident mask faltered. "Err, I might take you up on that."

"You bet. I'll personally put a bullet in the man who shot your father. I have killed before," he declared with casual assurance.

"You don't say," the Captain replied, voice uneven. His mind stormed a flurry, a tempest of emotions. "Tell me."

"It's this war really, kill or be killed. Our enemy could be our friends, if not for one defining issue: slavery. Both sides are continually lowering the bar, meeting an injustice with more odious injustices."

Jesse paused, and his eyes wandered, as though he were seeing the past replayed in his mind. His voice came out like he was narrating the vision. "We met Union soldiers on the field of battle. I killed their leader, the one brave warrior among them. In the face of defeat, he stood tall while his men panicked around him. Everyone congratulated me later, but I can't shake the look in his eyes. You could tell he was a strong, proud man. His face still haunts me."

The Captain was speechless for a few lingering beats. "You're not clairvoyant, are you?"

"Huh?"

"Nothing. I appreciate you confiding your thoughts to me." He still reflected on Jesse's words. It was not fair. Why couldn't Jesse have reminisced over a cold-blooded tale without any empathic undertones? He thought of Susanna's letter. Did her missives soften him up? Was killing this man truly the solution to his remorse?

Jesse gave a playful slap at the Captain's knee. "It seems we're linked in some way, as if we were destined to meet."

The Captain needed to change topics from the uncanny irony of Jesse's confession. "What's your motivation in this war? You honestly don't seem the most ardent proslavery guy. I see the way you are around Charlotte. You don't look down upon her."

"Hmm," he said and leaned back as if to ease his reasoning. "The Union came to my home. They almost killed Pa, and they abused and humiliated me. Like you, I harbor resentment. As for Charlotte, I love her like she's part of our family. Her daughter, too, but I do believe in slavery. Some states live off the land. We cannot economically compete without a labor force. Not yet, anyways, but I judge each man by his character."

Not bad, the Captain thought. There was hope. Again, he felt cursed by Jesse's penchant not to be detestable.

"You don't seem the Confederate type yourself," Jesse said. "I saw how you were with Elizabeth. Some of the men were offended."

"I believe you can't stop the future. England outlawed slavery, and no matter how this war goes, slavery will eventually be abolished here too. No offense, Jesse, and I salute you for treating Charlotte well, but economics is not a reason to enslave a whole race of people."

Jesse cut him off. "No offense to *you*, but while your vision may be noble, we the people of the land barely survive as is. The Union has their banks and their rigged money system. Yankee barons don't work like men. They don't toil the land or navigate the seas, nor does their livelihood endure the hardships of nature. They sit at desks and become rich off the labors of minions. The difference between their slavery and ours is that they exploit the system so they become kings while we're the serfs."

The Captain was unable to debate the merits of Jesse's rational. He'd spent much of his study time on science, humanities, and women, not economics. A different tact might suit him better. "You have more in common with the slaves than you realize. They're not part of the power elite. If the people of the land offered them freedom, imagine the power the combined plowshare could furrow in harvesting true economic equality."

This time Jesse was not as quick to reply. "It's complicated," he finally said. "I don't doubt the tenor of your rationale, but I advise you to keep these feelings to yourself. Words like that could be dangerous around the company I keep—especially Little Archie. He seems to detest you."

"I don't understand why," fibbed the Captain.

"Me neither. When he came back from Booneville, he praised you to the stars." Jesse lifted his cup for a sip of water.

"Maybe he'll love me after this gold heist." He paused and mentally calculated the time. Surely enough had passed. "As long as he listened and stayed clear of Albany, they should be okay."

Jesse gagged and spit water over his left arm to the porch floor. His jaw flexed. "Please tell me you're trying to turn the conversation humorous?"

The Captain's brow creased in feigned confusion. "Huh?"

"Albany?" His voice quivered like a five-year-old facing a trip to a dark, scary cellar.

"Yeah, if they let the gold pass Albany and congregate south, the ambush should be as smooth as a belle's behind."

Jesse's eyes implored. "A fierce debate occurred on the details of your plan. Little Archie said the ambush was to be outside Albany. My brother Frank was adamant that you said to avoid the city, but Little Archie's word carries more weight than Frank's, and Mason backed up Arch's account."

The Captain grimaced. A fleeting thought crossed his mind. Maybe he would not kill Jesse but instead torture him in some fashion. Yet looking at Jesse's concerned face, nothing sadistic came to mind, except perhaps making him sleep naked in a bed of poison ivy. The Captain wavered on the ultimate mission goal. The conversation minutes ago alone had to make him pause.

Jesse was as he said: a pawn; a tactically inferior chess piece. Jesse was not the king. That was Bloody Bill Anderson. Kill the head, you kill the body. The Bushwhackers' game should end once their king was vanquished.

The kid's face blanked like fresh parchment, and the Captain jumped from his chair. He extended his hand to Jesse and pulled the lad to his feet. "It's your brother. We have to go."

CHAPTER 57

Apparently the last time the two boys raced to a rescue, Jesse had taken it easy on the Captain and Fly Bait. Then, Jesse had increased his lead slowly. This time, with concern over his brother and friends, the lad was periodically out of sight whenever the wooded path looped and turned—with the gap between them growing.

When Jesse stopped to allow his horse a drink from a river, he could have set a hammock and caught a nap waiting for the Captain to arrive.

"Sorry," he said sheepishly.

"You and your warhorse are thunder." Jesse patted his mount. "We're lightning."

They set off, and again, Jesse surged ahead with a fierce determination.

Several miles farther, he found Jesse with his hand up, and he put a finger to his lips. A galloping sound approached. They dismounted and led their horses off the path into the nearby copse. Their eyes followed the sound as a scattered group of men scrambled in a hasty retreat. The Bushwhackers.

The first sight made the Captain curse inside. Little Archie. Maybe Cox and his Union force failed. He saw another figure and smiled before he put an arm around Jesse. "It's Frank!"

Jesse leaned his head into the Captain's shoulder. "Thank God." His voice shook. "For Mother, of course," he added unconvincingly. He pulled out from the embrace with a hint of regained masculinity.

The Captain watched the men approach, about ten in all. Some huddled over their saddle in pain, a few with clear signs of blood. The Bushwhackers had traveled with around twenty men, but the rest could have split off.

Jesse motioned toward the clearing. The Bushwhackers barely slowed as they passed the two men.

"Follow us," screamed Little Archie, his eyes wild with fear.

Frank's face was as pale as a Yankee desk jockey.

After a brisk mile, Little Archie stopped the men in wooded clearing.

"What happened?" Jesse demanded.

"Not now!" Little Archie yelled. "We need to cross the Fishing River and lose our trail."

The Captain saw stoneflies dance around the water's surface and wished to inquire about the quality of the fishing on the Fishing River but refrained.

Little Archie pointed at him and then a hunched over, bloody Bushwhacker. "You're the strongest. Please help Clell across the river."

Clell trembled in his arms as the Captain entered the brisk water. Blood seeped from the man, and red ribbons flowed downstream. He made sure to bob Clell's head under water a few times, eliciting gurgles and gasps.

Little Archie left two sentries, and the rest of the men brought their horses to a large cavern.

The Captain laid Clell on the ground, and one of the Bushwhackers administered to him. He sauntered by Little Archie and whispered, "Reverse Benedict Arnold."

The uninjured men gathered, and hot tempers whistled and boiled.

Frank screamed at Little Archie, "This is your fault!"

Little Archie wavered and looked down to the ground like it shifted under his feet.

"Bill's dead," Frank's voice cracked like bludgeoned ice.

The Captain had to bite his lip to suppress the grin. Bloody Bill Anderson—engineer of the Centralia massacre and scourge to Union—was *dead*.

Jesse recoiled like he'd been slapped. "How?"

Frank addressed the Captain. "You said to avoid Albany and stay to the south?"

"Specifically. The directions were clear as anyone's brains who'd say otherwise."

Everyone turned to Little Archie. Surrounded, his small shoulders sloped, and his body seemed to shrink within itself. He went to speak, but no words came out.

Frank nodded. "I said that, but he insisted we approach from the west. We ran into Union patrols, one fired on us, and we attacked. It was a trick. They led our men to a larger Union force. Some, like Little Archie, turned and fled. Others, like me, stopped to gauge what the majority was doing. Still others charged. Bill Anderson was killed. I saw it with my own two eyes."

Jesse shook his head in disbelief. "Say something, Archie."

The accused man's words came slowly. "I … think I … messed up."

The Captain puffed a heavy breath. "Messed up? Forget about the failed mission and lost gold, you served your leader on a platinum platter. You sabotaged the mission because you hate me!"

Frank nodded in agreement. "That's exactly what went through my head."

"Everything goes through your head," Little Archie muttered.

"Phew," scoffed Frank. "You're in no position to insult anyone. I was right to say, 'Stay away from Albany.'"

The Captain was pleased Frank stood up to Little Archie. "He's got a point."

Jesse's visage grew taut. "We have no leader. What do we do now?"

Little Archie's head perked up. "We have to continue the fight. I'm ready to assume the leadership role."

The Captain laughed. "Do what you want, men, but I wouldn't follow this chap from here to the wall." He gesticulated to the limestone not twenty feet away.

No one replied. The Bushwhackers hung their heads in defeat. The Captain considered his mission partially done until Jesse spoke.

"It's a setback, but we must not abandon our cause. Bill Anderson is cheering us on in heaven."

The men saluted Bloody Bill.

Jesse continued. "This country was founded on states' rights. The founders intended a weak federal government, but day by day, year by year, the bankers and bureaucrats sway the balance back to Washington. This fight is more than slavery; it's about each state deciding how they want to govern within the framework of the Constitution as written with the wisdom of the founding fathers. They send their sons and daughters from Massachusetts, New York, and Pennsylvania to our states to try to turn the vote and tide against what is in our state's best interest. I will die for Missouri before I sit idly by while liberty's wings are clipped, and our future's plucked away before we can take flight."

Frank embraced his brother. "You're right, man."

Jesse smiled and patted the Captain's arm. "These gold heists gave me an idea. What if we hit the Yankee barons where it really hurt?"

"In the funny bone?" the Captain asked hopefully. "I hate when I hit that."

"Me too," seconded Frank.

"No."

"In the balls?" Little Archie said and perked up.

"That does smart," the Captain said. "Ask Mason next time he's around."

Jesse did not tense up but stayed calm and shook his head. "The Yankee voyage westward must be capsized. Their ideals sunk to a watery grave. We become pirates of the land. We don't board ships; we raid banks. We go after the railroads that aid the engines of imperialism. We don't let the seeds of their corrupt capitalistic ways impede our growth as free men. We become outlaws. The Federalists have all the money. Let's rob the barons and hit them where it hurts."

"Brilliant," applauded Frank.

"I couldn't have come up with the idea if it wasn't for the Captain. I'm augmenting his plan."

The Captain bristled inside. Jesse was serious, and he did not want to take claim for this life crossroad. "Gee thanks, Jesse, but this one is all you. I disagree. You can still make things happen in America; the dream does not die on this war alone. I have some money I can give you. Get a girl, a house, and a family. You're a better man, Jesse James."

Jesse's hand caressed his chin slowly. "I value your opinion, my dear friend. I'm inclined to stand by my ideals but will consider your tidings."

The Captain gave a meek smile. "Thanks."

"Fuck that," Little Archie snapped. "I love your idea, Jesse. We'll form our own gang and rob the Yankee swine for every penny they print. We owe it the Knights of the Golden Circle and our future white brothers." He paused, his bluster apparently not burst. "And we'll all become legends."

A sly smile formed on Jesse's lips.

Little Archie crowed. "Generals Price and Shelby took Lexington. I wouldn't be surprised if the Confederate Army claimed victory in Missouri in a matter of days."

CHAPTER 58

Back at the Jameses' farm, the Bushwhackers received devastating news from Dr. Samuel. Two days after their comrade Bloody Bill Anderson had died, the Confederate Army was battered at the Battle of Westport. Rather than stand and fight like their Bushwhacker brethren, the Confederates journeyed to Mexico.

"Did you hear their migration song?" Frank asked as the men sat on chairs in the living room.

> I won't be reconstructed, I'm better now than then.
> And for a carpetbagger, I do not give a damn.
> So it's forward to the frontier, soon as I can go.
> I'll fix me up a weapon and start for Mexico.

"Those men have no valor," Little Archie sneered. "They fled like mice rather than fight like men. I always knew those army types lacked bravery, and it would take men like us to win this war."

"That's not what you said the other day," Frank reminded him. "You forecasted a glorious victory for the Confederates."

"Shut your big bazoo," piped Little Archie. "I was trying to stay resolute and confident after Jesse's proclamation. I still believe the Southern forces will prevail as the North presses further from the lands of their soft existence."

"Now what?"

Little Archie said, "We do the right thing. Steal, murder, and pillage."

The room quieted, and the mantel clock ticked.

Jesse's eyes found the Captain's. "I'm fighting. I won't surrender my beliefs to the Yankees. I know you won't, but I wish you'd join us."

He was disappointed. He didn't have to kill the boy, because Jesse would die like any other villainous scoundrel. "I won't. There's other ways to make a difference then by the barrel of a gun. For instance, I'm on my way to Lexington to work for the newspaper."

"That's wuss work," Little Archie decried.

"You shut your bazoo," Jesse said. "The Captain is not a wuss; just look at him."

Little Archie did not reply.

Jesse turned back to the Captain. "I'm not smart and educated like you. Maybe you can make a difference with your words. I can't. I'm a man of action. I have to follow my convictions, friend."

"We can only be friends if you're alive. I beg you to reconsider. I'll be in Lexington, a Confederate-sympathetic city. I need time to evaluate the mission to avenge my father."

Jesse tightened his face. "If you think about it, your mission is like mine—revenge."

"You're no different than us," Little Archie asserted.

"Except he's built like a mountain and educated," Frank observed.

Little Archie was smart enough not to rebuke him.

"I've said my peace on your decision," the Captain said. "I changed my mind about slaying the man who killed my pa. I actually could have killed him already. I observed him, and something you said made me pause."

Jesse's eyes narrowed. "What?"

"It's this war. Our enemies could be our friends, if not for this one defining issue. What if the person I was going to kill was a good man? He just happened to be born in a family on the other side of this war. You tend to follow your parents' ideals. Does anyone here have pro-Union parents?"

No one challenged the theory.

"Personally, I think this war is over. Contrary to Little Archie's hope, the Union Army is marching south at will. They have the money and the men, and it's only a matter of time before the white man picks his own cotton. Now you can go to Mexico like General Price or you can stay and fight a losing battle. Graveyards are filled with ideologues."

"That's us," saluted Archie.

No one joined in. The rest of the Bushwhackers were too fatigued or injured to comment.

The Captain focused on Jesse. "You know where to find me if you change your mind." It was time for good-byes. He had a nagging feeling that Bloody Bill's death solved nothing. He was letting Jesse live, with his life teetering on the sharp edge of a knife.

The sound of a door slamming open disturbed his thoughts. Mason entered the living room with a gaping grin. A large shadow loomed behind him, and he fingered the Captain. "Time to pay the piper."

A lumbering hippopotamus of a man filled the entire door frame.

The Captain reached into his jacket and pulled out the familiar gold sack. "How much?"

Mason looked back, his face furrowed in confusion.

So he explained. "When the citizens refused to pay the pied piper of Hamelin after he lured the rats away, he played a diabolical magic song. The town's children follow the pied piper and disappeared. So the moral of the story is 'pay the piper.'" He gestured to the large body mass. "Is he any good? Maybe we can start a folk band."

Jesse addressed Mason. "You two leave. How dare you bring trouble to our home?"

"Are you afraid my man will best yours? I'm beginning to suspect your admiration for him is fostered by some perverse relationship."

Jesse's fist snapped up like a prairie dog fleeing a badger-violated tunnel. It caught Mason's jaw, and he fell back and only avoided the floor by falling into his pet hippo.

"Leave," Jesse said.

"No," the Captain countered. "I'll fight this lump. Let's take it outside."

"No," both James brothers said.

Jesse explained. "That's Billy Joe Henry, the baker's boy."

"Three male names don't make him any more masculine. Let's go."

"Good thing Father is a doctor," muttered Frank as Billy Joe propelled Mason outside.

The hippo backed up twenty paces and waited for the Captain to come from the porch.

He was fairly certain he could match and beat Billy Joe in a straight fist fight. Billy Joe looked like he ate his father's bakery—a giant loaf of white bread. His best bet was getting the Captain down and using his superior weight as an advantage. The Captain thought that, like a hippo, Billy Joe would charge.

With his head down, Billy Joe ran at the Captain, who evaded the charge, but so could a gimpy tortoise. Billy Joe was slow as a day spent traveling in the sweltering heat. At the last moment, the Captain dodged to the left, ducked, and landed a short blow to Billy Joe's ribs.

The punch did not hurt the big feller much, but he did stop the pursuit. He shook his girth about and this time walked at the Captain.

"Crush him, Billy Joe," screamed Mason. As he spoke, his hand caressed his tender jaw.

The Captain laughed. "This landmass of lard?"

Billy Joe sneered as he walked forward. Mere yards away, he suddenly sped up. This time the Captain faked left and went to his right. He caught a glancing blow to a less fat-cushioned backside. He turned quickly and faced Billy Joe.

Billy Joe bunched his fists. The Captain did as well but bobbed his head and danced on his toes as the hippo took a long arching swing. The Captain leaned back and met Billy Joe's forward momentum with a right shot below the chest and then a left hook square to nose. *Crack.* Blood flowed from Billy Joe's nostrils, and he stumbled forward looking to grapple.

The Captain backpedaled away with a grin. As long as he stayed off the ground, he should be able to wear the oaf out.

"Hey, Billy Joe," he called. "I think I did you a favor busting the nose. You smell like a privy."

The taunt made the massive man snarl. Blood dripped from his nose to his chin. "You got a smart mouth, sonny."

"Actually I have a smart brain, not mouth. Furthermore, the weather is overcast, with hardly a ray of sunshine."

Billy Joe moved in, faked another punch, and tried to grab the Captain.

The Captain smiled at the obvious and jumped back. He shot forward with a strike to Billy Joe's face that flustered the big man, who held his nose and wheezed. Blood poured like a deluge.

"Jesse. Can you get your mother out here? I think Zerelda would offer a better challenge."

Both boys laughed, Jesse pointedly in the direction of Mason.

Billy Joe wiped blood from his face to a tent-sized shirt. He tried to press the Captain's back to the house, but the Captain scampered away, so the enormous man decided to stop. He waved the Captain in. "Come and get it."

"Okay," he said, and rushed in full speed.

Shock lit Billy Joe's eyes before the Captain ducked and rolled by, one leg braced in front of Billy Joe's, the other swung in from behind. The scissor motion brought the clumsy clod down to the ground. He tried to grasp at the Captain, who was quickly up on his feet. Two kicks stomped Billy Joe's back, and the Captain dodged away.

"Get up, flour child."

Billy Joe rose like a groggy hippo and warily put his hands back up.

The Captain sauntered by the spectators. "The biscuits are ready. Time to close up shop."

He moved to finish the fight. The James boys yelled Mason's name, and the Captain felt a foot slip between his stride. Unbalanced, he tumbled to the floor. Billy Joe lurched over and dropped on top of him.

"Humph," exhaled the Captain as the weight pressed upon him. "Holy baker's dozen. You weigh more pounds than a London bank."

"Now what?" Billy Joe breathed.

"This."

He arched his back. In one motion, he swung his legs up and over Billy Joe's head. With his thighs clamped over the other man's skull, the Captain rolled off his back and to his side.

While Billy's Joe's hands went to work on the legs, the Captain landed shots to his ribs. Each one was met with a groan, but this ground attack would take too long. He did not appreciate the dirt and blood stains he'd gathered either.

The Captain released his leg vise and sprang to his feet. He noted that the James boys had subdued Mason, pinning his arms behind his back. When Billy Joe rose, the Captain met him with punch after defenseless punch. Stomach, sternum, and face were repeatedly pounded.

Billy Joe teetered on wobbly legs, and the Captain landed another shot to his chest. With a gentle two-handed push, Billy Joe fell on his back. He was not seriously injured, but there was no more fight in him.

"Stick a cooking fork in him. He's done."

CHAPTER 59

St. Louis, by some margin, was the most metropolitan city in Missouri. Lexington was one of the state's next largest populated municipalities, and when the Captain rode into town, he was disappointed that he viewed all of Lexington with the swivel of his head. He'd been to London, New York, and other sprawling cities, and Lexington stood like a wart on Paris's large bosom.

The larger of the two churches could have fit in the Paris Notre Dame bathroom. There was one tavern, no fine cuisine, and the general store did not have provisions, such as wine or cheese. No naked ladies danced—even through a hole in the wall. In other words, Lexington was a Frenchman's *cauchemar.*

Union soldiers were stationed in small parties around the town. The Captain approached a church, still wearing his blue uniform. "Is Lieutenant Colonel Cox available?"

The oldest among them addressed him. He scratched at his light brown hair. "I don't recognize you. Which regiment do you march with?"

"None."

"Are you a deserter?" accused the soldier.

"No."

"Where did you get the uniform?" the soldier asked, eying the Union attire.

The Captain sighed. "My father was killed in battle. I wear this in memory of him."

The soldier's face tightened. "My apologies."

The Captain nodded his appreciation.

"Cox is in Richmond for a few days. You may have heard; he killed Bloody Bill Anderson."

"I wanted to speak to Cox, but I'll wait for his return. In the meantime, I'm here for work."

"I can get you into our regiment. You don't need Cox to enlist."

The Captain shook his head. "I got a job at the *Lexington Caucasian*." The soldiers glared at him.

"That's a Confederate paper," the leader hissed.

"I know." The Captain offered him a lopsided grin.

"We should burn the place down," declared one of the soldiers toward the back.

The Captain's brow sloped. "What, no free speech for the press?"

"No. Not to the sworn enemy of our country."

He produced the letter Cox gave him in the Kansas City bar, unfolded the paper, and handed it to the man who held rank.

The Union soldier read the letter, and this time his eyebrows arched. "Hmm," he said slowly. He folded and returned the letter, all the while chuckling. "My name is Rory Brewster. Whatever you need, let us know."

"What?" the soldier in back declared.

The Captain replied before Brewster. "I'd like to get a second set of clothes. Can you find something my size but more local in style?"

The soldier in back gasped. "Trade a Union uniform for rebel rag tags?"

"One last thing," the Captain requested. "I need a few volunteers who are willing to let me beat them up in the tavern later today."

The soldier snorted. "This is nonsense."

Brewster barked, "Shut up, Vance McCoy. This man has carte blanche. You're volunteer number one for the tussle in the tavern."

"I thought I had to go on the milk run," McCoy grumbled.

"*This* is priority." Brewster pointed at another soldier. "Weber. Get this man some new clothes."

"Thanks," the Captain said.

After the Captain dismounted Fly Bait, Brewster led him inside the church. "Tell me what you have in mind."

An hour later, the Captain emerged with new duds.

Brewster came behind him, shouting, "Confederate dog, leave this town!"

The Captain puffed his chest. "And what if I don't?"

Brewster's hands rested on his two revolvers. "You wait and see."

"I guess we will," the Captain challenged, but not before he shot Brewster a wink and smile.

Cox had detailed the Captain's mission and his assistance in the Albany ambush against the Bushwhackers. Brewster seemed to revel in the Captain's plans and assured full cooperation.

A few buildings away, the Captain found the town's journalistic juxtaposition, the *Lexington Caucasian*.

He knocked on the door. The man who opened it looked like a European dandy. A black top hat crowned a white curled wig, like fudge over tapioca. He wore a vermilion frock coat over a white shirt with more starch than a potato. An intricately knotted black cravat graced his neck.

The Captain suppressed an urge to tighten the knot further. Instead, he said, "John Edwards sent me here."

The man looked the Captain up and down, his eyes growing with each passing sweep. "Ah, my dear lad, you must be this Captain he told me all about." The accent sounded like the Captain's English professor.

"Only the good parts, I hope."

"Edwards's praise glowed like the star of Bethlehem. He raved about you and another chap. Jesse James, I believe."

The name needled the Captain like a mosquito hunting an armless man. He tried, unsuccessfully, to forget about Jesse, but hearing the name from another's lips stung even more. "I'm honored," he managed to say.

"Do come in," the dandy said, shutting the door behind him. "My name is Ashford Aberdeen. Can I offer you some tea?"

The man was bees-knees British, so the Captain mimicked Aberdeen's accent. "Blimey, bloke! I'm kip knackered and would be jolly chuffed for a spot of tea."

Aberdeen blinked twice through a quizzical glaze. His eyes cleared, and he clapped three times in succession.

A Negro bustled into the room with great haste like a naked woman beckoned. "Yes, Master Aberdeen?"

"Some tea and a light snack for our new employee. Perhaps the spotted dick."

The Captain feigned choking. "Excuse me, but I don't like my dicks spotted or unblemished."

Aberdeen rolled his eyes through a sigh. "Spotted dick is a steamed pudding with a mélange of currants." He pontificated like the Captain was a five-year-old foreigner.

"You don't say?" he said, figuratively pulling the man's white pantaloons.

Aberdeen dismissed his slave with a flippant backhand wave and motioned for the Captain to follow him. He pulled a key from his jacket pocket and unlocked a near door.

The Captain's eyes bulged in shock. The décor of the room was the antithesis of everything Lexington. Maybe he had been wrong to dismiss any similarities to London or Paris. It was like he had walked into a posh Mayfair parlor.

The Captain surveyed the splendor. A marble fireplace stood along the far wall. On the mantel stood silver candlesticks and an empty porcelain vase decorated with two painted pink roses. Above the mantel cantered the largest mirror the Captain had ever seen. It was clearly for show. Even as tall as he was, he barely saw his Stetson.

The ivory white walls were squared by windows covered with stiff velvet curtains hemmed with champagne fringes. A round oak table with clawed feet stood unabated like it might sprint from the room. Underneath, lay a cream-colored rug adorned with more flowers than a royal wedding. Above hung a grand chandelier made of bronze. The Captain hoped it was secure—or perhaps not, depending on the victim. If the monstrosity ever fell on someone, they'd be crowned to the ground.

"Impressive, isn't it?"

It really wasn't, the Captain opined. Sure it was exquisite, but less so than the wonders of Mother Nature. Sandy beaches lapped by blue water, autumn foliage on tree-topped mountains, pink sunsets over an ocean, the stars on a crystal clear night, a beautiful woman (Susanna)—these were far more appealing visuals.

The Captain was a simple man and also clumsy. He wanted to settle down in a large cabin, free of clutter where he could stumble about without fear of breaking expensive things.

He felt like saying, "I've seen better," because he had. Or: "The rumor floating around town is the Union Army is ready to storm the place and strip it bare as your dandy scalp." Then he considered sneezing and stumbling into expensive-looking plates hung upright on a wood table.

"I see you noticed my chiffonier," Aberdeen commented.

"Chef Onyay? My apologies, I thought the Negro was a slave, not a Parisian cooking prodigy."

Aberdeen's round face flattened. He walked and caressed the wood furniture supporting the plates. "This is a chiffonier."

The Captain nodded. "My apologies, I misunderstood your British pronunciation." In fluid French, he added, *"Je sais qu'un chiffonier est."*

Aberdeen peered at the Captain with healthy skepticism. He finally said, "I can see the wit and the intelligence Edwards told me about. You're educated but ride with rebels. Hopefully, I can not only guide and grow you to maintain those fighting instincts, but also refine you into a gentleman."

If the Captain ever dressed in similar fashion, it would only be on his wedding day. Instantly, he envisioned Susanna in a white dress.

Chapter 60

The Captain nibbled at the spotted dick and immediately gulped his tea. Such a name foreshadowed the disagreeable taste. If someone in the future offered him an aperitif called hairy bollocks, he'd decline.

"The dick is good, isn't it?" Aberdeen inquired.

He dammed his lips to prevent spouting his tea like a surfaced whale. Still, some dribbled from his mouth. "Fuck."

"I must work on your table manners. And a gentleman does not use profanity," Aberdeen reproached.

"Sorry, I choked on the spotted dick."

Aberdeen discussed the Union takeover of Lexington. He was quite concerned with his valuables and somewhat less about his newspaper. He boasted how influential the *Caucasian* was and how Lexington's population backed him.

"There's no other paper in town," he ratified.

"How, may I ask, did a man of your background end up in Lexington?" asked the Captain.

Aberdeen's head rocked back and forth like a pendulum of a cuckoo clock. "Our family came to America for the promise England lost."

"'O'er the land of the free and the home of the brave,'" the Captain sang.

"Let's hope America stays the brave. England lost her will and abolished slavery. A country needs its working class. They deserve a wage to eke out an existence. Trust me; I don't care about the impoverished."

The Captain believed him.

"I do resent the notion that a Negro is entitled to earn money for his labors, let alone having the same rights as even a white peasant. So we must win this war for the reason my family moved here."

Aberdeen spun a finger in a curl of his wig. "Traveling to California, I met a girl from these parts. Father wanted me to use my expensive education and start a newspaper in Kansas City, but this was close enough, so I stayed. I've been here four years now."

The Captain reflected on how his parents had met but pushed the thought away. He did not see a wedding band on Aberdeen. "Must be a wonderful woman to keep you here."

"She's a whore. She left me for a farmer who decided to move to New York for a different way of life."

"Makes sense," the Captain said.

Aberdeen's jaw dropped.

"Meaning, New York is a certainly a different way of life," he clarified.

The stuffy man rubbed his hands together and then spread them before him. "Let's talk about your job here."

"I have ideas for the paper." The Captain offered an eager smile.

Aberdeen leaned across the claw-footed table. "For instance?"

"Surveys from the town populace."

Aberdeen leaned further. "Hmm, that may be an excellent idea. The town supports our cause. What better way than defining it?" He tapped the Captain's hand with his powder-white fingers.

"I'd like to print letters from our readers that support the Confederate cause." He slowly pulled his hand from the table.

Aberdeen was pressed against the table, his frock coat creased. "Another excellent idea. It will also embolden the meek who support the cause yet sit on the fence."

"True, we need to make sitting on the fence uncomfortable. Barbed wire, perhaps."

Aberdeen mulled that over.

The Captain leaned forward, closing the space between them. "I might allow one of the letters to come from a Negro."

This caught Aberdeen by surprise, and he jumped back in his chair like the devil was before him. "Blasphemy. Now you've gone too far. None of them can properly read or write."

"Isn't that the point?"

Slowly, a cold smile crept across Aberdeen as he took the bait. "It might not be such a bad idea after all. Either it will be unintelligible or radical in the most primal of levels. The writings will further contrast the true inequality of the races."

The Captain gulped his tea to warm the chill emanating from his employer. "I know what you mean about the inequality of the races. I went to the new racetrack in Saratoga Springs, New York. Some of the horses were sleek machines, but most were farm horses built for work, not speed."

Aberdeen folded his hands under his chin and glowered like a provoked rattlesnake. "Don't mock me with intentional misunderstandings, boy. I am not one of your rebel ruffians."

"I'm sorry. That's just how me and my posse ride."

Aberdeen slithered back mollified. "I have some work to do if I'm to make you a poster boy for the Confederate cause. My standards are higher than those of our dear chap Edwards. After all, this is the *Lexington Caucasian*."

"I feel so blessed to be part of this esteemed journalistic enterprise," gushed the Captain. "Let's celebrate my first day with a few drinks at the saloon, shall we?"

Aberdeen leaned even further back in his chair. His head shook slowly from side to side as his tongue clucked *tsk-tsk*. "The saloon is no place for a gentleman. It's an establishment for drunken louts."

The Captain mimicked the admonishing sound of disapproval. "The saloon is the establishment of the people. The very people we need with us to win this war. No offense, sir, but these are the people you want to the fight for the Confederate cause. Words alone will not win the war. We should mingle with the people, let them know the Union may have taken this town, but they have not won her heart."

Aberdeen inhaled through his nose and then brought a handkerchief from his pocket and exhaled into the linen. The wet sound was presumably gentlemanly. He shuddered. "The saloon is a germ factory, a bubonic brewery."

He caught Aberdeen's eye. "Think how it can inspire the Confederate faithful to see the owner of the *Lexington Caucasian* mingle with the masses. What better message to show your defiance to the Union. Have one drink with me. What could go wrong?"

Chapter 61

The two men entered the saloon. Grousing under his breath, Aberdeen stood out like a peacock among pheasants. Union soldiers closed rank behind him like Joseph's brothers, envious of his dream coat.

The rest of the patrons watched eleven Union soldiers close in on the new arrivals. The townies sensed trouble and recessed to the corners.

"What are you doing here, Aberdeen?" asked McCoy.

Like a weasel, the dandy man twisted his body between the bar and the Captain. He whispered up to the Captain's ear, "I told you this was a bad idea."

The Captain addressed the question. "Let me break it down for you. We entered a saloon. We went to the bar, and we took money out. If you put two and two together, you get four. Also, if you read between the lines, there's space, and you'll draw a blank. Take a shot in the dark, even though the room is well illuminated."

"Let's go," whispered Aberdeen.

"Huh," a flummoxed McCoy said. "You're here for a drink?"

McCoy was not an ad lib aficionado, and the Captain clapped his hands with a mocking, deliberate slow pace. "With an aptitude like that, you'll attain the rank of private potato peeler in due time."

The soldiers stared confused.

He smiled back. "No hard feelings, fella. I'll treat you boys to a drink as well."

"We're not here for drinks." McCoy replied sternly, but the delivery was forced and over ambitious. The lad lacked acting chops.

Due to his monstrous size, the Captain had played Caliban in the Shakespeare play, *The Tempest*. He was widely praised for his acting prowess but grew bored despite his fascination with the story. He felt confined repeating the same lines. While he appreciated the literary genius of Shakespeare, he knew no one who talked with such flowery abundance. It became hard for the American maverick in him to resist changing some lines here and there. For instance, Caliban's passage:

> "All the infections that the sun sucks up
> From bogs, fens, flats, on Prosper fall, and make him
> By inch-meal a disease!"

The Captain wanted to modernize it to:

> "All the infections that the skin sucks up
> From the brothels, bordellos, bath houses, make Prosper's
> cock fall
> By a seven-inch-meal disease!"

That or simply, *"Die, Prospero, you fuck."*

After all, Prospero came to Caliban's island and enslaved him because he appeared different. That was, if you happened to consider being a son of a witch unusual. Caliban was put to servitude and forced to work for his new master. After he tried to have his way with Prospero's flirtatious daughter, Miranda, he was further humiliated by Prospero and ultimately obeyed his master again.

Despite the antiquated verbiage, Shakespeare was spot-on with his uncanny metaphorical parallel to the enslavement of the Negro race.

The Captain bunched his brow, breaking his reverie. He sized up McCoy. "Then why are you loitering about a drinking establishment?"

"To keep the peace and look for rebel traitors."

He grinned. "That's good to hear. Saloons need women, not wankers. For you swell chaps, I promise to look out for any rebel types."

The left side of McCoy's mouth angled up in a sneer. "I'm looking at some rebel dogs now."

"Let's go," Aberdeen urged, more loudly than before.

The Captain turned in every direction and then followed McCoy's gaze. He peered over Aberdeen at the portly saloon owner. "Him?"

"No. You and your pal."

The Captain pointed at Aberdeen and chortled. "This guy's a rebel? For what, dressing like a pimp Mary?"

Aberdeen gasped. "Hey. I'll have you know—"

"He owns the *Lexington Caucasian*," seethed McCoy with sudden realism.

The Captain stood tall and pressed his new, used clothing. The trousers fit fine, but the shirt sleeves fell short. Aberdeen shook against him with fright.

"I know. He's my boss," the Captain said matter-of-factly.

"Then you must be a rebel too," McCoy said with real disgust, his acting improved. Or, his anger was a natural manifestation of his dislike for both the Captain and his role in a soon-to-be public humiliation.

"The two of us might be the only unarmed men in this establishment," he said and lifted his jacket to show he was not carrying a weapon. "So kindly piss off, bootlicker, and let two kind citizens enjoy a glass of whiskey."

The Captain explained he planned to insult McCoy until the soldier threw a punch. He was just getting started, but McCoy appeared eager to accelerate the outcome. The Union soldier bristled.

"Time to learn some respect, rebel vermin."

McCoy lunged forward and floated his fist by the Captain. On the pullback, the Captain grabbed his arm, pulled the soldier in, and spun him back toward his mates. Like ten bowling pins, the Union soldiers fell.

Aberdeen sensed opportunity and tried to scurry to the door. Several Union soldiers rose to intercept old Aberdeen. The Captain could have intervened and gotten to his boss first, but that meant no joy for McCoy and his posse.

He had to make it look good, so he strode over as three men confronted

Aberdeen. Delaying him by design, the rest of the soldiers went to the Captain. The first punch struck Aberdeen in the face, and blood seeped from above his right eye.

Good start, thought the Captain. Aberdeen never labored, nor fought for the cause he believed in. He could afford to understand hardship and pain. He grinned when he saw Aberdeen knocked to the ground and get kicked and stomped.

The Captain screamed, "It's time you boys learned some manners." With Herculean force, he shoved his interceptors back. Two men fell, groaned, and stayed down. Six came back at him, and the first to arrive caught a soft jab to the head, and he fell back like he'd been struck by a locomotive. The next soldier was met with a knee to the stomach and doubled as if kicked by a mule.

One by one, the Union soldiers fell until there was only McCoy and the three soldiers attending to Aberdeen. McCoy charged forward as if an avenging angel, divine, and immortal. Again he threw an air punch, and with a little more inertia than his other strikes, the Captain planted a fist in McCoy's ribs.

The soldier fell to the ground and alternated between sucking air and screaming, "You dog."

Like Ukrainian Hopak performers, the Union soldiers danced on Aberdeen. The dandy no longer moved to protect himself from the onslaught.

The Captain grabbed two Union soldiers by the heads and rung them together. The last man standing pulled his gun, but the Captain swarmed the man before he could point. He knocked the gun away, and an elbow to the face sent the man down.

He went to Aberdeen and rolled him onto his back. The man's face was matted with blood. More importantly, so were his clothes. The nose was flattened like a boxer—more like canine than a brawler.

"Look what you did to this man, an upstanding citizen of this town. A town none of you live in. Shame on you," he reproached.

The Union men slowly rose and dusted themselves off. They held their hands against their fake injuries, except for McCoy whose suffering was no act. Like a good chap, he finished the job.

"Maybe you're right," McCoy snarled. "I threw the first punch, and you only defended yourself. I know when I've been beat by a better man. Take my advice, friend, and leave the *Lexington Caucasian* or we might change our minds about you."

"Fair enough," the Captain replied. "My offer to buy you a drink still stands."

Aberdeen garbled a protest.

"No thanks. It's best we leave." The soldiers filed out of the saloon.

The Captain called out, "Can I get a bucket of water and a bottle of whiskey to clean this man's wounds?"

CHAPTER 62

The two wealthiest men in the saloon did not have to buy a drink. First, the bartender poured the Captain and Aberdeen free drinks, "For ridding the bar of Union vermin."

"They're bad for business," the owner attested. "They take up space and don't drink. There's no entertainment like gambling or prostitution when they're here. My best customers stay away."

The second round was bought by the first man to approach them. He introduced himself as a doctor traveling to California. He had a medical satchel and attended to Aberdeen with bandages, ointments, and anodynes. Proud and loud, the doctor hailed the Captain and Aberdeen.

"An elderly man and a young lad defeated eleven soldiers. It was like the Battle of Thermopylae. You're Spartans, heroes! Take a bow."

Thereafter, every patron visited with gratitude and a round of drinks.

Initially, Aberdeen was petulant, hunched over the bar. He scolded the Captain for not avoiding the confrontation and often complained that he wanted to go home and sleep. Dr. Tristan vetoed Aberdeen's wishes. "Doctor's orders: drink whiskey to kill the pain."

That was all it took for Aberdeen to agree to stay. Six drinks and several well-wishes later, he glowed in the adulation, lit up like nighttime cannon fire.

"Did you see me trip the one guy up?" he asked. "I chopped him like this!" He swung his hand down like a cleaver. "Twenty years ago, I would

JESSE JAMES & THE SECRET LEGEND OF CAPTAIN COYTUS

have parried their attack for practice and then tore them apart like mere sheets of parchment."

"I missed that, my dear fellow," the doctor responded. "Your body got pounded like a human piñata."

Aberdeen's split and swollen lip drooped like a parched plant. "You probably had your view blocked. I got him good."

"My view remained unobstructed. I never took my eyes off you, chap. The beating appeared so vicious and unencumbered I feared for your life."

"Huh. Guess you missed it."

The doctor patted him on the shoulder. "Sometimes when your head gets kicked around like a ball, your perceptions become blurred and even imaginary."

"I can remember everything about my life quite clearly," he declared in protest, lip protruded in anger.

Aberdeen's swollen, discolored face glared at the doctor. The hellish visage reminded the Captain of the last play he acted in. Aberdeen glowered like Mephistophilis arguing with Dr. Faustus. Based on his prior success as the witch's spawn, Caliban, the Captain was asked to act the part of the demon, Mephistophilis, in the Christopher Marlowe play. Initially, he resisted the role, but the girl who assisted with costumes and makeup stimulated him to give it a go.

Three performances later, his acting career ended when he slapped the prissy actor who played Dr. Faustus before giving his speech about the perils of making a pact with Lucifer. The Captain reasoned that only a fool would make a deal with the devil and tried to knock some sense into the dense doctor.

The play's director pointed out that Dr. Faustus remained inside his magic circle and was thus immune from any demonic assaults. He didn't buy the Captain's rationale that his improvisation was a mere oversight. Nor did he subscribe to a rewrite, wherein the circle would negate any of the demon's magic attacks, but the Captain could still, on the physical plane, smack Dr. Faustus about.

The doctor addressed Aberdeen's assertion. "That's normal. The memories at the time of injury, however, are typically distorted. Let me not anger and fatigue you. I'll buy another round."

The Captain met the doctor through Brewster and took an immediate liking to the man. Dr. Tristan was heading east to join the major front of the war. His presence gave the Captain an idea, which he presented to the doctor, who obliged.

After treating Aberdeen with ointments, the doctor rubbed verbal salt into his patient's wounds.

The Captain appreciated Dr. Tristan's bedside manner.

Aberdeen tossed back his drink and grunted. "Like a hummingbird's wings, I must have moved faster than the eye can see."

It was hard to say that Aberdeen was saving face when his lumpy countenance resembled a bloody toad. He tossed back his drink and saluted Kentucky's finest.

Unrelenting, the doctor asked, "Can you show me one of those faster-than-the-eye strikes?"

"Think I'm a little too injured now, Doctor," Aberdeen said with a smile.

"Naturally."

Nine drinks later, he stood sheets to the wind … except, his balance was not undermined on a storm-wracked ship with masts unsecured by ropes or sheets.

Rather, he was piss drunk and something of a nuisance. He knocked the Captain's drink out of his hand when he reenacted for the umpteenth time his "Hermes-speed-like strike." The story changed yet again, and in the newest version, Aberdeen had been bluffing, feigning injury to tire the Union soldiers. He took the beating like the good Lord Jesus, only to rise and vanquish his foes. He even had the gall to refer to the Captain as one of his disciples.

The bullshit was thick with gravy on top. The Captain was amused until his drink was knocked from his hand. Spilled booze was as sacrilegious as spilled blood, and far less enjoyable than spilled seed.

Aberdeen put his arm around the Captain. For all to hear, Aberdeen cried, "You people will love my newspaper more than ever once this man," he pulled the Captain tighter to him, "puts his ideas in print. This is Captain Coytus, a legend in the making."

The older gentleman hoisted his drink, and everyone—but the whiskey-less Captain—joined. "To the Captain!"

"To the Captain," the patrons echoed back.

When Aberdeen finished his drink, he stirred the bar up to sing, "For he's a Jolly Good Fellow."

Three drinks later, Aberdeen boasted that he'd finish the job on the Union soldiers stationed at the church. He called for everyone to follow him.

Dr. Tristan consulted with the drunken self-proclaimed hero. "Even if you were healthy, the average female would imperil you. In your condition, I wouldn't tangle with the church mouse, let alone the soldiers."

Aberdeen lurched at the doctor, who stepped aside and watched the man tumble past him. Aberdeen fell and landed with a thud on the floor, wig askew.

Dr. Tristan shook his head and offered the Captain a faint, exhausted smile. "Get him home." Then, without another word, he gathered his belongings and left the saloon.

Although he did not move, Aberdeen's lips parted. "Let me at him. I'm only getting warmed up."

The Captain hauled his new boss from the floor, hoisted him over his shoulder, and said, "Let's call it a night, champ."

By the time the Captain had his passenger home, the old man was snoring. Aberdeen's slave met them at the door.

"What happened to Master?"

"He took a masterful beating."

The Captain searched for a reaction, figuring he would detect joy in the man's face, but rather his brow creased with concern.

"Is he going to be all right?"

"He'll live. What's your name, sir?"

"Jimmy Kemp."

"Jimmy, my father died fighting for a slave-free America. He didn't die in vain. This will be a land of liberty and justice for all men—and hopefully one day women too. We may be slow sometimes, but this great nation usually gets things right in the end."

Kemp's eyes narrowed with suspicion.

"I'm working undercover, Jimmy. You're going to see some big changes with this paper," he said with sly grin.

The long pause broke at last when the slave spoke. "I don't know. Master might look down upon me, but he's no cracker. He's too old and gentlemanly to fight."

"You should've seen him tonight. He took more blows than a blacksmith's anvil."

"I see."

"He now looks like the monster he is inside," the Captain sneered before turning his visage friendly once more. "I need to know, Jimmy. Can I trust you?"

"What is your name?"

"Call me Captain."

"Mr. Captain, answer me this. Where will I go if lose my master? A man needs to eat."

"Jimmy, a man needs to *live*. Sustenance from an odious slave owner, who deprives your own God-given dreams, is not living." The Captain pulled out his cloth sack and fished out two gold coins. "You have a good hiding place?"

Kemp's eyes widened. The poor soul lived in opulence but didn't have a nickel to his name.

"I do. Master never comes to my quarters."

The Captain frowned and pointed at Aberdeen. "Master," he scoffed. He jerked his hand back and forth in front of his crotch. "Master Beta is more like it."

"You can trust me," Jimmy said with a nod.

The Captain handed the coins to the smiling man. Both men's heads turned from a tap at the door. Before answering, the Captain found a key in Aberdeen's coat pocket. "Jimmy, can you get him into his bed?"

"Yes, sir, I can. Anything for you."

The Captain shook his head. "I want your trust only. You owe me nothing."

"Understood." He put the coins and key in his pocket and then lifted Aberdeen over his shoulder.

A second knock came from the front, and the Captain opened the door. "Thanks for making the journey, Miss Veronica Mosley." He nodded appreciatively at Brewster, who'd escorted her.

"This time, your work will be easy, Miss Mosley. Our Romeo is comatose." The Captain grabbed his camera. "Follow me."

CHAPTER 63

The Captain sat at a table in front of the *Lexington Caucasian* office. A sign read:

LEXINGTON CITIZENS ONLY:
Please take part in anonymous survey.
Vote and get free lunch!

Several residents stared over. A young man with a dark mop of hair approached. He had smooth skin and wrinkled clothes he'd likely slept in.

"What's this all about?" he mumbled with his head ducked.

The Captain gave a welcoming smile. "A proper newspaper should be a reflection of the people. We ask questions and tally the votes. You decide, we report."

"And where is this free food?"

He pointed down the street. "After you vote, I give you this signed declaration, which gets you a free lunch at the church."

The kid shifted about, looking to the Captain and then back to the saloon. "Are you the guy who took on twenty-five Union soldiers?"

He chuckled. "Looks like the tale stretched like a lemur's tail. It was around ten men."

The kid gawked, no less amazed. "How do I vote?"

"I hand you one question at a time, and you pick your choice and stuff the paper in the vase."

Aberdeen had unwittingly and ever-so-kindly volunteered an expensive-looking vase as a ballot box.

The Captain handed the lad the first question. The kid squinted at the paper. The Captain expected puzzled looks, but he overlooked one factor.

"I can't read," confessed the kid.

He took the paper and pointed. "This is yes; this is no. I'll ask you the question. You mark the answer and put it in the vase. Ready?"

The kid licked his chops. "Ready."

"Was Moses right to lead his people from slavery?"

"Of course," said the kid.

"To be anonymous, don't tell me your answers—just mark the paper."

The kid did as advised and slid the paper in the vase.

The Captain read the second question. "In a chess set, where one side has white pieces and the other side has black pieces, does the white side have a predisposed advantage?"

The kid's eyes crossed, and then he jotted an answer.

"If you believe skin color makes one human better than another, does the distinction also apply to fur? For instance is a white wolf superior to a black wolf?"

The lad scratched at his mop. Again, he penned his answer and filled the vase.

"Is a man with blond hair better than a man with darker hair?"

"Fuck that," said the kid as his hand swept through his dark mop. He stabbed at the paper with his pen.

"Who do you like better? The Negroes or the French?"

"Neither," said the kid, but he made a choice and dropped his selection in the vase.

"Make believe a white man raped a black woman. She has the baby. It is naturally of a mixed race. If you are proslavery, does that child become a slave? This question has three choices. Yes, no, or the offspring will be a part-time slave—three days a slave, three days a free man and alternate Sundays."

The skinny lad pondered the question for about a minute. After his stomach grumbled, he picked his answer.

"Who is smarter: the dumbest white guy or the smartest black guy?"

The kid answered, "Smartest Negro—you're funny!"

"Last question, and lunch is yours. Do you believe Jesus would be proslavery?"

The kid bit his lip so hard the Captain thought it would burst like a squeezed cherry. After almost a minute passed, he dropped his answer.

Two lunches were being served. One was normal beef stew; the other was spiked with prunes, raw cabbage, psyllium seed, dandelion root, and aloe. An Indian the Captain met while saving a fox from a trap swore the concoction was the cure for constipation. Brewster came up big by securing the ingredients. The Captain checked the kid for the spiked-special-recipe lunch and sent him on his way.

By midday's end, the Captain had handed out approximately one hundred free meal cards. Over eighty got the lunch special, which meant there would plenty of bowel-gunpowder-free leftovers for the Union soldiers and the poor, both black and white alike.

Back inside the *Caucasian* office, the Captain was eager to tally the day's votes. He found his hand too wide to fit through the mouth of the vase and only managed to pull but the top few ballots out. He called Jimmy, but he fared no better.

"Master might manage. He's thin as a corn stalk," Jimmy vouched.

"You're probably right, but I'd rather not tax Aberdeen while he's recovering." The Captain picked up the vase and examined it. "Shame, this rose is drawn with such detail."

"The old coot loves this vase."

After a weary sigh, he picked up the vase and smashed it to the ground. "That's what I figured."

CHAPTER 64

"Do I get a pay raise?" asked the Captain.

"Huh?" said Aberdeen as he lay in bed.

Jimmy spoon-fed him spotted dick, which seemed all the more funny with the picture the Captain took of Aberdeen, Jimmy, and Miss Mosley.

"You told me you never sold more than fifty papers in a week. The paper came out yesterday. We sold all forty original copies, printed one hundred more, and they're all gone. Your circulation is up like an erection."

Aberdeen jerked his side to side and moaned. "How? Most of this town is so broke they can't even afford a deformed slave."

The Captain leaned against the wall. "The credit goes to you, sir. At first I was mad you changed my questions and found your revisions to be silly with all due respect, but you insisted."

Aberdeen's head levitated from the pillow. "This better be one of your jokes."

He waved the charge away with his hand. "Sir, you sold more papers on Saturday than any newspaper in the state. I am attributing the success to you. If you want me to take all the credit, then yes, you should give me a raise."

"What questions?"

He pulled a sheet from his pocket. "Ninety-eight percent of the voters said Moses was right to lead his people from slavery."

"Why would I even care to ask something so ridiculous?"

"Beats me. My question was, 'Holy Moses, did you know God

threatened to kill Moses's son because the boy hadn't yet been circumcised?' I always wondered why a bit of skin mattered so much to God and wanted to know if others did as well. You took my idea and went on a different tangent."

"What else did I ask?"

"Fifty-eight percent of voters believe there was no difference between black or white chess pieces."

"Of course there's no difference, despite what 42 percent of the mental midgets say."

"I originally asked about the difference between white and black women's chests, but you refined the question to the game of chess."

Aberdeen frowned and waved him to continue.

"The public was evenly split on whether a white wolf was better than a black wolf."

Aberdeen rolled his eyes. "Please tell me this is a joke. The question is doggone dumb."

"My original question asked men if they liked a blonde girl with black fur—a wolf in sheep's clothing?"

Jimmy suppressed a grin and fumbled the spoon, and spotted dick spilled onto the bed sheet.

The Captain said, "Sixty-seven percent believe blonde-haired people are superior to those with dark hair. The original was, 'Do men prefer blondes?'"

Aberdeen wagged a finger. "I warned you about pulling my leg."

He pushed off the wall and playfully tugged at Aberdeen's leg. "That's pulling your leg, but all joshing aside, these questions were yours, sir. Right, Jimmy?"

Aberdeen fixed his gaze upon Jimmy, who tried to look busy and oblivious to the conversation.

"Jimmy, you know how I feel about liars. Well?"

"Master, I will do every chore you ask, but you know better than to ask my opinion."

"Of course I don't want your opinion, boy," scolded Aberdeen. "I want verification, not a viewpoint."

"Master, please do not sell me to a less gracious master than you, but what this man says is true. You said lots of things that did not make sense."

Aberdeen gazed at his slave crossly, but the larger man didn't flinch. Then he looked back to the Captain. "What else did we ask?"

"You loved the next question and did not change it at all. Fifty-one percent said they liked the French better than the Negroes."

Aberdeen's lips curled, and he tapped his chin. "That is a good question."

"The next question, a conundrum you claimed to ponder. Forty percent said the raped, mixed-race baby should be a slave. Seven percent said the child should be a free citizen, however 53 percent liked your idea about part-time slavery."

"I have never pondered such nonsense in my life," declared Aberdeen with disdain.

The Captain folded his hands in prayer. "My honor stands on General Stonewall Jackson's grave."

The injured man coughed like he'd inhaled bad tobacco. "At this rate, the general's grave must have rolled halfway to China."

"Yeah, maybe the Stonewall name is apropos, and he's resting against the Great Wall." His grin did not lessen Aberdeen's frown. "The next question was also an original. Eighty-four residents answered that the dumbest white man is smarter than the smartest black man."

This brightened the dimwit. "There's hope for this town, yet. It all comes down to education. All white men are inherently more intelligent than Negroes. You can train a dog to do a few tricks, but it's still a canine."

Jimmy let more of the spotted dick drip.

"The final question was only a slight alteration. Since most blacks worship the same God as white folk, I asked if both races are equal in God's eyes. You simplified that to, 'Would Jesus be proslavery?' Eighty-six percent envision Jesus as the sky's plantation owner, with Negro slaves picking cotton from the clouds."

Aberdeen nodded. "Like the gentleman I am, Jesus would be a civilized master."

The spotted dick dribbled downward, again. *Plop, plop, plop.*

"Speaking of Jesus, your idea about offering a reward to those who expose whites who engage in the sin of interracial sex was a stroke of genius."

Aberdeen's right eye dropped. "Dr. Tristan is a quack. He likely drugged me with a toxic tonic."

"You seemed so keen on this idea, sir. In fact, you insisted."

"Now that I think about, it is a lovely idea. We'll publically humiliate the traitors who trespass on decency with perverse bestial acts."

The rest of the spotted dick came down like a waterfall. "Oh, my God," Jimmy said. "Sorry, Master. Let me clean this mess up."

"You bungling buffoon! These sheets were imported from Egypt."

"Perhaps I'm to blame, sir. With the increased demand for your newspaper, Jimmy had to work overtime to print all the extra copies. So I made your meal today. My apologies; the spotted dick is more flaccid than usual. You like it nice and firm."

"True. Anything else you want to tell me?"

The Captain stuck his finger in the crease of a dimple. "Oh, yeah. I hope the vase on the mantel was not worth much."

Aberdeen's eyes bulged like a wet binding. "*What?* My grandfather bought that in Florence! The true worth is immeasurable when the sentimental value is calculated. What happened?"

The Captain shrugged with a sheepish grin. "In celebration of our newspaper's success, I drank a little too much. I became nauseous and panicked with thoughts of fouling the furniture. So—"

"You vomited in my vase? That's disgusting. Alas, surely Jimmy can wash it out."

"Yeah, well, it gets worse."

"Worse?"

"I went to clean the vase myself, when I was suddenly overcome by an emergency urine call."

"You washed out my grandfather's vase with piss?"

"I suppose I did. But tragedy struck when my penis got stuck. The fluted top allowed easier entry than exit. When I finally freed willy, I dropped the vase, and it shattered in pieces."

Aberdeen's hands found the top of his head as though he was holding his brain back from shooting like a cannonball.

"Wait a minute. I've dabbled with pottery before and did my best to fix your vase." He dashed from the room. He heard Aberdeen muttering as he returned with the vase over his head as he entered the bedroom. "See?"

The ceramic was crudely glazed together. Extra clay bonded various fracture points like mountain chains on a topographical map. Candlelight could be seen through small holes left by missing pieces. "I can improve upon this," he boasted. "When I'm done, it will appear as a work of great antiquity. No one quibbles over the cracks in Michelangelo's *Creation of Adam*."

Aberdeen banged his head up and down on his pillow but stopped to look at the vase again and thrashed about more. He pulled the sheet over his head. "Leave!"

The Captain and Jimmy shared a smile.

"Okay, you need your rest," the Captain said. "We can discuss my pay raise later."

The bed sheet rustled furiously like a cadaver returned to life.

Chapter 65

Jimmy brought the chamber pot into the room and placed it on a stand near the bed. "Let me help you, Master."

Aberdeen turned on his side and grimaced. "Every time I piss, it's like I'm shooting fire. Those Union cowards must have kicked me down under more than a few times," he said with a wave of his hand. "I seem to have strange, oozing welts on my privates."

Both the Captain and Jimmy stifled grins.

A splash was heard, and Aberdeen cried like he was passing stones. When he turned back, his eyes were watery, and his lips peeled back like a wilted flower. "Damn."

"My empathy, good sir," the Captain said. "A lengthy urine discharge is one of life's perverse pleasures."

Aberdeen huffed. "You're weird, son."

"Thanks."

"Where are we for the next weekly issue?"

"I am doing an article regarding the recent spike in dysentery disorders. Last week, over eighty people suffered bowel dysfunction. This matter should not be swept under the rug. Can you imagine excrement under your fine Persian rugs?"

Aberdeen coughed. "No."

"Me, neither. That is why I plan to cover this momentous issue."

"What else do you have?"

"I was toying with a joke of the week. Maybe we start with something like: what's a slave owner's favorite snack?"

Aberdeen shook his head. "I don't know."

"A cracker!" he said with a laugh.

"Let's pass on the joke of the week for now. Come up with a few better choices, and I'll pick one for a later issue."

"We posed a question last week. 'In one hundred words or less, explain what slavery means to you.' We got five responses so far. Four were from white folks, and one came from Minister Rapp. He supplied a passage from Frederick Douglass, which he said spoke for all of the oppressed." The Captain handed over several sheets of parchment.

Aberdeen read and thrust aside the first response and sped through the rest until he stopped at the last. "No, no, no. This won't do. These white men are illiterate simpletons."

The Captain tried to appear earnest. "I thought the letter from D.J. was at least understandable."

Aberdeen's mouth gaped. "The guy who said, 'Slavery means everything to me,' and repeated the word 'everything' ninety-six times to hit the one-hundred-word quota?"

"I found something sincere in D.J.'s simple eloquence. Plus, it was better than Jed's."

Aberdeen flipped through the letters. He read, stopping to spell out some of the words. "'Slavery meanz eyz werk les.' That's all Jed has to articulate on the matter. This letter cannot see the light of day."

"What if we put a warning on the front page of the paper, saying Jed's letter should only be read with artificial illumination, not daylight?"

"Don't be a fool."

"I'll try. What about the Frederick Douglass submission? The passage came from a book he wrote in 1845 called *An American Slave*."

Aberdeen turned to that piece of parchment and read with a hushed tone. "'I was broken in body, soul, and spirit. My natural elasticity was crushed, my intellect languished, the disposition to read departed, and the cheerful spark that lingered about my eye died; the dark night of slavery closed in upon me; and behold a man transformed into a brute!'" Aberdeen thrust the paper down. "I can't read any more."

The Captain gestured to for the letters. "I will, sir. I'm sure your eyes must be tired."

"My eyes are fine," he shot back. "We cannot print these letters. They undermine our cause. What else do you have in your hand?"

The Captain held a journal with a wax seal over leather strap. "This was left in front of the building." He waved another piece of parchment. "This letter came with it. The writer says they agree with the newspaper's campaign to disclose those who engage in interracial affairs. The letter specifically states this is not to be opened by anyone other than Ashford Aberdeen."

"Give it to me."

The Captain handed the package over. He stole a wink from Jimmy, who tried to look busy as he brushed imaginary dust from the wall with great diligence.

Aberdeen cracked the seal and then the binding.

The Captain had once rescued a frightened horse from a neighbor's barn consumed with flames. The creature's eyes reminded him of Aberdeen's as he stared at the contents of the envelope. His fingers shook as he turned to the next photo, and he began to pant.

"Are you okay, Master?" Jimmy asked.

He squealed like a poked pig. "Yes!"

He turned a few pages, and with each passing photo, gasped. When he flipped to the next page, he shrieked. Aberdeen shut the journal on his face and tugged the rest of the sheet over his head and wept. "Leave me in hell."

Chapter 66

The Captain wanted alone time, and Fly Bait needed exercise, so he left town. He found a brook filled with clear water over a stone bottom. The brook did not babble, at least not like any infants he'd encountered.

He let Fly Bait graze as he stretched out on a bed of pine needles, which made him think of the expression, "pins and needles." He loved to have fun with clichés and slang. Today, however, he did not feel spontaneous. His life rested on a bed of nails.

What was he doing? He set out to avenge the death of his father, had met the men responsible for the Centralia massacre, and had their leader killed. Despite ample opportunity to kill Jesse James, he'd let his father's killer live. He could have walked away and gone back to Booneville for Susanna, but instead he traveled to Lexington.

An ominous sensation lingered. The death of Bloody Bill solved nothing. For all the warm, fuzzy chitchat with Jesse, the lad was still a Bushwhacker. His chosen company dictated his future.

What did his mission have to do with the *Lexington Caucasian*? It didn't. He merely amused himself, hurting those who stood against his ideals. If that was his motivation, then why not follow in his father's footsteps—not walk bowlegged—and join the Union Army?

The truth was he felt no closure. Would Little Archie's death bring the fulfillment he sought? Would it be a Union victory? What would it take for him to return to his senses and go to Susanna? Jesse's death? Or was this mission with no discernible end, an evasion not only from love, but also responsibility? Was he nothing more than an aimless harlot masquerading in his personal pity party?

He didn't know, and this is what disturbed him.

Fly Bait horsed around nearby as he watched. Happy and content, the animal snorted and neighed with joy. The animal turned its head to the Captain, as if aware of the attention. He laughed, and Fly Bait nickered and shook his head, his black mane trailing like the tail of kite caught in a crosswind.

The horse that held his burden also unburdened his malaise.

He'd accelerate his plans at the newspaper and return to Booneville. Besides, he'd probably never hear the name Jesse James again.

Oh, Susanna, I'm coming from Lexington with a ring and bended knee.

Chapter 67

"You'll never guess who tried to enter town today," Aberdeen said. He lay propped up in his bed, his complexion gray, except for the dark bars under his eyes.

"Tell me a lost party of female Swedes. This town lacks temptation. I feel like a eunuch."

"Maybe if castrated, you might not always think with your privates," the gentleman snapped. "Jimmy should be back soon. He went to fetch some things from the store, so he can tell you."

"Tell me what?"

"Jesse James and his posse tried to enter town but were identified as rebels who have committed atrocities. They say Jesse travels with Little Archie Clement, who is a wanted man."

"I'm not surprised."

"The scuttlebutt is they're looking for you. Jimmy says one Union soldier named Brewster asked you to stop at the church for a chat."

Hearing Jesse's name so soon after he vowed to forget him foreshadowed something bad, and he didn't think he was being paranoid in thinking so. The Union thoroughly controlled Lexington. To risk coming here suggested urgency.

Perhaps in a week's time, he would check on the Jameses' farm before he returned to Booneville. He tried to dismiss the thought but couldn't. For some reason, his tie with Jesse James was not yet severed.

Aberdeen motioned for him to take a seat. "With Jimmy gone, I want to discuss something with you."

The Captain sat. "Shoot."

"I've been set up and blackmailed."

He feigned surprise. "Really?"

"Jimmy is part of the conspiracy."

"You think? He seems loyal to you. Even when I make fun of you behind your back, he always defends you."

"That's good to hear." Aberdeen paused. "I ... think."

"Why would you suspect Jimmy?"

The older man held up a bony finger. "You notice the crime is called blackmail, not whitemail?"

His forehead creased. "I didn't, actually ..."

Aberdeen nodded. "I suspect a *black* male is in on this blackmail. No one comes and goes in this house without Jimmy knowing."

"What do they have on you?"

"Scandalous pictures of me with Negroes. If I meet certain demands, the pictures will not be made public." He frowned. "I never had any dalliances with *those* people. Truthfully, I haven't been with a white woman in many years."

"I believe you."

"You do?" The wrinkles on his face perked with hope.

"Well, the part about the white women, anyway."

Aberdeen glared and went to speak, but the Captain jumped in first with a fib. "Sorry, boss. As for your point, how can there be pictures of you, yet you do not recall a photographer?"

"I've pondered the same thing. In none of the pictures is my face clearly visible, which is suspicious, but the suspect does look like me, and the pictures appear to have been taken in this very bedroom. I suppose someone with my physique and makeup could make a passable representation, or the pictures are me, but I was drugged."

The Captain dragged his chair closer. "Sir, I can't help you take care of the problem if you don't level with me."

Aberdeen squinted and pinched his lips together. "This better not be another one of your jokes."

"No, sir. But I did find it odd—you proposed the idea to publicize interracial affairs, yet black women visit you in the middle of the night. Once I chased them away due to your injuries."

"This is not a joke. Are you telling me the truth?"

"Yes. Everyone needs the release, brother, but I did find your exploits a touch hypocritical. No offense, sir."

Aberdeen waved away the apology. "I don't understand. Sex is not important to me at this age. I swear I never got intimate with any Negroes."

The Captain gave a firm nod and scratched his chin. "Is it possible that a week ago you were a raging hormonal stud and black booty your thing? Due to serious head injuries you suffered, these urges have been repressed."

"Nothing makes sense."

"Well, you're rich, sir; how much is the blackmail?"

Aberdeen scowled. "Today is my first one."

The Captain's brow slanted. "What?"

"As a sinner, I need to pray for my soul and ask for God's forgiveness."

He grinned. "Easy-split-*peasy*."

"At the *Negro* church," Aberdeen spat.

The front door shut. Both men turned their heads downward.

Aberdeen said in a hushed tone, "That's Jimmy. Don't say a word."

Minutes later, Jimmy knocked and entered.

Aberdeen glared at Jimmy and pointed a bony finger. "How dare you take part in this blackmail against me."

Jimmy's eyes dimmed with doubt. He shook his head in slow denial and caught the Captain's wink. "Master, what are you talking about?"

"The photos of me with Negroes."

"Sir, what pictures? Did we take a photograph together?"

"No, we did not. Sexual pictures, you imbecile."

"Master, Negroes don't own cameras. This must be a mistake," he said, but allowed doubt to creep into his face.

"Confess, slave!"

Jimmy's mouth hung open, but no words came.

"Tell me, now!"

The large man went down on a knee. "I did not betray you, but I may know who did."

"Who?"

"A Union soldier. I think he is one of their leaders."

"Keep talking. Why do you suspect him, or is this a canard to throw me off your scent?"

"No, Master." He gulped, like the next words proved difficult. "Some nights, when you had guests—"

"What guests?"

He shifted nervously. "You know …"

"Make believe I don't. Talk."

Still on a knee, Jimmy clasped his hands in submission. His voice came out like mouse squeak. "Negro women."

"Liar!"

Jimmy panicked and looked to the Captain. "You saw them too."

Aberdeen slapped the bed. "I talked to him. Now I want to hear from you. How does this connect to the Union soldier?"

"He brought them."

"Why did you fail to mention this to me?"

"I tried to once, but you wanted no part of discussing anything to do with the women. You called me insubordinate and sent me to bed without supper."

"You're cursed with the devil's tongue. How do you keep your lies as fresh as a spring breeze?"

"I never lied to you, Master. Never. You know that."

"How dare you presume to know what I know?"

"Sorry, Master. I only want you to believe me. I would hate to find a new master."

"Rise and get me the name of the man who you suspect is the culprit. Then I'll believe you."

Jimmy jumped up like an invalid touched by the hand of God. "I will, Master. I shall not fail you."

"You do that." Then, turning to the Captain, he said, "And let us two, white, free men discuss business."

Jimmy strode out of the room after passing one final uncertain glance toward the Captain.

The Captain was impressed with Jimmy's skills. He was a much better actor than Vance McCoy.

Aberdeen frowned. "A Union blackmail makes sense. I bet the dastardly doctor is involved. He's lucky I was drunk or I would have thrashed him."

"Dr. Tristan *was* squirrelly," the Captain said with a small head bob. "I think Jimmy is telling the truth, sir. Women did visit you. He also has a point about the camera. A white guy is behind this."

"I agree. It's not Jimmy's fault he's a Negro. God made him like all the other beasts of the planet, but he's blessed to be a human—ah, technically. Despite his inherited flaws, I trained him to a state of near civility. He may be a Negro, but he's smart enough to realize how good he has it with me. So I believe him too."

The Captain nodded. For a vain peacock of a man, humiliation could be worse than death—at least, he hoped as much. For all the vile men he met on this mission, from Badger Bob and the Booneville boys to Bloody Bill's Bushwhackers, this spindly old man was the most detestable of all.

CHAPTER 68

"That wasn't so bad after all," Aberdeen said as they left the church.

The Captain raised his brow in surprise. *Maybe you can teach an old dog new tricks.* "I also found the service moving."

"That depends on your context of motion. If you're referring to lots of jumping, shaking, clutching, and screeching, then yes, the Negro church was moving. If you mean spiritually moving, then I disagree. I found the ordeal disorderly and lacking tranquility to think and reflect."

The old dog still pissed venom.

"Considering you own a proslavery newspaper, I thought they treated you graciously."

Aberdeen stopped to stare at the Captain with an expression of disdain. "First of all, I'm a white male, and it's my divine right to be treated with respect." He picked up the pace once more. "All the contact with them people." He shuddered. "I'll need Jimmy to run a warm bath for me."

The old dog was a one-trick terrier.

"What about Minister Rapp? I found his sermon uplifting."

Aberdeen snorted. "You're easily pleased. The minister was a blowhard. Either Negroes have hearing impediments or all the screaming is for the benefit of the cognitively challenged."

After leaving Aberdeen to his bath, the Captain went to church to find Brewster, who was playing cards on the steps. For appearance purposes, he walked by without saying a word. Minutes later, Brewster met him in the minister's quarters.

"I suppose you're here about Jesse James."

"I am."

"The soldiers on the south side of town spotted him with a few other rebels. My men tried to chase him off, but he was persistent and held his hands up in a sign of nonaggression. He yelled your name and some message, but it made no sense—something about Mason Savannah. Does his message mean anything to you?"

"Jesse has a cousin named Mason, and I know Savannah, Georgia, but I'm not sure," the Captain said, yet something nagged him.

Brewster shrugged. "The only thing I can think of is the Masons, as in the fraternal order, and I'm not sure if you're familiar with another Savannah here in Missouri."

He pondered the meaning of Jesse's message, but on reflection, found everything even murkier.

"What's on for tomorrow, with Aberdeen?"

The Captain grinned. "A clothing donation for the needy."

The next day, he woke to shrieks of pain reminiscent of a trapped rodent. The cries were Aberdeen relieving himself, although there was no relief; for him, urination produced only agony.

Scents of bacon and fresh bread from Jimmy's breakfast wafted upstairs. Famished, the Captain hustled to the dining room. Aberdeen joined him minutes later, and his eyes burned red in his gray pallor like he'd spent the prior day at a sacrilegious black mass rather than at church.

"Is there an envelope for me?"

"Yes, Master." Jimmy pointed to the table.

Aberdeen frowned but picked the parcel up and took a seat.

The Captain ate and watched as he broke the seal, gingerly took out the parchment, and read.

"Shit on a roasting spit," he cursed and brushed his silverware aside.

"Sir, remember a gentlemen never utters profanities, especially in anger," reminded the Captain.

Aberdeen shook his fist. "Shut the fuck up. Got that?"

"Fuck, yeah."

Aberdeen scanned the letter again. "For the poor, I'm to gift twenty full outfits, right down to underwear."

"What a great cause, and you'll no longer look like the town outcast."

He snapped the letter down. "What did I just say?"

"You're gifting clothes to the poor."

"No, about staying quiet?"

"Oh, yeah. Sorry, boss."

Aberdeen grimaced. "My clothes are custom-tailored from the finest shops in Europe. Furthermore, I will be left with only three outfits."

The Captain cut the silent cord. "You told me not to speak, but I'm compelled to remind you that you can always buy more clothes."

"In these parts?"

"If you lower your standards."

"I'd rather stroll around naked."

"I'd rather you not."

Aberdeen rose from the table. "I'm not hungry. I'll be upstairs going through my wardrobe."

CHAPTER 69

The next morning was déjà vu. The Captain woke to Aberdeen the Rooster. The cock shrilled in the early dawn. Then they met for breakfast, and Aberdeen went right for the envelope. Right on cue, he read and cursed.

"They want me to serve a meal for twenty at the Negro church."

"That's nothing, boss," the Captain said. "We served more men when I did those poll questions."

Aberdeen glared at the plate on the table. "I'm to supply all the plates and silverware, which will not be returned."

"Sir, you witnessed my pottery skills when I fixed your vase. I'd be honored to make you a new set of plates to make up for the donated ones."

The old man put his head down and fled the room, yet later that day, he complied with the demands of the blackmailer.

The next day was another repeat: screech, breakfast, enter the rooster. Before Aberdeen opened the envelope, he said, "What indignity is next? I still cannot believe almost all the people we fed were wearing my clothes."

"Did you see the delight on their faces? Their joy must have made your sacrifice worthwhile."

Aberdeen did not reply and opened the envelope. "Fucking, fuckety-fuck."

"What?"

"Apparently a Negro family's shack collapsed. I'm to build them a new home. Until completed, I'm to house them here."

"Sir, that's not a problem. There's loads of space here."

"Until they leave, I'm to act as a servant, bequeathing all their desires."

"That does tweak things."

The bitter man addressed Jimmy. "I will pay whatever it takes. I want you to find someone who can build the quickest shit shack possible." He got up and left.

The next day was more of the same, except they had three new guests: mother, father, and daughter.

Aberdeen groused, "I've worshipped, provided clothes, fed the poor, and now I must shelter them. What could be next?" He opened the envelope, and the profanities came fast and hard.

"What's the deal, boss?

"I wrote an editorial, which claimed whipping is not cruel when disciplining a slave. Obviously, it should not be done for pure pleasure, but only responsibly. Nonetheless, I'm to receive ten lashes to my back courtesy of the Union Army." Aberdeen stared at him. "Try to tell me that's not so bad."

"I won't." The Captain winced. "It's going to hurt like a bitch."

Aberdeen went to leave but was stopped.

The male guest coughed. "You will stay, sir."

He smiled weakly. "I know it's rude to leave while everyone is eating, but I lost my appetite."

The man did not smile back. "I could care less about the presence of your company. Jimmy looks run down. He needs a rest, so you're going to clean up after we're done eating."

He glared. "I can't wait until you're gone."

"Likewise." The male guest scowled back. "A month is thirty days too long."

"*Thirty* days? My builder said the construction would take a matter of days."

"I modified the architectural plan," the male guest informed.

"Architectural?"

"Yes. My wife and I plan on growing our family and need more space."

"Okay, but that should add no more than a few days of delay."

"True, but the winters are cold here, and we want a fireplace like yours. We also expanded the kitchen some."

"Jimmy!" Aberdeen roared. "Talk to the builders. Tell them to get more men, work day and night, whatever it takes, but I want the home built as fast as humanly possible."

The guest's scowl deepened until his eyes were hidden beneath his brow. "You tell the builder yourself, but only after you're done cleaning up." He purposely swept his arm into a glass of wine, courtesy of Aberdeen's cellar. "Oops. I hear wine stains are hard to remove."

Aberdeen groaned and rubbed the bridge of his nose.

"As much as I despair over spilled liquor, don't fret, sir. I'd be more concerned with the whipping you'll get later," reflected the Captain with a smile of goodwill.

"Thanks for reminding me."

The next morning, the Captain and Jimmy helped Aberdeen down to the dining room. He had begged to be fed in bed, but the guests denied the request.

"I thought you didn't care about my company," he hissed as he tenderly seated himself. He did not lean back or seek any other comfort than to sit.

"I don't, but when I was a slave, and I'd been whipped, I was not allowed a day in bed."

"I'm older than you. Show some compassion."

"I don't, but you're lucky Jimmy does. He's convinced me to let him continue all chores."

Aberdeen's pained face washed with relief. "Thank you, Jimmy. I deserved one lashing for doubting your loyalty."

"You are fortunate," agreed the guest. "You will join us for each meal, but you may remain in bed otherwise."

Aberdeen twisted his lips and took the next envelope. "Two days left."

"Almost done, sir," encouraged the Captain.

"I'll give anything away—my best antiques, my finest art, my rare manuscripts, as long as I don't have to move." He ripped the envelope. "Jesus jump in a lake of fire. I can't."

"Do what?"

"I'm to participate in a sack race today and provide one hundred dollars as first-place prize money."

"I'll fuel you with so much whiskey, before you know it, the race will be over," assured the Captain.

Aberdeen shook his head so hard the Captain thought his thin neck might snap. "Whoever comes in last has to ride Old Man Cooper's bull."

"That's the bull that killed two men just the other day," Jimmy informed as he set a glass of milk before his master.

"Why hasn't the beast been put down?" Aberdeen demanded, his breathing rapid.

The Captain chuckled. "Darwin-style, they plan to weed out the weak by killing whoever is the slowest. You can't lose the race, sir."

"How much more can I endure? This has been the worst two weeks of my life."

"Don't say that, sir," implored the Captain. "That's when we first met."

Chapter 70

In the middle of town, the contestants gathered. The entries consisted of Union soldiers and strapping, fit farmers. No one was close to Aberdeen's age. Then his frown turned to a hopeful grin. A young boy no older than eight joined the participants. The age of the youth wasn't what cheered the old man; rather, he seemed pleased when the boy walked away from the sign-up table with a heavy limp and dragged his right clubfoot.

Jimmy tapped on Aberdeen's shoulder and pointed. "That soldier in the race is the man who brought the Negro women to you."

Aberdeen studied Brewster. "I still have no memory of him or these exploits."

"Maybe a ride on Old Man Cooper's bull is the remedy to jog the ole memory back," the Captain suggested.

"I'll pass on the medical advice."

The Captain pulled out his flask. "You need more booze if you're going to stand the pain."

Aberdeen grinned. "Much better bedside manner, Doctor." He took the flask and chugged.

A whistle sounded.

"You can beat the gimpy kid," the Captain encouraged.

The men lined up, and Brewster took a spot next to Aberdeen, who shifted down a few places. Brewster followed him until Aberdeen was the last man on line. The soldier stood next to him, and then the men stepped inside burlap sacks. The townsfolk gathered at the finish line, several hundred feet down the road. The whistle shrilled again, and the men were off to the cheer of the crowd.

The majority edged ahead of a few stragglers. The boy trailed the pack but not by much. Aberdeen cursed like a drunken sailor as he struggled forward. Just in front of them hopped Brewster, who lunged into Aberdeen's lane. Brewster corrected his course, but the boy caught them.

As they approached the finish line, the Captain saw sweat dripping down Aberdeen's contorted face. The boy had fallen behind again, and Aberdeen smiled, sensing victory. Again, Brewster impeded his route, but this time, he added, "Excuse me."

The boy crossed the finish line, then Brewster, followed by Aberdeen. The crowd cheered with delight, drowning out the old man's protest. After a minute, several men lifted Aberdeen off the ground and carried him to Old Man Cooper's farm.

"I won't do this," he cried as the men hoisted him onto the penned bull.

"Too late," Brewster said.

The crowd gathered at Old Man Cooper's farm cheered as the bull came out of the gate, bucking and charging. The beast kicked his hind legs, and Aberdeen rose off his back like a perched bird. Wingless, he landed hard on his back.

"Ouch," someone in the crowd groaned.

The bull came back. Lucky for Aberdeen, he was out cold, and the bull became disinterested and walked away.

The Captain pulled Aberdeen from the pen. "Way to go, boss."

When they got home, they found the final envelope nailed to the door.

"Read their sinister scribe to me," Aberdeen said groggily as they settled inside.

The Captain knew the letter verbatim, but he opened it and read. He summarized: "The message says that over the past several days, you learned what it feels like to be a slave. Frederick Douglass's passage on being an American slave will be included in tomorrow's paper. You're to write what it felt like to endure for a week what one race of people has been subjugated to for a lifetime." He paused. "That's a breeze, boss."

"That's it? There's always a hitch."

"No hitch. Looks like they want you to write a story on the evil of slavery, and you're a free man."

"If this week was a lesson, and this story, my test, they failed if they think I have changed my beliefs one bit. They will get their story. Leave me to think."

The Captain used the respite to return to the brook outside town. He kept thinking of Jesse's visit. The lad had come for some reason. What was it? Despite how many ways he spun the words, nothing connected.

Then, like the sound of a pulled cork, something popped in the Captain's mind: *Savannah* is *Susanna*. The other word was *Mason*. His heart began to race. No matter how improbable the connection seemed, that must have been Jesse's urgent message. Mason found his revenge in Susanna. Dread flowed faster than the brook beside him.

He mounted Fly Bait. "Go!"

As the Captain rode, he realized he wouldn't be around for the next issue of the newspaper. He had hoped, foolishly, that Aberdeen would pen a piece about the empathetic evolution of his mind-set. Whatever the result of the article, the Captain would release the salacious photos of Aberdeen. The owner of the *Lexington Caucasian* could not survive the scandal.

Chapter 71

The Captain charged into the Booneville sheriff house to find his former deputy doodling on paper.

"I wondered when you would turn up," Sheriff Less said. A concerned frown set upon his visage.

"Where is she?" the Captain asked. He'd first gone to her house but found the place deserted.

"I have no idea. The mother sold the home to a newcomer, who left to retrieve his family. The women left in the middle of the night, without word."

The Captain was thrilled the word "women" was plural. Susanna was okay. "What happened?"

"You don't know?"

Exasperated, the Captain huffed but realized it was not Less's fault. "No, tell me."

Less took a deep breath. "Few weeks ago, Susanna's mother came here. Said her daughter disappeared. We asked everyone in town, and she remained unaccounted for. We even got a search party going. After a week, I honestly thought I'd never lay eyes on her, again.

"Then, one day, she returned with a boy about your age. Turns out his cousin had abducted her." The sheriff's lips crimped, and his face drew tight as snare drum. His eyes fluttered closed for several long seconds before they opened.

Cold dread returned. "Go on," the Captain said, certain he did not want to hear what came next.

Less stepped around the desk, chair in tow. "Remember this chair? You once let me sit in it. I'd like you to take a seat now."

The Captain wanted to resist and yell at Less to level with him, but he sat.

Less took a deep breath. "Mason raped Susanna. He also disfigured her with a knife. Sliced her face."

The pain pierced him like a gunshot wound, and he gasped for air as remorse flooded him in a deluge of despair for his part in the tragedy. He was the agent who spawned her hellish ordeal, the saboteur who demolished her dreams by unleashing a nightmare. He imagined her beautiful face wrought with fear like a flower garden stuck by the first frost. No one deserved such a fate, least of all his angel.   •

"She'll carry a scar on her right side forever."

The Captain buried his face in his hands, but the haunting visuals still pierced him. A beach filled with litter, a sky blanketed with smog, a fractured diamond. Spoiled beauty. He had to look back to the deputy to regain his focus.

Less put his hand on the Captain's shoulder. "The only thing I can think of is to talk to the man who rescued her. His name is Jesse James. He said if you came here, to tell you he's sorry for what happened, and the family won't mind if you killed Mason in revenge—although he's gone missing. He asked for you to visit his farm."

"I have to go." The Captain rose. "Thanks. I hope that if we meet again, it will be under better circumstances, but I doubt it."

"We will," Less reassured. "This may hurt, but I hope you find Susanna, and when you do, that you still want her. She loves you so much. She came here almost every day, and we'd chat about you. You were like Jesus to her. She prayed for your return and her salvation. No matter who tried to talk her up, she did not care. You're all she thought about."

"Those words hurt, but I appreciate them all the same."

The Captain said good-bye and set out to find Jesse James, the man who killed his father and rescued his love—an impossible irony.

He rode past the saloon where he first met Susanna. Ingemar Skidmark stood atop a bale of hay before he jumped off and spun 360 degrees with a perfect landing. A few gathered children cheered, and Skidmark yodeled.

On his travels, he stopped to visit Jenny. "Meet Angus," she said and pointed at the new dog they bought to replace the one Mason had killed.

Grieved, the Captain was honest and told Jenny about Susanna and Mason's attack on her. "Please accept my apology, but I must cancel our dance date."

She shrugged. "Aww shucks, but I understand. Susanna must be a special lady."

When the Captain arrived at the Jameses' farm, Jesse burst from the house and ran to greet him. Frank trailed behind.

The Captain fell into a fierce hug with the two brothers.

"Let's go inside," Jesse said.

Seated in the living room, Frank explained. "Mason had been present when Little Archie and I recapped the night we all met the Captain in the Booneville bar. No one thought anything of it, but Mason later asked a few questions about Susanna." His voice faltered to a murmur. "I'm so sorry."

Jesse took over for his brother. "Mason's mother claimed Mason entered the barn with a girl. Curious, we decided to check how ugly the girl must be to bed Mason."

Jesse grew solemn. "When we got to my cousin's place, a girl screamed for help. We found them naked; Mason had a knife in his hand, and blood poured from the girl's face. He got by us and ran into his house and locked the door, but truthfully, we were more concerned about the girl. That was when Frank recognized her."

Frank apologized again.

"I left Frank to deal with Mason and brought the girl here. My stepfather treated her as best he could."

Frank grimaced. "Mason escaped out the back door."

"I brought Susanna back to Booneville," Jesse said. "She's aware Mason did this to her to spite you."

Susanna should know the truth. The truth hurt, but it paled next to the external and internal scars she'd suffered.

Jesse sighed, and his next words came soft and slow. "She said she loved you too much but asked that you never see her again. Not after everything.

Even if the terror subsided, her wounded face would always be a reminder she'd been soiled by another. I tried to talk her out of it, but she vowed to move and start a new life."

The lad dipped his head. "This is where I owe you an apology. I told her I was staying in Booneville, and if she left, I'd follow her. A few days later, she invited me for dinner as gratitude to my rescue. I think they drugged me, because I woke up, and they were gone."

He handed the Captain a letter. "She wrote what I just explained. How her exile is out of love, not blame. She wants you to forget her. Maybe one day, when you've moved on and have a wife and family, she would like to say hello. For now, she requests that you respect her privacy as she heals."

The Captain read the note, and her words read just as Jesse had said.

He requested time alone, mounted Fly Bait, and left. A mile from the farmhouse—and out of eyesight—he slowed the stallion's pace to a trot. The Captain lowered his face into Fly Bait's mane and let the tears fall.

Chapter 72

Winter moved to spring, and as the months slipped by, the Captain withered to a shadow of the man who had started his mission. He spent most of his time in the canvas-covered wagon alone, except for his new best friend, Jack Daniels. Brewster had gotten a cask from a startup Kentucky distillery and had given the booze to the Captain when he'd heard about Susanna.

The Captain drank the liquor every day until the demons quieted and he passed out. He'd wake the next morning, remember he was the reason Susanna had been assaulted, and start with the alcohol once more. If he hadn't provoked every perceived enemy with self-righteous indignation, Mason would not have had the impetus to find a way to hurt him through her. If the Captain had not fiddle-fucked around playing a comic crusader, Susanna would have been safe with him.

If … If … If …

He couldn't shake the image of Mason having his way with her. He envisioned her face, the fear, humiliation, the beauty made ugly. A spark snuffed, forever dimmed in a shroud of blackness.

The worst of it was how little he'd accomplished for all his bluster. The Bushwhackers under Little Archie acted as ruthlessly as ever. Over the past few months, they'd participated in a campaign of terror, murdering citizens, ransacking towns, and killing as many Union soldiers as possible. Jesse was no innocent bystander. He'd become Little Archie's confidant.

After all they'd been through, the Captain had accomplished nothing with these men.

As for the *Lexington Caucasian* ... well, despite his hasty exodus from Lexington, Aberdeen had the last laugh by selling the paper to a staunch Confederate sympathizer. Brewster begged him to return to his role as newspaper saboteur, but the Captain was unwilling to continue with the work, which he blamed for Susanna's plight. Again, he'd failed.

That's what it came down to. He was a failure—a drifter who thought life was one giant joke. Who was he to think he could make a difference? Naïve boy.

Charlotte brought him food and some newspapers she'd gathered. "You better eat. You're losing your Adonis build," she'd warned.

The war turned decisively in the North's favor, yet the nation remained divided, and would be long after the South's surrender. A Frenchman, George Clemenceau, covering the recent election, had been quoted as saying, "Any Democrat who does not manage to hint that the Negro is a degenerate gorilla will be considered lacking in enthusiasm."

He realized how futile his efforts had been when he read a new issue of the *Lexington Caucasian*, where the new editor printed, "We are opposed to a mongrel breed or mongrel government."[24]

The only change the Captain had managed was ruining Susanna's life, and knowing she had loved him made the despair worse.

Mason remained missing, but the Captain wasn't looking for him. Revenge had provoked the monster's wrath, and the Captain wasn't willing to let harm come to anyone else he cared for.

On an early April morning, Jesse came to the Captain's wagon.

"Join us for breakfast," he insisted.

Same question from a week ago, so the Captain gave the same answer. "No, thanks."

"Forget that you need to stretch the legs, talk to other humans, and eat a good meal. Your guilt-trip-to-nowhere is killing my brother. Frank thinks he should have caught on when Mason started asking questions. He's been so quiet, even Little Archie is begging him to talk."

---

24   Actual quote from the *Lexington Caucasian*.

That should have been funny, but when you're deep in a rut, even a lifeline can't pull you out, yet the Captain agreed to join the breakfast, though his heart wasn't in it.

"Look who it isn't," came Little Archie's voice.

Anointed leader, Little Archie had become a tiny tyrant. The men broke bread, and the Captain spread some honey while Little Archie recapped how they donned Union uniforms and raided Kingsville. They broke into homes, shooting sleeping citizens and torching most of the buildings.

"Let me ask you men something," the Captain said. "Do you really think you're going to make a difference in this war? The South is ready to surrender."

No one gave the question a second thought. Jesse answered for all. "We've been down this road. We fight for what we believe in until the day we die."

"Jesse's right," Little Archie said. "I contest the notion that the South is ready to surrender. There's no surrender in this fight."

Frank shook his head. "The South is losing battle after battle. Our only chance is to kill President Lincoln."

Little Archie scratched his head. "Okay, go back to mute patrol, Frank. You're a prophet of pessimism. Forget Lincoln; he's better protected than Fort Fisher."

The men continued eating. Also present were the Younger brothers, who looked a bit older than the last time the Captain had seen them. Crime was a Bushwhacker family business, it seemed. The Captain wondered if Little Archie had a brother. Perhaps, God wisely broke the mold after realizing what a defect the tiny man was.

Zerelda and Dr. Samuel entered the room. Samuel bore a deep frown, and Zerelda's face shaded red; veins bulged on her forehead and neck. In important matters, the masculine one was left to explain, so Zerelda did the talking. "Bad news, boys. General Lee surrendered. The war is over."

"I don't believe you!" Little Archie smashed his fist to the table. It barely shook.

"Believe me," Zerelda asserted. "First the North captured Fort Fisher, and bit by bit, everything fell. Once Grant took Richmond, the Confederate Army surrendered."

Little Archie scowled. "We couldn't trust the Confederates to get the job done. From the backwoods of every state, we will form a resistance, an army of Bushwhackers. We will strike their homes, their railroads, their banks, their Negroes, and their children on the way home from church."

"What about on the way home from school?" Frank asked. "School is five days a week, and church is only one."

Little Archie glared but bit his tongue with Zerelda in the room. "Coming from church sounded crueler. This is a rally cry, not a strategy session."

Jesse's voice came forth without emotion. "If we kill enough pro-Union sympathizers, then the Republicans will never win an election."

Despite the outcome of the war, the Captain did not revel in the victory. Jesse's words magnified his failures. He probably should have killed Jesse, but what would have happened to Susanna if Jesse had not been around to rescue her? Stuck in purgatory between right and wrong, he realized he would never kill Jesse James now.

CHAPTER 73

The Captain hitched up the wagon to Fly Bait. He needed to leave the Jameses' farm, not because he'd become a squatter, but because staying kept the wounds open and festering. Each day with the Bushwhackers was a reminder of his failures. He left a note with Jesse to contact him in Lexington if he or Frank received word from Susanna.

Despite the early hour, the Captain did not escape undetected.

"Leaving?" Jesse asked.

"Yes."

Jesse pulled him away from Fly Bait and toward the open field. "I'd like to chat before you go."

The two nineteen-year-olds sat against the trunk of a stout oak.

"You've got every right to leave. You can travel to Lexington. You can dig to China, but all you're doing is running from reality—escaping what's troubling you."

The Captain knew the admonishment to be true but did not reply.

"I'll give you my unsolicited opinion. Susanna loved you, but she would detest what you've become. She moved away, not because she hates you, but because she thinks the rape and scar make her something less than what you deserve. She wanted you to move on. Staying celibate, that is your choice, but you're dishonoring her unselfish wishes by wallowing in melancholy."

The lad had hit the mark again, yet the Captain remained quiet.

"Where is the swagger? The heart? The humor? Where is the guy with whom Susanna fell in love? If she saw you today, she'd be disappointed."

Jesse had diagnosed the situation about right, but the Captain had nothing to say.

"Okay, you still don't want to talk about her. What about your mission? Did you find your father's killer?"

The Captain finally spoke. "I did."

"And?"

"I let him live."

"There's the proof you've gone soft."

"That's where you're wrong—or then again, maybe you're right." He locked eyes with Jesse. "Pull your gun on me."

"I will not grant you a suicide wish."

"I didn't ask for you to shoot me. I asked you to pull your gun on me. I can only tell you what I need to say if you control the situation."

Jesse's eyes crinkled in confusion, but he took the gun from his holster and pointed it at the Captain.

He rose and backed away a few steps. "You can kill me at any time, but hear me out before you make a decision."

"What can we possibly have between us?"

The Captain lowered his head, avoiding eye contact. "I met the man who killed my father. He's my age, wise, and thoughtful, but misguided by his peers. Born in a different family, in a different state, in a different era, who knows what he'd be like."

"I sometimes wonder," said Jesse. "Imagine there's no war. What would I do with my life? I like farming and cattle, so I think I'd get myself a tract of land and raise a big ole family."

"You can still follow your dreams, Jesse."

"I can't. It's too late."

"It's never too late. I decided to abandon my mission. So can you."

Jesse lowered the gun. "I don't think so. You're an educated man."

"Education does not make an honorable man. Virtue does." The Captain eyed the lowered pistol. "Please raise your gun and point at me."

He squinted. "Why?"

"You killed my father, Jesse."

Jesse, unflappable boy, even-keeled in all situations, let his jaw hang like a feeding pelican.

"My father was Major Johnson, the man in charge of the Union troops at Centralia. I came here to kill you, Jesse, yet as I said, the man who shot my father is a decent man caught up in an indecent war. My father could have just as easily killed you."

The Captain exhaled the heavy weight upon his heart. "I decided not to kill you long before I left for Lexington and would never do so after you saved Susanna. Without her, I don't mind if I die, so you can kill me for all I care."

Jesse still gawked, dumbfounded, yet he held the gun steady and spoke. "I'm not going to kill you, either, but I may wound you," he said with a wry smile. "Were you responsible for Bloody Bill's death?"

The Captain figured he would ask, and he chose to lie, not because he feared injury, but more because he wanted the Bushwhackers fumbling in disarray and Jesse living an honest life. "If Little Archie did as I said, Bill Anderson would still be alive."

"So you're saying you were helping us, not setting us up with the gold heists?"

"I hoped to gain influence and steer you away from war. I tried and failed."

Jesse tossed the gun aside. He held his arms out to his sides, came forward, and embraced the much larger Captain with a marsupial baby hug. His voice stopped and started like a locomotive leaving a station. "I … am sorry … about your father. I've killed many men now, but only one face haunts me. He was a good man, better than I, and knowing he was your pa, I—I …" His voice broke, and he sobbed softly.

Both men agreed the Captain's revelation would remain their secret.

For the second time, they said their good-byes to each other. The revelation made the departure different but less awkward. For the Captain, the disclosure was a weight off his shoulders, an unburdened heart. It was the longest he'd gone without brooding over Susanna since he'd learned of Mason's deeds. Instead of despair, hope rekindled within him, a beacon in the endless gloom of the war.

The Captain finally took his leave. Frank screamed from the porch and ran to them, waving his arms in joy. Little Archie jogged behind.

Little Archie grinned like he had the best news in the world. "President Lincoln is dead. He's been assassinated."

CHAPTER 74

The Captain found himself in the same Lexington saloon. Despite the war's end, the scars lingered, and resentment soured the air.

After leaving the Jameses' farm, the Captain set out on a quest to find Susanna. Using Booneville as the compass point, he had charted a large circle in which he stopped at every town within the circumference. A photograph could have aided his search, and he lamented he did not have the camera until he'd met Cox. With her scar, however, Susanna should have been easy to describe and identify.

Yet she did not turn up.

He got his hopes up when one man acted certain he knew her location. The man took the Captain to a cabin with a roof that sagged like the man's jowls. A female was present, and she did have scars, but the wounds were old and suggested the pox, not knife work. Her body and general physique were nothing as the Captain had profiled. Her visage was lycanthropic, with a small shaggy beard and down sideburns, long and sharp yellow teeth. She looked werewolf-weird.

Turned out she was the man's wife. He begged the Captain to take her, swearing, "She gives as good as she gets."

Despite the hard luck, the Captain vacated his pity party. As he stood with his first drink in weeks, he surveyed the crowded saloon. A few caravans had pitched on the outskirts of town. Evidently, from the sound of the accents and tailored attire, a few visitors had wandered in.

A woman barged into the saloon and scouted the place until her eyes

274

locked on a man. She strode over. "You no-good, two-timing weasel! I know all about Becky Sue."

The man tried to quiet her, but she only became louder. A man to the Captain's right, with thick, wavy hair and a growing mustache, smirked.

"You know them?"

"No," the Captain answered. "From what I gather, she was to be his bride."

A bitter smile passed the man's lips. "A bride is a woman with a fine prospect of happiness behind her."[25]

"Evidently. This one is a beauty, though."

"Beauty is the power by which a woman charms a lover and terrifies a husband," he said with a chuckle.

The Captain joined the laughter with the man about ten years his elder.

"Women are easy. Love is a near unattainable allure," the Captain said, and thought of Susanna. Still, the bickering couple lightened his mood. "Seems they're off to a bad start."

The man beside him twisted a smile. "Love is a temporary insanity curable by marriage or by removal of the patient from the influences under which he incurred the disorder. This disease is prevalent only among the civilized races living under artificial conditions; barbarous nations breathing pure air and eating simple food enjoy immunity from its ravages."

The Captain heard bitterness in the man's tone but found his wit as sharp as an arrow. The Captain had once had a similar outlook, but then had met Susanna. Maybe this man was right, and Susanna's prospect of happiness was better without him. He refused to believe it. He truly had not wanted them to fall in love before he set out to kill Jesse James. He could have been killed, but as the mission petered out, he had realized what mattered most in life was love.

The scolded man had had enough. "Stop being a witch. Let's talk outside."

---

25   The quotes attributed to Ambrose Bierce have predominantly come from published sources. The author submits that the conversation here did take place. It is possible the author of the journals perfected the lines verbatim to Bierce's future writings.

The man next to the Captain sniffed. "A witch is an ugly and repulsive old woman, in a wicked league with the devil. Or, she is a beautiful and attractive woman, in wickedness a league beyond the devil." He paused and shifted his head, chin up. "A woman would be more charming if one could fall into her arms without falling into her hands."

The Captain guessed the stranger had difficulty with the fairer sex. He probably thought too hard. The Captain found women easily pleased by simple, thoughtful gestures. A good woman was hard to find, but they had it no easier in finding a good man.

The man put out his hand. "My name is Ambrose Bierce."

The Captain introduced himself, and Bierce flinched at the name "Coytus."

"You look run down," Bierce said as he studied the Captain.

"Despite the war's end, it's been a rough year."

"A year is a period of 365 disappointments."

"I wouldn't go that far."

Bierce bit his lip in consternation. "Didn't you write for the *Lexington Caucasian*?"

He was surprised this out-of-towner knew his journalistic deeds. "I worked there a few weeks, but my old boss fled town, and I have not reapplied."

"Those off-beat questions—that was satire?" asked Bierce, his brows arched. "You're pro-Union and worked at Confederate paper?"

He grinned mischievously. "You got me. How did you know? The writing always came out under Aberdeen's name."

"I met a Union fellow named Brewster. I served myself, and when I told him I was heading west to write for a paper in San Francisco, we got around to talking about you. You fight with the Union Army too?"

"Nope, despite my mischief, I was a noncombatant."

"A noncombatant is a dead Quaker," Bierce quipped.

"Are you a man of faith?"

"I'm a good Christian, but faith is merely a belief without evidence, in what is told by one who speaks without knowledge, of things without parallel."

"By the devil, you have a way with words," gushed the Captain. "You should create your own dictionary."

Bierce's brows slanted. "I like your idea. *The Devil's Dictionary.*"

"And I'm glad you liked my work at the paper."

"Brewster showed me the articles you were responsible for. You're funny, but take no offense; your writing is more than passable for the general masses but suffers what ails much of American speech and print."

"No offense taken. I'm not a writer by trade or education. My stint at the *Lexington Caucasian* was my way of trying to undermine the Confederates. It's more fun than traveling with a bunch of men fighting boredom more than battles."

He noticed Bierce's empty glass. "How about I get you another, and you clue me in on my flubs?"

"Deal."

So he ordered two more drinks and returned. "Fire away."

Bierce slugged whiskey and exhaled. "You wrote about the dilapidated Negro church. The word 'dilapidate' comes from the Latin word *lapis*, or stone structure. Thus, it should be only properly used to describe works done by a stone mason, not by a wood carpenter."

"I never considered that. Good point. Any others?"

"Quite a few," he said and laughed good-naturedly. "You wrote something about enemies hailing from the east. 'Hail' is sea-speech and comes from the custom of hailing passing ships. It will not do for serious discourse."

The Captain took the critique well. The man was clearly a physician of English, a man who cut and dissected with a precise knife in a quest to remove grammatical tumors plaguing the language. He nodded for Bierce to continue.

"You wrote, 'At this juncture, the Confederate Army looks like they will finish second in a two-man contest.' 'Juncture' means a joining. Its use to signify time, 'however critical a time,' is absurd. Then you described a fight in this very saloon. You claimed your boss was 'hit over the head' and knocked to the floor. If the blow was over his head, it did not hit him."

The Captain at first did not agree, but as he thought and visualized Bierce's words, he understood the technicality.

Bierce continued. "I also saw the word 'bogus' used, which is unfortunate. It is slang—the grunt of the human hog with an audible memory."

The Captain replied, "That's bogus," and snorted like a swine.

He laughed. "I also recall a sentence whereby a citizen had failed to note the hour. 'Failure' always carries the sense of endeavor; when there has been no endeavor, there is no failure. A falling stone cannot fail to strike you, for it does not try, but a marksman firing at you may fail to hit you, and I hope he always will." Bierce bit his lower lip and grinned.

The Captain laughed and toasted Bierce's glass. "Likewise, my scholarly acquaintance."

"Let's say *friend*," he said with a smile. "An *acquaintance* is a person we know well enough to borrow from, but not well enough to lend to."

The Captain laughed again. "My apologies, word-maestro."

"An 'apology' is to lay the foundation for a future offense."

Both men laughed. They ordered more drinks, and Bierce continued his witticisms. The Captain especially liked it when Bierce said, "'Philosophy' is the route of many roads leading from nowhere to nothing. 'Patience' was described as a minor form of despair disguised as virtue."

Bierce told him more about himself. The battles he fought and won, and the women he battled and lost. He'd suffered a head injury at the Battle of Kennesaw Mountain in early 1864, which took him out of duty until the Civil War's conclusion.

They discussed politics, which Bierce called, "A strife of interest masquerading as a contest of principles—the conduct of public affairs for private advantage." Despite admitting he was Christian, he called the institution of religion nothing more than a "daughter of Hope and Fear, explaining to Ignorance the nature of the Unknowable," and scoffed at those who pray to "ask the laws of the universe be annulled in behalf of a single petitioner confessedly unworthy."

The Captain admitted to not being particularly religious, but he did like to call God's name at least once a day.

When it came to the fairer sex, Bierce had suffered heart injuries that paled to his war stories. For all his brains, women made Bierce nervous. He took things too seriously instead of allowing things to run a natural course.

"Love is fun, if you don't analyze it." The Captain decided Bierce needed a one-night stand in the worst way. "Are there any women here you find attractive?"

Inebriated beyond discretion, Bierce peered around. "Several."

"Pick one, and I'll respectfully request her to join us."

"What? Pick a woman from a bar? That's not a place to find a wife."

"You need to forget about a wife and have fun. All the other stuff will work itself out."

For the first time, Bierce had no witty retort.

The Captain downed the rest of his whiskey. "What did you tell me before about a man who doubts himself?" He ordered two more drinks and listened.

"A person who doubts himself is like a man who would enlist in the ranks of his enemies and bear arms against himself. He makes his failure certain by him being the first person convinced of it."

"You only have to solve women if you make them a puzzle," said the Captain.

Bierce eyed him with admiration. "Maybe we can learn from each other." He pointed. "I fancy the brunette. Not the gal with the mustache disguising lip sores, the other one."

Chapter 75

Weeks passed after Ambrose Bierce had left town, but the Captain still thought of the word wizard. After his one-night stand with the brunette, Bierce seemed more relaxed. The Captain hoped Bierce found joy with the ease he found irony.

His new companion left with one last retort. Called a patriot for the wounds he suffered in war, Bierce bristled. He told the complimenting Union soldier that "patriotism" is "combustible rubbish ready to torch anyone ambitious to illuminate his name."

The Captain promised to write him in San Francisco, and Bierce guaranteed a newspaper job if the Captain chose a journalistic profession.

A knock came from the Captain's inn room door, breaking his thoughts. Brewster entered.

"Major Berryman says the Bushwhackers are outside town. Little Archie Clement demanded we surrender Lexington to him. Didn't someone tell those backwoods bastards that the war is over?"

The Captain and Brewster went to the church, where they found a grizzled vet consulting with his men.

The Captain shook the major's coarse hand. Berryman didn't appear fruity as his name suggested. He had large forearms and broad shoulders, and the creases in his face were like battle lines.

Brewster pointed at the Captain. "Major, this is the man I told you about."

"Your Bushwhacker friends committed crimes against humanity

in Kingsville. Now they're here, demanding our surrender." Berryman unrolled parchment.

> Sir: This is to notify you that I will give you until Friday morning, May 12, 1865, to surrender the town of Lexington. If you surrender, we will treat you and all taken as prisoners of war. If we have to take Lexington by storm, we will burn the town and kill your soldiers. We have the force and are determined to subdue any resistance.
>
> I am, sir, your obedient servant.
> —A. Clement

Berryman said, "It's a bluff. They don't have the men to take this town. We also received a second note." He handed the parchment to the Captain. "It's for you."

> Meet me on the north side of town at noon. I'll be alone. Tell the Union to lay down their arms. I spoke to Susanna and have a message for you.

"What time is it?" he asked.

"Almost noon," Berryman said.

"Your men know not to fire on him?"

"No. His crowd recently pillaged a town. This could be a trick, which is why I sent for you."

Frantic, the Captain's eyes grew. His words were fast but said with the steel of a direct order. "Jesse James must not be harmed."

Berryman clapped his hands. "Let's go."

The three men left the church, found mounts, and then raced northward. Gunfire sounded ahead and led the horseback men to a group of Union soldiers.

"What happened?" Berryman demanded.

"A rebel approached, and we shot at him," a baby-faced soldier said.

Berryman peered past the soldier, who answered to a shaggy-haired lad in the back. "Brady, what happened?"

The shaggy-haired soldier swiveled his head around. "Like he said, a rebel approached."

"How did he approach?" Berryman demanded.

Brady shrugged. "Slowly, with his hands up. He was saying something, but he never got close enough for me to understand him."

"Then what?"

"Someone fired on him."

"Who?"

"I'm not sure. Maybe Mack," he said, and his eyes fell on the baby-faced solider who had first answered.

Berryman glared at Mack and softened his gaze on Brady. "Go on."

"A few of us fired at him, including me. He was hit at least once but was able to flee. We saw you coming, so we did not pursue."

Berryman nodded. "Okay, men, pull back to town."

The Captain approached Berryman. "We need to find him, sir."

He shook his head. "I'd like to help, but we just shot one of their men. If I send only a few men, I'm putting their lives at peril. If I send more, the town is unprotected. All I can do for you is let him make his escape. God willing, the lad will live."

The Captain wanted to argue but was unable to rebut Berryman's rationale. "Thank you. I'm going to look for him."

The Captain was not an adept tracker but quickly found a trail of muddy horse prints mingled with blood. If Jesse was not severely hurt, then he'd backtrack to his posse. He might even return to his family farm. If his condition was dire, he'd seek immediate assistance.

The Captain aimlessly rode north, but he found neither Jesse nor the Bushwhackers. Not knowing what else to do, he set out for the Jameses' farm.

Jesse risked and perhaps gave his life trying to get news of Susanna to him. The Captain had been desperate to hear of Susanna's whereabouts, but now his thoughts were only on Jesse James. He had become much more than the man who killed his father. When it came down to it, he was the Captain's best friend.

He arrived at the Jameses' farm as night swallowed the sky. Zerelda greeted him at the door and waved him inside to the living room where Dr. Samuel was present. The Captain told them about Jesse's possible gunshot wound.

Dr. Samuel remained stoic as he stood like a totem pole while Zerelda tugged at her hair and balled her hands to fists. "He must be okay if he made an escape. Jesse's special. People will come to worship my boy's name."

The Captain left the Jameses' farm and returned to Lexington. There, he found Berryman and Brewster inside the church. His appearance did not elicit the usual grins. Both men fixed him with grave expressions.

"I have news for you," Berryman said. "Jesse spent the first night in a river and crawled to a nearby farmhouse in the morning." He paused, and his demeanor stiffened. "A bullet pierced his lung. I put out word that as long as the Bushwhackers are not aggressive, Jesse was to be brought here under the care of a doctor. His condition is such that the Bushwhackers put their hostilities aside and entrusted us with his life."

"He's here?" the Captain demanded as he turned to the door.

Berryman reached for him. "He is in bad shape. I advise you get the information you need from him quick. Doctor doesn't think he'll survive much longer."

CHAPTER 76

PRESENT DAY

Professor Gladstone stared out his office window. A cherry blossom flowered with spring splendor. Squirrels jumped about as two girls sauntered by. He felt like a prisoner looking out on the free world.

Ulysses Baxter sat in Gladstone's chair like a warden dangling the keys to the professor's freedom. Thus far, Gladstone resisted commuting his sentence by giving Baxter a perfect grade.

Baxter buzzed on like a faulty alarm clock. "If you think about it, my account of Jesse's ordeal at Lexington is the only one that makes sense. No historical record tries to explain first why the Union Army allowed him treatment."

"Coincidence," muttered Gladstone.

"They're not. The record is quite clear. It's almost like when Lee Harvey Oswald defected to the Soviet Union and then was permitted to return. I've filled so many historical holes that I should be unionized."

He grimaced. Baxter patted his own back so frequently he had to be a contortionist.

"What did you make of the Captain and Ambrose Bierce getting together?"

Gladstone frowned. "Since I don't believe the Captain existed, I didn't think much about it. Almost all of Bierce's dialogue came verbatim from his later literary works."

Baxter grinned. "Apparently, he likes to try out his material on those he deemed worthy. You never told anyone about a snippet of writings you had yet to publish?"

He shook his head and did not reply.

"You must be Bulgarian, because your headshake looked like a yes to me."

The professor sniffed the air for a compromise. "What if I give you a near-perfect grade, all my publishing contacts, and a lifetime recommendation and endorsement in all future endeavors?"

"Can you throw in a lollipop to sweeten that stinker?" Baxter said with a sour puss. "There'll be a bidding war from all the major publishing houses on mere content alone. My father will buy so many copies the book is guaranteed to land number one on the *New York Times* Bestseller List. The only one who benefits from linking our names would be you, sir."

The bugle boy trumpeted his own horn again, which made Gladstone want to kick himself. This nonsense had him conjuring cliché expressions.

"Ambrose Bierce disappeared in Mexico around 1913."

"I am aware of Bierce's fate," Gladstone said.

Baxter tapped at the professor's desk. "Consider the mystery solved. The end of my paper explains what happened to Bierce. I also solved the mystery of Maximilian's lost gold and the Wagons of Flour. Are you familiar with the legend?"

He'd thought he was, but the details escaped him. "Enlighten me. I'm sure you will."

"Maximilian was crowned emperor of Mexico when French Emperor Napoleon III decreed the throne to him."

"I know all that."

"Of course, how could I doubt your intellectual prowess on such trivial matters?"

Trivial matters? Gladstone glanced back out the window to distract his mind from the want to reply.

"Very well," Baxter said when Gladstone turned his back once more. "Maximilian was essentially lied to and had been told he'd been elected by the people. In reality, the Mexican government was indebted to France and refused to pay. Napoleon III wanted to recoup their loan and increase his own empire."

Gladstone sighed and turned his attention to a male cardinal with a bug in his beak. He loved birds and hated bugs, but he empathized with the insect. He, too, felt the bond of being prey.

"Do you know Maximilian's wife as well?" probed Baxter.

"Yes, the daughter of Belgian King Leopold I. Do you want her six names, or will her nickname, Carlota, do?" His smile reflected off the window.

"Wow. Without notes, I forget all her names. Have you ever thought about appearing on some TV game show like *Jeopardy?*"

"No, I haven't."

"You're probably one of those people that know almost everything about one topic, like history or math, but don't know jack about anything practical."

"I know a conman when I see one."

"Really? Is an interloper lurking outside? You're staring out a window."

Gladstone turned and looked at Baxter. He sighed again and hoped his stare got the point across.

"By any chance, is your first name Seymour?"

Gladstone had no idea where the kid was going now. "No, it's not."

"We have a neighbor whose given name is Seymour, but he goes by Sy."

"Yeah?"

"Sometimes there's something in a name. There's this dude named John who cleans the bathrooms at Fenway. Our neighbor's maid, Patty, bakes cakes. That pop star, Sky, is a total airhead. And have you ever met a thin Bertha?"

"No. I don't know any Berthas. Where is this going?"

"I noticed you sigh a lot. So I wondered if your name was Sy or perhaps Seymour?"

"Can you get back to Maximilian?"

"Can you sigh less? It's very disconcerting."

Gladstone peered back out the window. Just around the bend was the parking lot. He thought about making a dash for his getaway Lexus.

"Maximilian realized his Mexican reign neared its end. He dispatched his wife safely back to Europe with the hope she'd find assistance. None came, so he devised a plan to get an emperor's ransom out of a hostile country. First, the horde needed to be secretly moved from Mexico before Maximilian fled. Secondly, the Mexican ports were all being watched. So he planned to bring the riches through Texas and use the port in Galveston."

Baxter paused as if offering Gladstone the opportunity to comment. The professor ignored the impasse and instead dreamed of speeding on Massachusetts Avenue. Normally, he played sensible music, but in his reverie, he selected something more modern, fun, and decadent: The Beatles.

Baxter broke the silence. "Maximilian's fortune left in fifteen covered wagons. They managed to cross the Mexican border into Texas. You may recall, I mentioned how Generals Shelby and Price left for Mexico with their men."

Gladstone did not reply. His fantasy became reckless. He envisioned himself stopping for a drink at a gentleman's club instead of any old bar. He'd passed Emerald's plenty of times before. Today he would stop in for a beer and an eyeful of breasts.

"Well," Baxter said with impatient importance, "Maximilian's caravan met a group of Confederate sympathizers who were headed to Mexico from Missouri. You can Google that, Professor."

"I'll take you word on it." Gladstone was too busy getting something he'd only heard of—a lap dance.

"Although the caravan left Mexico—managed by Austrians—they were hardly safe. The Rio Grande was filled with villainous types. Indians raided migrating parties. So the caravan asked the Missouri men to guide them.

"The Confederates agreed and inquired as to the caravan's contents. The Austrians claimed the wagons held only flour, but of course, the Americans became suspicious. The Austrians were the only ones who ventured inside, and they bristled whenever the men from Missouri came near the wagons.

"As they approached the Pecos River in a desolate area known as Castle Gap, the Missouri men ambushed the caravan. Once most of the Mexicans and all of the Austrians were killed, the men checked the wagons and found money, gold, silver, jewels, and priceless heirlooms."

Professor Gladstone left Emerald's horny and raced down I-93. He wasn't speeding home, but rather planned to stop at the neighborhood coffee shop. A cute redhead usually worked there—well, mornings, anyway—but in a fantasy world, what difference does it make if she's working tonight? Her name tag read "Rebecca." She had a big smile and bigger breasts. Rebecca always wanted the professor. Okay, not really, but tonight she did.

Gladstone mused. *In a world where Captain Coytus is real, were his machinations any less probable?*

Baxter continued. "The fifteen wagons posed a problem. The story claims the men took whatever they could carry. They buried the rest of the treasure, let the oxen loose, and burned the wagons. They suspected one man of treason and shot him, then they rode on, only to be later ambushed and killed. The man who had been suspected of treason lived and went back to Missouri, and he told this story to a doctor.

"A story circulated as late as 1978 that the survivor came back to enlist the James brothers to reacquire the gold for the Knights of the Golden Circle. As with some legends, truth is hidden within a fictional account. My paper sets the record straight once and for all."

Gladstone was forced back to reality when, in his dream, the fantasy coffee girl splashed a hot cup of java in his face and yelled, "You dirty, old creep!"

"Can we wrap this up?" asked Gladstone. "I promised my son I'd go shopping."

"That's the lamest excuse ever. Would you choose to shop for toys over time spent with Galileo as he explained his controversial new paper, *Two New Sciences*? Or would you have accused him of heresy? Will history treat you with the scorn the Jesuits earned for their ridicule of Galileo?"

Professor Gladstone sighed.

CHAPTER 77

axter relinquished the chair back to the professor and sat at the edge of the desk. "Before I move on, do you want me to recap any of what I discussed thus far?"

The words spilled from Gladstone. "No, thanks. Truly."

"I understand there's a lot to absorb. This is your golden opportunity to ask questions and revel in the glory of discovery."

Professor Gladstone recalled the sensation of sitting in a dentist's chair. The thing with dental work was you had to endure; it had to end, eventually. One time, he lied and said the bite felt right on a temporary bridge just to end the visit sooner. To end this pain, he might have to utter another lie.

He looked earnestly at Baxter. "Forget the recap. I'm so captured by your story that I'm dying to hear how it ends."

Baxter puffed air. "You're being facetious, Professor. You already wrote an *F* on the cover. If you truly believe I'm lying, fail me. I dare you. I'm rich, and I'll never have to work a day in my life. I don't need this grade, and I don't need your attitude. When my paper becomes a sensation, I will inform every talk show host how you failed me."

"I don't want to fail you," he said, even though he very well did.

The boy continued his harangue. "I came to Harvard for one reason: to tell the Captain's story as the fount of the Baxter legacy." The lad paused to brush his hand over his duffel bag. "My father's great-grandfather is the one and only Captain. How do you think I got the journal and the other supporting evidence?"

After the lad dropped the bizarre bombshell, he reached into his jacket and pulled out a phone. "You talk to my father. You tell him the Captain didn't exist."

The last thing Gladstone wanted to do was chitchat with a billionaire tycoon.

Baxter held the phone but did not dial. "My family started their financial empire on stolen money. For years, we feared repercussions and kept the saga a family secret. Now, enough time has passed. The story deserves to be told." He held the phone up. "Shall I make the call?"

Gladstone flapped his hands about. "No. No, that won't be necessary. I don't want to fail you. I am prepared to give you an *A*, but you won't accept my offer."

Baxter rolled his eyebrows in consternation. "Why would I? You did not give me the professional courtesy of reading my entire paper. How can you grade me without knowing how the story ends?"

Gladstone was unable to break Baxter's logic.

"I solve three mysteries that are over a hundred years old: the disappearance of Ambrose Bierce in Mexico; the disappearance of Maximilian's gold; and the untold truth about Jesse Woodson James. Three cases cracked in one book. I'm like Sherlock Holmes, Hercule Poirot, and Shaggy, Scooby, and the rest of the meddling kids all rolled into one." His eyes narrowed. "The key difference, of course, is my work is nonfiction."

"Indeed."

Baxter smirked. "I admit I peeked at the list of Nobel Prize winners in literature. While I did not happen upon your name, I did find William Butler Yeats, Upton Sinclair, Herman Hesse, William Faulkner, Ernest Hemingway, Winston Churchill, John Steinbeck, William Golding, and Harvard's own T. S. Eliot. After I got to the last name and looked at the void below, I magically saw my name appear. It reminded me of those skywriting planes forming words across the blank yonder."

"Just like that, huh?"

"Yeah, or maybe like the old kid's toy Lite-Brite."

Professor Gladstone cringed. This paper would be his doom. He could forget about the vacated chairman position. He'd be lucky to be entrusted educating kindergarteners. He wished his office chair was an ejector seat to launch him from this room.

"I don't know this Lite-Brite," he finally said.

Baxter's head wobbled in wonder as he smiled. "Do you remember Hungry, Hungry Hippos? My father loves that game. He makes us play every Christmas Eve. He sings the old TV jingle, 'Hungry, hungry hippoooos'!"

"Interesting."

"Yeah, he's got a photographic mind with old television commercials. He also liked this other game, Connect Four. He always uses a line from the commercial: 'Pretty sneaky, Sis.'" Baxter tapped his chin.

"There was this other game: 'You sank my battleship,' the lad said with a deep tone of authority. Then the rest of us would say, 'Shhhhh.'"

Gladstone pitched in his chair like he was on the deck of a sinking battleship. "Sounds like a rollicking laugh-a-palooza, but what does this have to do with Jesse James?"

Baxter grinned. "Sorry. Jesse was close to death and at one of life's crossroads. History says he lived and went on to become the most famous outlaw in history. Over twenty-five movies have been made about his life. Many songs and books chronicled his fame. Everyone has it wrong.

"The common belief is Jesse Woodson James was killed by the 'coward' Robert Ford. Plenty of conspiracy theories tell a different story. Most claim James faked his death, and the body was someone else's. I will explain the truth and the reason everyone is wrong.

"Which is why I deserve a top grade," Baxter said. "Can you say, 'Summa cum laude'? Or as they say about the blonde, 'Summer, in Delta Gamma—Summer comes loudly.'"

Professor Gladstone shook his head with disapproval. "Yes. Indeed."

"Yes, indeed? You slept with Summer too? She's a screamer, eh?" Baxter winked.

Gladstone waved his hand back and forth like he was fanning a fire. "No. Will you please finish this story? I implore you."

Baxter rubbed his hands together, blew into them, and spread them apart. His chest swelled with pride, and he shook his mop. His hand motioned with each word.

"With extreme pleasure, I present the conclusion to *Jesse James and the Secret Legend of Captain Coytus.*"

PART VI

CHAPTER 78

JUNE 1865

For the first time since Jesse had been shot, the guard was dismissed, and the Captain entered his room alone. Jesse did not appear healthy, but like a raging forest fire that consumed all the available combustible material, a spark dimmed as the embers faded to ash.

The Captain pulled a chair toward the bed. A blanket covered Jesse up to his neck.

"I need to tell you something about Susanna before I die." Jesse's voice came out as a loud whisper.

"You're not going to perish," reassured the Captain, his words strong and resolute.

"I think you're wrong, cowboy. I travel to heaven for a cause I believe in. I'll go in peace." His eyes closed for several seconds.

"You died not in battle, but as a messenger. Are you happy with your choice to keep up the fight? Trails are paved with martyrs."

Jesse pouted. "Can you be less serious? I'm dying for a laugh. You hear any new jokes?"

He nodded with a smile. His friend didn't need a sermon. "A well-to-do Yankee couple stumbles upon hard times when the husband's business suffers hardships. The husband tells the wife over dinner that they need to fire either the maid or the butler. If they let the maid go, the wife will be forced to cook and clean, and if they release the butler, the husband will need to manage the grunt work.

"'Let's keep the butler,' the wife responded. 'I'll cook and clean.'

"'Thank you,' says the husband. 'Considering the difficulties between us, that's a huge sacrifice on your part.'

"'Dear husband, my decision is not a noble one. Without the butler, my vanity room will never be completed, and worse yet, I'll never have proper sex.'

"The husband acts shocked. He shakes his fist and mutters angrily under his breath. 'That settles it. The butler must go.'

"The wife smiles. She believes she tricked him into keeping the maid.

"The maid enters the room to clean up, but the man suddenly gets up and goes to the maid. He folds her over the table, and they make love right in front of his wife. As he's thrusting and groaning, he looks at his spouse. 'I'll still do all the grunt work, just as always. You fix your own vanity room, bitch.'" The Captain clapped his hands to punctuate the joke's conclusion.

Jesse wheezed into a laughing fit. "Thanks," he said when he regained his breathing. "It's the most I've laughed since I was shot."

"Show me your wounds. I brought a special dressing for you."

"Are you trying to complete your mission? Kill me once and for all?"

The Captain grinned. "Only after you tell me about Susanna."

"What's this ointment?"

"A honey imported from New Zealand."

Jesse pulled the blanket down, and the Captain removed the bandage. The open wound was surrounded by infection, and despite the stench of rotting skin, he applied the honey and reapplied the covering.

Jesse said, "I have a confession to make. I lied to you."

He chuckled. "You waited until after you got my miracle salve to confess."

Jesse stretched his mouth to an impish grin. "I hope to salve any wounds I opened." He paused, his chin pulled up and his steely blue eyes softened. "I've known where Susanna has been all along. It was true she fled without saying where she was going. Give me some credit. I can track down a mom and her daughter."

The Captain harbored no anger. He understood why Jesse lied.

Jesse exhaled like the confession was a weight upon him. "She said she did not want your pity and claimed she could not overcome the pain of your reaction when you saw her disfigurement. She wanted to move on and forget. When the salty tears fell down her face and into her wound, I decided to honor her request."

The Captain swallowed the hurt.

Jesse arched himself up further. "I thought you could get past Susanna, find another girl, but I watched what the news did to you. So I went to her. I told her you'd become as worthless as manure on infertile ground, and I feared for your life, since you no longer lived."

The Captain wanted to dismiss the concerns, but Jesse had not been far off the mark. "Thank you."

"You're not mad I lied about not knowing where she is?"

"No. I respect you more for keeping your word to her. Even when I fell apart, rather than tell me, you went to her on my behalf. We've both kept secrets from each other, and each time we confess the truth, our bond grows stronger."

Jesse leaned back down. "A bond is only as strong as its weakest link. I'm pretty weak. Since I'm going to die, can you honor a last request?"

"You're not going to die, but what do you want?"

"I don't want to die here, in a Union state. Let me meet my maker in free territory out west."

The Captain shrugged. "Why does it mean so much to you?"

"I hate losing." He frowned. "Mark my words, the day will come when only a Yankee baron can freely buy land in America. Everyone else will need a bank, a Federalist-invented institution. Indeed, my friend, you and I disagree on this war, but let's stick with the middle ground where we can tread without stumbling into each other."

"Agreed, partner," the Captain said and winked. "I'll get you out of here in a few days. Let the honey salve do its thing."

Jesse winked back. "Go find your honey, Susanna. Please don't buzz about too long. Bee-line back, and get me out of this hive. It's swarming with assholes."

CHAPTER 79

By means of an eyepiece, he studied her from a distance. She came out from the house in the early dawn and hung sheets from a line pegged between two trees. Her gaze darted about like she was cognizant of the surveillance or was on alert for predators.

When she returned inside, the Captain saddled up and rode to a small but well-maintained house and opened the picket gate. His hand went up to knock but then retreated like a turtle's head withdrawing. He coaxed his hand out again and knuckled the door three times.

Seconds passed. The wait seemed a lifetime before Susanna opened the door, and although she likely knew to expect him, she wilted in his presence. Her left hand flew to her open mouth, her right to the gash on her face.

The Captain took a step forward, opened his arms, and engulfed her. At first, her body was lifeless, like a puppet cut from its master. Her fingers twitched to life, clutching at his shirt, and then her head rocked slowly against his chest. She sniffled, and her breathing became rapid as she tightened her grip and let the tears come.

The Captain held her firmer. "I'm sorry." His head fell down to hers.

They stayed together until Susanna's mother finally interrupted. "Come inside and at least shut the door."

They obliged.

She smiled at them. "I'll leave you kids alone." Then she went to a back room.

They pulled two wooden chairs close and sat. Susanna still held her hand over her cheek.

"Let me see," he said.

Reluctantly, she lowered her hand. The scabbed wound ranged from her cheek to near the corner of her mouth.

The Captain wanted to joke that he hardly noticed anything—a mere scratch—or take the opposite approach: scream with fright and then laugh to cue her on the joke. Yet her ordeal was no laughing matter. There was so much he wanted to say, but sometimes actions speak louder than words.

"Please close your eyes, Susanna."

She blinked in surprise but complied.

"Imagine my face with your wound. Would that change how you feel about me?"

She shook with resolve. "No, but—"

"Susanna, I'm not here to pity you or make amends. I'm here because I love you and want you in my life forever. Please open your eyes."

She opened her lids, revealing watery orbs that peered at the Captain's extended fist. Her brow pinched in doubt. His hand opened one slow finger at a time. Like a pearl from a gaping oyster, the Captain's outstretched hand held a different gemstone—a diamond ring.

Susanna gasped and became still.

"You have every reason to boot this scoundrel from your life." He softened his voice. "I cannot change how I feel about you. It's like I've spent my life on a wayward journey to slay a mythological dragon, when all along a princess held the key to my dreams and ambitions. You're my princess. You're the woman I love." His tenor strengthened. "Will you please consent to marry me?"

"No," Susanna choked out.

"Wrong answer," a female voice sang from the hallway.

Susanna rolled her eyes. "Mom, a little privacy, please."

The Captain turned to the hallway. "Thanks for the comment." His vision returned to the gem he valued more than the ring itself. "Maybe she should stay."

Susanna smirked and shook her head. "No, sir. Let's take a walk out back."

Once outside, they strode to a small garden. Rows sprouted with new life, and to his right, a picketed pen housed several resting chickens. The Captain barely noticed, though. He still replayed the one fatal word: *no.*

They came to a felled tree and sat. The Captain thought about what to say next.

Susanna patted his leg. "Whether you truly mean what you say is immaterial to me. That you asked is all the satisfaction I can ask for. Thank you."

"Then, why—?"

One hand went to her scar, the other rested on her midriff. "I'm different now." He tried to protest, but she pushed his words away. "People will always stare at me. I can deal with that, but the scars inside will never heal." Tears dripped along her quivering face. "I'm pregnant."

The words hit like an uppercut to the scrotum. He put his arm around her and pulled her in close. "I still love you."

"If we were together, then this thing," she shuddered, "will always be with us. If we go our separate ways, it will be better for both of us."

"Speak for yourself. If this terrible event never happened, then would you have married me?"

Susanna appeared unwilling to answer, but his unflinching gaze brought her to say, "Yes, I would have, but—"

"But it did happen. If you believe the best way forward is without me, then I understand. Don't convince me I'll be better off. I want you and only you. I already fancy the scar."

Susanna pulled away and swatted at him. She put her hand back over her wound. "You were doing so well. Why'd you have to be a jerk?"

The Captain gave her sad puppy eyes. "I can do better. With or without me, you'll be taken care of." He pulled out his cloth sack. "Money can't heal, but the security can make life easier for you."

"You don't have to do this. We can manage quite well on our own."

"Listen, woman, you can deny my hand, and you can throw my gold down the well to make a wish you so assuredly deserve, but I'm leaving money behind. More will be delivered forever after."

"Not if we move from this town," she said and winked, then wiped her damp eyes.

"I'll find you."

"No, sir. If not for your friend Jesse, today wouldn't have happened."

The name again struck him, this time with remorse for his condition. He'd spoken encouraging words to Jesse, but his friend's condition appeared grave.

"Jesse may be dying. When he tried to reach me and tell me where you were, the Union soldiers fired upon him. He may have sacrificed himself for my love for you."

Tears again welled in Susanna's eyes.

The Captain told her about the Centralia massacre in Jesse's words and how he found Jesse to be different than his brethren and a product of his region. He explained his plan to defuse the Bushwhackers through the death of Bloody Bill and how he failed when Little Archie became the new leader.

He cocked his head at her. "I reflected on your letter that asked me what I'd do if I had grown up differently, with different parents or in a different state, such as Georgia."

She tensed, but with hope in her wide eyes. "Do you think he will live?"

"I'm not sure. I promised him I'd move him out of Lexington so he could be with his family."

"You should honor his request."

"Agreed."

Susanna nestled closer. "Before we got sidetracked on Jesse, you told me you were to do better and proceeded to make a feeble gold offer. Continue the speech."

Hopeful, the Captain's pulse raced. "'Four score and seven years ago, our fathers brought forth—'"

"Not that speech."

"Would it impress you if I recited Patrick Henry's speech, *Treason*? 'Give me liberty or give me death,'" the Captain boomed in deep voice.

"I'm ready to give you death."

"What if the speech was in a foreign tongue? A Roman emperor, perhaps."

Susanna purred, "Oh, I'd like hear a foreign tongue. Exotic sounds. We don't come across many Italians in these parts."

Over her shoulder, the Captain detected motion behind a nearby tree. He chose to ignore the vision. "Damn, you caught my bluff. I can't speak Italian. Would you settle for Pig Latin?"[26]

Susanna stared at him like he was playing the fool. "You're already swine, so ..."

He grinned. She was being her old self, and he believed—or, perhaps hoped—he could close the deal. "Pig Latin is a play on English words," he explained, showing the gist of how the words were altered, generally skipping the first letter of the word and adding it to the end followed by -ay. "Thomas Jefferson wrote to his friends using this system."

Susanna examined the ground. "You have socks inside them boots?"

He squinted with suspicion. "Yes. Why?"

"I wondered if your feet were cold."

The Captain breathed with relief. He pushed her hair back and looked into her face as if nothing else in the world existed. He went to one knee and summoned his most sincere expression. "Ouldway ouyay arrymay emay?"

Susanna snorted like a pig and grimaced. "Did anyone ever tell you you're a coxcomb?"

"No. Believe it or not, coxcomb is actually a new one." He again spotted movement, this time behind the closest tree.

Still on his knee, he said, "Susanna, if a genie gave me three wishes, I'd stop at one, for if you were my wife, I'd possess everything I desire." He kissed her hand. "Would you please consent to marry me?"

"No," she said and cocked her head and listened.

Crestfallen, the Captain misgauged his odds again. Perhaps Susanna needed time. "I understand."

"No, you don't," Susanna said curtly. "The first time, I said no because

---

26   The first published account of Pig Latin was found in *Putnam* magazine, May 1869; however, it is known that the language existed well before that date. Thomas Jefferson was known to write letters to acquaintances using the altered jargon to throw off unintended onlookers. My handwriting usually does the trick.

a lady always declines the first time." Her voice lowered. "This time, I said no because my mother is hiding behind the tree over there."

The Captain blinked. "You saw her?"

"Yeah. Seems I'm going to have a handful with you two together."

He swelled inside. *Together?*

"Mother, can you please go inside? I promise you can congratulate us shortly."

"Right answer," her mother replied and scurried back into the house.

Susanna smiled at him, their faces at equal height. "Can you try again? Don't pull the Pig Latin mumbo-jumbo or I'm going to hit you where it hurts. You'll talk pig squeal for days."

"Hmm, maybe I should reconsider. I don't believe in spousal abuse."

She smacked him. "Will you shut up and start talking?"

"Ouch." He rubbed his arm. "I think you bruised me."

Susanna shook her head in disbelief. "You're impossible."

"To resist? That's understandable based on your gender. Surely, therefore, you'll accept my vows of love and proposal of marriage?"

She rolled her eyes. "You're a splinter in the behind. How did my proposal go from so serious to a joke?"

"No idea," confessed the Captain.

"Keep it simple. Ask me again."

"Susanna, will you marry me?"

Again, tears came to her eyes, but this time her visage filled with joy. "Yes, but on one condition."

"Anything."

"If I'm going to be your wife, I should know your true given name."

The Captain winced, contorted his face, and chuckled. "Virgil."

She gave a lopsided smile. "For some reason, I had guessed Ulysses, but I guess the Captain will do. Now, kiss me, Captain Coytus."

The two were one for several minutes before their lips parted. Then they became three.

Susanna's mother draped her arms around them. "Congratulations!"

CHAPTER 80

The next few days passed like a fleeting dream, and they did everything together. The Captain provided a male hand to neglected chores. He chopped wood and fixed the side of the small barn where a fallen tree branch had cracked the frame. They played horseshoes (Susanna prevailed four games to his two), cards (he always won, but the game wasn't strip poker, so who cares). They got drunk, talked, laughed, ate. Then they slept together.

They were to set out before dusk. The Captain began to hitch the wagon to Fly Bait, but Susanna stopped him. "Save Fly Bait the burden of your wagon; it's housed more victims than a hospital."

She sat behind him and gave directions, and before long, they arrived at a wooded grove. Susanna set down blankets as the Captain built a fire. Once settled, they sampled wine and cheese.

Everything came naturally, like the rise and fall of the tide. After he pointed out constellations in the night sky, they fell into a comfortable silence. Their eyes spoke. They wanted each other—now. They moved together in perfect unison, like eagle wings on a downward dive, only to rise and soar again. Fireside, their love blazed with unshackled fury.

They were still awake when the sun began to rise. The Captain got up and added some wood to the dwindling fire.

Susanna said, "The sun's almost up; we'll be gone soon. Might as well let the fire die."

He nodded like he agreed, but a sly grin formed. "I'm worried about wolves."

"Wolves?"

"Yeah. The way you howled all night, I wouldn't be surprised if every wolf pack from here to Alaska is prowling outside camp now."

Her hand flew to her mouth. "I could kill you."

The Captain charged back and fell beside her. "When's the wedding?"

"Never!" Susanna giggled. "You have to go back and help Jesse."

The Captain unfortunately agreed. "Do you have any idea how hard it is to leave you?"

For the first time since she consented to marriage, she frowned. "I hate to turn serious, but I must confess something. I'd like to abort the baby." Grief rippled across her countenance.

He bit his lip. Many things crossed his mind, but at last, he simply said, "I support whatever decision you make. The baby is half you but will be all ours if you decide to give birth. If not, I understand."

"I'd rather not discuss this but wanted to let you know my thoughts." She paused. "One last thing before we gaze at sunnier skies. My mom told me that a beaver's testicles induce an abortion. Do you think that's true or an old wives' tale?"

He chuckled. "That went out in the early 1800s as far as I had thought."

"I figured," she said, and her smile returned.

The Captain grinned back. A finger went in the air. "That must have been an interesting test. I suppose doctors fed pregnant females a steady diet of beaver balls until they ruled out its noneffect on pregnancy."

"Disgusting."

"Maybe they mixed the testicles with spaghetti and claimed they were meatballs."

"Why do you think of such vile things?"

"No clue. Getting back to your original question, it has been reported that doctors are withholding a medical discovery. Frequent fellatio can terminate a pregnancy. They fear the revelation might stymie the birth rate, as men might prefer to be childless. Though again, it may be positive if the baby is unwanted."

Susanna's face creased. "Really?"

"I kind of made that up. But it does seem more believable than munching a beaver's bag.[27] I'm willing to test my theory," he encouraged with a playful prod to her arm.

Susanna looked to the brightening sky. "Dear God, what have I gotten myself into?"

His voice became low and booming. "This is the voice of God. Your path to salvation lies in following all of your husband's commands."

"Jesus wept."

The Captain responded with a kiss, and they made love again.

When they separated, he retrieved a jar from his bag. "Honey, this magic honey is imported from New Zealand." He lightly traced her wound with the ointment. He'd wanted to attend to the gash immediately, but she was sensitive about her condition, and he had decided to wait until she seemed more comfortable with him.

Susanna's eyes grew with hope. "Does it work?"

"You'll always have a scar, but this will help the healing."

Susanna frowned, but a smile was born. "Everyone, including my own mother, looks at me, and they see this." She pointed at the gash. "They either stare at me or avoid looking me in the face. You're different." She kissed him on the lips. "I love you."

They made love once more. As they lay in a blissful embrace, a rumble crackled from the sky. Dark clouds formed like ink blotches on blue parchment, and they broke camp before they headed back to Susanna's home. Breakfast was waiting. While they ate, claps of thunder boomed over the house.

---

27   The author confesses that he was startled by the discourse on beavers … Turns out, beavers' gonads have been, and still are, used for a variety of purposes. From chewing on willow trees, beavers' testicles contain salicylic acid, which is an active ingredient in aspirin. Today, the unfortunate male beaver still supplements many perfumes and flavors Phillip Morris cigarettes. If you smoke and were looking to quit, may that be the trick. As for abortions, since the Roman times, pregnant women sat before beavers' nuts roasting over an open fire in an effort to lose a baby. An auxiliary thought is that with all the males being killed, the few survivors have a lot of beaver to choose from.

When they were done eating, Susanna asked, "What would you like to do today?"

"How about a picnic by the river?"

She fixed him with a queer expression. "It's going to rain all day."

"A strong rain keeps the bugs away, especially the ants. I hate ants."

"That's a stupid plan."

"Okay. How about you wear your white dress, and we frolic about outside?"

"At what age do you expect to mature?"

Susanna's mother giggled from the kitchen.

"Don't encourage him, Mother," she reproached.

"Did I ever tell you I like to suntan in the rain? I never get sunburned."

Susanna's mother snickered at his comment.

Susanna shook her head. "Forget anything outside. I require a nap. Lay with me in the living room and tell me a good story."

After they were comfortable, the Captain said, "Jesse's brother, Frank, recounted a fascinating story." He recapped the entire saga of the Foo-Foo bird and even embellished a few twists to the tale.

After he stretched the story to almost a half hour, she said, "Does this story end? I need my sleep and am only awake to determine if the end makes sense or if I'm going to have to poison your dinner."

He continued right up to the present, even attributing Bloody Bill Anderson's death to the infamous Foo-Foo bird. "The moral of the story is if the Foo shits, wear it."

Susanna cast him the evil eye. "Mom, did the black nightshade sprout yet?"

"How could you joke about such a thing?" her mother lectured. "That was the funniest story I've ever heard."

Susanna shook her head and groaned and then aimed her finger like a gun at the Captain. "We're going to get married soon and move out. I will not be the outcast." She struck the table and pouted. Then she smiled, and the trio laughed.

CHAPTER 81

"I'm going to miss you," Susanna admitted. "Even if we never did marry, you gave me my life back."

The Captain carried buckets from the well to the house and rested. "I feel like the victim of Circe's charms and lack the desire to finish my odyssey. I'd rather sit on a porcupine than leave you."

She chuckled as she filled flasks for his journey. "Where do you want to live when we get married? I'd like to live in a place where people won't stare at me."

"How about up in the Arctic? We'll live like the Eskimo."

"Aren't those giant white polar bears up north?"

"Yeah. I met a Canadian who swears they're all left-handed. Do you think that means that if an obstacle blocked their path, they'd always bear left?"[28]

"I don't care, nor do I want to live in the Arctic."

"Does Mongolia or Siberia entice you?"

Susanna ignored him. "Someplace warm."

He snapped his fingers. "I know just the spot. Nice and warm, and no one will stare at you. In Arabia, the women wear veils. Your face will be hidden."

"Will you be serious?"

"Will you? I'll live wherever you want, love. Home could be an igloo

---

28   All polar bears are left-handed. Snapple Cap Fact #417. Did I mention I like iced tea?

in the Arctic or a tent in the Arabian deserts; it matters not. But you don't have to hide, sunshine. You're beautiful. You're not a freak, except for your unquenchable sexual thirst, but no one will know that except me."

Susanna stomped on his feet.

"Ouch!"

They walked over to Fly Bait and stocked the saddlebag with rations and water. When unburdened, the Captain kissed Susanna gently. She reached her arms around his waist. "Hug me, you buffoon."

Like a hammer to an anvil, a spark met every contact between them. Embraced, they rocked back and forth until a voice said, "You two are perfect together."

Susanna's mother arrived with bread she had baked for his journey.

"Thanks," he said, accepting the bread. "Take care of my girl for me."

"I *was* taking care of her. But she's her old self again, thanks to you. I think she'll go back to taking care of me."

They group-hugged.

At last mounted on Fly Bait and ready to go, the Captain waved at both women. "My body goes to Lexington, my heart remains here."

The journey to Lexington started uneventful, until ambushed by a tribe of Osage Indians. Their faces were colored with blue and green paint, and red along the hairline—warriors. They saw Fly Bait burdened with goods and raised their arrows. The Captain held a finger up. In their tongue, he said, "Story time."

The Captain was well versed in Osage legend and recounted the tale of the Fatal Swing. Osage legend told of a mother-in-law who doted over her daughter's husband. She cut the rope to the swing over a river, and her daughter fell into the river and drowned, but a god helped the husband rescue his wife from the depths of the river, and they returned to kill the wicked woman.

The Captain then told the story of what Mason did to Susanna, invoking the Osage legend. Several Indians nodded in sympathy.

Next, he talked about the Osage totem, the spider, a watchful creature of patience. He lumbered about like a bear. "I fell right into the Osage web."

The Indians grinned.

"Have you heard the legend of the Foo-Foo bird?"

They shook their heads.

The Captain pulled out a loaf of Susanna's mother's bread and passed it around as he told the joke. They didn't know the legend of Cinderella to connect the punch line from that story, "If the shoe fits, wear it," with the joke's reversal, "If the Foo shits, wear it," but they especially enjoyed all the parts where legions of white interlopers and neighboring enemy Indian tribes were wiped out by the Foo-Foo bird.

One large Indian said, "We insist you accompany us back to the village and retell the story of the Foo-Foo bird to the village elders."

The Captain obliged, and the chief laughed so hard throughout the Captain wondered what the man was smoking in his peace pipe. The chief then whispered in another elder's ear, who nodded. He pointed at the Captain. "Follow us."

He was led to a large felled tree across a wooden path. Bark had been stripped away from the center. Carved into the wood was a man on a horse, a deer, and a spider.

The village chief spoke. "Many moons ago, I chased a deer, when this tree fell, blocking my pursuit. I became angry. Then a spider spun a rope and came upon my shoulder. As I released him to the ground, I heard gunfire. I looked through the branches and saw several fur trappers. They spotted me and fired in my direction. As I fled, they came after me, but this tree blocked their pursuit. They tried to go around the side that had been rooted and toward the river that recently flooded. The trappers got stuck in the clay sand and began to sink. I heard their cries and the sounds of bears, wolves, and the spirits. Mother Nature took these men's skins."

The chief caressed the tree like a baby's cheek. "Like a spider, I have waited for someone to fall into our web. Together, every man can move this tree, but no man among us could do it alone, and a spider is not a pack animal. I have prayed for a sign when our people should move west. The spider told me not until this tree is moved off the path. You must try to move it, Captain Coytus."

The Captain factored the tree's dimensions. The trunk was as wide as his torso, and several branches as thick as his legs. No way was he heaving the tree from the path. "What happens if I can't?"

"Then you are unworthy, and the spider says you are prey." A frown creased his aged face. "We kill you." The tone came not as a threat, but rather a simple matter of fate.

The Captain approached the tree, put his arms around the middle, and then pulled it toward him. The branches caught on the trees on his side of the path, and the tree didn't budge. He walked toward what had been the top of the tree. One large branch forked around a midsized tree. The Captain jumped on the branch where it joined the felled tree. A kick then knocked the interfering branch off the trunk. He snapped off some smaller branches and got under the top of the trunk.

He thought of Susanna and the outcome of him failing to lift the tree. He did not fear death. What troubled him was what Susanna would think if he never returned to her. He motioned at the chief. "I told you about my woman. If I am to die, would you please get word to her that I perished?"

The chief said a command, and several bows pointed in the Captain's direction.

"I thought we were friends."

"The spider has no friends," said the chief.

The Captain always liked spiders, as they killed annoying insects like mosquitoes. He swore if he got out of this jam, he'd squash the first spider he encountered. He lifted the thinner top of the trunk and held it against his chest, closed his eyes, and took several deep breaths. He pushed and walked forward, the tree rising as he moved. The Indians stirred.

He ignored the cheers and pointed bows, kept his eyes shut, steadied his breathing, and lost contact with everything outside his body. Lost from the physical world, he was free, but not alone. The spirit of the earth surrounded him with a sense of purpose. A glowing figure appeared, one he mistook as the earth mother goddess. The illumination dimmed, and the angelic face was Susanna. She told him he could do this, how she believed in him. They would be reunited, their destiny unfinished.

The Captain roared and trudged forward in a state of anoesis. The tree creaked but continued its ascent until it hung over the path. With one final heave, the trunk fell on the other side bordering the path. A surge flowed out of him, and he nearly collapsed. A strand fell down from his shoulder to a nearby branch, and a black spider crawled away.

The Indians rallied around him and cheered all the way back to the village. The chief issued a few commands, and a bustle of activity ensued. He took the Captain aside.

"We never would have killed you. Man can do miraculous things when his life hangs in the balance. The spider adapts and overcomes its disadvantages. The spider cannot fly, so it builds a web to catch those that can. You are a spider. You are honorary Osage tribe member," he declared.

The Captain stopped and waited for a lithe Indian to make his approach. "We knew you'd move the tree. We made something for you while you accomplished your task."

The Indian handed the chief clothing, and the chief unfolded the garments: deerskin pants and shirt. "For you," he said.

Another Indian approached and handed the chief a feathered headdress, plain in the front, but red-dyed feathers sprouted along the back. The chief motioned for him to bow down. The headdress was placed on the Captain's head.

"Your Osage name is White Spider of the Night." He clapped his hands, and about ten Indian females lined up. "You take an Osage wife."

The Captain shook his head. "These are beautiful women, Chief. I do not want to offend thee, but I'm already in love."

He smiled. "You're a man of honor, White Spider of the Night. A spider's web is strong enough to take several preys but not many mates. You passed another test." He took a feathered necklace from his neck and motioned for the taller Captain to bow before he placed the feathered wreath around the white man's neck. "You are one of us."

CHAPTER 82

The Captain arrived in Lexington too late to call on the doctor's office and thought about going straight to the inn, as he was tired, but he went to the saloon instead, hoping for an update on Jesse's condition.

There was a sparse crowd inside; most patrons had long stumbled home by now. He didn't recognize any Bushwhackers or Union soldiers, so he started with the familiar saloon owner.

"A whiskey, please." When the man returned with his drink, he asked, "You hear anything about a man named Jesse James? Been holed up at the doctor's."

"They say he may die, but they've been saying that for weeks."

The Captain sipped his whiskey. The booze warmed him, as did the news that Jesse was still alive. A man sidled up next to him, and the Captain thought of Ambrose Bierce as he faced the man, but the face staring back looked nothing like the word maestro. This man had a mop of curly hair and a full, bushy beard—a mountain man.

"From over yonder, I heard you mention the name Jesse James. He a friend of yours?"

"He is. Is he a friend of yours?"

"No, but I know his father."

"Dr. Samuel?"

The mountain man shook his head. "No. He wasn't a doctor, he was a preacher. He went by the name Robert James."

"Did you go to his church?"

The man laughed. "Church? No. I fought for the American Army of the West. I met him in California."

"How long ago?"

"Three months ago."

"I thought he was dead."

The man's blurry eyes shifted about. "Er-r-r ... my time frame might be off. Maybe it was three years, not months."

The Captain steered the man to the bar. "I'm buying."

The man was clearly drunk and offered no comments on the Captain's deerskin Indian attire. Perhaps after they'd had a few more drinks, he'd put the headdress back on and check if the man noticed.

The Captain changed topics and joked about women and war and the subtle differences between the two. The man confessed it had been a long time since he'd had the company of a woman.

The Captain said, "I'm a member of this wild orgy club. Three women to every guy—and the gals are hot as a summer march in the American Southwest. A big guy like you could be king of the orgy mountain. Next secret party is in a few days."

The man leered into the distance and stroked his bristly beard.

"You suddenly seem parched. Let me get you another drink," the Captain said.

"I still have half my drink left."

"Kill it. The gangbangers I carouse with insist everyone is drunk at our orgies."

The mountain man killed his drink and took a fresh one when the Captain returned.

"Have you even been with three to ten women at once?" the Captain asked.

"No," the man slurred, "but I'm ready."

"I don't think you are. Drink up. Did I mention how beautiful these women are?"

"I think so." The man gulped at his drink, and the glass almost missed his face. Droplets of whiskey fell from his whiskers.

"Usually us men sit around and drink as the women get naked and saunter about and serve us food and more drinks. Then they put on a show for us. They do things together. Have you ever seen a woman have sex with another woman?"

The mountain man salivated like a starved man. "No."

"Imagine twenty goddesses doing ungodly things." The Captain whistled. "Heaven on Earth."

"Uh, hmm, err."

"At some point, we give into temptation. We're only men, after all."

"We are," the man said with a big gap-toothed grin.

"Because this is a secret club, we have to trust each other."

"Yes, I understand."

"No secrets between us."

"You bet."

The Captain winked at the mountain man. "By golly, did I tell you about the ridiculous redhead?"

"No."

"She likes us to dress up like Moses and bow before the burning bush. She yells Ten Commandments at us: 'Thou shall take the name of the Lord God in vain. With ecstasy thou shalt scream, 'Oh, my fucking God. Holy horny hallelujah!'"

The Captain snickered. "It's real hokey. I dislike wearing the fake beard, yet watching her handle five guys at once trumps the inconvenience."

The man's red eyes danced.

"We need more whiskey." He bought two more drinks. "Drink up, stud."

The man took a small gulp.

"You one of those quick-draw McGraw types in bed?"

The mountain man would have been less lost in an uncharted forest. "Huh?"

"Never mind. Oh, yeah, Jesse's father. What were you telling me before?"

He scratched at his beard in thought, not to capture whatever mammal was possibly lurking within. "I don't recall."

"The man you met in California."

"Oh, him," he replied, but lapsed into silence.

The Captain lowered his voice like a conspirator. "We're gangbangers, buddy. I thought we had no secrets."

The mountain man took a deep breath and let it all out. "Robert James hated his wife," the man said, spilling some of his drink and then the whole story.

"Jesse's father felt bullied and embarrassed by his wife's behavior. He had Confederate connections, and a plan was hatched to find gold in California, not solely for his own wealth, but another cause." He brought his coarse voice to a whisper. "He was part of some secret group but was not privy to the name."

"You mean the Knights of the Golden Circle."

"Err, yes, I believe that may be it."

"Go on."

"Robert James met another woman, one who truly carried the spirit of the Lord, as well as his libido. Being a man of God, he could not divorce, so he chose to fake his death. Robert cares for his children," the mountain man claimed. "He sent me with gold to give to his offspring. Frank, I understand, is in Kentucky with Quantrill. So I came here, but understand Jesse may die."

"Were you going to tell Jesse his father is alive?"

The man shook his head. "No. Robert may do so at a later time but still fears his wife. I was to tell them their father had found gold, and on his death bed, he asked that it find its way to his children."

CHAPTER 83

The next morning, the Captain went to visit Jesse. The doctor informed him that his friend was still close to death but that the infection seemed to be subsiding. "Nothing we can do to heal his lung," the doctor lamented with a sigh.

The Captain put his headdress on and knocked on Jesse's door.

"Enter," Jesse moaned.

He sauntered inside, singing an Osage Indian song.

A huge grin broke on Jesse's face as the Captain danced about the room in a wild frenzy. He tried to scuttle down in his haunches like a spider, but he got up when he realized he couldn't mimic all the limbs and ended up looking more like a turkey with feathers coming from his head.

The Captain switched to English. "I am White Spider of the Night, shaman of the spirits, heavenly healer." He circled his hands over Jesse's injuries. "Ohm-mm-mm," he hummed three times. "The spider ate your infection and webbed your lung. You will live but need several months to heal." He delved into his spastic, no-rhythm dance again.

Jesse laughed so hard he put the pillow over his face to stop himself, due to the pain.

The Captain stopped his theatrics and took a seat. "Doc says your wound is better."

His friend removed the pillow. "Maybe the honey is magic. So was your grand entrance. What's with the getup?"

"I'm an honorary member of the Osage Indians." The Captain told him about his experience with the Native American tribe.

Jesse grinned. "Wait until Frank learns his long-winded joke helped you and is now being told throughout the Osage Nation."

Jesse momentarily shut his eyes. When he opened them, his skin was taut, and his vision focused. "Last night, the doc came in and told me a man was here to see me. Claimed the guy was drunk, unarmed, and had something to give me from my father. Naturally, I let him in."

The Captain knew all of this because he had walked the mountain man to the doctor's office.

Jesse reached under the blanket and held a cloth sack. The crease in his chin revealed pride. "My father found gold before he became ill and died. On his death bed, he requested the gold find its way to his children."

Pink colored his pale cheeks, and he glowed. "I feel better about my pa now. He left on a secret mission, one he could not even tell his family. They joined the California gold rush to help finance the Knights of the Golden Circle."

The Captain patted Jesse's bed. "Great news, friend. I remember when we talked about our fathers. This must be a better closure."

"It is."

"I have more good news for you."

Jesse straightened and tilted his head. "Yes?"

"Doctor told me you were still unfit for travel. I took him out to my wagon and showed him the bed inside. He's agreed to let me take you home."

An hour and an enormous grin later, Jesse was inside the canvas-covered wagon. They left town, but not before Fly Bait relieved himself on the doorstep of the *Lexington Caucasian*.

About halfway home, three men jumped out of the woods. Two had pistols, one a rifle, and all wore long coats and had red handkerchiefs covering their noses and mouths. The one with the rifle snickered. "What's in the wagon?"

"A dying man," the Captain said. "I'm bringing him home so he can be with his family before he departs to heaven."

The man gestured his rifle at the wagon. "Check inside," he said to his cohort. "And if someone is inside, don't get brave or your friend is a dead man." He leveled the rifle at the Captain.

A short, wiry man inspected the wagon. "He's telling the truth. There's a man under a blanket. He's awake but looks in a bad way."

The man with the rifle nodded and eyed the Captain. "What's in those saddlebags?"

"Books and journals in this one," he said and slapped the leather casing on his right. He patted the left bag. "Only food and water."

"We'll take the food. You keep your books. Do you have any money? Don't lie—we're going to search you."

The Captain detected movement in the background. "No," he said and brushed his deerskin clothes. "I live off the land. I have no need for money. You're robbing the poor."

"The wagon cost money."

"The wagon is not ours, but rather the doctor's in Lexington. You can take it, but I must profess that would be a cruel thing to do to a dying man."

"We don't care. You might be a dying man, too, in a few moments."

The Captain grinned. "Actually, *your* life is the one in peril."

The man with the rifle laughed through his handkerchief. "How so?" He steadied his rifle.

Buzzing ripped through the air, and arrows struck all three men. Two fell over, arrows stuck into their backs. The one with the rifle staggered but stayed on his feet. One arrow pierced his shoulder, another struck his buttock, and he screamed in pain.

Indians moved out from the wooded copse onto the trail.

The Captain chuckled and pulled out his cloth sack. "By the way, I lied." He spilled a few gold coins in his hand. "I have more gold than a leprechaun."

The man tried to use the rifle to brace himself up but crumbled to the ground.

The Osage Indian chief strode over. "Since we saved your life, you will now have to move another tree. This one is much larger."

"What?"

The chief laughed, and his men joined in. "Foo-Foo," he sang. "I'm joking, White Spider of the Night."

CHAPTER 84

With the morning sun at their backs, the Captain had the wagon within sight of the Jameses' farm. "We're almost there."

Jesse whooped.

"Wow. Your home added marble pillars and a moat with a drawbridge and portcullis."

Jesse laughed. "I think my mom would like to be Queen Zerelda."

The Captain did his best to feminize his voice. "Do all your chores, Jesse, or to the dungeon you go."

Someone appeared on the porch, used his hand to shield the sun, and peered at the approaching wagon. He jumped up and ran toward the stables.

The Captain patted Fly Bait. "Come on, boy, give me all you got." He wished they could jettison the wagon to gain speed. He was still too far away, and Mason escaped on horseback.

The Captain bit his lip. He'd told himself revenge would solve nothing, yet seeing Mason in the flesh broke the resolve. Hate manifested from every pore on his body, and the scab ripped from an old wound.

He brought Fly Bait to a stop. Others ventured from the house to the porch: Zerelda, Dr. Samuel, Charlotte, Dottie, and a lad whom the Captain did not recognize. Zerelda stepped down first, her eyes wide with question.

"Do you have any news of my son?"

Jesse's voice moaned from the wagon. "This is the ghost of Jesse James. I am back to haunt you for the crimes against me while living. When I was five, I asked for marbles for Christmas, and I got a bag of small rocks instead. At seven, I wanted new shoes and got Frank's hand-me-downs. At eleven, I asked for a drum and was told to use Frank's head, as it was hollow. Then, at thirteen, after someone put a beehive down the outhouse, I was forced to stand naked in front of my family as Dad pulled beestings from my butt."

Zerelda ran to back of the wagon and peered inside. Her hands went to her head, and she squealed. "Welcome back, son!" She reached in and held his leg.

After they secured Jesse in his bed, the Captain settled in the living room with Zerelda and Dr. Samuel.

"Thank you for bringing my boy home," Zerelda said.

Dr. Samuel called the wound "serious," but she disagreed.

"He looks fit to fuck," she said, which quieted her husband.

The Captain at first discounted Zerelda's diagnosis, yet if the girl were lithe and creative, Jesse's mom might have been figuratively correct.

"I suppose you want to hear about Mason?" she asked.

He nodded. "I reckon I do, ma'am."

"After what he did to your girl, thinking he was a wanted man, he went into hiding. His victim never pressed charges, and he eventually returned home. Unfortunately for the family, their slave burned down the house. Mason spied the guilty Negro nearby and shot him, but he was unable to put the fire out."

"Where was the rest of the family?"

"They were at church, but Mason was sick and stayed home."

Hate returned. "Why do I disbelieve Mason's version of events?"

Zerelda's hand went to her mouth like she'd just heard a man refute the Holy Bible. "You're influenced by Mason's misdeeds to your girl. I understand your bias against his word."

The Captain slowly shook his head. "Mason killed your neighbor's dog because she rejected his advances. Next, he abducted an innocent woman and raped and scarred her for life. Later, he almost burned down his barn to keep his rabid dog from killing him and his sister as he waited for King to transform into a vampire." The Captain tilted his head down. "Excuse my skepticism, ma'am."

Zerelda's jaw jutted in defiance, but her jowls sagged, and she relented. "I have to believe him. Until the family has a new home, they had to split their kids up. I have three. You met Mason and his sister, and I have their brother, Hank."

The Captain's expression softened. "You know Jesse is prudent and wise. Don't listen to me; listen to him. Mason is trouble."

Zerelda cocked a fist. "He'll behave."

He believed her.

"Mason won't be a problem," Dr. Samuel added, though he sounded meek.

The Captain did not believe him.

"You know about my late husband?" Zerelda asked.

"Yes, I met a man who told me the same story."

"Tell me about this mission," she huffed with disdain.

In his mind, he said, *Well, ma'am, no man likes his woman to boss him around. They might put up with it if she's so beautiful that to bed her you'd swim the breaststroke across a pool of piranhas with only your pecker exposed. But since you're a troll with tits, he split.*

The Captain instead said, "Yes. Being a Confederate sympathizer, his church secretly stockpiled Confederate guns. A traitor reported your husband's misdeeds to the Union. The Knights of the Golden Circle had planned to send men to California to find gold for their cause and asked your soon-to-be arrested husband if he wanted to go."

To sweeten the deal, he hammed it up. "Your husband did not care about himself, but he cared about you and the children. Even if he gave up the guns, the Union would have tortured you looking for more. He didn't want you to suffer. He loved you."

She puffed a raspy chuckle. "What a stack of buffalo chips. Robert didn't love me; he feared me. Good thing he did, as he eyed every Sunday church girl like dessert. As for his mission, who knows? He went west one way or another. I barely grieved the coward's death."

Both parties are better off, thought the Captain. *Sometimes you fall out of love.* He wondered if that could ever happen with Susanna and dismissed the notion as impossible.

CHAPTER 85

The Captain spent the night in his wagon, restless and unable to sleep deeply. Mason never returned. In the morning, the Captain went to Jesse's room for another good-bye—this time for good. Jesse would be in no shape to make their wedding.

"Good morning," the Captain said with blustery cheer. "Rise and shine. Oh, yeah, you can't, you invalid." He shot Jesse a broad smile.

Jesse grinned back. "I'm glad I've been upgraded from cadaver to invalid."

"I was optimistic you'd live. You, on the other hand, seem bent on death."

The other boy's mouth slanted. "I want to live but don't want my life stolen from me. I yearn to be with my friends, fighting the Yankee cultural incursion. I wonder if I'll ever be healthy enough to join the Bushwhackers again."

The Captain cracked his knuckles. He heard the same speech before, but for the first time, he grew angry. "We're still young, Jesse. You're going to grow up one day and realize life is much more than this losing battle you wage. The war is over, brother. You lost. What are you fighting? Damn, if you are so hell-bent on dying for this lost cause, I should have killed you myself, you obstinate jackass."

Jesse looked on throughout without a twitch, his face impassionate. His voice came out monotone, as if mesmerized by the Captain. "I told you I would die before I'd accept Yankee tyranny. My father was a man of God.

He met his maker on a Confederate mission. When I die, I'll meet him in heaven, knowing I'm there for fighting for the same ideals."

"Well, you better stay alive then, because your father's not partying at the pearly gates."

As if broken from a trance, Jesse lunged from the bed. For the first time ever, his face seared with anger. "How dare you suggest my father's in hell!"

The Captain had no intent of mentioning Jesse's father. It just came out. Now Jesse's interpretation begged an explanation. He probably could navigate around this whirlpool, yet the cat was out of the bag, even if a pussy had not hopped out of the sack.

The Captain patted his hair down and sat in the chair beside Jesse's bed.

"Apologize," the other demanded.

He took a deep breath. "Remember when you lied to me about not knowing Susanna's whereabouts?"

Jesse's brow furrowed. "Yes. Are you justifying your slight?"

"No, I'm not, Jesse. What I'm going to tell you might be difficult to fathom."

Jesse rested on the bed again, with his chin propped up, his eyes sharp. "I'm all ears."

"No, Frank is the one with elephant ears." He grinned.

No smile met his.

"Tell me what you have to say."

"I planned to tell you this later, when you healed and were out of this home, away from your mother."

"What? Now you want to insult Ma?"

"No, Jesse." He proffered his hand. "Take this."

Jesse waited a few seconds, still glaring, but took the Captain's hand.

He became serious as he stared at his friend and tightened his grip. "Your father is alive."

Jesse tried to pull his hand away, but the Captain held tight.

"No." Jesse shook his head. "No, no, no. What's your game?"

The Captain held his grip and gaze. "Jesse, I would not fib about such a thing." He explained how the mountain man had tripped up. "A traitor broke your father's coterie. So they faked their deaths and traveled south. He sent a man to get word to his family but learned Zerelda had remarried. He decided to let it be, the mission too important to jeopardize. Your father took the gold to Mexico to meet Confederate leadership that fled there after the war."

Jesse stared back, and his visage fell like candle wax as his cool demeanor melted away. He sniffled a few times. As though dark, threatening clouds, his eyes unleashed a deluge of tears.

The Captain offered a faint smile. "He's alive, Jesse." He got up, leaned over the bed, and hugged his dear friend. "Let it all out. I can only imagine what's going through your head."

Jesse sobbed for a few more moments but pulled back, eager with questions. "Where is he?"

"Your father journeyed to Los Cabos, Mexico. I reckon he's there by now."

"You referenced my mother before?" Jesse questioned with an arched brow.

The Captain returned to the chair. "Your father found a new woman and probably remarried. Technically in the eyes of God, he's living in sin, circumstances permitted. He does not want to complicate things with your mother either, as her marriage would be illegitimate as well. He had some other rationale, but the mountain man was explicit your father did not want her to know."

"How come this mountain man, who, by the way, had a name—Alvin—did not tell me my father was alive?"

The Captain's visage twitched. "Alvin? That's his name? I never asked, and I gather why he didn't tell me. Alvin sounds like a low-level banker, not a rugged mountain man."

"True." A sly grinned crept across his lips. "A night out with you is dangerous. Alvin was sloshed."

"His name is Alvin. Obviously he can't drink."

Jesse chuckled. "Did you order him not to tell me about my father?"

"No. Your father planned to reveal the truth to you, but at some later date. He felt it was too dangerous to do so now. Hopefully one day you can ask your father himself."

Jesse bit his lip and spoke through it. "I have to find him."

The Captain shook his head. "You need to heal, chap."

"As soon as I'm better."

The Captain chuckled inside but hid his amusement with a grim gaze. "No way. You're a badass Bushwhacker. You need to stay and fight, not vacation in Mexico like the Confederate-Army types who bailed when the tide turned against them."

"This is different."

"Different? Would Bloody Bill Anderson cut and run from battle for a tender, heartwarming reunion with his pa? Would Little Archie Clement say, 'Later guys; turns out my father lives on a beach in Mexico—I need to work on my tan and sample some of the tequila I keep hearing about. Hope you live to twenty—cheers.' What about the Younger brothers? You're going to let them get older while the only thorny issue you'll face is a cactus after nightfall? Or—"

Jesse silenced the Captain's sermon. "I know you're trying to prove a point. What would your advice be otherwise?"

"I'd go to the ends of the earth to see my father again."

CHAPTER 86

The Captain left the house after yet another farewell to Jesse. He found Charlotte feeding Fly Bait and mimicked the sound of a horse neighing.

"Thank you," he said and nickered. Then he shook his own mane and walked over. Despite his banter, she seemed only to force a smile.

"What's the matter?"

"Do you think Jesse will live?"

"I do. He'll be in pain for a while, but eventually he should be fit." Charlotte's care for the boy always amazed the Captain. She saw the same things he did—a decent lad at heart, raised with a Confederate conscious. Like Susanna wrote, *What would he be like if he grew up in a different climate?*

"Good. I'll have him around for a while."

The Captain grimaced. "You won't, actually. He's going to Kansas to live with one of his other cousins. Jesse and his friends committed some heinous crimes around here. It's not safe for him to stay."

Charlotte's jaw jutted. "I don't believe Jesse did these things."

"He did. His gang tortured and killed not only soldiers, but civilians. He may be the best of the lot, but he's no angel."

Her hands went to her hips. "That's his mother. She made her sons into fighters."

He scratched his head, tilting his hat to the side. "I don't get you, woman. I understand as a slave, you had not much of a choice but to stand by the family. The war is over. Leave. I'll give you the money to travel and get yourself settled."

"No," she said without a thought.

The Captain pressed on the brim of his Stetson and tugged at his hair. "No? You and your daughter could have a different life."

She wagged a finger at him. "You know nothing about me. Are my parents alive, and if so, where do they live?"

The Captain shrugged.

"Do you know who my friends are?"

"No."

"Do I have a new lover?" She didn't pause for his reply. "Perhaps I have someone who is very dear to me who depends on me. Don't so easily judge. Thank you for your offer—it is most generous, and I understand your heart is in the right place—but my answer is no."

"What if I bought you your own place, away from zany Zerelda?"

"No."

"Is Dr. Samuel your new lover, by any chance?"

Charlotte's eyes grew, and she uncorked a punch, not full force, but not exactly a love-tap either.

"I'm sorry," he said and laughed.

"The truth is, my pa is still alive, and I help take care of him. My minister built a home to care for the elderly." She paused as if unsure how to say what she wanted to. "The minister's wife died a few years ago, and well, we've become close." Embarrassed, a smile split her lips as she dropped her gaze to the ground.

"You little vixen," he cooed.

Charlotte struck him again, this time harder.

The Captain wondered what quality he possessed that made women feel the need to strike him. Perhaps he had to tweak his charming techniques.

She grimaced. "The reason I'm sad is Minister Faye has also become ill. If something were to happen to him …" She shuddered, unable to finish the thought in words.

The Captain frowned. "I'm sorry. I do hope he recovers, but can I at least make a donation to the church? To help in case hard times come to bear?"

"May I ask where you got all this money? You told me your parents were not wealthy."

He nodded. "They weren't. My ma worked for a wealthy man whose wife had died, and my ma helped raise his son and take care of the house. I used to go there with my mother, and I became friends with the boy, Timothy. I came to learn some local ruffians bullied the boy. One day, playing ball, a few decided to venture over. A few punches and kicks later, they crawled away whimpering.

"Timothy told his father. Mr. Townsend asked to speak to me one day, and he thanked me for helping his son. No longer timid and shy, the boy hardly shut up anymore according to his father. 'He mostly talks about you,' he had said to me. Then the father asked me something I did not expect. 'What do you want to do with your life?' I told him I wanted to be a hero and help people. He agreed that was my fate but insisted upon the importance of education.

"I told him Mother always read to me as a child. I remember curling up beside her as she made words form magical splendor. Mr. Townsend said as long as Tim and I remained friends, he would sponsor my formal education.

"I didn't care about the promise. I liked Tim. He found me funny, which is a quality I cherish in a person. For the next five or six years, we were tutored together. We even traveled to England for a year, where we studied under the man who taught Mr. Townsend as a child. When my father left for the war, I visited the Townsends almost every day."

The Captain paused, because what happened next still pained him. His voice hitched. "They were in a stage coach when a violent storm broke. The horse panicked, strayed off the trail, and fell down a gulley. The horse, driver, and Timothy were killed instantly. Mr. Townsend died weeks later in his home, but before he did, he left the bulk of his personal wealth to me."

Charlotte's dimples pocketed. "Out of tragedy comes goodness. You do the Lord's work with your endeavors. You *have* become a hero."

"Thanks. Or are you buttering me up for a fat donation to your church?"

She smiled with sweetness. "How did you guess?"

CHAPTER 87

The Captain journeyed back to Susanna in good spirits. Finally, Jesse's days with Archie Clement and the Bushwhackers were over. After he healed, he planned to reunite with his father rather than continue his Confederate crusade.

The Captain also was pleased he had helped Charlotte. Hopefully, the minister, like Jesse, recovered for her sake. He could tell she fancied the minister, and he wished the two of them a lifetime of love.

Yet the real joy would be seeing Susanna. He recalled his trial with the Osage Indians when he moved the tree. In her, he found the resolve to clear the trail. He was glad they'd waited to be intimate; the night was much more special.

One thing nagged the recesses of his thoughts—Mason's residency at the Jameses' farm. Something told him Mason's return spelled trouble. Because of Mason's jealousy of his cousin, the Captain believed he was capable of killing Jesse and passing the death off as an aftermath of his already punctured lung. His crimes against Susanna proved testament to his rotten timber.

The Captain hoped he never set eyes on Mason again, but if he did, he'd kill the scalawag. Still, dwelling about Mason didn't solve anything and only made him angry. So he thought of bliss—lying naked with Susanna.

The open sun glared, but a brisk breeze dissolved any heat. Like a dog, the Captain reveled in the glory of a fine summer day. Every so often, his reverie broke as he thought he heard something beyond the prattle of the wagon. He hoped if bandits pursued, a tribe of Osage tracked the travelers.

He turned around a bend and came to a wide river, which required a ferry to cross. The Captain paid the fare and loaded his cargo on a floating dock that was pulled across from a rope pulley. A ferryman was consistent, easy business, but you had to stay armed and alert. Scoundrels frequently targeted their earnings.

As they crossed, he spotted beaver dams upriver on the near side. He didn't detect any activity though. The colony had likely been trapped and killed, and he found the beaver ghost town unsettling and looked away.

The Captain's eyes turned to the creepy ferryman. Black, stringy hair hung around a pale face that sloped from a high forehead down to sharp mandibles, reminding the Captain of the maw of a praying mantis. His attire was all black, as were the few remaining teeth.

Between the vacant beaver dams and Charon, the River Styx ferryman, the Captain chose to turn and face Fly Bait's behind. The horse's tail whipped up for an extended hello.

The Captain arched his head and gazed at the only pleasant sight available, the afternoon sky—blue with barely a cloud. His eye caught the attention of the strangest bird he'd ever seen. Although it flew high above the earth, it was still visible as the sun almost radiated off its silver frame. The odd bird appeared round and flew in crazy zigzag patterns. After a few moments, the bird flew with great speed to the west and out of sight.[29]

The Captain was relieved when they reached the other side and he touched down once more on terra firma. He rehitched the wagon and took a dark wooded trail that had him wondering if Hades waited at each turn of the path. Eventually, he came through the woods and out onto a more open plain. The warmth of the sun again settled his thoughts on Susanna.

A nervous excitement coursed through him at the prospect of seeing her once more. He hoped she felt the same joy. He was almost upon the house when she sprung from the ranch. Her ecstasy as she raced toward

---

29 People have researched ancient texts, paintings, and monuments with intent to prove that aliens and UFOs have long been part of our history. Could this passage, found in the primary-source documents, be evidence of the *Chariot of the Gods*?

him made the Captain feel like the most loved man in the whole world. She clapped her hands and screamed in delight.

Susanna almost reached him when she stopped so suddenly she fell to one knee. Her mouth quivered, and her breathing became rapid.

"No," she moaned as if caught in a bad dream. Her eyes closed, and she fainted.

The Captain leapt off Fly Bait and ran to Susanna. He picked her up and cradled her in the arms. Had he read her expression wrong? She'd appeared excited to see him, but as she got close, her face froze in horror. Maybe the sight of him triggered a flashback to her ordeal.

He turned to the house, and a voice called from afar. "Hey!"

The Captain squinted as he peered toward the sun. A man on a horse waved. "Thanks for helping me find where my girlfriend moved. I'm sorry, *ex*-girlfriend. Do recall who had her first."

The Captain shook with anger.

"I loved how after I spilled my seed in her, she begged for more. She even asked if I could rustle up a few friends." He snickered. "I took her virginity and made her a proper whore."

Desperate, he wanted to attack, but he had Susanna in his arms, and Fly Bait was still hitched to the wagon. He cursed.

Mason waved. "I'll be around."

CHAPTER 88

Nobody spoke as they ate, eyes fixed on their meals. The only sounds came from silverware striking china. The Captain belched loudly once, for which he apologized. Other than the one gastric outburst, the house was eerily quiet as Susanna's mother took the plates from the table.

Susanna appeared as in a fugue. Fearful spasms periodically dotted her visage as her mind revisited the attack upon her. Her plate was still half-full when she slid the china forward and gestured she'd finished. Her mother didn't mention starving children in some remote outpost and instead cleared the dishes.

"What are we going to do?" Her broken voice was filled with despair.

With equal measure, the Captain was eager and yet dreaded the start of the conversation. He did not press, for Susanna's emotions needed time to settle.

He reached for her hand. "Let's lay all the options on the table. We can stay here and take countermeasures or move away."

"If we move, he'll find us again."

"I believe we can evade him. For instance, if we took a train east, and he did not board—that would be verifiable enough. I'm not saying I want to do this yet; I am just laying options out."

"And if we stay?"

"We warn the sheriff, and I stay here on alert. Perhaps get a few dogs."

"That's a wonderful idea," Susanna's mother said from the kitchen.

"Mrs. Dooley got these two dogs shipped from New York called pugs. They're adorable."

"Pugs are slugs, ma'am. They'd be as much of a deterrent to an intruder as a welcome matt. Something like a German shepherd would do."

"We'd always live in fear, wondering," Susanna said, her chin taut.

An idea had occurred to him. "I think you should return to Booneville. The sheriff can ensure your safety while I find and kill Mason."

"No. The sheriff can't protect us day and night."

"Maybe he's bluffing," her mom said. "I bet his aim is to scare us. He's a coward and will probably never come anywhere near here again."

The sound of shattered glass broke the conversation. A large stone bounced into the living room.

The Captain jumped from the chair, picked up the rock, and ran for the door.

"No!" Susanna screamed. "He could have a gun."

He opened it, but no shots were fired. A figure ran away from the house, and the Captain sprinted in pursuit, his legs fueled by fury. He closed the gap, and Mason resorted to frequent direction changes, but that only delayed his eventual capture.

Within range, the Captain lunged and tackled his quarry. Mason grunted hard as the Captain landed atop him. The Captain threw a hard punch into his quarry's jaw.

"Please, stop," a voice begged.

He stopped and peered into a bloodied face. He looked closer, wondering if the dark was played tricks on him, for his quarry wasn't Mason. He thought he recognized the face, but the name did not come. "Who are you?"

"Hank James."

"Why did you throw a rock through my window? Did Mason tell you to do that?"

"No. Mason threw it. He told me to let you see me, and then hopefully you would follow. He said he wanted to talk to this girl who loves him. He said she hated you, and Mason came to rescue her."

He'd been tricked. Anger and panic pulled him off Hank, and he sprinted; his legs and mind raced back to the house. He could only think the unthinkable. Too much time had passed.

The sound of two successive gunshots shredded his hope. Mason may have killed Fly Bait, nullifying any pursuit, or worse yet, he could have murdered two women.

He desperately willed himself to run faster. Mason left the house alone and detected the Captain's return before quickly mounting his horse.

Too far away, the Captain bit his lip when he realized Mason would escape again—this time with two dead women on his hands.

He ran into the door. Blood splattered across the porch. Inside, the kitchen table was flipped on its side with the top facing the door. Susanna rose from behind the wood barricade. A gun pointed from her hand, and her mother emerged from the closet. With shaking hands, she closed the front door.

Susanna grimaced. "I can't believe I missed. He dove as soon as I came up with the gun."

"There's blood. You must have just grazed him though, because he moved okay."

She gritted her teeth. "I think the decision is obvious. We have to move."

CHAPTER 89

Sheriff Walters personally dropped off the letter the Captain had waited for, and he read. Everything was in order. The house had a new owner. The Captain visited the local church, spoke to the minister, and learned that a family lost their home not to fire, Indians, termites, or neglect, but rather something new in frontier America: banks. Blight struck the family's crops, and they were unable to bring produce to market. They fell behind on their loan. Now they would have a new place to live. No loans. No interest.

They decided to move no more than a few towns away, a large ranch with acres of farm land. With the war over, many soldiers needed work. Brewster hired a crew to pose as laborers and act as security against Mason.

They also purchased two German shepherd puppies; their fur was mostly black, with silver and tan markings. The dogs had boundless energy and were seemingly always hungry. They barked a lot and already had small bellies.

"I want to name the bigger one with more silver Ryan," Susanna had declared.

"I'll name the other fellow Rex."

The Captain knew the marriage was off indefinitely. Despite her smarts and heroics in thwarting Mason, Susanna remained on edge. Mason's specter followed them like a black cloud. The time was not right for a proper wedding.

They had their first true fight, which was over the plan.

"I instructed the locals to pass word to Mason where we moved. This way Brewster's men can take him out."

"You want to use us as bait," Susanna said, her eyes growing in disbelief. "Let's move far away."

"Where?"

"Mason is a strident Confederate and would never go to a place like New York City," she asserted.

The Captain had other ideas. "Should my plan fail, I'll find and kill Mason myself."

Thereupon, the fight ensued.

Susanna's face had furrowed with determination. "I want us to live in peace. Sure, I'd have no remorse if he died; I aimed to kill him myself, but I don't want you to leave and play avenging angel again. Every action has a reaction. Think about how we got to where we are today."

Her insinuation was clear: the Captain had provoked Mason to go after her. The assertion rang true—he'd confessed as much—but she always rationalized the apology away. How could he know Mason would react as he had? Yet wasn't that her recent point? *You don't know.* The truth hurts. She was right, but he felt some masculine underpinning that prevented him from admitting the cold truth.

He simply said, "We'll never rest until he's dead."

"You can serve your bullshit, but I'm not indulging," she said, storming away.

The Captain went inside their new home, and Susanna's mother smiled at him. "Lovers' quarrel. Every couple has them. I won't interfere. Just a little advice—most of the time there's a middle ground, a compromise of sorts that keeps both parties happy.

"My late husband did not get along with my mother, but through no fault of his own. No one was good enough for me in her opinion. When my father passed, Mother needed help to get through a day. I asked to take her in, and my husband resisted and offered to pay for a caretaker. When he saw how important the matter was to me, he relented. Every time my mother was cross with my beloved, I did things to make it up to him. Some I could mention, others I'd rather not," she said and giggled behind a screened hand.

The Captain found Susanna asleep in her mother's bed. Quietly, he carried Ryan and Rex and plopped them next to her. He hunkered down and peered over her backside. The two puppies rushed to her face and licked her.

She woke with a gasp. "Yuck!" she said with obvious jest. She puckered her lips, and the puppies continued their lick attack. "Now where is that rascally father of yours?"

The Captain popped his head up and caught Ryan's eye. The puppy bounced with his tongue wagging, and the Captain caught a few licks before he picked up Ryan and playfully crashed down on the bed with him.

Susanna rolled over. "Sneaky devil—using these cute, innocent creatures to lather me up."

He adjusted his face like he'd been hurt by the remark but smiled the reproach away. "You're right. In my mind, I was going after Mason for you. To avenge his crimes against you as well as end any future affronts. The reality is I was doing it for myself, to ease my own guilt. I can justify an eye for an eye all I want, but if there is one person I should listen to, it is you."

She peered at him and relented with a nod. She leaned closer and kissed him on the lips. "I'm proud of you."

"Yes. So instead, I'm hiring a band of mercenaries to kill him rather than do the deed myself."

She drew away from him. "Really?"

"No, but I thought about it."

"I'd rather you not."

He nodded.

Her lips pressed into a line. "He also is the father of my child. I want to live in a place far away and never hear his name mentioned again."

Again, the Captain had not thought everything through. He cursed himself and maneuvered to firmer ground. "So here's what we're going to do. We're going to ride out the winter here. I hired some men for security. As soon as spring sets in, I'll move to any place in the world with you. Until then, I'll never leave your side."

She sported an impish grin. "You better leave my side. A lady needs her moments of privacy. And, in case you didn't notice, we sleep in separate bedrooms. Mother gave us one night in the woods. Even if we live under your roof, she requests we don't live in sin."

"Winter is made for snuggling."

"Don't complain. She'll find ways to leave us alone but pretend otherwise. Plus, my stomach is already starting to bulge. You'll want no part of me."

"Sure I will. It's amazing what the dark can do." He flashed his toothiest grin.

She pushed him hard, and he dropped off the bed. Rex and Ryan found his fall amusing and leaped on his chest. The Captain stared at their pointed ears, excited eyes, and canine smile. Their tails swayed side to side. He laughed, and both dogs licked him vociferously.

CHAPTER 90

Rory Brewster and his crew arrived the next day. Details were worked out, and they agreed that at night, three men would stay in the farmhouse. Three others would stay in what had been the servants' (read, *slave*) quarters. The last two would stay in the main house, in the first two rooms down a long hallway. All the shifts rotated, except for Brewster, who was stationed in the main lodge.

He had other tidings. "Your boy Jesse is a wanted man." He went on to explain what the Captain already knew. The Bushwhackers had committed atrocities. Both sides had. The difference was these happened *after* the war ended. Their actions during the war were largely forgotten, but the Missouri authorities viewed these recent crimes differently. "They're not going to let this matter rest." He paused. "You know where he is?" It was not a question, but an assumption.

"Jesse is wounded and mending."

"I respect you, but don't let friendship cloud your judgment. His injury doesn't negate justice. Let the court hear him out, if he's innocent."

"You're right, of course. He's not innocent either, but I'm the reason Bloody Bill Anderson is dead. Jesse's not like the rest of the Bushwhackers. He's a good lad who got caught in a bad crowd. After he heals, he's going to Mexico to live with his father and start a new life. Let him be."

Brewster nodded. "You've forgiven him for your father's death. Who am I to judge?"

"You're not judging. You're asking reasonable questions, friend.

Susanna's mother taught me to find compromises. Talk to your superiors and tell them that if they forget about Jesse, I'll deliver them Little Archie. And they'd better kill him, because they'll never take him alive."

An imperceptible nod. "I'll have a letter dispatched immediately."

As winter's icy grip took hold of the frontier, the men prepared to hold it at bay. They stocked enough food to feed their small army and cut enough wood to furnace a ship sailing all seven seas. Besides the reassurance the provisions and company provided Susanna, it was fun having the others around. Usually several men would eat dinner at the dining room table. Stories were told, some even true, but laughter always permeated the room like a sweet fragrance. The Captain loved to watch his future wife enjoy herself.

There had been no sign of Mason. The Captain was not sure if that was good news or not. He had no doubt Mason would try something dastardly before long. The Captain did not inform Susanna of his bit of camouflaging: he'd left instructions that if someone of Mason's profile came looking for them, to tell the inquisitor of the town to which they'd moved. The Captain wanted Mason dead, not so much for revenge, but to end the ordeal with certainty.

They celebrated Christmas in fine style. Susanna and her mother cooked a feast worthy of serving the immortals on Mount Olympus. The venison stew was the best he had tasted, and the apple pie disappeared faster than an erection exposed to subzero temperatures. The Captain secured a case of Bordeaux wine that was nearly depleted by dessert's end.

Mother and daughter surprised all the men with new wool sweaters and mittens.

Brewster drifted to the back while the delighted men tried on their gifts. "Hey," he called. "Look what we have here. Mistletoe." He pointed to some greenery fastened to the ceiling. "Hmm, there's only one couple here. My Celtic ancestors have been doing this for centuries. It's up to you to maintain this holiday tradition." He smirked.

Susanna batted her eyes at Brewster. "I used to like you." She punctuated her sarcasm with a whimsical laugh.

Brewster walked over with a twisted grin and tugged the couple toward the mistletoe.

The pair faced anxious faces. "This is embarrassing," Susanna muttered.

The Captain grinned back. "Suppose we give them a show then?" he asked, but gave her no time to react as he moved in. He picked her up and raised her above his head, tilted his hands, and her face descended to his.

"I could kill you."

"First, kiss me." He put his mouth over hers, and his tongue explored while hers receded. Emboldened by the wine, they kept at it. Her arms wrapped behind his head, and her tongue met his in a passionate dance.

Lost in love, the clapping and hooting distracted them like the crash of a fallen feather. They finally separated when Ryan and Rex hopped at their feet. The dogs looked at the grinning crowd as if suddenly aware of their presence.

"Good Lord," Susanna's mother said.

New Year's Eve was even more festive, and the food equally delicious. Four soldiers who had girlfriends brought them to the party. This time, the men drank whiskey, and the women rejoiced with the devil's wine, champagne.

The Captain left and returned with his guitar. Cheers erupted as he merely strummed a warm-up chord. He opened with, "Yankee Doodle." Everyone danced and sang along, including Susanna's mother. After a few more upbeat songs, he slowed things down with, "Meet Me by the Moonlight." The couples came together in a slow waltz, and Brewster whisked Susanna's mother in for a dance, and the two seniors of the crowd laughed like children.

Susanna disappeared for a bit and then reemerged with her guitar.

"Check her out," Brewster saluted.

The Captain did. Despite her worries over the pregnancy, he found her as beautiful as ever. They practiced a few songs together over the week, starting with, "Oh My Darling, Clementine."

The men clapped and whistled to the song's conclusion. They bowed and rejoined the party. Those without dates began to play some silly drinking game with a deck of playing cards. A short while later, a young feller, Aidan Mack, without a whisker on his face, ran to the front door with his hand clamped over his mouth.

"Ah, an Irish lad who can't hold his booze," Brewster lamented with an Irish brogue. "His mother must be English."

Mack returned, his hands shaking with wild abandon. Spittle hung from his lips and chin. His pale face was augmented by red, wild eyes.

Brewster chuckled. "The drink made a demon out of him."

"The stable!" he screamed. "It's on fire!"

Despite drinking more than anyone in the room, Brewster snapped to attention. His eyes came alert behind the watery glaze. "Men, grab your weapons. DeMayo, you got the front door. Two of you stay guard here. The rest, get to the stables and try to put out the fire." He pointed down the hallway. "Women, go to the last bedroom."

The men filed out, and the woman retreated to the back. Susanna's face disappeared from view. The expression was one the Captain hoped he'd never see again—fear.

CHAPTER 91

The party was snuffed out like the barn fire.

Lit bales of hay had been stacked against the stable wall. Fortunately, the mischief had been discovered before the barn wall caught fire and had spread to the animals and stores. That was the good news. The bad news was a horse's throat had been slit—Brewster's horse.

"If God can't turn Mason's heart, may he turn the lad's ankles and neck," the ex-soldier said, accented in Irish brogue. "Did you read the note?"

The Captain nodded but said no more.

Brewster did not pry.

> If the child is a boy, would you be so kind as to name him Mason Jr.? It would mean a lot to me. My only wish is he grows to look just like his pa.

The Captain deposited the note in the fireplace. Some things were truly best kept from the ones you love.

The next week passed unlike the prior month. The happy banter became long bouts of silence, and grins became grimaces.

A doctor moved in to assist with the pending birth of Susanna's baby. He was a little startled with the armed men about, but he got over his apprehension after one delicious dinner. "How can I ever eat my wife's cooking again?"

Brewster signaled to the Captain one morning. His face was uneven, but he'd been scowling since he lost his mount. "I finally got a reply on that Jesse-Little Archie trade-off. They rejected the offer, claiming they don't need you to get to Little Archie. It's only a matter of time before he's found. As for Jesse, they said not revealing his whereabouts is treason, yet out of respect for your father's sacrifice and your part in Bloody Bill's death, they won't press the matter." He shrugged one shoulder. "Sorry."

The Captain moped around the rest of the afternoon while Susanna spent the day in her room with the doctor. Whiskey seemed the answer, so he went to his room and drank himself to sleep.

In his dream, Susanna screamed in anguish as he struggled to locate her. The long hallway had hundreds of doors rather than six. Every door opened to Mason, who smirked and disappeared in a puff of smoke. On the second-to-last door, Mason said, "I hope my baby boy likes sucking on his momma's tit as much as his daddy did."

The Captain jerked opened the next door, and this time, Mason grabbed him and shook him, saying, "Wake up. Wake up."

The Captain swung a slow dream-induced punch that connected. *Ha.* Mason cried out like a girl.

"Ouch! Please, wake up."

He opened one eye. Susanna's mother stood over him, caressing her jaw. She placed a finger in front of her lips. "Shush." Her face drooped.

He pulled himself to a sitting position but kept the blanket around his naked torso.

Susanna's mother sat at the edge of the bed. "I have some news," she murmured, sighing deeply as though she had a deep burden to lift. "Susanna lost the baby." She paused to let the news sink in. "Doctor says the cord got wrapped around the baby's throat. Nothing he could do."

The Captain shuddered. How much more could Susanna take?

"My daughter's going to need some time alone. She's in the bath now. She said to tell you that she'll call upon you later."

The tidings made the Captain's hangover worse. He sat with his hand bracing his forehead for a long time before he fell back on the bed.

He fell asleep and soon found himself in the familiar hallway. This time all the doors hung open, and Susanna screamed, "Mason's coming. Shut the door!"

He heard Mason cackle, and he sped down the hallway, closing doors. With each door he shut, Mason's voice sounded successively closer. The Captain raced faster. Only a few open doors remained.

As he reached the last one, Mason stepped into the hallway and grabbed the Captain by the collar and laughed. Mason opened his mouth to speak, but the Captain did not want to hear what he had to say. He crashed his forehead into Mason's face. *Crunch.*

"I told you," sang a woman's voice.

The Captain opened his eyes. Brewster had both hands over his nose, and blood dripped through his fingers. Susanna's mother handed a cloth rag to Brewster to help dam the flow. She bustled from the room.

The Captain realized what he'd done. "Sorry. I'm caught in this nightmare. I keep lashing out at what I think is Mason, and well …," he said, leaving the obvious unfinished.

Brewster laughed. "Don't worry. My nose breaks like the wind after the army bean stew is served. Next fight, I should break it myself beforehand and then smile at my opponent as the blood stains my grin red."

Brewster grabbed the almost empty bottle of whiskey on a dresser. "This should take care of the pain." He gulped down the last of it. "Don't worry about me. Go see your woman."

Chapter 92

The Captain opened her door, and to his astonishment, Susanna sat in front of an easel, her face blocked, only the top of her blonde hair visible. He shut the door behind him and waited, unwilling to take another step until she beckoned him.

She rose, and her visage was not what the Captain expected. Her eyes glistened like black opals caught by sunlight. She appeared worn but not fatigued—like a warrior with a lot of fight left. Her smile wasn't broad or forced, but rather complacent, at ease. She covered the easel and motioned him to the bed.

The Captain obliged.

"As you know, I lost the baby."

"I'm truly sorry."

"Don't be. It's God's will and also mine. A piece of Mason would have hovered over our lives. I am at peace knowing my body rejected the child."

He listened to her words and knew them to be true. She had not shed tears over the loss. The worried, harried expression she bore for the past week had disappeared, leaving her reassured, confident.

"There is so much I can say, but I'll start with … you are one incredible woman."

"Stop right there," Susanna said with conviction, her jaw firm. "For me, I'd rather not discuss any of this. I need to move on."

"I understand." And he did. "We'll get through this. In a few months, we leave Missouri forever."

The house seemed to dispel some of the bad air Mason's attack had left lingering. The first heavy snowfall blanketed the earth, and a snowball fight commenced. Susanna insisted on not only participating, but also playing against the Captain.

The dense snow easily packed into projectiles. He noticed his aim was true, except when he was gunning for Susanna. Most of the men instinctively took it easy on her, throwing snowballs with less power. She did not deserve the mercy, however, as her accurate throws came with considerable speed, especially when she put the Captain in her sights.

Their fun stopped by the approach of a man on horseback. The plump figure and long blond hair did not match Mason's profile, yet several of the men went ahead to greet the visitor, many of them wary. The Captain and Brewster hung back, remaining in front of Susanna. They could not hear the discussion.

After a moment, an ex-soldier, Eli McEntee, left the greeting party and returned to the trio. In his hands, he held a box adorned with a red bow. His lower jaw hung limp. "Can I talk to you men alone?" he said, eyeing Susanna.

"No, you may not," she barked. "What's in your hands?"

McEntee flinched and looked at the Captain, who nodded to continue. "Mason paid the man to deliver this gift." He swallowed a few times. "It's supposed to be for the baby."

Susanna strode forward and took the box from his hands. She marched over to the courier. "I'm sorry you had to make the trip. Please tell the man who sent you that I prayed to God to not bring his baby into the world. He answered my prayers, and the baby died at birth."

The courier blanched but finally said, "I don't know if I'll ever see him again."

"You will," she said with certainty.

When the visitor left, a lull settled in, but a snowball from Susanna's hand to Brewster's head ended the doldrums. The air soon filled with volleys of snow. When everyone tired, Susanna suggested they build a snowman. The Captain figured the men would have found the task silly, but they reveled in the idea. Soon, a six-foot snowman with a pipe and a hat stood guard in the front yard.

While January had been pleasant enough, February was unforgiving. The temperature plummeted so low the Captain was able to walk on the surface of the two feet of frozen snow. The winds came like the howling breaths from testy Nordic gods sharing the weather of Nilfheim with the residents of Missouri.

All the men moved into the main house, where the fireplace was continually stocked with as much wood as the hearth could accommodate. Shifts were taken to keep an active guard, despite the doubt any man would travel in the frigid conditions.

The Captain was playing chess with Susanna when Brewster came in from the cold. He moved his limbs slowly, as if checking whether their mechanics still functioned. "Some idiot is approaching. My men went out to meet him." He reopened the door and stepped back outside.

Minutes later, Brewster reappeared. "The near-frozen fool says he needs to speak to you. His name is Frank James, says he's Jesse's brother. Is this true?"

The Captain launched to his feet and grinned. "Let me see him, and I'll tell you."

Brewster snapped his fingers. "Frank James is a wanted man, and a reward's posted for his capture."

"I'll match the reward."

He snapped his fingers again. "It's not the money, you see. It's the moral principle."

"I'll get a priest to bless the clemency of your good deed."

"Priest? I just need a sacrament. Get me enough whiskey to outlast this winter, and you got a deal, partner."

CHAPTER 93

After a hug and a hello, Frank stood by the fire and defrosted. A puddle formed at his feet, and Susanna helped him from his coat and boots. Despite his frigid condition, his smile and eyes glinted warm. "Good to see you again," Frank repeated for the sixth time.

Susanna returned, "I'll leave you men be."

Frank put his hand up, slowing her departure. "Before you go, I wanted to tell you, Jesse sends his greetings. Need I remind everyone who was present the night you two met?"

She smiled. "You James boys seem to share some destiny with the Captain. There are too many uncanny connections."

Seconds later, her mother appeared with a tray in her hand. "Help me with these snacks."

"You have it good, my friend," Frank said.

When they were alone at last, he began by telling the Captain of his travels with William Quantrill, the famed rebel leader. They'd been in Kentucky, attacking Union interests. "I went home in January to recruit more men. I was born in January, as were both of my parents, so in addition, Quantrill sent me to enjoy my birthday."

The Captain pulled two cigars from his front pocket, gave one to Frank, and then motioned to the glass of whiskey Susanna had poured. He lit Frank's cigar, and the men toasted glasses. "Happy belated birthday, Frank."

Each downed his drink.

Frank had stopped shivering and rubbed his belly. "That's the cure for frostbite."

The Captain poured another round.

Frank savored a sip this time. "When I got home, I found out that Jesse had been shot and that our cousins now live with us, although Mason remains unaccounted for."

"He's been busy harassing us."

"That's why I'm here. I had to leave; our home is being watched by the government. So I visited my cousins where Jesse is recuperating. He told me Mason visited him, and how he bragged how he'd joined the Bushwhackers and how Little Archie already recognized his talents by making him his new right-hand man."

"I believe that. No offense, but Little Archie has the acumen of an ant. That he's taken to Mason shows he's short not only in stature, but judgment as well."

Frank jacked his shoulders. "Little Archie upped the attacks after the passage of the Thirteenth Amendment."

"You guys need to move on. Slavery's been abolished in much of the world already. America was late to the dinner party. Sample the humble pie, and you'll realize the just desserts are actually not bitter after all."

"To be honest, I never admit this to the guys, but I think slavery is wrong. Our cause is complicated, however."

The Captain chuckled and said, "Yeah, yeah, I've heard it all before."

"There are more urgent matters to discuss, but let's get back to the Thirteenth Amendment, which abolishes slavery and involuntary servitude, *except* for those punished by a crime. Think about that for a moment. The winners of this war—the politicians, the judges, and the police—are in power. They can arrest who they want. In fact, my brother and I are both wanted. The government is the new slave owner. Now they got cheap labor."

"You're just like your brother."

"You mean I'm right."

"You have a point, but I disagree with your methods to illuminate with blood. Forget this debate. How is Jesse doing?"

"He looked bad to me, but he says he's getting better. He's frustrated being confined to a bed, says he misses the fight. But now he's consumed with seeing our father."

The Captain recounted what he'd already told Jesse, and Frank sat for a long while, sipping his whiskey as he considered everything that had been unloaded upon him. His gaze centered on the crackling hearth.

"I'm going with Jesse to Mexico."

"What? Shouldn't you be getting back to Quantrill? Surely you're not abandoning your great and just cause for a tenderhearted reunion with Pa?"

"Good try, but Jesse told me you gave him the same speech."

The Captain snorted. "Brothers."

"Funny you say that, as Jesse and I talk about you like you're family."

He was touched. "I hope you two find your father in Mexico." He stopped as an idea germinated, but he left the seedling unplanted for now.

"Thanks," Frank said, and his visage grew rigid. "Back to Mason. He told Jesse he's not done with you. Jesse begged him otherwise, but he refused. Jesse wanted to kill him right there. A pistol was stashed under his pillow, but Mason had one in his hand. It was a race Jesse could not win."

Frank paused, his jaw clenched. "Mason paid people to look for a couple fitting your descriptions. No offense, but Susanna's scar stands out like an albino in Africa."

"The analogy was perhaps overreaching, but no offense taken."

"You're smart to station men here. Mason knows this, and he'll either wait you out or come up with some new plan."

"Let him try."

Frank turned his hips and went into his right trouser pocket. He pulled out an envelope with a wax seal. "This is from Edwards. I didn't read yours, but Jesse got one too. Open the envelope. Nod if the letter has anything to do with a certain French emperor of Mexico."

The Captain broke the seal and unfurled the letter. He read and nodded several times before he reached the conclusion. "Interesting."

"Will you join us?"

"I'd have to think about that, Frank. It may never even happen."

"True. If it does, though, Jesse will be healthy by then, and we're headed south to find our father anyway. We might as well rest up in southern Texas before we continue to Mexico."

An earlier thought connected to a new one. "Frank, I may join you after all. Keep me informed of developments."

"I'll try. The only reason I was able to travel here was this weather. There are no patrols about. A purse over your capture is no way to live."

The Captain raised his glass, signifying another drink was in order. "I have an idea. I help you, you help me."

"What do you have in mind?"

CHAPTER 94

Frank refused the offer to stay and wait until the bitter cold passed. "The weather permits my best chance to travel undetected, and I want to see my father again."

The Captain empathized, as he often fantasized receiving the same news—his father on a secret mission and still alive.

Wishful thinking. He'd viewed his father's body; though his mother resisted, he insisted. Mother had been right. Seeing his hero dead, the closed, lifeless eyes, the waxen skin, and grim expression that belied the perpetual smile he fashionably wore had imprinted bitter memories.

Frank only accepted a flask of whiskey and a hug before he left.

The Captain read Edwards's note again and fed the letter to the hearth. Apparently, the French-installed emperor of Mexico, Maximilian, was on the verge of being overthrown in the revolution sweeping the country. Ferdinand Maximilian Joseph was an Austrian, who married the daughter of the king of the Belgians, and King Leopold I. Maximilian's wife's name was Marie Charlotte Amelie Augustine Victoire Clementine Leopoldine. Friends, writers, and people with common sense called her Carlota.

The French had a presence in Mexico, and with the backing of the conservative natives and Napoleon III, they made Maximilian the emperor. In only six months, the people began to turn against him when the expected land reforms never came. Maximilian recognized his rule teetered on borrowed time.

Many of the Confederate leaders who fled to Mexico allied themselves with him. The pay and the perks could be good when your boss was the emperor. Maximilian had a problem, though. He wanted to sneak a bonanza of wealth out of Mexico before he left, and he planned to stay visible so the people would not know he'd robbed the country of its treasures.

Maximilian's plan was to load caravans and have a small party of loyal Mexicans—as well as a few trusted Austrian soldiers—bring the cache across the Texas border. They would then travel to Galveston, which had a port and thus a means for getting the goods back to Europe. Thereafter, the emperor would make his escape.

Texas was filled with bandits and Indians who preyed upon traveling parties. So Maximilian asked Edwards and General Shelby for help. He requested that the Americans meet the caravan at the border and escort it to Galveston.

Edwards assured Maximilian that he had a crew perfect for the role, and he had picked Jesse and the Captain as the point men. What Edwards did not tell Maximilian was that Galveston would see three feet of snow before the town saw the Mexican mother lode. The Bushwhackers would kill the caravan commuters and secure the treasure for the Knights of the Golden Circle.

What the Captain never told Frank was that he had other plans for the Mexican treasure. Instead, the Captain did tell Frank his plans for Mason. The younger James was dubious at first, but the more he thought it through, the better he liked the idea.

Now came the hard part—selling the idea to Susanna. He went to her room, where she sat at her easel. She covered her work and rose to greet him. "My love."

"You know why I call you honey? 'Cause honey is the only food that never spoils."[30]

She flashed a coquettish grin. "You lay it on syrupy-like, honey."

He gestured at the easel. "I thought about dabbling with drawing and painting myself. I have some familiarity with the arts."

---

30   The only food that does not spoil is honey. Snapple Fact Cap #26. If only beer had fact caps as well, who knows how many more footnotes I could have conjured?

"Splendid. We can work together."

"Excellent. I hope you'll help me."

She laughed. "Help you? I'm just trying to learn myself."

"I prefer classical geniuses, such as Michelangelo and Da Vinci, not some of this new dung where it looks like someone vomited on a canvas. My former art instructor was a fanatic, said arts starts with the human anatomy. Take Michelangelo's *David*. The feet, legs, torso, buttocks, stomach, ribs, shoulder, and face—all are human perfection. Well, except for his penis. It is rather small."

Susanna shook away the last comment. "Where are you going with this?" she asked, wary with suspicion.

"I want to create the *Statue of Aphrodite* in honor of you. So if you would be as kind to pose nude for me, I will set about creating a goddess of marble."

Her eyes bulged. "Nude? What?"

His head teetered. "Perhaps some attire is in order. A grape-leaf band around your head would bring the Greek motif to fruition. Use a bow as a prop." His brow creased. "Did Aphrodite carry a bow?"

Bewildered, Susanna's face crimped.

He shook his head. "No, Artemis had the bow. I believe Aphrodite was an outright nudist," he said with a sly grin. "Were you aware the Romans had to place guards around the Aphrodite statue so men didn't masturbate on it?"

Susanna rolled her eyes. "I don't know such vile, decadent things."

"I made that up, but knowing those horny Romans, it may be true." He feigned a serious expression. "What do you think about my nude idea in general? My Aphrodite."

"Didn't you tell me when you broke the owner of the *Lexington Caucasian*'s vase that you put it together like a blacksmith rather than an accomplished potter?"

"Yeah, I'm a butcher when it comes to art, yet with this project, I'm determined to take as much time as needed to sculpt a masterpiece. Might be years of work, but I'm ready to labor before your naked body until I have something that at least looks bipedal."

Susanna scolded him with a cocked finger. "I'm not even replying to your nonsense."

He took her hand and led her to the bed. They sat. "I do have something serious to discuss."

Her shoulders sagged, drawing her inward. "I don't like the sound of this."

The Captain told her what he had in mind. She sat silent and listened, and her manners never betrayed her inner thoughts. He left pauses for her to assert herself, but she remained quiet.

After he finished, she nodded and said, "Yes."

The Captain peered into her eyes in hope they might unlock the mystery of her mind. "Really?"

"You're asking my permission for something you already decided to do."

He cut her off. "Not true. If you say no, I will stand by our original plan."

"That may or may not be true, but there'll always be something else." She moved her hand into his and offered a soft smile. "This is who you are. You like to be the hero."

"No."

"Shush. Let me speak. I can't change you, nor should I. You may be mad, but you're an agent of good. Wherever you are, you try to right what you think is wrong. You could use your charms for misbegotten gains, but you'd rather help the downtrodden."

"Thank you."

"Shhhh. This plan is as foolhardy as I've ever heard. We may never see each other again, but I've falsely thought that before." Her hand tightened around his. "I'm past doubting. The good Lord's blessed you. I believe in you and will pray for your safety and success."

The Captain began to reply, but she leaned over and surprised him with a kiss. After several seconds, their lips parted.

"I like when you quiet me with a kiss," he confessed.

She offered a sly smile. "It appears I'll be kissing you a lot."

"I'll make sure I talk even more."

"Impossible."

"You're probably right," conceded the Captain.

CHAPTER 95

The frigid cold persisted into early March. Icicles the size of lances hung from the roof's edge, and no one stayed outside for long. Even Ryan and Rex were quick about their business before sprinting back inside. The two started to fill out and were quick learners. If any man feigned striking Susanna or her mother, they took an aggressive posture. Interestingly, if Susanna faked punching the Captain, no matter how he howled in pain, the two dogs jumped about like it was playtime. They brought joy to the monotony of being weather-bound prisoners.

By mid-March, the cold climate at last relented. Three days of warmth melted most of the snow, creating marsh-like conditions. The Captain thought it was funny when he tackled Susanna into the wet slop. A curse and a kick near the groin suggested she did not enjoy the revelry as much.

Susanna cleaned up inside, and Brewster's men alerted them to the approach of a man on horseback. The Captain, covered in mud, waited and watched. Brewster and two of his men met the visitor. They talked for a while, and the man left.

Brewster came back to the Captain, sporting a wry grin. "Little Archie's been quite the bad boy. I understand the governor is livid that he hasn't been apprehended, let alone anyone else associated with the Bushwhackers. The authorities in charge of the manhunt have agreed to accept the proposal. The James boys are pardoned of all crimes the day Little Archie is captured or killed."

"You know I don't need to accept that offer anymore." The Captain had already explained his plan. He needed men to pull the caper off, and Brewster had agreed to the adventure along with several of the ex-soldiers.

Brewster eyes twinkled. "You despise Little Archie."

"You got a point. He's so dumb, he's dangerous. Okay, tell them we got a deal. I'll set up the when and where and pass the details on."

"Good call."

"Now that the weather's passed, we'll wait a week or so for the ground to firm, and then we go."

"My men are ready."

Mason had not been heard from, but the weather had been inhuman. Now that the cold passed, the lug was bound to appear again soon. It would be a long week.

This time, the Captain sold the house. He needed to pay his hired men. They would be protecting the woman he loved, and he wanted them well motivated.

The two lovers spent each passing night like it was their last. They explored each other's bodies and minds like adventurers discovering uncharted territories. Nothing was rushed. Every touch brought togetherness, until they unified as one. They never dwelled on the sadness their separation would bring. Instead, the unspoken brought a higher state of ecstasy, as the two knew what they would be deprived of before they could be reunited once more.

Each night, the Captain would sneak back to his bedroom. Well, *sneak* is the wrong word. Susanna's mother told him he could visit but requested he find his way into his own bed before the sun rose. He lustfully agreed with that arrangement. After he left Susanna's room, two others would replace him. Susanna slept easier with Ryan and Rex as company.

The day finally arrived. Nervous anticipation hung in the cool air like a flock of birds set for their annual southern migration. Good-byes were given and received as old friends who expected to reunite soon chatted and shared drinks.

Everyone cleared some space for the last farewell. The Captain opened his arms to Susanna and pressed her into his chest. He played with her hair.

A small sob escaped her, and she turned up to him with watery eyes. "I'm sorry," she said. "I promised I wouldn't ..."

"I'm sorry, sweet Susanna. I lied. I'm never going to meet you in Mexico. I met this sexy Osage Indian gal, and ..." He stopped when hurt washed over her face. "Sorry. That was a bad, All Fool's Day joke."[31]

She pinched his arm. "You're a fool."

"A fool in love."

Susanna reached up and brushed his face. "Only after we're gone, go to my bedroom. I left something for you."

They kissed.

The Captain led her to his wagon. Inside, Rex and Ryan bookended his soon-to-be mother-in-law. Susanna kissed him again and hopped inside.

"Pull out!" the vanguard ordered. The wagon rolled forward, surrounded by a twenty-five-man escort. Through the open flap, both women waved. The Captain and Brewster waved back.

"Give me a few minutes," he requested as the wagon vanished over the horizon.

The Captain left Brewster and went inside the house. He passed through the living room and thought of the good times he'd had there, as well as the bad. A lot had happened in a few months.

He felt like an interloper as he entered the bedroom without Susanna present. The void of her not being within was magnified by the bareness of the room. Gone were the dresser and the doll her father bought for her fifth birthday. The only object left was the easel.

The Captain had wondered why she had always covered her work but had never pried. She claimed more than once she was embarrassed but hoped someday she'd create something worthy of hanging on a wall.

He slowly walked around the easel.

His jaw dropped.

At first he thought a mirror had been placed on the easel, but his Stetson was on a hook near the front door, not his head. He stuck out his tongue and wiggled his fingers. The canvas didn't mimic his gestures.

He'd seen acclaimed paintings before, and her hand created something

---

31 All Fool's Day became April Fool's Day. The author thoroughly believes this holiday gets the shaft and should be celebrated with the same vigor as Thanksgiving and qualify for a day off from school or work.

suited for European galleries. Damn, he looked good. She portrayed him as half-royalty, half-god.

The Captain touched the painting, letting his fingers thumb the top of the canvas like a book binding, and discovered more paintings stacked behind his portrait. He moved his self-image to the floor, resting it against the easel leg. He gazed at a landscape that was not a random backdrop. He recognized the hills and the stream in the foreground—the site of their first real date and also where her father's murderers met their maker. The painting was like a photograph, except for the color.

He might have stared for hours, but one painting remained. He carefully picked the landscape up and then almost dropped it as his knees buckled, yet he managed to rest the second painting against a free easel leg. Needing to catch his breath, he willed his eyes not to glance up.

He finally raised his vision to the bottom of the painting. Before they strayed an inch higher, he spotted a folded note.

My Captain,

I started this painting of you the day you left Booneville. I finished the painting of me just days ago. I know I am a mere amateur, but I admit, I am proud of the one of you. I started painting because I wanted something to remember you by, in case we never saw each other again. When I believed we'd never meet again, I would stare at you for hours. I wanted to take "you" with me to Mexico, but you're in my heart, so I'm willing to part with it. The worst painting is obviously the one of me. Sorry I'm not naked, but just for you, my Adonis, I put a leaf band around my head.

I love you!
Susanna

He refolded the note and put it inside his trouser pocket. He then examined the final painting. Susanna was wrong. She'd saved the best for last. He put his fingertip to her painted face and traced her scar.

He had no idea how much time had passed. His rapture broke when he heard Brewster cough from the open door. The Captain turned, and Brewster said, "Everything okay?"

He motioned Brewster into the room. "Look at this."

Brewster walked around the easel and stopped, shaking his head in wonder. "Did she do that?"

"She did."

He whistled. "I have news for you, son—you better marry that woman. I'm ten years your senior, and I'm still a bachelor. Trust me, a good woman is hard to find. A great one is near impossible. An extraordinary gal like Susanna is one for the ages."

CHAPTER 96

The Captain and Brewster arrived in Lexington without incident. No bandit attacks, no Osage Indian interventions. Fortunately, Hades drove the spooky ferryman off, and instead they had a curious chap ... who, if you counted his teeth, head hair follicles, and entire word vocabulary, the sum was less than twenty. No matter the question, he answered, "Wagh!"

"What's your name?"

"Wagh!"

"So, Mr. Wagh, what do you call a guy who's still a virgin, reeks like a mountain of manure, and is as bright as Satan's asshole?"

"Wagh!"

Once they arrived in Lexington, the Captain left Brewster and went to the *Lexington Caucasian* building. He knocked, and a familiar face answered. The Captain said, "Welcome back from Mexico."

Apparently, beans, guacamole, and salsa were part of an acceptable walrus diet. Edwards had packed on considerable blubber in Mexico and was almost a manatee in proportion.

The Captain entered the foyer. "Where's the new owner?"

"I don't know. I got here two days ago," Edwards said. "I found a note that said he left on urgent business but to use the facilities and the slaves—I mean help—for any meals."

The truth was Berryman and some of the soldiers who had worked under him had abducted the new owner.

Inside the greeting room, Frank and Little Archie were playing checkers.

"King me," Frank said.

"This game is stupid," protested Little Archie. "Just like backgammon and chess. Give me a deck of cards any day."

Both players moved to stand and greet the Captain.

"Continue your game," he said.

"This game is over," Little Archie said.

"Sure is," he agreed. "You got your butt kicked bronco style."

Little Archie seethed but said nothing.

Edwards left and returned with two platters of appetizers. On one silver tray were anchovies on a wafer; on the other platter were crackers and a pile of caviar. Although near-famished, he decided to pass. Besides Edwards, everyone abstained.

"Don't you have any normal food?" Little Archie groused. He took a plain cracker and squinted at the caviar. "What's this slimy shit? Fucking fish balls?"

"Fish eggs, better known as caviar," informed Edwards.

Little Archie scooped a smidgen of caviar onto the cracker. He took a whiff as he slowly brought the cracker to his mouth. "Phew, hope it tastes better than it smells."

The Captain had seen a sword swallower make a hastier meal of steel than Little Archie did with his dotted cracker. Archie finally nibbled a bird peck off the cracker, all grain. He ventured further and got a smidgen of the caviar on the next bite. His lips puckered, and his cheeks slackened and then inflated. Little Archie spat the snack onto the floor. He reached for the water pitcher.

"Yuck."

For a rare moment, the Captain liked Little Archie. Serving aristocratic hors d'oeuvres to Bushwhackers was like pacifying a den of cougars with steamed veggies.

"You don't have any walrus burgers do you?" asked the Captain as Edwards stared at the grounded food.

Three quizzical glances sped his way.

"Never mind."

Frank ate a cracker. "It's good if you don't put the fish balls on it."

Little Archie emptied the pitcher. "Thanks, Frank. I've sampled a cracker before."

Edwards finished the rest of the platter before he got to the meat of the matter. "I'll be notified in advance, but I expect the Mexican treasure to be moved in May and reach Texas in June. You'll need to kill them all—no survivors. The Mexican bounty is enough for the Knights of the Golden Circle to maintain Confederate ideals and build a new strong South."

Little Archie licked his lips. "Good. After the war ended, things didn't seem too bad with these Black Code laws, but now there have been rumblings that the Republicans want to end segregation. I thought America was the land of freedom. They're taking our liberty away."[32]

Oh, the irony, thought the Captain as his temporary goodwill toward Little Archie evaporated. "America was founded on religious freedom. It's expanded to cover skin color, and gender is next. I cannot grasp why some white men who believe in their inherent superiority would fear equal opportunity for all."

Everyone stared at him, some glaring, others slack jawed. Little Archie glowered with anger, yet Edwards appeared flabby and flabbergasted.

Frank tilted his head down to disguise a smile.

"Surely you don't discount Caucasian superiority?" Edwards probed.

The Captain cocked his head at Frank and Little Archie. "I ask you, gentlemen. You've heard Charlotte's daughter, Elizabeth, play the piano. Can anyone here play with such precision?"

"No," Frank conceded.

"Of course I can," Little Archie asserted.

The Captain laughed at him. "You're lying. The saloon's got a piano, and I have the sheet music Elizabeth played. Since you're not happy with the food here, let's get a bite at the saloon. If you can play, then I'll treat for all the food and booze. If you can't, then the bill is on you."

---

32 The Black Codes were laws passed by Southern states following the Civil War. The legislation was designed to deny blacks freedoms, primarily with regard to labor. Corporal punishment was used to enforce the codes. In other words, not much changed down on the plantation.

Frank chuckled. "I can't lose on this bet." He tapped Little Archie. "Hope you have enough money, because you'll be treating."

Little Archie was so steamed that the Captain expected to hear the whistle of escaped water vapor. "Button it, Frank," Little Archie said. He focused on the Captain. "So what? The Negro can play a piano. She took lessons. You can train a monkey to do that."

"No, Small Arch. You can't train a monkey to play Chopin." The Captain pontificated like Little Archie was a five-year-old. "It's never been done. Nor can they read, write, or learn skills unique to *Homo sapiens*. But you made an interesting point: Elizabeth was taught."

He turned his attention to Edwards, who licked his lips like he desired another round of ocean snacks—perhaps sea cucumber seasoned with plankton. Walruses also ate crabs. Based on the way Edwards scratched his crotch, the Captain ventured that he had his own breeding colony.

"Edwards, you're an educated man and a gifted writer."

Edwards put up a modest hand, but his face filled with pride.

"I'd like an honest answer. I trust you've seen Frederick Douglass's work."

A small nod confirmed Edwards had.

"Can Douglass write better than the majority of white Americans?"

Little Archie interjected, "First, how do we really know Douglass even wrote anything at all? It could be a Yankee liberal plot to fool the ignorant into accepting equality. Second, there's no way any Negro can write better than me."

The Captain again laughed. He reached into a bag he'd brought with him and took out parchment, a fountain pen, and ink. "Here you go, buddy. Dazzle us."

Little Archie seized the offering, set the parchment on the table, and stared at the pen like it was the schematic of a locomotive engine. He opened the ink well and dipped the pen with the skill of a chopstick virgin. He moved the pen just above the parchment and fidgeted like he was considering a dissertation in Latin.

"What's the problem?" asked the Captain. "I know you can write. You dispatched a note to the City of Lexington."

"Jesse wrote it," informed Frank.

Little Archie grumbled, shook his head, and then touched the pen to the parchment. He hunched over and plopped his arms on the table as a screen. He went to work. *Snap!* "Oops. This crummy pen broke." Little Archie grinned in apparent victory.

The Captain smiled back. "Don't worry." He reached into his bag and procured another pen. "Here you go."

Little Archie cursed. "I'm having a hard time gripping the pen. It hurts my hand."

He winked. "I figured your right hand would find the width familiar."

Laughter boomed from Frank. "Maybe that's how he hurt his hand." He jerked his hand up and down from his lap.

The Captain grabbed a folded newspaper near the end of the table and slid the paper to Little Archie. "Read something for us?"

He rubbed his chin and peered at the printed words like it was a Sumerian Cuneiform tablet. Then he grinned. "This story is about Negro-loving traitors." He looked at the Captain but inched his chair back from the table. "Perhaps *you* should read it."

The Captain didn't take the bait and instead laughed again at Little Archie. "How about I get the Negro minister to read for us? Then you can explain how you are intellectually superior to him. You're a small man, with a small mind, who only grows by oppressing others."

Little Archie touched his holster.

"Runt, before your gun moves an inch, I'll be all over you like flies to a little shit."

Edwards's head bobbed up as if he surfaced the ocean for air. "Enough! How can I jeopardize this mission to men who are ready to kill each other?" He glared at the Captain. "What happened to you? You even worked at this paper. What happened to your job? Were you fired due to these abolitionist views?"

Little Archie smiled. "Yeah?"

Frank stayed silent.

"Actually, things started well. My ideas resulted in the largest circulation in the newspaper's history, but your friend, Aberdeen, got caught in a scandal foisted by some Union soldiers."

"What scandal?" The enormous man fingered his mustache in wonder.

The Captain stared right into Edwards's eyes and gave him a knowing smile, like the two were in cahoots. "Aberdeen was photographed having sex with Negroes, both women and men."

"Bullshit," Edwards said. After he spoke, he tilted his head at the Captain, who reached under the table into his magic bag. Worry crept across Edwards's face.

The Captain pulled out photos and passed them around the table. "See for yourself." He pointed at Little Archie. "I know you've never had sex. Don't get all excited and spunk on these pictures."

"Fuck you," spat Little Archie.

The Captain eyed Edwards and nodded.

"Shut up, Archie," Edwards scolded.

He gazed at each man as they gawked at the photographs. "Aberdeen fled and closed the paper. Apparently, he found a buyer, but I'd left town by then."

Edwards frowned, drawing his moustache downward. "You mentioned the Union was behind this scandal?"

"Yes. They selected high-profile Confederate advocates and enticed them with Negro prostitutes. If the guy took the bait, then they photographed the escapade. They mailed these photos to Aberdeen and essentially blackmailed him until he fled."

"Understandable."

The Captain again captured the other man's eyes. "The photos sent to the *Lexington Caucasian* not only included photos of Aberdeen, but of other prominent Confederate champions. I recognized most, and one is someone I know quite well." He slipped a sly smile toward Edwards. "In fact, I brought some of those photos with me as well."

"Let's see them," an excited Frank said. "This is funny."

"I think we've seen enough," Edwards pronounced.

He arched a brow. "You sure, Edwards? I bet you'd recognize one guy in particular."

"No, no, no. That won't be necessary."

"Please," Frank begged.

"This man will be of a particular interest to all." The Captain feigned a move to his bag.

"I just ate, and I can be repulsed no further," protested Edwards.

"You don't have to look," Frank said.

"That is true," the Captain agreed, and reached down once more.

Panicked, Edwards shook like he was naked, wet, and cold. The Captain thought the man's heart might fail, so he relented and compromised. As it stood, Edwards had a purpose in the Captain's plans. "Yeah, come to think of it, we've seen enough."

"What about the guy we know?" Frank inquired.

He tipped his Stetson. "Later." He drew Edwards's attention to him with a smirk. "We got sidetracked when you questioned my loyalty to this mission due to some personal beliefs. We also established Little Archie can't read or write and is likely a backwoods by-product of incestuous breeding."

Little Archie jumped from his chair and balled his hands into fists.

The Captain had only to glance at Edwards.

"Sit the fuck down," he thundered.

Little Archie pouted and sat.

The Captain returned to his inquiry. "Back to Frederick Douglass. Can he write better than most Caucasians?"

Edwards rolled his tongue around his mouth before he answered. "Yes, agreed."

"In fact, as talented as you are, my friend, I reckon Douglass is even a more gifted writer. Surely you would agree?"

The two Bushwhackers turned to the floundering walrus, who gulped and grimaced like he'd mistook a rock for a crustacean.

Edwards eyed the Captain, who in turn looked down at his bag.

"Douglass is a better writer," he said with haste.

The Captain clapped his hands. "I think I've made my point."

"Indeed, you have."

"One last thing. Every mission needs a leader. I'll never follow another man's command. Therefore, I must lead the Mexican mission."

"Hell, no," Little Archie protested. "I lead the Bushwhackers."

"Furthermore," the Captain continued, "Jesse will be my second-in-command. Together, we will assemble who's coming with us."

"Jesse reports to me," Little Archie protested.

"And while Jesse and I will make all decisions, Frank will be charged as the rest of the men's direct superior."

Frank grinned.

Irate, Little Archie squawked and shuffled in his chair.

The Captain mirrored Edwards's eyes. "It's your call, sir."

Beaten, Edwards looked down at the table as if the top was a chessboard and he'd been checkmated. He gazed back to the Captain. "Captain Coytus, you are hereby appointed command of the Mexican treasure heist."

Frank clasped his hands in prayer. "Now that's been settled, can we see more of those salacious photographs?"

CHAPTER 97

The Captain started his leadership with marching orders. He informed the two Bushwhackers that he had private business to discuss with Edwards. Despite his wager with Little Archie, he gave them gold and told them to treat themselves to lunch. He considered it the right thing to do. After all, the meal would be Little Archie's last supper.

Little Archie was told to return with a steak for the Captain, and Frank would retrieve Jesse and safely get him to the Jameses' family farm, where they'd reunite for the mission.

After the two men left, the Captain handed the lurid photographs to Edwards.

Now that he possessed the photos, Edwards scowled, "Why do I think that you framed all of us?"

"It's logical, but you're wrong. I know who did this, so did Aberdeen. Sir, if I was culpable, I could have truly harmed you. I kept my promise. I never told a soul about the time I walked in on you with a Negro prostitute, nor did I show anyone these photos. After Aberdeen left, I confronted the man responsible. His name is Rory Brewster, and I persuaded him to destroy all your photos for five ounces of gold. Frank and Jesse know my loyalty is genuine. If anyone flubbed, then it's that mental midget, Little Archie. He's the reason Bloody Bill Anderson is dead."

Edwards bobbed his head. "I'm wrong to mistrust you. Aberdeen sent a letter to me and raved about you. He said you were brash but brilliant and a possible poster boy for our cause."

"Sir, I readily admit I do not believe in the inferiority of the races. Neither does Jesse. He fears Yankee capitalistic superiority. I'm here because my father died in the war," he said and bit his lip with a pained expression. "You have no obligation to include me in this mission. I have my own gold and a woman I can't wait to see again, naked. But if I am to go, then I must be in charge. I am not taking orders from Little Archie. I'd rather follow a blind man through the Black Forest."

"Is that the truth?"

"So help me God."

Edwards licked his lips and sprouted a devious smile. "Okay, I'm taking no chances. You're excluded from the mission."

The walrus would have made a terrible poker player. His shifting eyes and unconvincing inflection spoiled his ruse.

"I understand, but I do offer this advice. Put Jesse in charge. He's smart and won't take unnecessary risks."

"Good counsel, son." Edwards spread his hands and smiled. "You passed my test. I want you to lead the mission."

The Captain widened his eyes in feigned surprise. "I confess slight hurt, but I'm not one to show my emotions."

"Thank you for keeping those photos secret."

"I hope the trust I showed you can be reciprocated."

Edwards pinched his brow with skepticism.

"The favor is not for my benefit, but rather for the James boys. After we secure the Mexican treasure for the Knights of the Golden Circle, they're headed to Mexico."

"Why?"

"To find their father."

Surprised, Edwards accidently yanked the left side of his mustache and yelped. His fleshy face twitched. "He made it to Mexico?"

The Captain was ready to reply and stopped. "What do you mean he made it to Mexico?"

"I knew Robert, the reason he went west, and why he faked his death. He must have arrived after I'd left." He paused and frowned. "Looks like I'm losing the heroes I wanted to depict in my eventual newspaper."

He grinned. "Maybe not. Enter Jesse Mason James and his brother, Hank. They'll assume Jesse and Frank's identities. Make them legends."

The Captain looked at his timepiece and calculated; it should only be a matter of time.

"Why?"

"Jesse and Frank are wanted men, which might compromise the mission to steal the treasure and thus jeopardize the future of the Knights of the Golden Circle. Their father faked his death for the K.G.C. Like father, like sons. Write the cousins up big, and hopefully they'll die quick, and you can make martyrs out of them."

"These two cousins are going along with this?"

"Leave that to us."

Edwards patted his girth like he was thinking about the Captain's steak that would never come. "You can count on me to do my part. I have faith you will do yours."

Edwards reached into his suit jacket, withdrew some papers, and unfolded two maps. His finger pointed at Mexico City and traced north, then slightly east. "This is the expected route the caravan will take. Not the most direct, but one they feel is the safest." His finger dragged over to the Mexican-Texas border. "Here, due east from San Antonio, is the border town of Presidio. Meet the caravan here."

Edwards looked at the Captain to make sure he followed and then slid the maps across the table. "Don't attack right away. The Austrians will be wary, so earn their confidence. Remember, you must ambush them before San Antonio."

"Another reason why I need to be in charge. Be honest. If you were the aristocratic Austrians, and you met Little Archie with human scalps hung from his mount and attire fit for a vagabond, would you trust him?"

"No. Do you think he should even go?"

He faked considering the question. "I suppose so. If things get messy, then Little Archie is fearless and the type of guy you want in those situations. As long as he stays quiet, we'll be okay."

Edwards toyed with his mustache. "Anything else you want to ask me?"

"The photographs of Aberdeen included black women *and* men. If you don't mind me asking, besides pounding plump prostitutes, do you also fancy men?"

Edwards's mouth hung open like a hungry nutcracker. He worked his jaw as though trying to remember how to form words, but gunfire broke the impasse.

Alert, the Captain sprung from his chair.

Edwards ducked under the table.

"Stay," he said, knowing the only way Edwards would move was if he located a safer hiding spot.

The Captain went through the foyer toward the front door, and more gunshots fired. *That could be bad.* He opened the door.

Little Archie crawled on the ground in the middle of the street. Several men stood over him with their guns drawn. Archie cursed at them and tried to reach for his fallen pistol. Another shot fired, and Little Archie went silent—forever.

"Sir, it's Little Archie. I think he's been killed. I'm going. Should something happen to me, get word to Jesse."

Edwards started to say something, but the Captain shut the door behind him.

He strode over to Little Archie's killers. Brewster came closer but stayed back like a bystander. The Captain gesticulated like he was in an argument, but he congratulated the men.

The door of the *Lexington Caucasian* cracked open, and he saw Edwards peek out, so the Captain continued the fake argument.

Loudly, he said, "I'm taking his body back to his family and friends. He deserves a proper funeral."

One of the men shook his head and grunted. "His body is coming with us."

A fake fight ensued. The Captain knocked down several men before one of the fallen rose with a pistol to the Captain's head. The fracas broke up, and he retreated back to the *Lexington Caucasian.*

Little Archie Clement, the tiny turd of terror, was finally dead.

CHAPTER 98

The Captain met with Sergeant Joe Wood, the man assigned to kill Little Archie. His demeanor was as hard as his physique, but a few glasses of whiskey loosened him and his tongue up.

"These Bushwhackers must be eradicated like locusts. They'll ravage our way of life. Thanks to you, we got Bloody Bill and Little Archie. We take out a few more, like the Younger and James brothers, and the problem will go away."

The Captain wanted to protest and point out that the James brothers had been pardoned, but he took another angle. "Are the James brothers next?"

"Yeah, their place is under observation. Only a matter of time."

He wondered if Woods was unaware that Little Archie's death had provided amnesty to the James brothers. "When's the last time you talked to command?"

"Days ago. I was told we had an informant who would provide a time and a place, which turns out to be you." Woods stopped, pursed his lips, and stifled a curse. He shifted and played with his collar in discomfort. "Oh, yeah, you're the guy who made the deal for the James boys. We're not going for them anymore."

The Captain bluffed. "I don't care if you kill them later, but I need them alive a little longer. I have an issue with someone, and they can put me in touch with that person."

Wood mulled over his words. "When do you plan to meet them again?"

374

"In about a week."

"Oh, that must explain why their amnesty had been denied."

The Captain realized he'd been lied to, the agreement a ruse to get Little Archie. He considered Brewster's loyalty, and after his meeting, found Brewster at the inn with an Irish lass named Maggie. Brewster cursed like a drunken pirate when he learned he'd been double-crossed. "I swear fealty to you and the mission."

The Captain believed him.

The next few days passed like swallowed glass. The Captain sat around the *Lexington Caucasian*, desperate and helpless. The James boys were in danger, and yet he couldn't leave until Edwards received the rendezvous date for Maximilian's treasure caravan.

On the fourth day after Little Archie died, the message finally arrived. It was go time. The Captain found Brewster in bed with Maggie. Though he hated to pry apart a tryst, his fear for the James boys superseded his friend's personal pleasures.

After he dressed, Brewster met the Captain outside the inn. "I have a favor to ask."

"Yeah?"

"Can Maggie come with us? I have never been in love like this before."

The Captain did not want to deny his friend's wishes, yet the road ahead was paved with danger.

A pair of Irish puppy eyes implored. "She's a trained contortionist—one in a million. Please?"

"You know the risks we face. The decision is yours."

Minutes later, Maggie saddled up behind Brewster, and they set off.

About a mile from the farm, the Captain held his hand up, and they slowed. He listened as gunfire popped in the distance. The Captain knew the terrain and pulled binoculars from his saddlebag. He told Brewster and Maggie to stay put and then dismounted and went off path, into the woods. He approached from the north, the closest the copse came to the Jameses' farm.

He pulled out his eyepiece and peered through it. Three men protected the road ahead. In four groups of three, men surrounded the house.

The Captain retreated back to Brewster and Maggie and relayed the situation. They hid the horses and discussed a plan.

Maggie said, "What if we disposed of the three men ahead? If we get them and steal their clothes, then you could upset the balance of the attack."

"Stupendous idea, honey, but how do we accomplish that without alerting the other men?" Brewster asked like a general speaking to a private. "Surely they'll see or at least hear our attack."

She snickered and hung her arms down and hunched. "Me, caveman. Attack," she said and spun one of the strawberry blonde locks above her shoulder. "You men think with your groins. Let's use that to our advantage." She told them her idea.

The Captain liked her strategy and decided it was worth a gamble.

"Not on your life," Brewster protested. "We'll think of something else."

She addressed the Captain. "What do you think?"

"I think it's a splendid—" he paused to absorb the glare emitting off Brewster. "Err, a splendid way to jeopardize matters."

Maggie laughed. "You two are funny, but you know I'm right, and your friends don't have time for us to squabble." She began to undo the lace under her neck, which stitched the top of her dress.

"No," Brewster said.

"Shut up, Lord of Love."

The Captain squinted at his companion. "Lord of Love?"

He threw up his hands. "She's crazy."

Maggie smirked. "True, but the nickname came from your lips. Not to mention: the Minister of Midnight Moves, Bishop of the Bedroom, or—my favorite—Captain Cunnilingus."

Brewster shrugged and laughed at himself. "Hey, I wanted to be a captain too."

Maggie backed up two paces and pulled the dress over her head as Brewster groaned to no avail. Nearly naked in undergarments, she handed the dress to the Captain and pointed up. "Throw my dress up on that branch."

The Captain tried not to, but he stole a glance before he jogged away. Maggie's body was marvelous. On the third throw, he hooked the dress on the desired branch and ran back.

"Hide," she ordered. She gave Brewster a quick kiss and ran down the road.

While peering from the bushes, the Captain heard her shriek. In a few minutes, she ran back with the three others.

"There," she said and pointed at her dress. "He threw it up there."

One man said, "You don't suppose this could be a trick?"

"No, everyone in the house is accounted for. She came from the other way. No lady would go this far—"

Brewster whispered, "They obviously don't know Mags."

"She's got big boobs."

He faked a punch in reply. "Am I supposed to say thanks?"

The men walked under the branch but were unable to reach the dress. One man got on another's shoulders. The guy on top said, "Get me a stick, Rick."

Rick scouted the ground and snatched a branch. "Got one."

As soon as he turned, the Captain and Brewster sprung from the shrubbery. The Captain punched the back of Rick's head as he ran by. The man fell, and Brewster stayed with him.

When her coconspirators leapt from the bushes, Maggie shoved the two man totem pole. The low man swayed and almost regained his balanced when she went to his back and pushed again. The driver stumbled, and the passenger was ejected to the ground.

The Captain went to the driver as he got back to his feet and booted him in the gut before following with an uppercut to the face. Good night, his day was over. The next guy began to back away, but three quick punches brought the man down.

None of the clothes fit the Captain, but he managed to get a shirt and coat around him. He looked like a man in kid's attire. The Captain retrieved the horses and stood on Fly Bait. With the stick, he freed Maggie's dress.

After they questioned the remaining conscious men, they gagged and tied their hands behind their backs and around a small tree. Once Maggie dressed, she was given a gun and tasked with guard duty.

Gunfire sounded from the Jameses' farm, and the Captain and Brewster ran.

Chapter 99

The Captain knew the farm better than the men sent to capture or kill the James boys. The men Maggie guarded claimed the man in charge of the siege was an ex-Union soldier named Mark Greyson. He was stationed with two men behind the house and faced the back door. Three other men were at the stable, and three at the front.

The Captain went to the stables first. The men positioned there watched the side house windows, which meant their attention would be forward. He hoped the animals and occasional gunfire would obscure their movements. Out of the woods, he and Brewster crawled through high grass. They avoided the mud pit and went to the right along a wooded rail until they reached the far stable wall. Around the corner, the men were audile.

Brewster's brow creased. "How are we going to get them without causing a ruckus, let alone avoid being shot?"

The Captain arched his brows. "Any chance we can send for Maggie?"

The other man's lips parted into a toothy grin. "I hope we're never in a similar situation, and Susanna is the only gal around."

The Captain told Brewster his primitive plan and then waited until a round of gunfire discharged before he climbed atop Brewster's shoulder. The roof's edge, however, was still out of reach. There was no time for a new plan. Balanced, he leapt as high as he could. His hands found the ledge, and he crawled up the slant and then down the far side of the roof.

He peered downward. Three men pressed against the corner stable wall. One of the men glanced around the corner and nodded. The other two brought their arms around the corner and fired shots through the house window.

The Captain positioned his body, took aim, and fell. His feet struck the far one, his elbow the nearest, but his rear end landed squarely on the middle one's head.

Brewster arrived before the Captain shook off the pain. Two of the men were walked into the stables and gagged. The one whose head was up the Captain's ass had to be dragged in. The Captain and Brewster spoke to the men and explained how they'd been double-crossed on the Little Archie deal.

Brewster pointed at the Captain. "Think about it. This man's father died fighting for the Union at Centralia. He's also responsible for the deaths of Bloody Bill and Little Archie Clement. We are not your enemy."

The Captain reached into his dwindling gold purse. Just as he did with the three men they left with Maggie, he gave each man a gold coin. "I apologize for any pain I caused. You will be set free without further harm."

"How are we going to get those guys in back?" asked Brewster.

"We're not." He took a blue Union service scarf off one man. "I'm going to talk to the man in charge. You stay with these men. That's our leverage. I'll threaten to kill them if he doesn't listen to reason, but even if I'm killed, do not harm these men."

The Captain left the stable and walked toward the back, arms in the air. He called out, "Mark Greyson, my name is Captain Coytus. I'm walking toward you, unarmed. We need to chat."

No reply came, but he did not stop. Two men remained hidden behind a tree, their guns aimed in his direction. One stood in the open, lean and wiry, with a narrow face, poised like a fierce mongoose.

The Captain held his arms over his head and waved the blue scarf as he went forward. "Greyson?"

The man nodded, and his eyes narrowed as he recognized the scarf.

"I already captured your men up the path and in the stable."

"How do I know this to be true and that my men are alive?"

The Captain yelled out, "Brew, fire a shot and then ungag a man and tell him to yell something. Have him sing for us. 'Buffalo Gals' would be nice. I like that one."

A gunshot blasted from the stables. Seconds later, a voice called out, "This is Hal. I was thrown out of church choir, so don't make me sing. We're okay, but Jenkins will be sore for a few days."

The Captain explained the double-cross to Greyson, who listened without interruption. When he finished, Greyson said, "Judging by your actions and your words, I'm inclined to grant your wishes. If I get whiff that this double-cross story is farm fertilizer, I'll be back."

The Captain directed him up the road and then released his men.

Reunited, Brewster, Maggie, and the Captain entered the Jameses' house to thunderous applause. Frank rounded on the Captain with a vise-like hug. Jesse was timid in his approach, still too hurt to entertain any serious body contact.

Someone snaked toward the door. The Captain pushed Frank aside and tackled the passerby into a table, which collapsed as if made from chicken bones.

The Captain felt a rage of unbridled anger as his blows rained down upon the man beneath him. He heard voices begging him to stop, but the pleas registered like muffled cries from the shadows of a dream, until one voice broke through the shroud—a female's. One he recognized, but it was not Maggie or Zerelda. He remembered the sound of her wail from the day he and Jesse rescued her from the rabid dog, King. Mason's sister, Dottie.

The Captain got off of Mason and trudged outside.

CHAPTER 100

The Captain found solace with Fly Bait. The horse tilted his head downward, and his big, brown eyes reflected like still water at dusk. Fly Bait breathed with small hitches like a somber, sleeping child. The Captain patted his muscular neck, and the horse nickered.

Both human and horse jumped in surprise when two gunshots came from the Jameses' home. Mason emerged from the house, ran to the Captain, and stopped fifteen feet away. He leveled the gun. Blood trickled down his forehead and streaked his swollen blotched face like red lightning. His lips protruded like bloody meat cutlets.

All at once, everyone emerged onto the porch. Jesse, Frank, and Brewster aimed their guns at Mason. Zerelda held Hank at gunpoint, and Dr. Samuel did what he did best in a conflict—nothing.

"Don't do anything stupid, Mason, or I swear I'll kill you," Jesse shouted.

The Captain slowly backed away from Fly Bait. Mason had already shown his cruelty to animals when he killed his neighbor's dog. Despite the Captain's plan, Mason would die if he harmed Fly Bait, but he moved back for another reason as well.

Mason had no reason to follow. He had the gun, the great distance equalizer. The Captain needed to be either really close or far away to neutralize the advantage. Unless Mason was a miserable shot, neither approach proved practical. Mason had the gun; he was in charge. He read the Captain's retreat as fear.

The Captain backed up a few more steps and stopped about ten feet from Fly Bait, who tilted his large head at the Captain as if he sensed the danger. Mason shuffled forward, keeping a fifteen-pace distance.

The Captain wondered how far fleas and lice could jump.

"I'm serious," Jesse said as he followed the slow procession away from the farm.

Mason's bloody maw grinned like a lower-planed demon, frightening yet pitiful. "Maybe I don't care if I die," he responded and spat blood to the ground.

Brewster grunted. "Then I'll kill you now."

"No one is killing anyone," shouted Zerelda. "Not on my land."

The Captain took two more paces backward. Like tethered twins, Mason moved, keeping the same equidistance.

"Then I'll wound him and kill his horse."

Just as the Captain had feared. He took four pronounced steps back. *That should do it,* he thought, but this time Mason stayed put. The Captain needed him to move just a tad more and forget about Fly Bait.

"You can't fight me fair. You went after a girl. You're afraid of me," he taunted. "Look at your trembling hand."

Mason took a few steps forward, his lips curled in anger. He swayed the gun from Fly Bait to the Captain. The dirt kicked up as a bullet ricocheted near Mason's dancing feet.

Brewster whistled. "Drop the gun or I drop you."

Mason took one last tentative step, and Fly Bait's right leg kicked back, catching Mason midriff. The gun left Mason's hand and glided skyward as he fell backward and landed with a heavy thud, and heavier groan.

The Captain laughed and looked at Fly Bait, who shook his mane and neighed. "I knew your ninja skills would come in handy one day. I truly must rename you, buddy."

Mason was carried inside and rested on Jesse's old bed. Zerelda's pinched expression showed her displeasure as the sheets soaked up Mason's blood, but she held her tongue. Dr. Samuel examined him and pronounced that—other than some cuts and bruises—the only concern was a probable cracked rib from Fly Bait's mule-like kick. Fortunately, the wound was in the same spot where Jesse's ribs had been injured by the bullet. The Union knew about that injury from Jesse's time in Lexington. After the hoof print faded, the blow would be suitable cover when Mason was killed or captured in the near future.

The Captain did not explain his ability to mesmerize people, because he did not want anyone to connect the dots to his manipulation of Little Archie, so he lied and concocted a ridiculous story, but one he expected them to swallow like sweets.

He opened a saddlebag he had taken off Fly Bait and withdrew two flasks of whiskey mixed with herbs. "You have to trust me from here. These two secret elixirs were crafted by none other than Sir Isaac Newton and the British Royal Society. Newton was an alchemist who tried to create potions that could turn metal to gold or give the drinker eternal life." He shook the flasks. "These will make a man lose his entire memory for up to an hour, and while the mind is a blank slate, I can create new memories and a new identity. Mason and Hank will believe they are Jesse and Frank as long as everyone plays their part."

"Why must you be alone with them?" asked Zerelda.

"The window of supposition is short. The subject must see one face, hear one voice. Trust me—if I wanted Mason dead, I would kill him. This is about your son's future and the biggest treasure heist in world history."

Everyone bobbed their head as if in prayer.

The Captain slapped his hand to his forehead. "Oh, before I begin, I have bad news. Little Archie was murdered."

Frank's and Jesse's eyes bulged. The Captain pulled out the *Lexington Caucasian*.

"There's no writer mentioned, but Edwards wrote this."

He handed the paper to Frank. Zerelda punched her hand in anger. Jesse sat still, expressionless.

"I tried to get the body, but his killers forbade me."

Frank handed the paper to his brother. "I can't read too well."

Jesse's eyes scanned the paper, and his chin drew up. "He resisted arrest, and they killed him. He died an honorable death. Little Archie's a crow. You can't cage a crow unless you clip the wings that make him soar."

The men saluted the life of Little Archie Clement. Zerelda and Dr.

Samuel left to fetch Mason's mother. Maggie, who'd tended to Mason's sister, joined the men and sat alongside Brewster.

The Captain slipped off to start with Hank and held his hands up, nonthreatening. "I just want to talk," he said and took out his timepiece.

In mere seconds, the man's eyes rolled up, underscored by white. His orbs fluttered and centered, like facing morning light.

Even with his patient under hypnosis, the Captain learned nothing. Hank was as deep as a follicle, rooted only by his adulation of Mason, so the Captain planted fake childhood memories and a future that promised misdeeds and a timely funeral.

Mason was another matter. He cursed, and his eyes repeatedly closed in anguish. The friendly approach did not get his attention.

"By the way, did I mention that if you come near my horse from the rear, he has a habit of delivering a brutal back kick? I never fail to warn my friends."

"Eat shit and die."

"You think? From a palate standpoint, it's disgusting. Still, I think the digester would survive the experience. A kid I knew once ate a buffalo chip some boys told him was a beef jerky patty. The only thing he suffered was bad breath, but that's to be expected."

"Fuck yourself and the horse you rode in on."

The Captain gave a thumbs-up. "Now that makes more sense, but a guy can't literally fuck himself, now can he? As for my horse, he doesn't like being approached from the rear, as you may recall."

Mason glared.

"Any other pearls of wisdom?" He had Mason's attention now and arched the timepiece back and forth.

Mason's words came out slow and slurred. "I—I—I'm going to, to kill … kill … kill you one day."

"Follow this gold watch. You feel yourself going into a deep sleep."

Mason's eyes tried to resist, but whether he shut them or looked away, they refocused and shifted back and forth with the pendulum.

Unlike Hank, Mason's mind was not an empty vessel, but more like a pig sty. His thoughts reeked as though a toxic sludge of waste. The Captain learned he liked the taste of his own semen and became aroused whenever his mother breastfed his younger siblings. He appreciated a woman's figure, but he despised them for it and often dreamed of raping and disfiguring any pretty belle he encountered.

The Captain went to work, keeping Mason's ruthless nature intact, but refined it—sort of like the real Jesse James. With Little Archie dead and the war over, it was up to Mason to lead the Bushwhackers, and a new strategy beckoned. Attack the instruments of Yankee interests: banks, railroads, and the leaders who perpetuated the North's cultural infiltration.

Like Hank, Mason was given the necessary childhood background, parents, siblings, and false memories. The injured rib was in truth a gunshot wound suffered months ago.

"Oh, and that swell guy, Captain Coytus? He's your hero."

A grin lighted his face as he brought Mason out but left him in a fugue. His work was done.

Chapter 101

While Mason and Hank slept, the others—Jesse, Frank, Zerelda, Dr. Samuel, Brewster, Maggie, and Hank's mother—gathered in the living room to discuss the plan and the payout. Mason's parents were hardly distraught to lose their two boys. They acknowledged Mason was responsible for the house fire, and their fee was light.

Zerelda and Dr. Samuel were another matter. They agreed to the plan for the sake of their sons, but at the same time, she was losing them, possibly forever. "Money can't replace my boys."

The Captain joked, "We could forgo the compensation," but an icy stare revealed some payoff in fact would do. Everyone believed Mason and Hank would be dead in less than a year, and the Captain paid accordingly.

Hank emerged from the room, and the Captain changed topics. "So how about them Yankees?"

"An evil empire," Zerelda spat with venom. "May the South rise again."

"Who are all these people?" asked Hank.

The Captain answered, "Besides your aunt and cousins, these are friends of mine." He gesticulated. "Meet Rory and Maggie."

Maggie nodded, and Brewster stood and proffered a hand.

Hank took the hand and nodded at the Captain and then back to Brewster. "Any friend of his is a friend of mine. My name is Frank."

Everyone but the Captain gawked at Hank.

Zerelda composed herself and said, "Are you hungry after your nap, son?"

"Famished." He came over to his seated mother. "Mother, do I tell you enough how much I love you?"

"All the time, Frank."

Hank leaned over and gave her a back-thumping hug and then pecked her cheek. "You're the greatest, Ma."

"Thanks, son," Zerelda replied. She peered at the Captain, half-amazed, half-unsettled. "Let me get up and have Charlotte make you something to eat."

Hank backed up and kneeled with his hand extended. "Let me help you off your throne, Queen Mother."

She gazed at the Captain with a slanted brow. "I think you went a bit too far. Any way you can tone the mamma's-boy act down?" She read the Captain's face and frowned. Accepting Hank's helping hand, she rose. Hank kissed her hand before he released it, and Zerelda left the room muttering.

Hank addressed Dr. Samuel next. "Where's Jesse? In bed?"

"Yeah, but he should be better in a few days."

Jesse winked at the Captain and whispered, "He doesn't even notice his mother."

Mason's mother grimaced. "Shush. Let's keep it that way."

Hank took Zerelda's vacated seat.

"Dr. Samuel, we have a long trip ahead of us; may we check on Jesse before we depart?" the Captain requested.

Everyone but Brewster and Maggie went to check on Mason, who was awake but groggy.

"I wanted to say bye before I left," the Captain said.

Mason's eyes blinked away the haze. "Leave? With Little Archie dead, I figured I'd take charge of the gang. I wanted you to be my second-in-command."

The Captain shook his head. "I ride alone."

Hank said, "Can I be your number two?"

Mason shrugged. "I'll think it over and see what comes to pass."

Maggie snickered, which caused Brewster to giggle.

The Captain examined the man who had raped the woman he loved. He hadn't killed Mason but had assuredly scripted his future to end in arrest or death—a fate befitting his crime. Again, he presumed Mason's time was short. Hopefully, Mark Greyson reported back to his command, and his orders to acquire the James boys would be reaffirmed. The only benefit to dragging their capture out several months was knowing Zerelda would go crazy. He wouldn't put it past her to do the deed and kill Mason herself.

The Captain wanted to walk out on the bastard forever. "I'll stop by next time I'm in town."

"Please do," Mason begged. "Can you do me a favor and send for my mother? I had a dream that God told me I don't show her the love and affection she so richly deserves."

He suppressed a grin. "I'll request her immediate presence."

He passed on Mason's request to Zerelda, who cast a meaty finger at him. "I could kill you."

A lie fluttered from his mouth. "My apologies, but I must explain. In my time spent with Frank and Jesse, one thing was a constant—their love and affection for you. They know the hardships you endured, and I tried to instill those memories in Mason and Hank. How that manifests is unpredictable."

Her slow nod indicated reluctant acceptance, and still muttering, she went to Mason.

Brewster gawked. "Remind me to never get on your bad side. The poor woman."

The comment was punctuated by Mason's loud voice. "Mom. I conjured a poem for you!"

> When you're lying by my side,
> Heart is on a bucking stallion ride,
> And every night I close my eyes.
> Thank God, I'm the luckiest guy!
> When they open in the mornin',
> I see you, my angel adoring.
> Every day I pray to the Lord
> That he reattach the umbilical cord.
>
> Oh, Mommy. Mommy, Mommy, Mommy.
> Ohhhhh, Mommy!

A female retched; Zerelda emerged from the room and ran out the front door. From the window, he saw her vomit over the porch railing.

Brewster whispered, "You wrote that song, didn't you?"

With a wink, he quipped, "I'm miffed she didn't get to hear the second and third verses."

CHAPTER 102

Like the vanguard of a small flock of migrating birds, the Captain rode up front alone. Behind, Brewster and Maggie rode side by side, trailed by the real Jesse and Frank.

Brewster and Maggie flirted with each other while Jesse and Frank remained quiet, lost in the pain of separation from their mother, while thinking ahead to the gold heist and being reunited with their father.

The Captain tried not to think about Mason, but he did. He patted Fly Bait once more, as he'd done every so often, for his heroics. More than once, he said, "You might have saved me from taking a bullet."

In honor of the deed, he kicked about a few replacement names for the heroic stallion, but nothing seemed appropriate. As they got closer to Booneville, he only thought about Susanna, and the memories of the first time he saw her flooded him and refreshed his demeanor.

In the shadowy dawn, the outline of a church appeared—the place where he had met Susanna on their first date. The absence of her pained him, but he reminded himself that she was what he fought for.

"There's the saloon where we first met," Frank called out. "Last time I was here, we celebrated a Confederate victory. Seems so long ago."

They entered the saloon. The corner table where once Frank, Little Archie, and Edwards sat was occupied—the same table where he learned who'd killed his father. He viewed the corner where he once played guitar and sang for the patrons. Between stood the table where Frank had crashed into Badger Bob. It did seem a long time ago.

Brewster's men were easy to spot along the back wall. The Captain walked over but was intercepted by Katherine—ex-sheriff's wife, ex-lover.

She grabbed his arm, and life vacated her body like she'd touched a wraith. Color drained from her face, and her posture slumped into him. "He's back," she murmured. "He came back yesterday."

"Your husband?"

"Please don't utter that word. I got so used to thinking I'd never see him again." She still gripped his forearm. "Things didn't go well for him in Massachusetts. He was greeted with open arms, meaning surrounded at gunpoint. They chained his leg to a post and made him live in a pigpen. He ate with them, slept with them, probably had sex with them, being the swine he is. He claimed he will hunt to the ends of the earth to find you."

The Captain laughed. Seemed his friends back east had shown the sheriff worse hospitality than he'd requested.

Her eyes fluttered. "Thing is, I just met a man I adore. He's brought me flowers and chocolates, all so fragrant and sweet. He's leaving town soon but said he'd come back for me." She bit her lip and frowned. "Doesn't matter now."

The Captain tilted his head toward the back of the saloon. "Is the man you met here right now?"

Her dimples creased. "Yes?"

"Would you like to join your new Romeo on this journey?"

She went to speak but shook away whatever she wanted to say. "How can I?"

"Easy. I'm riding with those men. We leave at dawn. There's already another belle with us." He pointed toward Maggie.

"What about my husband?"

"I'll save him the labor of traveling the ends of the earth looking for me. I'm going to pay him a visit. You go home and get a good night's rest. See you in the morning."

He went to the bar and tipped for a few wash rags and a rope coil. "Any chance you have an apple?" Smiling, he left the saloon and strode to the place where he actually held his first legitimate job—even if the means to be anointed sheriff proved illegitimate. Around back, he found one of the stakes he'd made in preparation for his showdown with the men who had murdered Susanna's father.

The Captain burst into the jailhouse like a tornado. The sheriff sat in his favorite chair with his legs propped on his desk. The Captain breezed over, grabbed the sheriff's ankles, and pulled them over his startled, seated figure. The chair tipped and crashed on top of the screaming sheriff.

The Captain looked over toward the near wall. "Hello."

Deputy Less shook his head and grinned.

"Arrest him," groaned the sheriff.

He pulled the chair off the sheriff. "As crooked and decayed as your teeth are, you still have a bite. That won't do." And he swatted away the sheriff's protective hands before grabbing him by the back of the head and taking a well-aimed power punch to the sheriff's mouth. A crack reverberated through the room, and the sheriff gagged and spat what sounded like pebbles to the stone floor.

The front upper teeth were either missing or jagged remnants. Satisfied, the Captain shoved the apple in the sheriff's mouth and tied the rag around the fruit. He bound the sheriff's hands behind his back and his feet together.

"What are you going to do?" asked Deputy Less.

"A pig roast," replied the Captain. He grabbed the stake and slid the wood on the cross beam of the cell door across to a shackle bracket on the far wall. Then he went back to the sheriff, who was significantly thinner since his travels east. Either pig feed was an improvement to his diet or the faster, smarter pigs left him only crumbs.

The Captain carried the sheriff into the cell and held his body on the stake. He wrapped rope around the torso and snaked it up to his head and then back to the feet before he stepped back and admired his work. "A fitting end. Why do you think my friends made you live like a pig? Now I have to get some kindling." He motioned for Deputy Less to follow him.

"I have a new job offer for you, Deputy Less." The Captain told him about the mission to Mexico. "So how about leaving this dump and joining us?"

"My wife is half-Mexican, and she is bored of Booneville."

"This place is as stimulating as conversing with a mime. Do you blame her?"

Deputy Less shook his head.

His brow lifted. "Can you do me a favor? Locate that ski nut, Ingemar Skidmark. Also, please ask the sheriff's wife if she can find the Viking helmet the sheriff wore on All Hallow's Eve."

Deputy Less smiled and left.

The Captain returned to the jailhouse with some cut wood, stacked a few logs under the sheriff, and crumpled the *Lexington Caucasian* in the center. "Now I just need my flint."

Despite the apple lodged in his mouth, the sheriff moaned with a desperate fear, like a basset hound that had picked up the scent of a bear instead of a dead grouse. His red, moist eyes drooped at the corners. Sweat beaded on his forehead, and gravity rained droplets to the stone floor.

The Captain strode over to the desk and slid the sheriff's favorite chair over. He eyed the chair and then the sheriff. "May I?"

Not that it mattered, but the sheriff nodded.

The Captain sat and shifted about. "Hmm, this chair doesn't support my back properly." He vacated the seat and held the chair's arms and pushed at the back. "If I could just get—oops." The wood back snapped from the seat of the chair, and the Captain tossed the broken piece to the side. "Guess I'll just stand."

He leaned against the bars, his right foot crossed over the left and rested on the toe end. "A rumor's floating around town that you're going to kill me."

The sheriff shook his head. "Wah, wah, wahhhh."

"I think you're lying to me. You did want to kill me, didn't you?"

"Wah."

"That's what I thought. Yet things have changed, haven't they?"

"Wah."

"Indeed. And now you want my mercy?"

"Wah!"

"Do you know why I dispatched you to Massachusetts to live like a pig, only to come back and be roasted like one?"

"Wah?"

"When I lived in England, a corrupt cop worked the wharfs. Everyone in London knew he was dirty, on the graft. His plump cheeks, pointy ears, and upturned nose combined with his greasy groveling earned him the moniker Pig. You're his American counterpart." The Captain kneeled and struck his flint a few times near the newspaper.

"Wah! Wah! Wah!"

"Really? You knew who killed Susanna's father and did nothing. I had to clean up the mess, you filthy pig." He struck the flint again.

"Wahhhhhhhhhhhhhhhh!"

CHAPTER 103

Dawn of a new day, and the Captain stood in front of the jailhouse.

The sun hid behind hills that glowed orange like they were ablaze with holy fire. Bats flew overhead, returning to their lair for a daylight snooze. A large crowd gathered in the town center.

The Captain spotted Katherine and handed her a piece of parchment. "Your husband wrote a letter, which was ratified by the minister. The declaration confesses to his infidelity and abuse. This constitutes legal separation from him."

"Infidelity? Him? I was the unfaithful one."

"The devil is in the details. Your husband confessed to sins that would make Satan blush."

Her eyes circled like pinwheels powered by the hot air. "Where is he now?"

"He's tied up at the moment."

"Did you hurt him?"

"Like a baby, he'll need to eat soft foods for the rest of his life."

Katherine's eyes narrowed. "Why did you want the Viking helmet?"

"Ingemar Skidmark is with him. I wanted to make sure your husband gets the tender loving care he deserves."

A man walked over and put his arm around Katherine. He extended his hand. "You must be Captain Coytus," he said with an off-the-boat Italian accent. He sported dark, wavy hair so abundant that it looked fertilized. "My name is Antonio Natoli."

The Captain took Natoli's hand. "*Paisan*, marry this madonna. She'll explain," he said and left the two alone.

Brewster chatted with a stout man whose belly was as big as his beard. A cunning sparkle lit the man's eyes, and Brewster introduced Atticus Huth.

Huth spoke to Brewster. "So *this* is the guy who could handle the Huth, eh? By the size of him, I reckon you're right. Perhaps, when I was a younger man," he said with a reminiscing laugh as if a good scrap was something he enjoyed like the English fancied tea.

The Captain and Huth shook hands. Both men gripped the other, and when Huth squeezed, he squeezed harder. Huth released the tension first and laughed. "Strong as an ox."

"We leave in fifteen minutes," the Captain said with some sorrow. He had hoped for one late arrival. "I have to talk to someone."

Deputy Less and a woman—presumably his wife—talked with Jesse, Frank, and two lads the Captain did not recognize. He had forgotten the deputy and Jesse had met back when Jesse had rescued Susanna.

"You must be the lovely Mrs. Less," the Captain said and took her hand to his lips.

"Carla," she purred. "Thanks for the invitation. I've always wanted to go to Mexico."

The Captain pointed to Brewster and Maggie, and then to Natoli and Katherine. "Ride next to them. Maggie and Katherine would enjoy the female camaraderie."

Next up on the introduction tour came the lads. Frank gesticulated at the two strangers. "This is Wood Hite and my cousin, Dick Liddil."

"Is this a joke?" asked the Captain.

His brow creased. "Huh?"

"No offense," the Captain said to the shorter man with the rounder face, "but really? Dick Little?" He snickered. "Good luck with the ladies with that advert." Then he nodded to the other guy with the long, clean face. "Wood Height, on the other hand, sounds like a guy who's packing some lumber. With a name like that, you're bound to do better with women than short stub over here."

Wood Hite laughed. No one else did. "You might be onto something. I get all the girls, and poor Dick's a virgin."

The Captain nodded at the affirmation. "Must be tough having a small whizzer. Perhaps they have group therapy where you can get the moral support you need. Like, Short Cocks Anonymous or something." The Captain giggled through his last few words. No one joined in the hilarity, not even Frank.

"The names are Liddil and Hite," Frank said, and spelled them out.

He still found the whole thing funny. Being as no one else did, he asked, "You boys coming along?"

They both shook their heads, but Jesse answered. "They're sticking around to keep tabs on Mason and Hank—possibly identify their bodies at some point. Hopefully soon for my poor mother's sake."

The Captain saw recognition in the James boys' eyes as they looked past him.

"What are you doing here?" Frank said. "You can't leave Ma."

The Captain turned and grinned. Charlotte and her daughter, Elizabeth, walked over.

"I'm not," Charlotte said. "But she is, though it breaks my heart. With you boys leaving and slavery ending, your parents can't run the farm and feed her. I want a better life for her. God willing, we'll see each other in time."

The Captain had hoped Charlotte would join them too. The mission was dangerous, and watching a young girl separated from her mother could be a burden, but Elizabeth had grown up in a time where she knew only war and cruelty. She appeared too grown up for her age, so he figured she'd handle it. She had to.

"Before you take her, my daughter has a confession to make. Something she did wrong, and she needs to expel the guilt."

Elizabeth's lip trembled, but she held her posture and gaze. "Jesse, I owe you an apology."

His brow pinched together, and a crease formed above his nose. "How so?"

"I was the one who put the beehive in the privy hole."

He jumped up like he was relieving bees stinging his backside. "You? Why?"

"The hive was meant for Dr. Samuel. He always wakes up first and visits the outhouse. That was the only day you ever beat him there."

Jesse gave a wry smile. "I woke up sick."

Charlotte prodded her daughter. "Tell them."

For the first time, Elizabeth's stare wavered, and her voice came out like fractured glass. "He touched me in ways he should not have."

"I want her out of that house," Charlotte said with defiance.

"Bull," Jesse said.

"Is it now, Jesse?" probed the Captain, and he eyed Frank. "You viewed the photographs of the owner of the *Lexington Caucasian*, Aberdeen. I told you we were sent other pictures as well. One was your father, Dr. Samuel."

Frank nodded. "I believe you. He's not my real father, anyway."

Jesse nodded. "My own mother told me he's not interested in sex. Their marriage was for convenience and stability, not love or passion."

"I think he found other outlets. Pedophilia peccadilloes," said the Captain.

Jesse nodded once more and smiled at Elizabeth. "I'm not mad at you. Shame your plan didn't work out though. He deserved the pain and humiliation." He winced, cast an awkward grin, and laughed. "I thought they'd be plucking stingers out of my butt forevermore."

Everyone chortled, including Elizabeth.

"We'll watch over her," he promised.

"I know you will," Charlotte said. She hugged the men good-bye and took her daughter aside. The Captain heard them both cry and proclaim their love for each other. He still wished Charlotte would join them, but he knew her reasons. Such a decision had to be hard on both of them.

CHAPTER 104

The road was hard.

The Captain had hoped so, as muddy trails made travel difficult. Their caravan was jubilant, all twenty-one men, three women, and two youths, as Katherine brought her son along. Stories, pranks, jokes—Frank recanted the Foo-Foo bird saga—singing, dancing, guitar picking, card playing, juggling, hearty meals, and hard liquor passed the time.

They started in wooded lands, came to stunted trees, to sparse brush, and then cactus—something most of the caravan had never seen, whereupon came the first injury since their journey commenced. Frank, under the influence of whiskey and his drunken brother, decided to hug a cactus.

"Ouch!" he screamed, and ran back wincing, but laughed the incident off … until the next morning when he sobered up. "Son-of-a-backwoods-bitch ballocks-bastard," he wailed in pain.

He walked back to the offending cactus, cussed it out, pulled out his gun, shot the cactus a few times, and limped back.

Everyone laughed until he revealed the red and inflamed puncture wounds. The Captain poured whiskey on the ailment, and the caravan moved on.

Cheers erupted when Huth announced that Presidio was a few miles ahead. They skirted the town from the west and set up camp near the Mexican border. Now they just had to wait.

The Captain pulled Frank and Jesse aside. "We need to talk." He led them near, but not too close, to a cactus. "I have a confession. You'll probably be angry, but now's the time to come clean."

Jesse glowered. "If you lied about my father …"

The Captain stopped him with raised hands. "I assure you I told the truth about your father. My deceit is with Maximilian's treasure. The booty is not going to the Knights of the Golden Circle."

"What?" both brothers said.

"Sorry, boys, but the Confederate South is not going to rise again. The men with us, and some others waiting in Mexico, will split half of the loot. The rest is to be divided evenly among us three. Thus, you both will receive a sizable portion of treasure. If you want to throw your share down the Confederate well-to-hell, God bless, but we're going to be living in Mexico, at least for a while. We might as well live like kings. I hope you agree, and we can remain friends forever, but I understand if not. I did lie."

As usual, Frank was an easy read. Jesse's face was as blank as a cloudless sky.

"The Knights of the Golden Circle, who?" Frank deadpanned with a wide grin.

Jesse stood impassively as his brother endorsed the plan. He blinked once and spat on the ground. "When the war got rough, we stayed and fought. The Confederate generals and their army flocked to Mexico like doves in defeat. They long ago abandoned the cause, and you know what? So have I."

Jesse walked closer to the Captain, and his tight face unbuckled. "You've been right all along. I see it every day in Elizabeth—the way she looks out at the world with hope and promise. She's smart, funny, and sweet as a sugarloaf. She told me she'd teach me piano to make up for the pain my butt endured from those bee stings," he said and laughed. "My brother is right. Fuck the Knights of the Golden Circle. They got more than they deserved from us Bushwhackers."

On the seventh day, the Captain finished no work and rested siesta style. He lay in the only available shade, under his wagon. Four days had bypassed the rendezvous date, but the mood was still chipper. The biggest laugh came when someone decorated a cactus with clothes and then told Frank it was a friend in need of a hug.

The Captain appreciated the solitude. Being responsible did not give him much time to dwell on his separation from Susanna, which he supposed was a partial blessing, but here and now, he conjured her face in his mind's eye. He imagined conversation, intimacy, and her soft sleeping breaths.

He lapsed into a blissful sleep but woke to the sound of shots.

"Over here!" Huth shouted.

The Captain rolled out from under the wagon and followed the man's gaze south. In the haze, dust kicked up in the sunlight, blurring the shape of an approaching caravan.

Huth walked over. "You ready?"

He saddled up Fly Bait and along with Huth, Brewster, and the James boys, they went out to meet the approaching caravan comprised of fifteen wagons. Even from a distance, the distinction between the Mexicans and Austrians was apparent. About ten men wore loose-fitting ponchos. A few, including two in the front, wore blue jackets with some fancy embroidery, reminding the Captain of fine dinner linen. A red sash covered the waist, and blue pantaloons with silver stripes covered the legs. On each head sat a red cap, but only one man had an attachment that hung off one side. It looked like the tail of a horse's ass.

The caravan slowed as the welcoming party arrived. They appeared haggard, like men who had forfeited sleep and sustenance to realize their mission. The Captain introduced himself.

"The name is Coytus. Captain Coytus." He gestured behind him. "These are my men who will protect you. We have abundant water and food supplies at our camp."

Almost all their faces swept with relief. The guy with the horse tail—which was actually a silly golden frond—remained stern, hand on his rifle.

"*Ich bin Otto Kriegsmann.* I am in charge of this mission and will remain in charge. *Das ist verstanden, ja?*"

The Captain replied. "*Sehr gut, Herr Kriegsmann.*"

Kriegsmann slowly shook his head back and forth. "You Americans, so lawless that rank escapes you. Not *Herr Kriegsmann.* I am *Zugsfuhrer Kriegsmann.* I lead the caravan."

"Excuse me, Master Corporal. We Americans are ignorant on

landlocked, second-rate empires that don't pose a threat to the United States."

The other man stiffened further, which seemed impossible.

The Captain reversed course and exchanged pleasantries, but Kriegsmann did not pick up the conversation. He barked out orders, and the caravan moved toward the camp.

With the caravan in camp, Kriegsmann, for the first time, seemed eager to chat. He pointed to Maggie, Katherine, Carla, and Elizabeth. *"Was ist das? Ist das drei fraulien und a schwartze kinder?"*

"That's no mirage, Zugsfuhrer. Yes, three women and a child. You might be surprised to guess that none of the women is her mother."

Kriegsmann ignored the last comment. "Ah, concubines for the voyage. Good. As leader, I might use them."

"Sir, one is married, and her husband is here. The other two are attached to men on this mission, and the black child, as you called her, is a juvenile we're taking care of."

"So the child is unattached?"

"She's a *child*," he admonished. "Too young for her first kiss."

Kriegsmann puckered up. "She has to learn someday."

He made a fist. "You'll kiss these knuckles first."

Kriegsmann took a step back. *"Ich bein der fuhrer, hier."*

Despite the threat behind Kriegsmann's words, he stood tall. "Our Confederate liaison told us to escort you, not provide prostitution services. You can find all the women you need in San Antonio."

Kriegsmann's broad shoulders filled out his military jacket, which looked more suitable for a dinner party—whether guest or waiter, the Captain was unsure. He rubbed his peppered gray chin. *"Sehr gut!"* ("Very good," but his tone sounded like he'd said, *"Sehr schlect,"* "Very bad").

"What do you have in those wagons?"

"Flour," answered Kriegsmann. He may have been a fine military strategist, but apparently his ordered mind was not regimented in the art of bullshit.

The Captain repealed his smile. "Flour? Are you fucking kidding me? We rode all this way to escort a portable French bakery?"

Kriegsmann frowned and bit his lip. "This *ist* special flour."

Mouth open, the Captain nodded. "You have that magic flour that has the power to make bread that never stales and for some reason makes woman incredibly horny?"

Kriegsmann nodded back and grinned. "*Ja, voll.*"

The Captain matched the other man's grin. "I made that up."

Kriegsmann cursed under his breath.

He gestured at Katherine. "She makes cakes, pastries, and other fine baked goods. How about you toss us some flour and let her bake us a big ole cake."

"*Nein.*"

"Nine cakes might be a good idea. We have a lot of mouths to feed."

Kriegsmann tightened his grip on his rifle, as though he thought about using it. "We have no time for cakes."

"How about a few muffins then?"

"*Nein.*" Kriegsmann cursed. "That is *no*," he added to ensure there was no misunderstanding.

"A cupcake?"

"*Macht schnell.* Get your men ready."

CHAPTER 105

"Your turn," the Captain said to Huth.

The big man let a hearty chuckle rip. "How about I tell Kriegsmann I crapped in my trousers and hoped to use the privacy of their wagons, since women occupy ours?"

Brewster laughed. "Brilliant."

The Captain snickered. "I suspect the tight-ass Zugsfuhrer will prove unsympathetic."

The men kept their pace, and Huth drifted back. The men had been taking turns to find ways to get near the wagons. Not because they wanted to confirm the wagons' contents, but to get a chuckle out of watching Kriegsmann squirm.

The Captain went first, telling Kriegsmann he wanted to brush up on his Spanish and asked to chat with one of the Mexicans.

Request denied. "You can ask them anything you want in San Antonio," Kriegsmann ably deflected.

"Would it be permissible to ask them the secret to good guacamole? I'm dying to know," he said.

"Later," snapped Kriegsmann.

Frank went next. He fell back and told Kriegsmann he wanted to chat for a moment. Frank gushed how much he loved Kriegsmann's homeland and claimed he felt the Zugsfuhrer began to warm to him. The goodwill ended when Frank started to ask about kangaroos. "Kangaroos live in Australia. I'm from Austria, *dummkopf*," spat Kriegsmann.

"Are there koala bears in Austria, or is that Australia too?"

Kriegsmann glared. "Australia, *Arschloch*!"

"Oh, forget it then. No wonder you left your country. Austria's boring," Frank had said and left a fuming pack of Austrians.

Brewster told Kriegsmann he worked as the traveling priest, on-hand to bless the mission. Tomorrow happened to be Sunday, and he hoped to perform Holy Communion. If only he had flour to make the proper sacrament, God willing.

Kriegsmann's mouth parted in glee, and he reached into his saddlebag and came out with a loaf of bread. "Here you go, Father."

Brewster crossed himself. "We are consuming the body of Christ, not your lunch."

Kriegsmann's shoulders momentarily eased before he feebly told Brewster he would try to get him some flour when they set camp at nightfall.

Jesse went last and told Kriegsmann he was a wainwright by trade and hoped to inspect the wagons as a professional curiosity. "They're different than the Murphy and Prairie wagons I build."

Kriegsmann looked to the cloudless sky, but the sun leveled his vision. "We are moving now and have no time for delays. You can inspect the wagons in San Antonio." He glared. "Tell your friends that unless the matter is urgent, the next man to come back here will be shot."

The Austrians did not shoot Huth, but his urgent request to change his soiled trousers had been rebuffed. The men laughed when he told them Kriegsmann's response was simple and curt.

"Tough shit."

A female whistled. "Lord of Love, I'd like to ask you something."

Brewster smiled sheepishly and fell back in line. Minutes later, he reappeared with Maggie.

She said, "The Austrian said the next man would be shot unless the matter is urgent. You tried urgent, but you haven't tried a woman yet."

"What if he agrees?" groaned Brewster.

The men agreed to keep a watchful eye on the proceedings as Maggie drifted back to the Austrians.

"Rumor has it, you want to fuck me," she said boldly and loudly.

Kriegsmann flinched. "Who said such nonsense?"

Her hand went to her jutted hip. "The Captain. If you're not man enough to admit your desires, you're not man enough to please me. Bye." She prodded her horse forward.

He called out to her. "My apologies, Fraulein. He said you were attached, and I am a gentleman."

She scoffed. "I'm not married yet. Maybe I'm looking for a better lover." And she swept her hand across her midriff as her tongue circled her lips.

Kriegsmann patted his jacket over his heart. "I can assure you, I am. In San Antonio, I will show you what a real man is."

Red hair bounced as she shook her head. "He plans to propose to me tonight. If you want to be my savior and convince me, you need to show me what you can do *now*. Let's hop in the back of one of those wagons." She flashed a coquettish smile. "Trust me, I'm worth it."

Kriegsmann stammered and spat words Maggie did not understand, but she ventured it was not the Germanic version of "O' Tannenbaum."

So she raised her hand and twirled a finger. "I changed my mind. You're too stiff, except where it counts."

Laughing, she raced back to the front of the caravan and recounted her exchange with Kriegsmann, causing her audience to erupt in belly-bursting laughter.

The Captain spied the ravine ahead. The settling sun glowed orange beyond the peaked ridge. "Okay, men, get ready."

The trail became an old, dried-up river bed that snaked through a gulch for about a mile. Halfway through the arroyo, boulders crashed ahead of the caravan. While easily passable on horseback, the wagons' forward progress was effectively blocked. Indians appeared on both sides above them.

"Fall in, and circle the wagons," screamed the Captain.

Kriegsmann yelled, "I am the Zugsfuhrer! I issue commands." No one stopped to listen. "Gather behind the wagons!"

The men all bunched together. The Captain position himself behind Kriegsmann, the rest of his men near each Austrian. He nodded and grabbed the back of Kriegsmann's head and violently twisted it as gunshots drowned out the sound of a snapped neck. In a matter of seconds, every

Austrian soldier was dead. The men then surrounded the stunned Mexicans. They took their weapons but assured them no harm would come to them.

The Captain waved up to the Indians. "Thank you."

A short, stout Indian in a feathered headdress came to the edge of the ravine wall. "White Spider of the Night, we will make sure you have safe passage to the Mexican border."

The Osage Indian chief had told the Captain his daughter had married into a southern tribe. Like marriages between royal families to broker alliances, Indian elders gathered to find ways to unify against a new common enemy—the encroachment of the white man. The Captain had made an arrangement with the eastern Pueblos. For a few gold coins, guns, and pouches of tobacco, they agreed to assist his caravan. For the Pueblos, it was a win-win; namely, some white men would die, and the rest would leave the country.

He approached the Mexicans. "Do you men know what's in these wagons?"

The Mexicans exchanged glances among themselves. One spoke up. "We were told Maximilian's belongings."

"You were lied to. The wagons hold treasure—some personal, some accumulated from plunder." He eyed each man. "He also smuggled out artifacts sacred to the land of Mexico."

"*Mios Dios,*" the man said. His comrades spoke quickly to each other. "Señor, we know nothing of this. I swear. If we knew, we would have killed the Austrians ourselves."

That was what the Captain had hoped to hear. "We're headed to Mexico to return what Maximilian stole from your people. His personal belongings are now ours. If you help escort us through your country, we'll make sure you're rewarded for it. You boys okay with that?"

A chorus met him. "*Si, señor. Si, si, si!*"

The caravan returned the way they'd come.

CHAPTER 106

Blue water peeked out between rocky hills dotted with palms, cactus, and exotic flowered shrubbery. The cool breeze flowing off the ocean rejuvenated the weary travelers. "Viva Mexico," the men sang.

The caravan neared the border of Los Cabos.

So close.

The final words spoken by Emperor Maximilian were, "Viva Mexico." Once Napoleon III pulled the French troops out, he could not fight off the rebellion and was captured and executed by a firing squad.

Two of the Mexicans stuck with the Captain's party to act as guides. The rest took three wagons and returned treasure native to Mexico, including Mayan and Incan gold artifacts, to the new president, Benito Juarez.

Rich in money and beauty, the caravan almost floated the last few miles. Curious, Elizabeth looked about and squealed with glee at her destination. The Captain held his arms around her aboard Fly Bait.

Brewster and Maggie planned an immediate marriage. They flirted so much that several of Huth's men carried the couple to the Captain's empty wagon and demanded they get some of the love out of their system.

The James boys were elated with the prospect of seeing their father, who for years they had believed dead. They discussed their anticipation with questions, such as, "What's the first thing you're going to say to Pa?"

Deputy Less and his wife, Carla, seemed reinvigorated from the monotonous mold their life had been cast into. They talked about all the things they wanted to do, none of which involved chores and sitting around the house like drab furniture.

With Maximilian's cache, the Captain became one of the richest men in all of the Americas. The newfound wealth was a boon, but he had different booty on his mind; one more glorious than gold, with a sparkle that outshined any precious gem—Susanna.

The caravan came around a bend, where merchants gathered. They all bore friendly smiles and gestured at their goods: strange fruit-filled wicker baskets, as well as tables and poles with ponchos, sombreros, and color blankets. Elizabeth became excited at a table displaying beaded jewelry and seashells. The Captain bought her a necklace of aqua blue stones. For himself, he sampled some tequila he found to his liking and purchased all ten bottles in stock. For Susanna, he purchased a shell. In his pocket, he fingered a necklace he'd taken from the inventoried wagons when they determined what should be rightfully returned to the Mexican people.

After a short respite, the caravan moved on, encouraged by news that a new settlement of Americans lay just down the road. The Captain got the caravan to sing "Oh, Susanna" when the outpost appeared ahead. In response, two hounds barked a duet.

A man atop a wall surrounding the compound called out, "Open the gate! They're here!"

Two large wood doors swung open, and two dogs burst from the gate. They pranced about with excitement and then zeroed in on the Captain; they charged. He dismounted with Elizabeth and was besieged by sloppy licks from Ryan and Rex, who battled for his face.

Elizabeth laughed, and Rex jumped on her with a wet kiss. The Captain walked Fly Bait through the open gate to cheers. People raced from their homes to greet the new arrivals. The caravan stopped in a courtyard in the center of a small village. The Captain recognized several faces, some of whom had protected their home in the harsh winter.

Like being guided by a divine vision, his eyes followed intense brightness to Susanna. She ran toward him, her arms stretched wide. Her checkered dress fanned up behind her tailwind. With the two German shepherds at his heals, he sprinted to meet her. Susanna jumped in the air, and he caught her against his chest. He kissed her as he twirled in a circle.

He wanted to tell her how much he missed and loved her, but the kiss spoke for the both of them.

Their courtyard courtship ended when Ryan growled and Rex bit the bottom of his trousers. He returned Susanna to the ground. The two dogs stopped their aggression, sat, tongues out, tails wagging.

She chuckled. "They've become quite protective of me. They don't let anyone get too close to me."

"Err, where do they sleep?"

"On either side of me."

He leaned down and patted his two beasts. "The big alpha dog is back." He took her in his arms again. Rex yelped, but they settled down when her sweet voice reassured them. They sat with their tongue dangling out of toothy grins.

Susanna's mother appeared with a tray of warm biscuits. She handed the platter to her daughter and opened her arms to the Captain. "You made it," she said and hugged him. She took the tray back.

He looked into Susanna's eyes. "Would it be funny if I confessed I founded my own harem but hope you'll join our merry crew?" He accepted one of the biscuits.

Her mother giggled.

"Would it be funny if I lifted my sharp, bony knee into your crotch?"

"No, I like my prank better," he said with an impish grin. "The last thing I want to do is leave you, but I must." He explained the immediate need to secure and divide Maximilian's hoard. Then he told her about the daughter they'd adopted. He didn't ask Susanna's permission; he knew she would accept unequivocally. "You are going to adore Elizabeth."

Susanna had an idea and explained it to him. "Have some of your friends put her gift in the living room while we have dinner on the beach."

"Let me introduce you to her first."

The Captain jogged over, with Ryan and Rex, to Elizabeth and lifted her high onto his shoulders. He ran back to Susanna, and Elizabeth giggled as she used her hands to blindfold him. Although he could see well enough through her small fingers, he meandered about with his hands, as though feeling the way in front of him. Her giggle became full-throated laughter.

"You better not drop her," Susanna said with the caution of a mother.

Elizabeth, at the helm of the ship, gave directions until they navigated back to Susanna. The Captain brought her down with the speed and fluttering trajectory of a fallen leaf. Susanna hunched down to meet her at eye level.

Elizabeth did not waver with timid trepidation and gave Susanna a wide smile. "You're even more beautiful than he boasted."

"I love her already," she said and opened her arms. "Come here, cutie." Elizabeth stepped into a warm embrace.

"The men have some things to do. How about I show you our home and your new room? Then we'll cook a meal, and the three of us will have dinner at the beach, watching the sunset."

Elizabeth backed up with a grin that made the whole world seem a better place. "Can they come too?" she asked and pointed at the dogs.

"They can come, but watch your dinner," Susanna warned. "Those two are sneaky devils when it comes to food. One will charm you while the other makes off with your meal."

The little girl's grin turned upside-down. Her voice came out soft. "That's all right. I understand them: how to live off scraps, how it feels to be punished but remain loyal and attentive to my masters."

The Captain went to speak, but Susanna's mother responded first. "Honey, those two dogs are her best friends and are treated like royalty."

Susanna smiled in acknowledgment and offered her hand to Elizabeth. "You will be our princess."

Elizabeth's smile returned. "I know." She gesticulated at the Captain. "He treats me great and always makes me laugh. He's so funny."

Susanna rolled her eyes. "My girl, I hope over time you realize that encouraging his warped sense of humor is not necessarily a good thing." She gave the girl a smile to let her know it was all a big joke.

Well, sort of.

CHAPTER 107

"Y̶ou've waited over ten years to see your father, and you can wait another day. We have to divide the loot, and you two are getting a large share. You need to be there," the Captain told the James brothers.

Jesse nodded like he agreed, but he ultimately disagreed. "It's only been months since you last saw Susanna. Would you wait another day or trust us to divide your portion?"

He could not deny his companion's point. Thus, he replied, "I'd wait a month before I'd let two villains, wanted by the state of Missouri for unspeakable crimes, divide a deck of cards behind my back."

Frank's eyes dragged downward. "Gee, that hurts. I thought we were friends."

"He's jesting, and even if he wasn't, we'd still trust you to be honorable in our absence," Jesse said.

"I will. If everything goes well, bring your father back for the party tonight."

"Dad's a minister. He doesn't drink," Jesse stated.

The Captain fixed his hand like he held a mug and raised and tilted the imaginary beverage to his open mouth. "More for me then."

He wished both brothers well and went to Brewster's new home. The wagons were parked out front. In attendance were Brewster, Huth, and two of the lads—McEntee and Demayo—who had guarded the Missouri home when Mason had been on the prowl.

The Captain realized it had been the first time he thought of Mason in a long while. By now, his nemesis surely was in jail or dead. They planned to send correspondence north to Zerelda to let her know the boys were safe as well as check up on Mason and Hank.

The Captain explained the James boys' absence. No one complained, nor did anyone give a hint that they should be disadvantaged. While they had given the wagons a cursory examination, they intended to chronicle every item, down to a gold thimble they had found in an ornate box.

Five hours later, the men stopped and marveled at what they had uncovered. The entire first floor was coated with loot, including every flat surface available: tables, seats, shelves, and beds. A pathway snaked through Brewster's home from the front to the back door.

The inventory included gold and silver bars, as well as coins from many countries, including Spanish doubloons, British sovereigns, and Austrian Maria Theresa Thalers. The value of the coinage cache alone was larger than most North American banks held.

One wagon was filled with enough swords, bucklers, and helmets decorated with gold and precious gems to arm a band of crusaders. A plush velvet box held two jewel-encrusted gold crowns. Another styled box, rectangular, held a scepter and orb. The Captain wanted to request the scepter and orb and perhaps a crown. He envisioned himself tormenting Susanna as the king of their castle.

Satchels, likely filled in haste, contained every imaginable piece of jewelry. A mine's worth of gems, such as diamonds, pearls, sapphires, and rubies, bulged hard-to-lift cloth sacks. Over twenty paintings were stacked on the kitchen table. He was certain he recognized a renowned neoclassicist artist's handiwork.

McEntee became excited when he thought he found a unicorn's horn, but the Captain assured them the long ivory horn had come from a narwhal—a type of whale rather than an equine creature.

One wagon possessed nothing but religious artifacts. Folded in a leather strapped crate were vestments and robes and other holy garbs. Another larger crate held a gold baptismal ewer. There were over thirty crosses, almost all of which were adorned in gold, silver, and gems. Boxes etched and painted with crosses held bones and hairs of various saints.

Someone would have to travel to the Vatican to view a more copious reliquary display of icons.

One plain wood cross appeared so antiquated that the Captain wondered if it was the first-ever Christian cross miniaturized to represent the symbol of Christ and his crucifixion. In the same crate, they found a strained nail as well as a shaft of dense wood.

"Jesus Christ," Brewster said in awe.

The Captain tallied the final item in his journal, a gold-cast replica of Paris's Notre Dame Cathedral. He scanned through several pages. "Incredible. This is some payday. Tax-free, to boot."

Brewster chuckled. "And we still have four more wagons to unload."

They decided to meet the next morning and finish the job. The Captain requested a favor of Demayo and McEntee, who obliged with glee. He gave them money from his own pocket and left to meet Susanna and Elizabeth.

With the shell he purchased in hand, he sidled through the back gate and walked down to the beach. The sun hung on its descent, and a pinkish-orange glow lit the near-cloudless sky. On the beach, the two women stood between the water and a nearby fire. Ryan and Rex ran out from the ocean, and one appeared to drop something at their feet. Susanna picked an object up, took a few steps, and hurled it back into the water. The two dogs ran in pursuit.

Elizabeth noticed him first, and she patted Susanna's arm. They clasped hands and ran to a set blanket. The Captain sprinted over, dropped the shell, and lifted both females off the ground. "Aaarghhhh," he boomed in a deep, raspy voice. "I am the monster of Mexico."

He shook them a bit. Elizabeth giggled while Susanna gave a sarcastic laugh. "Ryan! Rex! Save us."

In seconds, both dogs snapped at his feet with low growls rumbling from their maws.

The Captain lost his ogre voice. "Hmm, seems I have some work to do with these guys." He returned the girls to their feet and picked up the shell with a sleight of hand. "This is for you," he said to Susanna.

"That's sweet of you, but I hope you didn't pay too much. I have ten bigger shells I found all by myself."

The Captain raised a brow. "This is a special, magical shell, rumored to have been touched by the hand of Merlin himself." He grinned down at Elizabeth and noted that she had kept the secret of the shell purchase from Susanna.

Susanna's eyes narrowed at the shell in the Captain's hands. "Let me guess. You put your ear on the opening, and you hear the ocean?"

"No, ma'am. Give the greatest wizard ever some credit. This shell bears incredible gifts."

He handed the conch to Susanna, who accepted the offering like it was the beehive Elizabeth had shoved down the privy several years ago. When she turned the exoskeleton over, her mouth opened almost as wide as the conch shell's aperture. She eyed the Captain, the corners of her mouth creased with joy, and then pulled at what dangled from the shell. Out came a pearl necklace.

"Abracadabra," he bellowed. "I told you it was a magic shell."

She examined the necklace and shook her head back and forth. "Beautiful," she finally said. She came forward, and the Captain leaned over to accept her puckered lips. "Thank you," she squeaked like her lungs were bereft of air.

He took the necklace from her and eased the pearls over her head and down around her neck.

"Woo, so pretty," purred Elizabeth. From out of Susanna's vision, she flashed the Captain a cute smile of conspiracy. "Can the shell make me something too?"

"Um, the magic shell needs to sleep awhile now. However, before I came here, the shell bore a gift to you as well, but your present was too big for me to carry, so I left it at our new home."

"What is it?"

"That, my dear, is a surprise."

"Then let's hurry up and eat!"

The Captain noticed an omission. "Where's your mother?"

Susanna chuckled. "She has a male friend, Henry, with whom she spends all her time. She basically moved in with him, but remember, they're just friends."

Susanna, with Elizabeth's help, served a meal of chicken fajitas and a portion of fish so soft it flaked apart with minimal fork contact. Elizabeth squealed in delight when she did not have to share her food, as each dog got a plate of chicken.

The Captain hummed with pleasure. "This place is the most beautiful spot in the world, and here I am with the two most beautiful gals imaginable. How about we stay here all night and sleep under the stars and listen to the sound of the ocean?"

"No," said Elizabeth with the last morsel of food in her mouth. "I want to go home."

The Captain and Susanna laughed, knowing full well she wanted to see what he'd brought her.

"Don't listen to him, honey. What did I tell you about this giant galoot? He has a party to go to while us girls bond."

They returned home, and Elizabeth raced through the door and screamed in delight. Before the Captain and Susanna reached the foyer, they heard notes being played. The Captain recognized the E-flat major key of Chopin's waltz, Opus 18.

Susanna prodded him to slow their pace. Her wide, wonderstruck eyes stared at him. "Listen to her play that piano. She's incredible."

"She certainly is." This time he initiated the kiss. "So are you, my sweet Susanna."

CHAPTER 108

G as pole lamps lit the crowded courtyard. Remnants from Maximilian's reign, such as the gas lamps, had been sold off by the reinstated Mexican government, and the initial caravan was fortunate to acquire royal European furnishings at peasant prices. They also hired a Banda band, which once had played in Maximilian's court. Bodies swayed to the polka-like beat, and hands clapped along.

Having eaten already, the Captain passed three tables of meats, cheeses, fruits, and baked desserts and went to the five tables stocked with beer, wine, whiskey, and tequila. Self-serve-style, the Captain poured himself a glass. The Bordeaux, also purchased from Maximilian's estate, were gifted to the former emperor by Napoleon III.

He did not seek out company yet, still caught in the afterglow of his two gals. Despite the courtyard festivities, he wagered the girls would have as much fun making dolls, drawing pictures, and likely poking fun at him. He sipped his wine and thought of Charlotte and how she must miss Elizabeth. At the same time, he considered himself fortunate to raise her daughter.

He meandered closer to the music. A clapping throng formed a circle around Huth, who displayed some adept footwork as he marched to the beat like it was a military drill. Brewster and Maggie joined the dance, and the crowd whistled and cheered. Katherine and Antonio strutted out, pumping their fists. Carla dragged Deputy Less out, and the ovation increased. Then a few other couples joined in. One pairing included a white man in his late forties and a Mexican female at least ten years his junior. They twirled and spun like synchronized Swiss timepieces.

On the far side of the circle, the Captain spotted Jesse and Frank, and their adoring eyes told him who the dancing man was. He arced around to the James boys. "Is that your father?"

"Would you believe it?" Frank gushed. "He's a changed man."

"He's better than I dreamed," Jesse said through a whisper.

The trio watched Robert James and his new sexy wife take center stage as the other actors drifted out of action. No one looked more relieved than Deputy Less, who had stumbled throughout.

"Who brought the professionals?" Huth shouted with mock lament. Everyone laughed, except the James boys, who glowed like the gas fire lamps.

"Her name is Rosa," said Frank. "They're truly in love."

"She has so much energy for a little thing," Jesse commented.

The woman moved with the grace of a feline.

"She's beautiful," gushed Frank.

Jesse beamed. "Those large eyes are like black pearls in heavenly white clouds."

The Captain would not vocalize his thoughts, but on an attraction basis—Robert James's wife upgrade was like a toadstool to a desert rose. He suspected the personality change was like sticker-bush to sugarcane.

The song ended, and applause sounded through the courtyard. Robert bowed, and his wife curtsied. The couple waded out of the circle and joined the group.

Jesse introduced the Captain. "Meet my friend I told you about."

Robert shook the Captain's hand. "Please excuse me, but I'm parched and need a drink." He looked at his woman. "Tequila and pineapple, Rosa?"

"Why, of course," she purred.

"That shit is delicious," he said and departed.

Rosa was an eyeful, but the Captain was fascinated by Robert James. Although he'd never met the man, he believed Frank's claim that his father was a changed man. Not only did Robert have a younger, prettier wife, but the Captain guessed that when attending to his former ministry, his hair was not down to his shoulder. Nor did he likely perform sexy public waltzes with Zerelda, the dancing bear. Being a man of the cloth, he had abstained from decadence, perhaps even fun. Now the man drank and cussed. Robert James had shed his cocoon and let his wings expand.

Robert returned, and the Captain left, allowing them to catch up on lost time. He liked the James boys' father, especially when he said, "My faith in God has not wavered, but I no longer see the devil's hand in every pursuit of pleasure. God wanted mankind to have laws and morals, but he also wanted us to have some fun on the mortal plane to balance the hardships mankind faces."

"Amen," said the Captain.

Robert also confessed to having abandoned the Confederate cause once the army surrendered and fled south. "I left my children for a bunch of cowards. Down here, in all this sun, blue water, and palm trees, you neither think nor care much about the war anymore," he explained.

The Captain understood. Los Cabos was a tranquil paradise where conflict seemed another planet away. His thoughts were broken by a loud cheer. Two cactus piñatas hung from a stone arc in the courtyard *omphalos*.

Brewster stood in the circle with a stick in hand. "Frank, since you're the only man I've ever seen assault a cactus, how about you take the first whack?"

The younger James handed a glass to his brother. "I'd be honored," he said to laughs. He took the stick and brandished it at the lowered piñata. "You should see what I did to your cousin." He pulled the stick back, screamed, and struck the cactus.

A crack sounded, followed by snickering and laughter. The cactus still dangled from the rope, unblemished. Half of the broken stick remained in Frank's hand, and he examined the break with his eyes and finger. "Ah," he said with a knowing smile.

Brewster handed him another stick. "Hack this cactus."

Frank took the stick and applied some pressure. Satisfied, he drew back and again hit the cactus; his follow-through brought him underneath it. The stick held, but the piñata was punctured. Sand rained down on his head, and the crowd howled.

"I got sand in my eyes!" cried Frank as he rubbed at his sockets.

The laugher increased.

He dusted himself off, and the second cactus was lowered within reach.

Frank warily swung again, this time with less force, his arms outstretched to keep a distance. *Crunch*, a metallic *ding*, and the clinking increased as objects poured from the piñata.

He looked down. "Money!"

Nearly the whole crowd surged toward him. Heads and bodies collided like billiard balls.

The Captain didn't help the chaos when he announced whoever found a silver coin with a Z carved in it would win a gold-cast dragon that had come from China. The courtyard murmured. "A carved Y wins an exquisite gold candelabrum." Excitement grew. "If you find the silver coin with an X, you win a fur coat and matching cap made from Arctic fox." The announcement drew little applause.

In a mass of bodies, Frank's voice sounded. "Shiver me sphincter! This is Mexico, not Manitoba."

"Sorry," the Captain said. "The fur ensemble and a leaky chamber pot made from fool's gold were to be tonight's door prize." He furrowed his brow. "But the party's outdoors with no closed passageway to exit, so the idea of a door prize seemed silly."

Almost everyone was still on their hands and knees, searching for unclaimed and loose-fingered coinage.

"If you find the X, you'll receive a voodoo hex and never again have sex."

"The curse of Little Archie lives on," joked Frank.

The Captain winked at Brewster, who nodded and took a box from Demayo's hands. He opened it and handed it to the Captain.

"If you find the X, you win this jewel-encrusted crown." He raised the crown over his head. The light from the gas lamps reflected off the sparkling array of gemstones.

The scavengers paused to view the grand prize. "Oohs" and "aahs" stirred through the crowd. Then a "Hol*eee* shit" that the Captain could swear sounded like Robert James. The brief pause ended, and the buzz was resumed as the partygoers swarmed the ground like worker bees.

Three ex-Union soldiers won all the grand prizes, yet anyone who dared the piñata stampede ended the fracas a few coins richer. Despite the alcohol consumption, the distribution of a small portion of Maximilian's coins proved the best tonic of the night.

CHAPTER 109

Frank was having a little fun on some unexpected drunkards. He made a few men chug whiskey upside-down. The men were brought back to their feet and spun in a circle. He ordered them to race across the courtyard arch, and the winner would receive ten gold sovereigns. None finished. A few lost teeth.

The Captain had used the same ploy on Frank when they'd first met in Booneville. He smiled when he recalled Frank crashing into Badger Bob's table. The memories brought him to Susanna.

"You're home early," she said. "Sounds like the party is peaking."

He sat in a chair across from the couch she reclined upon. "The party is roaring like a horny lion. Unfortunately, no single women were available, so I decided I could at least get lucky here."

Susanna flung a pillow into his grin.

"Humph! Must I be emasculated? I confessed that I'd rather be with you."

"No, but it's nice to hear you say that." She motioned toward him. "Can I have that pillow back?"

He cocked his arm and sped it forward, and she flinched, expecting a fast return, but he stopped his arm at the last moment. The pillow arched slowly back until it hit Susanna's forearm shield and fell to the floor.

"Nothing is simple with you."

"Just my husband rules: you provide meals and sex at the snap of a finger. I, on the other hand, promise to commit adultery less than ten times a year."

She picked up the pillow. "Your face wants this back."

"My face would rather hit those two pillows," he replied, his eyes drifting down to her chest. He smacked his lips and returned his gaze upward. Instead of her face, he saw beige fabric. The pillow bounced off his head.

"Hmm, seems my romantic overtures have flopped. Tell me about your evening with Elizabeth."

Susanna shook her head in wonder. "She played piano for me, and I read to her." She pointed to a table with dolls made from husks. "We made those. I also designed a dress I'll make for her."

He'd seen similar dolls at the merchant depot just outside Los Cabos.

A small frown crept across Susanna's face. "She told me a few stories too; she's been through too much for her tender age. Mostly though, we chatted about good things. Life here, what she wants to learn and do. We talked a lot about you. She adores you like the father she never truly had."

Touched, he dipped his head.

Susanna chuckled. "You know what else she said? She sees us as her new parents and would love a brother or sister."

The Captain jumped out of his seat and stepped over the table, scooped Susanna up, and hoisted her over his shoulder. "Let's give the girl what she wants."

CHAPTER 110

The crowd gathered around the courtyard. A trellis of flowers covered the stone arch. The cobblestone walkway was speckled with rice like the first flakes of a snowstorm.

A five-piece orchestra, also holdovers from Maximilian's reign, started to play, and a hush fell over the crowd. The front gate opened for the fourth time that day. Elizabeth walked in wearing a light yellow dress and a flower in her ear. On either side of her loped Ryan and Rex. The trio reached the courtyard and stopped before the arch.

On Elizabeth's left stood the three recently married brides, Maggie, Katherine, and Susanna's mother. Behind them was their shared maid of honor, Carla, and a lady Susanna's mother had become friendly with, Josephine. To the right were Antonio, Brewster, and Henry trailed by the best men, a *paisan* named Anthony Mannino, Atticus Huth, and a chap named Theodore. Dressed in full minister garb, Robert James stood in the middle.

Elizabeth wiggled between the women and Minister James.

The bridesmaid and best man strolled forward next. The crowd howled as Jesse and Frank walked arm-in-arm. Jesse wore a suit, another purchase from the Maximilian liquidation sale. Frank also had a snazzy three-piece, but the formal attire was covered by a white lace dress. He sported a female wig, fixed with auburn curls. Around his neck gleamed a sparkling necklace. Frank blew kisses to the crowd as the two brothers walked to the arch.

Someone yelled, "I got first dance with Francine!"

Susanna did not have a chance to bond with the other women as did Maggie, Katherine, and Carla on the journey to Los Cabos. When the Captain told his future wife he planned to ask Jesse to be his best man, he jested Frank should play the part of the bridesmaid. She loved the thought, which had been a rarity in her reaction to his ideas.

When they asked Frank if he would do the honors, he was overcome with emotion and hugged them both. Now dressed as a woman, he looked like his mother, Zerelda, only prettier.

The brothers reached the arch; Jesse went to the right and joined the men while Frank sashayed over to the women.

The music changed, and in came the Captain. The gate shut behind him. He wore standard trousers and his father's Union jacket. None of the suits from Maximilian's minions fit. Ironically, Jesse suggested the Union jacket as a way to honor Major "Ave" Johnson. Susanna agreed, but she usually agreed with Jesse, leaving the Captain to half-wonder what he was doing wrong.

He positioned himself next to Minister James.

The gate swung open again, and a gilded stagecoach trotted inside. The horse, Sir Johnson, formerly known as Fly Bait, nickered and shook his mane. The driver, Deputy Less, dropped to the floor and then opened the stagecoach door.

Apparently the stagecoach was a sky chariot in disguise, because out floated an angel.

The crowd gasped, and the Captain almost fainted he was so spellbound by the majesty of her beauty.

Susanna wore a cream-white satin dress with a pearl white-laced trim and neck insert. The sleeves tapered to white gloves. Blonde strands fell from her head like rays of the sun, and she walked forward, chin up, eyes bright, and a smile on her face that could have swallowed the world.

Minister James patted the air for quiet and welcomed the bride and groom. "Should anyone object to this wedding, let them speak now or forever hold their peace."

The Captain cringed.

"I do," a voice yelled. "I—"

The crowd hushed.

"Forget it, Patwell. Please," begged the Captain.

"Do I still keep the money?"

He shrunk in his skin. "Yes. Just don't say anything else."

Susanna's eyes strayed to heaven.

"What is going on?" asked Minister James.

"I think I know." She eyed the Captain. "But why don't you tell him, my love."

He shrugged. "I thought it would be funny if someone objected." No one appeared amused, but then again, he faced all women and a minister. "So I paid Patwell to object and gave him some witty lines for why the marriage should be annulled. In hindsight, I realized the idea was better on paper, but an unworkable draft nonetheless."

Minister James let out a low chuckle. To Susanna, he said, "You must be blessed with immeasurable patience."

She shook her head. "Not really. I start with ignoring him and proceed to projectiles."

Now Minister James tilted his head to the side. "Well, God bless the two of you."

This was the fourth wedding in succession, and out of respect for all parties, Minister James vowed to keep his blessings short. Like the first three processions, he read passages from the Bible. Now, as he read from his used but unblemished Bible, the Captain recognized Romans 12:1–9, but barely. The sight of Susanna diminished all other senses.

Minister James then spoke from his heart about love, commitment, and other nuances of marriage, including children. Susanna nodded along and smiled as the minister spoke, but for the Captain, the words came in fragments, as though his ears were periodically dammed with fingers.

Minister James motioned them to move in, and again, the words did not register. A poke to the back from Brewster imported the message. The minister asked a bunch of questions, but all the Captain heard was Susanna say the words, "I do."

Then the questions came his way. Previously, he planned to answer in Pig Latin, but he now opted against the notion and wondered if he was maturing.

"Do you take this woman to be your lawful wife?"

He locked eyes with the only woman in the world for him, the one that set his heart aflutter. All he had to do was utter two simple yet profound words, and he would finally be married to the love of his life.

"Can you give me a second?" He fumbled in his pocket.

The crowd groaned, and Susanna rolled her eyes.

At last, he pulled out a gold coin. "Heads for a shared bed—tails and I bail."

Susanna took the flower from Elizabeth's head and threw it at the Captain. "Sorry, my love, but I passed the ignore stage."

Her mother giggled.

The Captain handed Susanna the coin, and she took the offering with reluctance. Puzzled, her eyes strayed to the object in her hand, and she gasped.

As emotion rippled across her visage, the Captain said, "As for my answer, of course I do. I love you, Susanna."

The crowd cheered.

"Finally," Frank said. "I want to get out of this dress and wig."

Susanna flipped the coin over. Her face trembled as she began to cry. "I love you too."

Elizabeth gave the rings to Minister James and grinned at the Captain. She'd seen the coin he had designed. One side depicted Susanna's visage from the painting she'd left for him. The other side of the coin said, "*To my wife; I love you.*"

They helped each other put their wedding rings on to a chorus of cheers and whistles.

Minister James let out a soft, pleasant laugh. "This has been the most interesting wedding I have ever serviced. May I present to you, for the first time, Mr. and Mrs. Johnson. You may now kiss the bride."

PART VII

Chapter 111

Summer 1880, Spring 1890

Sixteen years later, the James boys looked less alike than ever before. Frank had packed on weight and lost much of his hair, yet his demeanor remained vibrant and happy. Jesse was lean yet muscular, his sculpted face handsome yet haunted. Frank married a native Mexican, whom his new mother-in-law introduced him to sometime prior. Jesse had many suitors, but no relationship lasted more than a few weeks.

The Captain sat with the two brothers on the beach, drinking tequila, telling stories. A week had passed since their father, Robert James, died of unexpected heart failure. The day also marked the first time Jesse had left his house since his father's passing.

Robert James was the first resident of their compound to die, unless you counted Sir Johnson (Fly Bait), Ryan, or Rex.

The animals were remembered by six mutts and two colts Sir Johnson had sired.

Susanna's mother and her new husband, Henry, had voyaged to England and never returned. They had traveled Europe, sending letters and parcels home, until their journey through life ended.

Robert James was the oldest, so statistically it made sense he passed away first, but then again it didn't. The man maintained his physique with vigorous walks and a healthy diet. He was a firm believer in God and presided over every baptism—including Frank's three children and the Captain's son, as well as every wedding and church service since their arrival in Mexico. Adored as the town's true treasure, everyone shared in the James family's grief for Minister Robert's passing.

Over the years, their compound received a steady stream of newspapers from the United States, albeit the paper often arrived months after print, though even so, the men relished news from the States. Electricity became the new rage, with the Edison Illuminating Company leading the way. Another president, James Garfield, had been assassinated the prior year. Tsar Alexander II of Russia was also murdered, but no one in the compound cared.

"*He wuz uh stupeed, peeg, eediot,*" Brewster said in his best Russian accent.

The interesting man the Captain met in the Lexington bar, Ambrose Bierce, now wrote for several San Francisco news journals and had acquired the nickname Bitter Bierce for his sardonic view of life. The Captain wrote him a letter, which was returned, edited, along with a biting critique on modern society. They maintained regular correspondence thereafter, with each subsequent reply revealing a diminishing quantity of edits, until the Captain received a letter back that simply said, "Bravo!"

The conversation soon turned to a regular topic, Jesse James.

"I cannot believe Mason is the most famous man in America today, let alone still alive. Edwards did some job making a hero out of a criminal," Frank said and sipped his tequila.

The Captain scratched at his clean-shaven chin. "In hindsight, I should have programmed Mason to fancy cliff diving or sword swallowing. I never dreamed he'd prove so resourceful, and the authorities so inept. The Pinkerton Company has fumbled the raids like fools. For starters, you cannot have the word 'pink' in your designation and pretend you carry authority."[33]

---

33   Allan Pinkerton started America's first detective agency (rent-a-cop). His agency protected President Lincoln at his inauguration, and Pinkerton served in the Union Army. He took up pursuit of the James gang. One of his detectives went undercover as a farmhand, and was discovered and killed. Pinkerton organized a raid of the Jameses' farm, and an incendiary device was thrown through a window. Zerelda was injured and lost an arm. Her third son, Archie, died. The botched raid was a disgrace to Pinkerton, and he abandoned his pursuit of James family members.

Frank laughed.

"Our poor mother," Jesse said for the countless time over the past fifteen years, especially when Zerelda had lost her arm, as well as her new son, Archie (named in honor of the sniveling Little Archie Clement), in a Pinkerton raid.

The Captain never had sympathy for Zerelda because, by all accounts, she reveled in Mason's exploits.

Frank echoed his thoughts. "Ma loves the fight. She wouldn't want it any other way."

They heard a shout, and the men turned. Brewster ran across the beach toward them. He waved a newspaper of his own. Out of breath, his eyes settled on Jesse, and he handed him the newspaper and said, "I'm delighted to report that you're dead."

Color raided Jesse's cheeks as he read. "Mason's dead! Two traitors shot him in the back." He raised his glass of tequila. "To my death."

The men drank with him.

Jesse held up a finger and refilled their glasses. "To my rebirth."

The men continued to drink and discuss Mason's historic life of crime. Jesse's words appeared literal. Like a phoenix, his namesake's death lit life into his ashen complexion. An hour later, close to sundown, he asked to speak to the Captain alone.

"What is it?" the Captain asked once Frank and Brewster were out of ear shot.

"Mason's notoriety hung the albatross of guilt around my shoulders. A weight I was unable to shift off my soul." He gave a sideways smile. "I know you have no love for my mother, and I understand why, but she's still my mother," he said and sighed. "I never met her son, Archie, but my half-brother died due to Mason's actions. That could have been me. It's who I wanted to be."

He did not speak out of regret, but with relief, and finished his thoughts. "Until this burden lifted, I feared I'd bring nightmares to the one I love."

The one he loves?

"Please, don't punch me, but I wanted to talk to you about Elizabeth."

"Elizabeth?" he said with surprise, yet as the name escaped his lips, he realized the revelation was obvious. Throughout Elizabeth's childhood,

Uncle Jesse doted on her. As she reached maturity, the relationship changed to close friends.

"I realize I'm ten years older, but if things worked out, I think I could be a good husband to her. And you wouldn't make a bad father-in-law, I confess," he said with a light smile.

Protective of his girl, the Captain knew that Jesse was true to his word, not a womanizer like someone else he'd once known.

"I appreciate you had the respect to bring this to me first."

"Of course, Dad," Jesse said.

"Although she's not our offspring, Elizabeth is very much our daughter. We're not related, yet you're like my brother. I bless your request and wish you success. If Elizabeth rejects the advances, then I implore you continue to treat her as you always have. She does love you—but whether that extends to romance is another matter. Thus far, she hasn't shown a lot of interest in men. I'm not sure if she's busy with her hobbies or surrounded by a bunch of white guys." He punctuated his off-color comment with a laugh.

Jesse grinned with insight. "We've talked. She would welcome some black folk around here, but she's not uninterested in white men either. She is absorbed in her favorite pastimes, but she once said, under the influence of tequila, that she fancied one man—yet he never made a move, as it's not proper for a lady to initiate." His face firmed. "I hope I'm that man."

The Captain watched Jesse travel back to the compound and then turned to the ocean, wide as far as his eyes could see. All these years, and he still found a tranquil harmony in the clear blue water. Whoever first equated blue for sadness was either color blind, afflicted with blue balls, or dressed as an infant in his sister's pink hand-me-downs and became psychologically scarred by the assigned-masculine color.

After all, what was better than a clear blue sky? Gray would have been more apropos for gloom, which was how Jesse looked as he walked back to the Captain. He had been gone under an hour.

Although father and daughter had never discussed the matter, the Captain knew Elizabeth's answer. At least, he thought he did.

Jesse's last few steps labored like the ball and chain were already attached. He trudged over, head down, not meeting the Captain's eye.

The words came out slowly and pained like his lung was still punctured. "She said no."

The Captain grinned. "I knew it."

Jesse finally made eye contact. "You did?"

"Sure. She's way out of your league. I know you're lying."

"What? How?"

"She said yes, only because she's too kind to break your heart."

Jesse did a double take when the Captain held out both hands.

"Come here, son. Welcome to the family."

CHAPTER 112

DECEMBER 1910

The Captain's arthritic hands trembled as he opened the box and found Susanna's journals. He thought the well was dry, but tears fell when he cracked the first binding and read her handwriting. She had chronicled his life from the time they'd first met in Booneville, over forty-five years ago. Like her paintings, her writing breathed with realism.

An hour later, he closed the first book. "You're amazing," he said to the empty room, yet he felt her spirit alive with him. "Won't be long before we're together again, love."

In response, a breeze blew through the open window.

He lay on the bed and used his sleeve to wipe his wet face. The respite marked the first time he'd been alone since they'd buried her. His son, Ulysses, and daughter, Elizabeth, were present, along with Maggie and Brewster. Most of the rest of the faces were children of their original migrants and business associates.

There had been many funerals over the past ten years. Five years ago, Frank James fell over dead as he played with his grandchildren. Jesse passed in his sleep at Elizabeth's side. His death had been hard on her, but fortunately, her two daughters and five grandchildren kept her busy.

The Captain visualized Susanna's face as she had looked when he first laid eyes on her in Booneville. The face morphed into a knife wound and then the scar that never faded. He recalled the pain she endured during labor and then the joy on her face when their only son was born into the world. The one-way changes of time never robbed her beauty.

He knew he'd cope, but the loss was even more profound than he had guessed. When illness took her, he stayed by her bedside for a week until her last gasp. "I was the luckiest woman ever." She went to say more, but no words came.

A knock pounded from downstairs and then the deep sound of Ulysses's voice. "The Captain? Virgil Johnson? No one's here by that name."

A muffled reply came.

"Please have some respect. My father just buried his wife."

Again, the Captain could not hear the other voice.

His son said, "I'll give him the message."

The front door shut.

The Captain was curious about the visitor, who had referenced the Captain's moniker *and* given name. Many years had passed since he went by the name Virgil Johnson. After the Maximilian caper, most of the men changed their names. The Johnsons changed to the Baxters—a name Elizabeth chose, as it was her true father's surname. The James family became the Jones clan. Brewster became Sullivan.

His son's footsteps padded upward. He still saw Ulysses as his boy, but everyone else viewed him as the head of a growing economic empire. Ulysses's son and daughters utilized their wealth while hiding the truth of their fortune. When word spread of possible oil fields near the central gulf coast of Mexico, they purchased much of the land.

American speculators came by the droves, and a bidding war broke out. Rather than maximize their windfall, they sold the land at handsome profits and became silent partners. The oil enterprise soon reached into Texas and California, and their investments spread to banks, textiles, shipping, hotels, and always real estate. Throughout, the family always stayed in the background and let their investments work.

A knock at the door came, and the Captain eased off the bed. He sat on the desk chair where Susanna used to write. "Come in."

In walked his son, Ulysses. The boy was a perfect balance of both parents. He was built like the Captain and possessed a similar wit. Ulysses had Susanna's sharp nose and calculated judgment.

"A man from California called upon you. He's even older than you," he said and chuckled.

"Be careful, boy. You've got some gray at the temples."

"That's what a Stetson's for."

"Soon you'll need a sombrero."

"Hardy, ha-ha," mocked his son.

"Was this man named Ambrose Bierce?"

Ulysses scowled. "You know that insufferable man?"

"I met him once, and we stayed in contact. Ambrose has bad luck with women. They cheat on him like he's a test in an unsupervised classroom. After his latest marriage failed, Bierce said he contemplated leaving America, as he put it, 'a land occupied by unscrupulous she-devils.'"

"She-devils?"

"He's a pretty well-known writer in America. His nickname is Bitter Bierce."

Ulysses bobbed his head. "Well, he's at the inn." His expression turned soft, the small smile gone, and he sat on the bed and clasped his hands. "You okay, Dad?"

"In her memory, I will be. Do me a favor, son."

"Anything." His red eyes pleaded.

The Captain tapped the box with Susanna's journals. "A time will come—not in your lifetime, nor your son's—where the truth about Maximilian's stolen cache can no longer hurt the family. When that time comes, I want your mother's writings to tell our story. It is not only our story, but the truth about Jesse Mason James and Jesse Woodson James."

The Captain smiled at his only son, and his hand stayed on the box. "Most of your mother's writings are about me, but every good story needs a great character."

PART VIII

CHAPTER 113

PRESENT DAY

"So that's the story. The whole truth and nothing but the truth," Baxter said like a lawyer who filibustered his way through the closing argument.

Gladstone noted the boy had left out, "So help me God."

"So the history books only need to exchange Mason for Woodson, and the story of Jesse James is, in essence, the same."

"You don't say," Professor Gladstone said. He felt like he was in Guantanamo Bay and being subjected to intense interrogations until he provided the answers his inquisitors demanded.

Baxter droned on. "Documented expert testimony exists, backed by computer analysis, that the face in the photos taken after Jesse James was shot is Jesse *Mason* James. The claims made by the investigator, however, surmise Jesse Woodson James was the criminal who killed his cousin Mason and then used Mason's body to fake his own death."

Baxter, for the first time that afternoon, grimaced with vulnerability. "I don't make a big deal about the photo analysis, as another comprehensive study claims the body is another relative altogether. So I'm not hanging my hat." He paused and winked. "Although, I'm not wearing one on this photo analysis. I merely mention this tidbit as yet another pebble in the fortress of facts scaled and built throughout my paper.

"Furthermore, I uncovered Ambrose Bierce's final resting spot. He'd

438

left for Mexico around 1913 and was never seen again. Add the truth of Maximilian's lost treasure, and you've got the icing on a cake layered with substance. Even the worst baker couldn't fail with all the ingredients I had at my disposal."

Smug, he cocked his head. "So let's cut through the chase and slap an A+ on my paper. Trust me. I got better things than to sit in this dreary dump."

Heated, Gladstone sagged like a warmed Popsicle. His ex-wife believed in some psychobabble about the laws of attraction and the ability to will things into reality. He envisioned a scruffy student pulling a fire alarm and concentrated hard, but nothing happened. Maybe the fire alarm was too improbable, but then again, wasn't winning the lottery? Something his ex-spouse continually claimed was around the corner.

He considered other possible interventions: a terrorist campus takeover (but wimpy eco types, not jihadist killers), a meteor strike, DEFCON 1, but nothing realistic came to mind. Damn his former wife. Then a thought occurred to him. The irony. He saw his ex-wife injured—nothing too serious, perhaps a broken foot from a fall. The phone on his desk would ring, summoning him to pick up their son. He concentrated. He believed. A force flowed through him.

The phone rang, and Gladstone jumped in his chair. It worked! He casually put a finger up for Baxter's benefit and answered. He hoped his ex-wife was not too hurt. "Hello?"

"You guys still running the two-toppings extra-cheese pie and chicken-wing combo?"

"Huh?"

"Is this Carmine's Pizzeria?" asked a raspy voice.

"No, this is the Harvard history department."

The caller laughed. "Sorry, Professor Happy Rock. I meant to call you next. Is Ulysses still there? He's not answering his cell."

"The name is Gladstone, and yes, Ulysses is still here."

"Why are you detaining him so long? Should I be concerned? Is this, like, a hostage situation?"

His face flexed with exasperation. "No."

"Can I talk to him to ensure what you say is true?"

"Are you crazy?"

"Ulysses is," the voice asserted. "I told him not to show the paper to you without an agent present. I knew you'd try to find a way to enrich yourself off his family secret."

The caller kept flapping, but Gladstone removed the phone from his ear and angled it toward Baxter. "Can you tell your friend you're not a hostage, and we're merely haggling over your grade?"

Ulysses grinned. "I'm okay, Chainsaw. I should be out in a bit."

Gladstone put the phone back to his head. "Satisfied?"

"How do I know his reply was not coerced at gunpoint?"

"You really are crazy."

"Am I? Is my concern any more preposterous than haggling over his grade? My mother is lead editor of the *New York Times* Book Review. She's acquainted with everyone in the publishing industry. Ulysses's story is going to make a bundle. More importantly, I can't wait to tell her how rude and condescending you were to me. Hope my commentary does not influence your next book review in any way, however. The last one was bad enough." A punctuated sarcastic laugh was heard, and the line went dead.

Gladstone dropped the phone into the cradle.

"Don't mind Chainsaw," advised Baxter. "He means well."

"Why do you call him Chainsaw?"

The student tipped an imaginary glass to his lips. "He's a drunk, always buzzing," he said and lolled his head, as if tipsy. "Chainsaw is lead guitarist in the band The Happy Humpers. He's already asked to get one of their songs on the eventual soundtrack for the movie adaptation of my novel."

Gladstone wheezed.

"I'm more concerned with getting the right actors. Do you think it's possible if I surround myself with an all-star cast, I can play the Captain? I realize it's the lead, but I believe I'm literally born for the role. Plus, with all the sex scenes, I could get to see a few Hollywood hotties naked."

Professor Gladstone had once read that if someone on the phone announced they planned to kill the president, then the Secret Service would arrive in minutes. Nope, that wouldn't work either. They'd lock him up, and he'd assuredly lose his job. In the end, he had to assign a grade.

Baxter went through his bag and pulled out gold bars, coins, jewelry, and photos. "I have all the evidence you need. Want to take a look?"

Gladstone sighed in defeat. "You win, but I strongly advise losing the ridiculous footnotes and corny clichés." He took out his pen, crossed off the F, and wrote A+.

EPILOGUE

Six Months Ago

Ulysses Zeus Baxter's opponent bent at the haunches and placed a white dimpled ball on a spiked tee. His molted, patterned, green Callaway golf shirt stretched across his body like a watermelon skin protecting mushy innards. The guy had the whole country-club look going. The pleated plaid trousers, white tasseled golf shoes, and a salmon visor, which was odd, because he had dark shades covering his eyes. The frames said Armani.

They were at the first hole of some Greenwich, Connecticut, country club his opponent belonged to. Zeus forgot the club's name already and renamed the joint Chateau la Snobbery. So far, he'd seen nothing but assholes. His opponent introduced him to a group that teed off before them: Biff, Cole, Wally, and Bart. He had no idea why all four of them had cardigan sweaters tied over their shoulders, and wondered if the look was coordinated or simply Greenwich fashion happenstance, like Scots in kilts.

He didn't arrive in his normal attire: jeans, shorts, or—heaven forbid—sweatpants. He wasn't wearing one of his many customary T-shirts either. Instead, he wore a muted blue polo, and it even had a collar. Other than weddings, funerals, and court dates, he was proud to avoid the stuffy servitude of being a collared man.

His opponent reached into a deluxe golf bag, which might have sheltered a poor family in cubic footage. Top-of-the-line clubs, costing more than the median American's yearly salary, poked their covered heads out like a large family stuffed in a flashy convertible.

Zeus had a good set of clubs himself, but his were several years older. Not an avid golfer, he preferred mountain climbing, rugby, or hockey, although at forty-three, those days were passing like a milkshake through a stomach pumped full of antibiotics with unfortunate side effects.

His opponent golfed several times a week. This was his country club, his course, yet he would still lose. The visiting man never lost a wager. His opponent was Dillon Wilshire, lead investment banker at a white shoe boutique named Wilshire Worldwide.

Dillon's father ran the show, but his son turned the company into a Wall Street powerhouse. In reality, Wilshire Worldwide only had four offices, just two of which were outside the United States. Besides their Wall Street and Greenwich offices, they had a third in the Cayman Islands and another in Beijing. A corporate jet made the world a smaller place.

Dillon Wilshire was obsessed with the notion of bringing Zeus's company public. It was not the first time the company had been approached, nor would it be the last. Forbes ranked them as the largest privately held company in the United States. By comparison, runner-ups—Cargill, Bechtel, and Price Waterhouse Cooper—looked like roadside lemonade stands.

The family always resisted the temptation to bring the company public. They employed over four thousand people, and the salary structure and benefit package were second to none. Poor work wasn't tolerated, but firings or layoffs were rare. Every employee had been interviewed by him or his father. Their policy was simple and stemmed by something his family always believed in: don't hire assholes.

Therein lay the problem. Dillon Wilshire was a genuine, certified A-hole.

He had met Wilshire in the clubhouse at a Los Cabos golf resort while Wilshire was on vacation. He, on the other hand, had an estate nearby, which was actually a mini-compound, part of which was free to all company employees.

Wilshire sandbagged him while he enjoyed a glass of a specialty Jack Daniels the bartender recommended.

"I know everything about you," Wilshire had gushed. "My firm has done its homework on your company."

Wilshire had invited himself into Zeus's conversation with a lady, who shuffled away when Wilshire said he wanted to talk business. He told him he didn't want to talk business, but the obstinate businessman persisted. Zeus realized he would need to be intoxicated to endure the overbearing blowhard before him and had ordered another JD and then instructed the bartender to ensure he never saw the bottom of his glass.

Wilshire requested a concoction that turned the bartender into a chemist as he crushed, mixed, and stirred ingredients into some cloudy elixir. By the time Wilshire had been served, Zeus was ready for a refill on his bourbon.

Wilshire bragged about his firm in such nauseating detail Zeus was certain he could write the Wikipedia company profile.

Annoyed, Zeus asked, "What's the bottom line, Dilbert?"

"It's Dillon."

"I know."

Wilshire shrank back, allowing a comfortable distance at last, but his eager smile returned. "Why don't you and your wife visit my country club? No business talk, just to see if we hit it off."

Zeus frowned. "We won't hit off, and I'm not married."

Wilshire, it seemed, hadn't ground his way to the top by letting initial rejection impede his goals. The art of the sale was overcoming the refusal. His eyes darted to Zeus's hand. "Sorry, I saw the ring and assumed—"

"I thought you did some homework and knew all about me?"

Wilshire blinked. "We did." His voice hitched.

"My wife died almost fifteen years ago."

Wilshire eyed the wedding band, and his gaze darted back up.

"I will not take this ring off unless I remarry. You were probably in college then and too busy feeding off the silver spoon to notice all the press coverage, but your old man, sure as shit, would remember," he said. "You failed your homework assignment, Dilbert."

Wilshire tapped his temple. "My apologies, my mind is distracted. A dear friend is close to death."

"Someone assault him?"

"No. Cancer."

"Oh. I thought being a friend of yours, somebody likely beat the snot out of him."

Wilshire laughed. "You're funny, in a tough way. You have a magical gift of speaking to the heart of matters, without the flowery fog that only clouds the meaning of the message."

"Exactly. If you ever hear me use the two words, *flowery* and *fog*, together, you'll know I'm full of shit."

"I love your tenacity. Please come to my country club and give me an opportunity to spend a fun day of golf with you. Afterward, I'll elaborate what our company can do for you."

Zeus asked, "Is your country club any good?"

He held up an index finger. "Blakemore Gardens Country Club is rated the top course in the northeast." This time he held up two hands, seven raised fingers. "Seven times, the US Open has played Blakemore. Are you an avid golfer?"

"No. It's kind of boring, really. I just like to walk the courses and enjoy the scenery."

"Then you'll love Blakemore Gardens," vowed Wilshire.

He raised his brows. "Is it a private club?"

"Naturally. Membership is tightly screened, and the fees are high." He swirled his cocktail at Zeus. "Keeps out the riffraff, if you catch my drift."

"Unless you're talking about the cloying cologne you're swimming in, I don't."

Wilshire scratched his scalp with a puzzled expression, as if the reply was spoken in Japanese.

Zeus sputtered his lips. "Let me see if I can recap your pitch: you want me to visit the best country club in the northeast, which happens to be private, to convince me to take my private company public?" He gave a sarcastic chuckle. "That's some horse-shit-radish you're marinating me in."

Wilshire's jowls jiggled. "One is a business, the other is a club."

"Does the country club turn a profit?"

"Of course, but we always reinvest to keep Blakemore Gardens the pinnacle of the golfing world."

"Like any good business. I got a deal for you. Open the country club to the public, then I'll follow the model."

Wilshire's face still shined, but his visage waxed. "I can't make that decision on my own. I am only one of twenty charter board members."

"I figured as much. Sell them on the idea. That would convince me."

His countenance sagged. "I can't."

"Have a good day," Zeus had said and left for the restroom.

Sure as another lost New York Jet season, Wilshire found the urinal beside him.

"Let's start over," pleaded Wilshire.

"First, let's not. Second, why are you looking at my dick?"

Wilshire's eyes darted up and then down on his own discharge. "I wasn't."

"You're not one of those bathroom stalkers, are you?"

Wilshire jiggled his fleshy face about. "Please. God, no."

Zeus flushed, washed, and returned to the bar. Before he arrived, Wilshire's labored breathing sounded behind him, and he decided to change tactics.

"I'll make you a deal. You're probably unaware, judging from your research thus far, but we own a couple of recording labels. One of which has some of the best gangsta raps stars out there. You know that brother, Donald Dick, who raps in a duck voice?"

Wilshire shook his head, eyes wide.

"He's the brother who stirred a controversy when he rapped, 'Fuck politics, hate that crap, though I must admit, the first lady, I'd tap.' Yeah, we got him and other studs of syntax."

Wilshire's lips moved, but no words came.

"We also have a heavy-metal label. One of our bands is a punk-metal band called We Are Rebellious. I'm guessing you're not hip enough to know, but they have that song they play in all the swank clubs, 'I Wanna Be a Gynecologist.' We have black-metal bands too. They wear corpse paint, metal spikes, and reversed crosses."

Zeus patted Wilshire on the back and gave a brotherly squeeze. "The rap-and-metal community feel rejected by mainstream society. Let's play a round of golf at your country club. You win, we talk business. You lose, your club entertains me and twenty guests. Dress code null and void, of course."

Perspiration beaded above Wilshire's lips, but his eyes began to dance. "What's your handicap?"

Zeus's brow pinched. "Like picking horses at the track?"

Wilshire shook his head. "When you play a round, what do you usually score?"

"To be honest, I don't golf more than a few times a year."

"Have you ever taken lessons?"

"In golf? Heck no. But I don't want you to think I'm trying to shark you. I'm good at all sports. I can hit the ball a ton. I am six and a half feet tall and weigh two-sixty. What are you, five seven and close to three hundred on the Richter scale?" he asked as his eyes circled Wilshire's rotund frame. "There is not a sport, other than the Coney Island Hot Dog Eating Contest, that you could beat me in."

Wilshire smiled, perhaps confident he could indeed win. That or he'd try to renege out of the wager if he lost. "I think I can agree to those terms."

"I hate to be a stickler, but unscrupulous sorts exist that welch on verbal commitments. Thus, we'll have our attorneys draw up a document binding our agreement," he said.

Now, several months later, Wilshire took his practice strokes, rolling his ass and hips like he had a large hula hoop around his waist. He pulled grass from the ground and tossed it to the air. Wilshire's eyes followed the grass as the blades descended a little to the left.

Zeus hoped his opponent didn't repeat this routine every shot or it would be a long day.

Wilshire connected with the ball. It went a fair distance and rolled just a tad off the fairway. Good shot. Heck, considering Wilshire's bloat, perhaps a great shot. Zeus planted his tee in the ground and topped it off with a golf ball.

He thought of a joke he'd heard once.

The poor play basketball, the working class play football, the middle class play softball, and the wealthy play golf. The moral of the story is: the further you go up the ladder, the more your balls shrink.

Zeus took one backstroke and blasted the ball. It sailed one hundred yards farther than Wilshire's and landed about sixty yards from the green. "I'll take that. The nine iron is my best club."

Game on.

Wilshire opened the conversation as expected—small-talk banter, which covered sports, hobbies, family, and children. The discourse was warm, buttery bullshit, extra salty. Wilshire was impressed that the strange man's son attended his own alma mater. Wilshire then bragged about his three spawns. Naturally, they excelled at everything: piano, archery, horseback riding, sailing, and violin. In short, they were groomed to exhibit etiquette and chivalry.

Polite monsters, in other words.

Wilshire flexed into his warm-up routine again before smacking a straight shot that landed twenty yards from the green, dead center of the short bunkers. In the healthy walk to the next ball, Wilshire confessed he had been on the losing end of the vote to ban golf carts at Blakemore Gardens. He went into a longwinded explanation about why, with certain guidelines, motorized carts should be permitted. "What do you think?"

"Unless you're handicapped or elderly, golf carts are for pussies."

Wilshire didn't follow up on his inquiry.

Zeus's second shot arched up like a lazy fly ball to the outfield, where it dropped and rolled a few yards before settling ten feet from the first pin.

Wilshire brought his third shot on the green, but on the far side, about fifteen feet from the pin. His putt came close, a few inches shy, and he put the give-me away on his fifth stroke.

Zeus concentrated on his third shot. He hated putting. Being tall, he did not like hunching over the ball, and his putt landed a foot short. He sank his fourth shot.

"You're up one stroke," Wilshire said with a grin, perhaps sensing his opponent's game lacked finesse.

By the second hole, Wilshire was back to his spiel about the wonders of his company. "This time I did my homework," he said with a sheepish smile. "You care about the people who work for you. You need to go public. On the IPO date alone, every employee will be rolling in so much dough you'll be the envy of every baker and banker in town."

"What town?"

"Any town, it doesn't matter. It's an expression."

"I know. I like to have fun with clichés, as did my father, and his father before him. Take 'clean as a whistle,' for instance. What makes a whistle so fucking sanitary? What if the previous blower had a cold or herpes? And what about the saying, 'it's for the birds.' Why birds? Why not something more trivial or useless, like armpit hair? Or, what about politicians?"

Wilshire grinned.

"Or investment bankers."

Then he frowned.

Their second hole was a par five. Wilshire gambled his third shot, and from his angle, the left side of the green was the safest approach with lots of room. The flag, however, was on the far right side, where the green ran downward to a deep bunker, and Wilshire's ball rolled into the trap.

"You got me by two strokes that hole," he said, grin diminished. "I need to make up ground. This is one of my best holes."

"Then it must be a glory."

They both pared the third hole, and Zeus kept his lead.

He tilted the brim of his baseball cap. "My friend, Satan's Anus, from the band, Whore Hounds from Hell, is going to love this joint. He's hoping I win in the worst way."

Wilshire rubbed at his eyes as if he might wake from a nightmare. "I have to turn this around."

On the next tee, Wilshire took his warm-up routine to an absurd length. His club arced back and forth so many times, Zeus thought he counted sixty seconds on a grandfather clock.

Wilshire tried to change his luck and switched his gloves. He opened a new set of golf balls and then studied the greens like a battlefield commander. Ever the sport, he stood in a brook and whacked the ball out rather than accept the obstruction penalty.

After the ninth hole, Wilshire was down by six strokes. There was no more small talk about families. Nor was there more big talk about business. Wilshire drooped as he carted his gargantuan golf bag along like an SUV towing a U-Haul.

On the tenth hole, Zeus intentionally sent a hook shot that drew far to the right and into the rough. He kicked at the ground in mock disappointment. Wilshire tried not to smile, but his strut to the tee showed a man who sensed an opportunity. He went through his warm-up routine so long he could have been a rusty relief pitcher. His first strike was a dud, and he topped the ball. It bounced straight, but only a hundred yards.

There was no helping Wilshire, nor did he try again. It was better keeping his opponent quiet. At the last hole, down by nine strokes, Wilshire gave a tepid grin. "Okay, I lost. How about I throw you one hundred thousand dollars, and we call it even? I promise to never bother you again."

Zeus tightened his lips. "Please. I make more on dividends every month. My friends are coming here. We signed a deal."

"One million?"

"Nope."

Zeus sank the final shot of the match, and then they entered the clubhouse in silence, the establishment stocked with squares and rounds. No one said hello. Wilshire avoided eye contact with everyone.

Zeus brought both his work and personal phones with him just for the occasion. He reached inside his pocket and tapped a button. Guitars screeched, and he pulled out his other phone. "Sorry about the ringtone."

Wilshire slouched against the bar.

"Oh, look who it isn't." Zeus spoke into the phone, his voice booming. "Satan's Anus, what's up, bud?"

A few people glanced over with pursed pusses.

"Yeah, I won," he said into the phone, and he shrugged at Wilshire, who looked like he'd rather be shopping for vasectomy doctors.

He tilted his head, listening to nothing. "You want to bring your anaconda to Blakemore Gardens Country Club?" He waited a beat. "I don't think they have a hedgehog problem here." He scratched his head. "Oh, you founded a hedgehog breeder, and you'll release hundreds of them? Sure there's a pond your anaconda can swim in." Another pause. "The band arriving on Harley-Davidsons shouldn't be an issue, but driving on the golf course itself is probably a no-go."

Now almost everyone in the clubhouse bar focused on the newcomer, and they glared. Noses upturned like their stiff upper lips were coated with smelling salts, and mouths murmured soft, unheard pleasantries.

Zeus was nonplussed. "Hey, Anus, let me go. I got a call on the other line." He faked connecting while a frantic Wilshire patted the air down in a gesture for quiet.

"What up, Dawg?" Zeus sang with volume. He covered the phone and boomed, "Would you believe it? Dawg E. Stylin' is on the line!"

Zeus feigned listening and nodded a few times. "The thing is, Dawg E., while I'm not certain if Blakemore Gardens has specific rules on drug use, marijuana is against the law." He paused. "I know. Just keep it cool, and you can get away with blazing all the bud you want, bro. As for the blast-beat boom box, that might not comply with country-club etiquette. Your topless-striper entourage should float, however. This place is a sausage factory, so I suspect they wouldn't mind a little entertainment." Pause. "Sure, I'll take a lap dance."

He was having so much fun that he didn't notice someone approach from behind until he was tapped on the shoulder. Zeus moved the phone from his ear and spoke to the shoulder-tapper. "Excuse me, can't you see I'm talking to someone more important than you?"

He returned to the phone. "Gotta go, Dawg E. Some guy here seems upset with our chatter." He paused. "That will not be necessary, but I'm flattered. I can handle this myself. Cheers."

Zeus grinned at Wilshire and the shoulder-tapper. "Would you believe it? Dawg E. Stylin' just said he'd personally get the Bloods and the Crips to make peace for a day and visit here if anyone gives me trouble. I swear, it warms my heart to know Dawg E. Stylin' sees me as a brother."

The newcomer had close-cropped hair, too long to be military, but too short to be cool. He had black-framed glasses perched on his sharp nose, as though he were used to looking down at people. But he was three inches shorter than Zeus, so he pushed the frames back and looked up.

"Who said anything about trouble? I came over only to ask you to speak a bit softer. That's all. A request from one gentleman to another."

"Sorry. I'm hard of hearing. Too many mortar blasts from the war. It gets pronounced on phone calls."

Wilshire seemed to know it was bullshit from the cocked brow, but a cold stare kept him silent.

The shoulder-tapper addressed Wilshire. "Is this your guest, Dillon? He does appear familiar, I must say."

Wilshire looked like he'd rather acquaint his wife with his mistress. "Farnsworth, let me introduce you to—"

Zeus interrupted. "Farnsworth, here's the scoop. If I desired, I could buy this joint and do lots of things. Low-income housing for starters, or how about a clinic mall? One-stop shopping for drug addicts, alcoholics, manic depressives, broke gamblers, and my favorite—sex addicts. Then again, I'd love to turn Blakemore Gardens into a public course," he said and winked at Wilshire, who covered his face in his pudgy hands.

"The only reason I graced this dump was to play this man a round of golf." He pointed at Wilshire. "He'll explain the terms of our arrangement." He waved at the gaping onlookers. "Adios."

Just like the first time they'd met, Wilshire chased after him. "Stop. You can't do this."

Zeus turned. "Do what?"

"Ruin me."

He scoffed, "Ruin you? You're not losing a dime on this deal."

Wilshire's fleshy countenance shook. "My reputation will forever be tattered, the loss of business unfathomable."

Zeus cocked an eye at him. "Trust me; no one thinks you hang out with rap and heavy-metal stars. You're a yuppie snob, just like them. They'll understand you made a business gamble and lost."

Wilshire grabbed Zeus's hand, and his eyes swelled. He began to kneel, but Zeus pulled away.

"Our wager was ratified by our attorneys. If I lost, you'd enforce the contract. You're not getting out of this. I had much more to lose."

Wilshire huffed, sweat dripping from his chins. "Five million dollars. Please take the money and run."

Zeus shook his head. "Nada. You keep the money and run. You could use a cardio workout by the looks of things."

He drooped like a parched plant. "Fifteen million dollars. Please, I beg you."

Zeus rubbed his jaw. "Something's not right. I can't grasp why you'd spend that kind of money to avoid unconventional guests at your club."

"Some club members are my clients, including the president, and—" Wilshire stopped, forced.

Zeus was pretty sure he knew why Wilshire did not complete his thought. "I was under the impression the country-club seal and president's signature implied the president was well aware of this bet. He endorsed your side of the agreement." Zeus paused and arched his brow. "Or didn't he?"

Wilshire nodded. His face trembled, and his eyes blinked back tears. "Can we talk in private?"

The men left the club and found a tavern. Broken, Wilshire was no longer full of shit, piss, or even vinegar. He almost enjoyed Wilshire's company. Maybe it was the twenty-five-year-old scotch Wilshire splurged on.

This time when he talked of family, it was the truth. He loved his wife, but she didn't love him, only his money. He hated to admit it, but he preferred his youngest son over the eldest, whom he termed a "freeloader."

In the end, Zeus let Wilshire wiggle off the hook for his forgery of the president's signature. No rap or metal stars would visit the country club. They never were going to anyway.

The men came to a new arrangement, a performance-based bet that could cost Wilshire millions. Top score was a free 10 percent stake in Wilshire Worldwide, but Wilshire rued such an achievement impossible.

They didn't leave as friends, but they left on better terms.

PRESENT DAY

Seated on Dillon Wilshire's yacht, Long Island's Gold Coast beckoned with an effluvium of inherited money. A crew of landscapers worked an estate like greens keepers preparing for the Masters. The sun was nearly down, and Ulysses Zeus Baxter had yet to hear from his son, Ulysses Hercules. Wilshire held a glass of white wine and wore the same business grin he had sported way back in Los Cabos.

"Maybe he's afraid to call you," Wilshire suggested. "I told you, Professor Gladstone is a tough cookie. Doesn't fail many students, but anything above a B is a rarity. I was happy to pay the five million to charity if he received a B."

Zeus merely nodded. He trusted his son would deliver, and his phone chimed. He eyed Wilshire as he took the call and pressed speakerphone.

"What's the word, son?"

"Sorry, Pops. I got held up celebrating the A+ I got on my history thesis."

Zeus pumped a fist. "Way to go, son! Congrats."

They chatted back and forth and parted with plans for Ulysses to spend his summer vacation in Europe.

"My boy did it—top score. That's 10 percent of your company, Dillon."

Wilshire played with the white sailing cap perched on his head. "How do I know your son didn't cheat and hire a ghostwriter? Or a famous historian, perhaps?"

Zeus laughed. "Are you kidding me? No one in their right mind would take responsibility for writing a story called *Jesse James and the Secret Legend of Captain Coytus.*"

ACKNOWLEDGMENTS

The author would like to thank the primary editor for this book, Kira McFadden. Great job, Kira! I would also like to thank Timothy Staveteig and Evah Graves for their edits, counsel, and hard work in making this a better book. I would also like to thank the editorial staff from iUniverse for further polishing and improving the story. A special thanks to Mallory Rock for her talents in creating the book cover. I would also like to thank, Michael Dadich, author of the award-winning fantasy *The Silver Sphere*.

I would also like to thank Michael Brewster, Brian Dunn, Chris McEntee, Steve DeMeo, Joe Shavel, Jason Ernie, and Randy Morgan for all their laughs and friendship. To my team, Mike Cassano, Roopesh Amin, Rise Hall-Noren, Lauren Klein, and Zack Lajka—you guys rock! Congratulations to Rob & Katie, our friends from across the pond. Thank you for all my awesome Stoke City gear!

To my parents, I would have to write a much larger novel than this to document all you have done for me.

Dr. Roiland, Melissa and I would like to thank you for all you did for Paola. You are a fantastic vet and a special person.

A sincere thank-you to all my readers.

I read quite a few books on the famous outlaw Jesse James, some historical, some conspiracy-minded, but the spine of this novel was based on the acclaimed work of T. J. Stiles: *Jesse James: Last Rebel of the Civil War*. If you are looking for a more detailed and accurate account of the life and death of Jesse James, I strongly recommend Mr. Stiles's book.

Printed in Great Britain
by Amazon

72102536R00277